Dead Girl Walking

Dead Girl Walking

Christopher Brookmyre

Atlantic Monthly Press
New York

First published in Great Britain in 2015 by Little, Brown

Published simultaneously in Canada
Printed in the United States of America

ISBN 978-0-8021-2364-0
eISBN 978-0-8021-9141-0

Atlantic Monthly Press
an imprint of Grove Atlantic
154 West 14th Street
New York, NY 10011

Distributed by Publishers Group West

groveatlantic.com

15 16 17 18   10 9 8 7 6 5 4 3 2 1

For Marisa

Murder Ballad

Her world collapsed around a single moment. A single act. That was all it took for what she understood as reality to be altered for ever.

She watched the blood splatter from the girl's open mouth like vomit, engulfing and uncontainable. The knife must have gone in right to the hilt, driven as it was by so much force, like he had been trying to punch right through her. She tried and failed to apprehend her thoughts before they turned to the massive organ damage necessary to have precipitated such an eruption. The girl would bleed out in a matter of minutes, maybe seconds.

There was no numbing moment of disbelief to anaesthetise her fear. This was real. This was now. She was better wired than most people to fundamentally understand this.

Just as she had learned that dreams can come true, that things you have merely fantasised about can suddenly become everyday reality, so was she starkly aware that the darkest dreads could be made manifest too. Most people's dreams didn't come true. Most people didn't get to play their music to thousands of people in city after city, night after night. Most people didn't see a human being murdered before their very eyes and know that they were next.

The girl now slumped to the ground, collapsing in stages; one hand clutching her stomach, the other extended to steady herself, as though a fear of toppling over were the chief of her concerns. Then she flopped forward on to her face, folded up like a doll.

The attacker barely cast a glance towards his victim. Now that she had been dealt with, and was no longer of value to him, the girl ceased to merit his consideration.

In those brief seconds, she thought of the years she had lived, and of all the time and effort it had taken to reach this stage in her career. The doors that were opening. The places she was yet to go. It seemed so unfair that all of it could be gone in the blink of an eye. Yet she knew just how sudden, how arbitrary and capricious fate could be.

Watching the blood pour from a scared, astonished mouth, she had just as immediately grasped the implications for anyone who could testify to having seen it happen.

He was moving forward, simmering with an aggression he could tap into at will. Those muscular arms, that body honed and sculpted to brutal purpose.

Killing machine.

She thought she saw movement from the floor, but it was just the blood pooling around the girl's waist.

She felt a cold, iron paralysis, a crippling fear of flight that fear of death could not overcome. She was petrified. She was powerless.

She was next.

The payment was gone, the only leverage, and it had bought nothing.

That thought seemed almost random, flashing past like just another piece of debris in the vortex of this tornado. Once upon a time, the notion of losing that much money would have been catastrophic. Right now it was barely relevant.

It didn't look like she would be needing it.

Investigated Reporter

They didn't look like cops. Not at first, when he walked to his seat on the other side of the table. More like lawyers, surrounded as they were by piles of notes and stacks of folders, binders and hardbound volumes. They seemed a little swamped, a little distracted, referring to various loose sheets and plastic-wrapped documents as he sat down, as though they had to remind themselves of who he was and why he was there.

It wasn't like any interview room he'd been in before either. It was a bright and airy upstairs office, lots of windows, a couple of framed prints and the walls covered in a recently painted soothing shade of light blue. All very neutral, very non-threatening.

This was in marked contrast to the language and tone of the missives by which he had been compelled to come to London. They had made it clear that if he didn't cooperate by travelling voluntarily, he'd be doing so in the back of a van. Yet now they were acting like it was at his own convenience. He even had an appointment. It was like visiting the proctologist; all very polite, respectful and professional, but ultimately you knew that the point of the exercise was for someone to ram their finger up your arse.

'I'm Detective Sergeant Ben Mitchell; this is Detective Constable Audrey Pine. We are both with Metropolitan Police Specialist Operations, operating under the auspices of the Westercruik Inquiry, whose full powers we are at liberty to command.'

The preamble went on for a bit after that, like the terms and conditions you never read before clicking Yes to installing a piece of software: the details and the legalese weren't important, as you both knew there was no option but to proceed. The appointment thing was a bit of paradoxical mummery to establish their credentials too. Its purpose was to underline that he was not even that

3

important in the greater scheme of what they were about here and to remind him that this thing was a juggernaut, so step carefully lest you end up under the wheels.

It was Pine who spoke first.

'Alec Forman,' she stated matter-of-factly, like she was taking the register.

'Present,' he replied, eliciting a grimly weary look. She wasn't in the mood for humour. That was fine, because neither was he.

Pine looked late thirties or early forties, pale and skinny with a dyed-blonde bob. She might have been younger: her impassive expression and a complexion betraying a committed smoking habit were probably putting a few years on her. She seemed all the more pallid next to Mitchell, who was brown of skin and jet black of hair.

'You've been publishing under that byline for roughly the past three years.'

When I've been published at all, he thought.

'You've been in journalism more than two decades. You've worked in London, Los Angeles and Scotland. You've largely been freelance since the mid-nineties. You started off in Glasgow then moved to London when you were hired as an investigative reporter on the . . .'

On and on she went, with the expression and the tone of voice that conveyed an indefatigable stamina for bureaucratic detail, far more than a mortal man like him could possibly endure. His only salvation might be her need to nip out for a fag. If she had Nicorette gum, he was doomed.

He wasn't so sure about her strategy, it had to be said. She just kept telling him things about himself, which didn't strike him as a likely means of tripping him up. There were a few hazy periods, granted, but he was generally accepted as the world authority on the subject of his own life.

These were mere overtures, however. They were circling, trying to make him wonder where they'd come from when they finally decided to attack. Either that or the plan was to remind him of just how far he had fallen in order to have made the desperate mistakes that had ultimately brought him to this room.

'Your time in London, working for the Exposure team, you carved out a bit of a name for yourself. You were very much ahead of the curve.'

Mitchell was speaking, glancing back down at a document as he did so, like he hadn't had enough time to prepare for this. Aye, right.

The journalist occasionally known but decreasingly published as Alec Forman still said nothing.

'In fact, you were cited by name several times during the Leveson Inquiry and reference was made to quite a range of, shall we say, improvisational methods of procuring information. It was alleged that, in order to stand up your stories, you employed computer hacking, unauthorised, invasive and covert electronic surveillance, even burglary. This is going all the way back to the early nineties. You truly were a trailblazer for all that ultimately became rotten about modern journalism.'

No, they didn't look like cops: not until they started asking questions, at which juncture the humourless condescension was unmistakable. They must teach it at Hendon.

He knew he was being goaded and he ought to deny the cop a response. Maybe three years ago he'd have been strong enough to resist. These days his skin had worn a lot thinner from being the whipping boy.

If you prick me, do I not bleed? If you wrong me, shall I not fuck your shit right up?

'Those were allegations made by individuals and organisations bearing long-term grudges about having their own sharp practices exposed.'

'Your editors at the time stated at the inquiry that highly sensitive documents and other evidence frequently came into your hands through unnamed sources: sometimes documents and evidence that had previously been quietly resting in a safe.'

'Yes, and they were so uncomfortable about the provenance of my information that they said absolutely nothing about it until they were in front of an inquiry and needing to offer up a sacrificial goat.'

'So where did all those documents come from?'

'Unnamed sources. Many and various sources. That's journalism, or at least it was, once upon a time. As far as I remember it, no specific evidence was produced to support these allegations.'

Mitchell glanced intently down at the fire hazard of loose leafs in front of him, like there might be a citation there that would refute this last statement. There wasn't, but he had a pretty good comeback nonetheless.

'In the year 2000 you were found guilty of breaking and entering, were you not? You were jailed and served a total of seven months.'

Mitchell ran a finger down the sheet he was looking at, like he was double-checking.

'Oh, sorry, that's not strictly true. Part of that prison time was while you were on remand for a charge of murder.'

Mitchell spoke with a very measured pronunciation, like he savoured his own elocution. There were trace elements of Brummie in there, but mainly his accent spoke of good schooling and attention to detail. He seemed dynamic and determined, a permanent searching seriousness about his expression.

Mitchell looked a good bit younger than Pine, but was clearly the one in the driving seat. Probably highly ambitious and dexterously political too, to have got himself a gig on this inquiry. His suit looked good on him as well, the bastard.

Oh, Christ.

He winced inside as the import of the moment struck home. Comes to us all, sure enough: he had just told himself the polis were looking younger.

Somebody shoot me in the fucking head, he thought.

'Does it mention anywhere in your documentation that I was completely exonerated?' he asked, trying not to sound rattled but succeeding only in alerting Mitchell to the fact that he was.

Mitchell responded by stepping things up.

'Did you break into an apartment in Knightsbridge while it was being used for sexual liaisons by Sir Anthony Mead?'

He responded with a blank look, then wondered if that appeared more guilty than an outright denial. Acting like you don't know who Anthony Mead is: yeah, that'll fox him.

'Did you break into Anthony Mead's home?'

'I couldn't even tell you where that might be. Home Counties are all the one to me.'

That was payback for Pine saying London, Los Angeles and Scotland. Really sticking it to them here.

'So you know his house is in the Home Counties.'

Shit.

'Did you plant a bug or a DVR to record him?'

'No.'

'Did you hack his mobile phone?'

'No.'

'Did you hack Angela Goldman's phone?'

'No.'

'Did you break into Angela Goldman's flat?'

'No.'

'Were you aware that Angela Goldman was having an affair with Anthony Mead? Did you use this information to blackmail either of them into revealing his encryption password?'

Round and round they went, back over the same ground several times. He figured it couldn't be to see whether he contradicted himself, as it's hard to contradict one-word answers, especially when the answer is almost invariably no. He couldn't be sure what the endgame was, what agendas were at work, but he did know there was one thing they would definitely be seeking, sooner or later. He was also sure they wouldn't be getting it. It was one of the few things he *could* consider himself sure of these days.

'How did you feel during the Leveson Inquiry?' Pine asked.

'I wasn't watching it through my fingers, if that's what you think. I wasn't watching it with a bucket of popcorn either, though if I was I'd have been throwing it at the screen. It was like Glastonbury for humbug and hypocrisy. An all-time-great line-up of self-serving wankers.'

'Not your profession's finest hour.'

'Look who's talking. Met, did you say?'

He'd have given them points if one of them had said touché. They just stared back, that cop thing where you don't know whether they're playing the humourless bastard angle to keep you uncomfortable or whether they simply are humourless bastards.

'The real damage came after Leveson for you, though, didn't it?' asked Mitchell. 'You used the phrase "sacrificial goat".'

'Yes. Kind of like the "one bad apple" defence synonymous with accusations of police brutality or corruption.'

Mitchell didn't bite.

'It seemed expedient for a lot of your former employers to distance themselves from you.'

'Aye, but give them credit for an impressive exercise in having their cake and eating it. They denied they knew how I operated, but made me the totem of everything they now considered verboten.'

'But the bottom line was that you were effectively unemployable. Was that when you started using the name Alec Forman?'

He said nothing. They knew this shit. It was written down in front of them. Were they trying to get him to relive the moment? Start blubbing right there at the table and open up to them when they offered a hanky?

'It was also around this time that your marriage broke up, wasn't it?' asked Pine; though again, she wasn't really asking.

Still he said nothing, but this time because he really didn't want to go there.

'You're divorced now?' Mitchell enquired casually, like he needed to dot an i.

'Separated.'

Christ. He had got a lump in his throat there, and he hoped it hadn't been detectable in his voice. What the hell? He hadn't felt like this in ages. Why was it threatening to surface now, in front of these bloodless stiffs? And where were they going with this?

Well, he knew the ultimate destination, but was starting to get confused by the route, like a tourist being gypped by an unscrupulous cab-driver.

'Did Leveson and the resulting fallout contribute to the break-up of your marriage?'

'We're still married,' he replied.

Aye, right, said another voice.

'That kind of exposure must have put an intolerable strain on your relationship,' Pine suggested.

'We were having problems before that. It certainly didn't help,' he conceded, hoping the acknowledgement would get them off the subject.

Fat chance. Mitchell had good sense for this stuff. He knew when to press home.

'Was your ex-wife aware of your methods?'

Fuck you.

'Or was she appalled to learn of them through the same channels as her friends, her colleagues, her family?'

Fuck you.

'Did she feel ashamed? Was she angry with you? Did you feel shame for what you put her through?'

Fuck you. Fuck you. Fuck you.

(Yes. Yes. Yes.)

'She's not my ex-wife,' he managed to state.

Mitchell consulted the documents again.

'You haven't lived together for some time. More than a year, I believe.'

'What's it to you?'

'Listen, I'm not some automated vessel of the state on a bureaucratic errand. I've a task to carry out, but I'm not without sympathy. We deal in human emotions here in this job: when you strip away the extraneous detail, that's where the answers usually lie. I'm trying to develop a picture of your state of mind, post-Leveson, post your separation, when you began working on this story.'

'I had been working on it before either of those things. The time-frame isn't as simple as you think. Proper investigative journalism can be a very long game. It's about cultivating contacts, following up small possibilities, keeping track of things that might not immediately appear significant.'

'And yet you stepped up the pace rather precipitously, didn't you? In a manner displaying an impatience and a failure of judgement quite out of keeping with your previous record. That's what I'm getting at. You were trying to get back in the game with one swing: prove everybody wrong about you being washed up; show the world – show *Sarah* – that there was a massive, moral, public-interest justification for the methods over which you'd been vilified.'

He said nothing, trying to remain impassive, but he was struggling. Especially when Mitchell spoke her name. That wasn't the worst part, though: the worst part was that the fucker was right on the money.

'A conspiracy orchestrated by British and US intelligence and security forces to blame terrorist organisations for atrocities they themselves carried out. That's real tinfoil-hat stuff.'

'The story I was working on was a little more nuanced than that, but I know how it looks. We all know how it looks.'

'Well, on the plus side, on this occasion we are prepared to believe that you got the crucial evidence from an unnamed source.'

Finally. Fucking finally. Let's get to it, then.

'Who gave you the laptop?' Mitchell asked.

He sighed, slumping a little in his chair, assuming the posture of a broken man. It wasn't a tough sell. He *was* a broken man.

'I have this friend who's a keen golfer,' he told them with an air of surrender. 'I mean, really keen. He'll play in a hurricane, torrential rain, freezing winds, anything. One day I saw him heading to the links with his clubs when there was snow on the ground.'

It was the turn of Mitchell and Pine to look like they weren't sure where this was going, but having worked so long to get him to open up, they were prepared to be patient.

'I asked him what the hell he was doing and he said he had this new ball with a GPS tracker. Even in the snow, he could locate it anywhere. Amazing. So I asked him what you just asked me: Where did you get it? His answer was the same as mine.'

'What?' Mitchell asked, intrigued.

'I found it.'

They didn't like that. He knew he was bringing down upon himself the full pompocalypse of criminal law and cop-grade self-importance, but it was always going to come to this anyway.

'Did you enjoy prison?' Mitchell asked.

When they started asking really stupid questions was when you knew you'd truly pissed them off.

'Do you want to go back there?'

'To be honest, if it was between prison and connecting in Terminal Five at Heathrow, I'd choose T5. Just. So no.'

'You are far from being the focus of this inquiry, but if you obstruct it you will feel the full force that it can bring to bear.'

He folded his arms and sat back in his seat.

'I'm not naming my source. I don't care what you threaten me with.'

'I'm not bluffing here. When I report back, there is every chance they'll escalate this. This inquiry is going to need heads on spikes by the end, and it'll get them one way or another. One of them doesn't have to be yours. They're after bigger game here. Who gave you the laptop?'

'I'm not naming my source.'

They sat in silence for a long couple of minutes, Mitchell and Pine staring at him every time he glanced up. They were like disappointed parents waiting for a huffy kid to apologise.

'It doesn't have to go this way,' Mitchell said eventually. 'You could still have a career again. There is a lot of unseen influence at play in these things. If you were to cooperate, then who knows what doors might open . . .'

Mitchell said this with a shrug, trailing the bait, saying let's negotiate, if that's what it takes.

He just shook his head.

'You're right. I've been desperate. But not that desperate.'

'Then you're finished,' Mitchell said.

'I can leave?'

'I mean in journalism. Under *any* byline.'

He gave the cops a wry, humourless chuckle.

'That was already true when I walked in here,' he told them. 'You haven't taken anything away from me, officer. In fact, you've already proven things aren't quite as bad as some people made out: after Leveson, there were those who said I couldn't get arrested.'

Mitchell looked at him with almost pitying disgust.

'You haven't *been* arrested, Mr Parlabane.'

The mixture of bravado, anxiety and defiance was already turning into something cold and sour in his gut before he left the building. He had stood his ground and made it through his first tangle with the Westercruik Inquiry, but when he walked back outside, the same reality would be waiting for him: one in which he was a disgraced and disparaged hack nobody in the business would ever go near again.

And it wasn't because of burglary or computer hacking or any of the other shit that came out in the wash. He hadn't hacked any murder victim's phone, or pursued any illegal activity just to find out whether two D-list celebutards were shagging. He had nothing to be ashamed of there.

There were plenty of guys who had done horrible shit and walked back into jobs as soon as their jail time was over. In the perverse and hypocritical world of journalism, the Leveson Inquiry had merely proven their mettle regarding how far they'd go to get a story; not to mention how they could keep their mouths shut to protect the cowardly pricks upstairs.

It wasn't even that he had broken a golden rule and become the story. That was consequence rather than cause.

His sin was far worse than that.

It was that he'd been played.

He got scapegoated. He got screwed over. He got angry. Fair enough. But then he got desperate, and then he got played. There was just a memorial plaque now where his reputation used to stand. His judgement would be forever suspect.

In the past it was at times such as this that he would have sat down with Sarah and talked things through. Then, everything would look brighter after two hours of blethers and a bottle of wine.

Now that was over too.

He filled out some paperwork and then went for a slash, trying not to catch his reflection in the mirror as he washed his hands.

He saw Pine on the steps just outside the main entrance, smoking a roll-up. It looked oddly studenty; he'd figured her for Marlies or B&H.

'I can see why your wife left you,' she said.

Disarmingly, it didn't sound like a dig. It was like she was concerned.

'There's stubborn, and then there's pointlessly self-destructive,' she added.

'What does that mean?'

'It means, I don't get why you're prepared to take the fall for someone who burned you. You were set up and your source left you twisting in the wind. Whoever he is, he ruined any chance you had of resurrecting your career. You could go to prison and yet you still won't name him.'

'As someone smarter than me once said, principles only mean something if you stand by them when they're inconvenient.'

'Principles strike me as a luxury you can't afford any more, especially when they're the principles of a profession that's chewed you up and spat you out. Why would you stand by them now?'

'Because they're all I've got left.'

The Opposite of Journalism

Parlabane took another sip of his coffee and wondered how long he could spin out the process of drinking it: a delicate balancing act between having no plausible justification for remaining seated in this café and discovering just how lukewarm a latte his palate could tolerate. He had just missed a train back to Edinburgh and now had a couple of hours to wait before the next one. Time was, he'd have seized the opportunity to take a wander around a gallery or browse a few record shops, but he was low on funds and lower on motivation.

Sitting in a railway station café seemed appropriate: a neutral space, transitory, temporary. He didn't belong anywhere right now. He wanted out of London, but there wasn't much waiting for him back in Edinburgh either.

Since he returned from his disastrously vainglorious quest to 'get back in the game with one swing', as Officer Mitchell astutely put it, he had spent recent weeks crashing in spare rooms and on settees while he tried to sort out something more permanent. He was not so much reaping a dividend of long-standing good-will on the part of old friends as feeling like a charity case. They all wanted to help him out because they felt sorry for him, but though they were prepared to offer him a berth, it was horribly awkward. Christ, it wasn't like anybody wanted to sit up late with a couple of bottles, blethering like they used to. How could they?

'Well, Jack, what will we talk about first: the break-up of your marriage or the death of your career?'

He wasn't enjoying the coffee, or the joyless atmosphere of the café, but nor was he in a hurry to get on that train. He knew he wouldn't be travelling hopefully and he wasn't looking forward to what awaited him when he arrived. At least sitting in this place he had an excuse for doing nothing.

There was a line between reasonably describing one's status as freelance and more honestly calling it unemployed. He had crossed it a while back and was now wandering the hazy borderlands of the next such marker: the one that lay between the terms 'unemployed journalist' and 'former journalist'.

It was busy on the other side of that line, the arse having fallen out of the industry as it struggled to accept that we were effectively in the post-print era. There were still jobs to be had, filling up the content-ravenous beasts that roamed the new digital landscape, but not for journalists. Parlabane's problem was not so much that nobody would hire him: it was that the job he did no longer existed.

He felt the buzz of his mobile from his jacket pocket. The absence of a ringtone was a legacy of times when it went off so often that the noise was as irritating as it was unnecessary, and the device seldom off his person anyway. Nowadays the fact that it was still only on vibrate was mildly embarrassing: on the rare occasions that it sounded, it merely served to tell him he was kidding himself.

The screen showed a number rather than a name. He sighed. That most likely meant he was dealing with a misdial or about to hear some recorded spam. He answered anyway.

'Hello. Is that . . . Jack?' asked a female voice.

'Depends,' he replied, instantly regretting it for both its pitiful defensiveness and the fact that it made him sound like a twat. 'Who's this?'

'It's Mairi,' she said.

'Mairi who?' he replied, thinking it was turning into a knock-knock joke. Punchline: 'Mairi whoever you like, Sarah's divorcing you, arsehole.'

'Mairi Lafferty. Do you remember me? Donald's sister.'

Donald. Jesus.

It was a sledgehammer to the psyche when he realised his old friend had been dead longer than he ever knew him. And to that Parlabane could add the survivor's guilt of realising how long it had been since he'd even thought of the guy.

15

'Mairi. Sure. I haven't seen you . . .'

(. . . since the funeral.)

'Yeah,' she said, not wanting to go there either. 'You're in Edinburgh now, is that right?'

'Not this second. I'm actually at King's Cross, waiting for a train.'

'Don't get on it. I need to talk to you about something. In person.'

Parlabane hadn't seen Mairi in fifteen years, but they had clearly been kind to her. She stood in the doorway of a Hoxton flat dressed in black designer jeans and a leather jacket, her hair in a tinted black bob that looked expensively tasteful, matching her skin tone so as not to draw attention to the dye-job. He knew she had to be forty-one or forty-two, so she was maybe on the cusp of dressing a little young for her age, but she was carrying it off.

Back in another lifetime, Mairi had been Donald's trendy little sister: brassy, stylish and constantly insinuating herself into her big brother's world, where she wasn't welcome; at least not in Donald's view. There was one lurking in the background of every male adolescence: the mate's younger sister who you secretly fancied but you knew it was wrong and anyway it was never going to happen. She was way too cool for you, and even if your seniority gave you some cachet, you didn't want to be one of those creepy guys dating a girl three years younger.

So how old did that make him feel, to recall a time when three years seemed like a major difference?

She beckoned him inside and led him to the kitchen. On the way there, he had briefly wondered why she had a couch in her hall, before realising that the narrow passageway was actually her living room. She got a couple of beers from the fridge and placed them on the kitchen table alongside a blue folder and a small pile of magazines. *Mojo* was on top, *Q* underneath, and possibly *Tatler* at the foot of the pile. This last immediately made Parlabane think Mairi must be doing very well for herself, as in his experience the only people who read it were women of her age who fitted that description, or much younger ones hoping to marry men who fitted that description.

16

They traded small talk, which mainly consisted of Parlabane asking Mairi sufficient questions about herself as to prevent her from reciprocating. He felt acutely conscious of it *being* small talk, and yet it felt all the more necessary in order to paper over the weirdness. This wasn't merely two people who hadn't spoken in fifteen years, but two people whose cumulative conversation prior to that could comfortably have been transcribed on a Sinclair ZX80.

'So what is it you do with yourself?' he asked, not having gleaned much data from his brief transit through her home. A glance at her left hand established the absence of any significant rings, but although that didn't preclude the existence of a significant other, this really wasn't an area he wanted to get into.

'I'm in the music business. I've got my own management company.'

'Oh, wow,' he said, pitching at impressed but not surprised, hoping not to sound patronising. 'What's it called?'

'LAF-M. As in Lafferty, Mairi, but pronounced like *la femme.*'

'Which acts do you manage?' he asked, hoping to hell he had heard of one of them and that it wasn't some *X-Factor* maggot he wanted to machine-gun.

'I started off managing Cassidy. Remember them?'

Parlabane did. They were an all-girl vocal group who had enjoyed a number-one hit around 2002. They had been indistinguishable from their peers and would have barely stuck in his memory but for the fact that they had also hit the top ten with an utterly unlikely cover of 'She Knows' by Balaam and the Angel.

Now, more than a decade later, Parlabane finally worked out why.

'"She Knows",' he said. 'That was your idea.'

Mairi nodded but didn't elaborate. They both knew she didn't have to. Donald had been a big Balaam fan, spending hours back-combing those goth-locks of his before a police regulation shearing saw them gone for ever.

'And what about these days?' he asked.

'We'll get to that,' she replied. 'It's why I'm here. I want to offer you a job.'

'In music management?' he asked, laughing.

'No. Something a little closer to your normal beat. I'm prepared to pay you a daily rate of three hundred pounds, plus expenses.'

Parlabane tried to remain impassive, but there was little point in pretending it didn't sound generous. However, it did also sound temporary, so he didn't reckon she was about to pitch him a gig as a press officer.

'My normal beat? Investigative reporter?'

'Investigative, yes. Reporting not so much. In fact, you might say it was the opposite of journalism, because the point is to keep it quiet.'

'I thought the opposite of journalism was royal correspondent, but I'm listening. What is it you want me to look into?'

She winced rather apologetically, picking at the foil on the neck of her beer bottle.

'I'm afraid I can't tell you until you agree to do it. This is something that would be a big story if anyone found out, and I need to prevent that from happening. Discretion is everything here. I'm sorry.'

'So let me get this clear: you want me to look into something that would be a big story, but I'm not allowed to tell anybody?'

'I know it goes against the grain, Jack, but that's why I'm prepared to pay.'

'So why not hire a private investigator?'

'It's delicate. I need someone who can investigate people without them realising they're being investigated. A journalist asking questions would be perfectly normal, and you've got a plausible pedigree.'

So she knew about all the soft-soap stuff he'd written for the music glossies. It had been during a time post-Leveson when he still had friends in the industry and his hard-bitten reputation was actually a plus point for the magazines when they were pitching to bands for an interview. Even then he had regarded it as a form of selling out, but that was *before*. These days he'd bite your hand off if you offered a gig interviewing One Direction for *Hello!*.

'Why don't you just tell me, Mairi?' he reasoned. 'There's something redundant about demanding a non-disclosure agreement from a guy that nobody would listen to even if he did disclose it. Which I won't, by the way. You've come to me in confidence.'

Mairi sighed and gave her head a tiny shake.

'Sorry, Jack. I can't do that. No offence, and I appreciate how it must sound, me not taking you at your word after all you did for Donald, but that's just how this has to be.'

Christ, he thought: how big must this story be if she's prepared to walk away, after admitting she was low on alternatives?

Even as he asked himself this, consumed by the eager curiosity he had been addicted to for decades, he realised that she *wasn't* prepared to walk away, and not because she was bluffing. She had known before she called him at King's Cross that it wouldn't come to this, because he would be the one to fold.

'Okay,' he told her. 'I'm not fighting off alternative employment offers with a shitty stick, but then I think you probably knew that.'

Just to underline that she did, Mairi produced the pre-prepared NDA from inside the blue folder.

Parlabane paused only a moment over the document before applying his pen, pondering whether being paid *not* to write a story marked a new low.

'At least I don't need to sweat that this is some Mephistophelean deal. I sold my soul so long ago I'd need to ring my accountant to find out who bought it.'

Mairi didn't laugh, nor even smile.

'If that were true, I wouldn't have asked you here.'

'So why *have* you asked me here?' he enquired, having signed for the right to do so.

Mairi slid her copies of *Q* and *Mojo* out of the way and pointed, rather unexpectedly, to *Tatler*, which she spun around so that it was facing Parlabane the right way up. He scanned the tag lines, picking up on the words 'Savage Earth Heart's warrior women', which was when he realised that one of the two figures posed in ancient battle dress on the cover was Heike Gunn. He hadn't recognised her at first, not so much because of the Roman costume, but due to her signature porcelain-blonde curls having been replaced by flowing locks dyed a cheap-looking shade of pink.

'You manage Savage Earth Heart?' he asked, impressed, but this time unable to conceal the surprise in his tone.

'For the past two years, just about.'

'I gather Ms Gunn's a bit of a control freak.'

This was the polite version. 'Manipulative psycho bitch' was the phrase that best suited the accounts he'd heard.

'She takes on too many burdens,' Mairi replied, with what sounded like dutiful neutrality. There was something else there too, but he couldn't pinpoint what.

'She emptied one of the founding members, if I recall. Who's playing fiddle for them now?'

Mairi pointed to *Tatler* again, indicating the other cover girl. Parlabane belatedly noticed that the object she was balletically thrusting towards Heike was not in fact a sword, but a violin bow.

'Monica Halcrow,' Mairi said, slightly incredulous, slightly irritated. 'You telling me you didn't see the photos?'

Parlabane realised he was a few pages behind and haemorrhaging 'down with the kids' points.

'What photos? Safe to say I've been focused on other stuff recently.'

'Never mind. What's more pertinent is that the third album – *Smuggler's Soul* – is due for release in just over a fortnight, coinciding with a thirty-five-date US tour. It's the first major-label release of a three-album deal with Sentinel, who are putting serious marketing muscle behind this. The band have just completed a sell-out tour of Europe and the new single, "Stolen Glances", is currently top ten in seventeen territories. The world is at Heike's feet.'

'It certainly sounds like it. So what's the problem?'

'I don't know where the fuck she is.'

The Money Trench

Maria glanced down briefly at the NDA then back at Parlabane, all having become clear.

'I take it this isn't simply a case of not taking your calls? I mean, if she's just finished a European tour and she's got all this action coming up, is it feasible she's on an islet in the Maldives where she knows there's no mobile reception?'

'She's missing, Jack, and you are now one of a very exclusive number of people who knows this. She went missing in Berlin, final day of the tour. The last person to see her was Monica, that morning. Heike's final words to her were: "See you at the sound-check", but she never showed up for it. They had to cancel the show: tour manager told the venue she had a throat infection so that it didn't become a story. Nobody's seen her since. She didn't turn up for the flight home and her neighbours say she hasn't been back to her flat in Glasgow. There's been no answer on her phone, no reply to emails, no tweets. It's like one minute the eyes of the world were upon her and the next she's vanished from the face of the Earth.'

Mairi sounded exasperated, but Parlabane could tell there was genuine worry there too. This wasn't merely a business matter needing to be dealt with, albeit delicately and discreetly. None-theless, having been played to disastrous effect so very recently, he couldn't help his suspicions.

'No offence, Mairi, but the first thing that comes to mind is that this is a publicity stunt, and if that turns out to be the case and you have roped me into it . . .'

'A publicity stunt?' she responded, with sufficient outrage as to indicate the 'no offence' disclaimer hadn't cut it. 'Are you fucking kidding me, Jack?'

Nonetheless, this would be precisely how he'd expect her to respond if indeed this was a ploy.

'You're in the music business, Mairi, *a cruel and shallow money trench, a long plastic hallway where thieves and pimps run free, and good men die like dogs.*'

'*There is also a negative side,*' she responded archly, completing the quote. 'I'm familiar with the words. I just didn't think you were quite as cynical as Hunter S. Thompson.'

'I'm simply telling you how it looks from here. Two weeks before her biggest-ever album gets released, Heike's manager is asking a journalist to look into her sudden disappearance; and how better to disguise her true intentions – not to mention bait the hook – than to get him to sign a non-disclosure agreement. Then, when the story breaks, you can even get out of paying him.'

Mairi swallowed back whatever she was about to unleash, professionalism taking over.

'Point taken,' she said, just about keeping her voice steady. 'But I want you to ask yourself: after what you did for Donald, do you actually think I would try to use you like that?'

Parlabane met her gaze and answered honestly.

'After what I've been through lately, I truly don't know what anybody is or isn't capable of any more. But because I don't want to live in that world where my accusation is true, I'm going to take you at face value.'

She nodded subtly by way of acknowledgement.

'That said,' Parlabane went on, 'could it still be a stunt that you're not in on?'

She didn't even think about the question, which told him she'd asked it herself already.

'Not a chance. This is Heike we're talking about. After the shit she's been through with the media, and given how much she likes to micro-manage everything down to the last press release, there's no way she'd willingly put herself at the centre of a storm she couldn't control.'

Mairi glanced down at Heike's photograph on the magazine: elegantly poised, as graceful as she was formidable.

'The very reason I'm worried is that this isn't like her,' she said. 'I need you to find her, but I can't let it get out that she's missing, and you know how little it would take for a rumour to start in this business. The band don't even know. I got Jan, the tour manager, to tell them she had been in touch to say she was ill and had flown home as it was the last night of the tour.'

'They bought that?'

'They knew there was something iffy about it, but they've all been around Heike long enough to have witnessed her, shall we say, self-protective side. Besides, they're all governed by the golden rule that what happens on tour stays on tour. But *something* must have happened. I heard through other sources that Heike had a minor breakdown on-stage in Hamburg, two nights before she went missing. I can't get anything out of the band, though, and if I push hard on the subject, they'll get suspicious. That's why I need you.'

'Why are you so desperate to keep it quiet? Surely the more people who know someone as recognisable as Heike Gunn is missing, the greater the likelihood of her being spotted.'

'I can't have this turning into a media circus. For one thing, once it's all resolved – *inshallah* – I don't want Heike thinking that we in any way milked this. But to be brutally honest, I don't want the record company spooked. Nobody at Sentinel knows about this, and if it all blows up they might get very nervous about authorising that seven-figure marketing spend.'

'Well, that tracks, at least.'

'What?'

'She's your meal ticket.'

He thought Mairi might bridle at this, but she seemed to let it bounce off her.

'Heike is a lot of people's meal ticket, and that has to be quite a responsibility. Like I said, she takes a lot on her shoulders. She's got a tough reputation, but she's far more fragile than people assume. I'm worried about her, Jack. I need you to bring her home.'

Running Away with the Circus

I will always associate the sound of the fiddle with my grandfather.

It was the sound I heard whenever I went to his house, and whenever he came over to ours. I mean, it wasn't like he carried the thing about with him all the time, just that I have a more vivid recollection of those visits when he had his violin with him. Looking back, these are probably brighter memories because they were social gatherings, and when I was really wee, I loved a busy house and a crowd of familiar faces in the living room and the kitchen.

When I got a bit older, I was less comfortable with such shindigs, as I would be asked to demonstrate how my own playing was coming along. It felt horrible to be put on the spot, and sometimes I would compound my faulty fingering as I got more and more flustered. But when I was playing well it was a thrill to be getting it right in front of other people. Even now, whenever I'm in front of an audience there's still this tension between my fear of flustering under the spotlight and the way adrenaline can bring out a level of performance that would be impossible if I was by myself.

Even when I got more confident and my abilities were really starting to develop, I would still get butterflies whenever I was asked up in front of family, mainly because I could feel how nervous my mum was. She was always anxious that I should play well, especially in front of Granda.

They sometimes say that talent skips a generation. I don't know about that, but I'm sure my mum believed it. Growing up on Shetland, where the fiddle is practically a way of life, she was always worrying she had disappointed Granda. She had put in the hours and achieved a certain competence, but she didn't have a gift and she didn't have a passion. That was why she was so adamant that I'd be a great fiddle player, and so hard on me about practising.

She desperately wanted my playing to please her father in the way hers never could.

I could always sense that she was on edge whenever I played in front of him, or even in front of anybody who knew him; which on a place like Shetland didn't leave out many people. And just as she didn't want to disappoint her dad, I never wanted to let down my mum.

It's why I've always been a bit of a goody two-shoes. I was never in trouble as a child, not even a hint, because my mum is a teacher. At primary school, while the other kids knew that their carry-on might earn them a punny but that would be the end of it, I just assumed that if I stepped out of line, it would get back to her before I even got home. And at my secondary school, where she actually taught, I reckoned she would find out in the staff room by the end of the next interval.

So I was hard-working, well behaved and a bit quiet. Too quiet still, I think. I'm shy, which is hardly a vice, but sometimes I hate myself for shrinking into the background when I've got something to say. I know it's easier for other people, but deep down I know I'm being cowardly.

I can take the spotlight if I'm playing my fiddle, but otherwise, those sidelines look quite comfy, thank you. That's why folk were amazed to learn I was joining a band: not just doing session work in a studio, but actually going on the road. They could picture me taking my place in the orchestra, even travelling to the Mod each year, as it was easy to imagine me playing my wee part of something so respectable. But a band?

They'd even double-check the word, carefully chosen by me. A *band*, you say? Yes. Not a group, as in folk, or a quartet, as in string. A band. As in . . . well, let's let the critics argue about that one. (Rock? Indy? Grind-core death metal? Maybe not the last.)

And if folk who knew me were amazed, there aren't the words to convey my own levels of surprise, which continued to plague me all the more the closer it came to the start of the tour.

I know I was in denial during the rehearsals. It didn't feel that different to studio work: just a bigger soundproofed room, except more of the floor was messy with flight cases and there was no recording console.

Whenever we all sat in the pub afterwards, or went for a curry, it went through my mind that I was about to go away for months with these people I barely knew. And this wasn't going to be like going on tour with an orchestra. This was . . . well, I didn't know, and was trying not to let my imagination run away with me. How wild could it get? I asked myself. We were never out that late on those pub nights. Damien, the lead guitarist and the most rock-looking guy in the band, was always imposing a curfew by buying the 'last round', reminding everybody of their professional obligations to turn up to rehearsals on time in the morning and to be able to give our best.

It wasn't Mötley Crüe I was going out there with.

People still loved winding me up about what I was getting myself into though, especially old orchestra colleagues and friends from back home. All the usual rubbish about throwing televisions out of hotel windows. Yeah, yeah: sex, drugs and rock 'n' roll. Please. My fiancé Keith was always making duff jokes about it, failing to hide his own unease. When he wasn't acting like he couldn't take it seriously, he was acting like it wasn't happening at all, or that things would get back to normal once it was over.

We never discussed what 'over' would mean.

I got more nervous and more impatient the closer I came to that opening night. I just needed it all to be under way. Then, only a few days before we were due to kick off the tour, Granda died.

It wasn't exactly out of nowhere. He was ninety-two and he'd been fading over the past three years, requiring him to move into assisted accommodation and then into a nursing home, but it still felt sudden, as he hadn't been ill or anything.

Dad came back for the funeral, flying in from London. First time I'd seen him in close to a year. He fronted up I guessed as a gesture of respect and affection for Granda. Given the way he'd acted over the last few years of their marriage, nobody was going to mistake it as a show of support for Mum.

I admit I got a weird buzz from the look of shock and worry

on his face when I told him why I'd be flying out first thing the next morning.

Aye, Jamie, your first-born daughter is running away with the circus. Suck it up.

Then he kind of neutralised it by telling me that he had Savage Earth Heart's last album on his iPod. Actually he said 'the' album, obviously ignorant of it being their second, but then that went for just about everybody who bought *The Venal Tribe* after 'Do It to Julia' got used on that American TV show. No matter. The point was, if my dad listened to them, then how hell-raisey could Savage Earth Heart be?

It was a good funeral. We do generally give good funeral in Shetland, which is not to say that we sent Granda off to sea in a floating pyre, but that it was more of a celebration than a wake. I saw lots of familiar faces, got a lot of hugs, and we all cried good tears, warm tears, the kind that make you feel better.

Despite the temptations of such a gathering, maybe haunted by the image of Damien standing over me and glancing at the clock, I got myself a comparatively early night. Keith came up to bed around the same time too, under the pretence of making sure I was all right but actually a bit frisky. The combination of such an emotional day and a few too many drinks had much the same effect on me.

We had sex for what was actually only the third time. (I'm not even sure if the second one really counts, as he barely got it in. Things were even tighter than the first time, as I kept tensing up.) It went better than on both previous occasions, but to be honest, it still didn't feel anything like as good as before we lost our virginities. Prior to that, there had always been the thrill of pushing things to the next stage, then for a long time just getting good at what we did do.

This is not a blog, by the way. I mean, it *is* a blog, obviously, but that doesn't mean it's for anyone else to read. In fact, it's absolutely NOT for anyone else to read, so I suppose it's a diary then, but that doesn't sound right.

27

Whatever.

The point is, I'm writing it for myself. I'm writing it because I think the next few weeks are going to pass in a blur, and I want to get all of this down so that I'm able to remember it when I'm older. When I have kids and grandkids, I want to be able to look back and tell them: you know, I was actually once a rock star – sort of.

Plus, I reckon it will give me something to do on all those bus journeys, which look like being a big part of my life in the weeks to come.

The sun was shining when I reached Bristol, hazy in the late afternoon. Through the cab window I caught a glimpse of the water and a trendy development: all glass frontages and renovated dockside buildings. It looked a nice place to go for a wander, but the cab veered away from it like it had just been teasing me. I recalled Damien the guitarist describing the reality of tour travel: 'You think you'll be seeing the world, but you'll mostly be just missing it. And your day off will be in Gdansk.'

The venue for this, my first night on stage as part of Savage Earth Heart, was the Academy. The place looked shut, all the doors closed tight. The band's name was picked out in black plastic letters on a white, backlit (but currently unpowered) marquee sign. The words 'SOLD OUT' ran underneath, causing me some anxiety. For others they might be a source of pride, but I knew nobody was coming here tonight to see me. My role was just to fill out the sound (and hopefully not bugger it up) for the person they *were* paying to listen to.

I found my way around to the stage loading bay, where the doors were wedged open, ramps running up into the truck's rear doors. I expected to be challenged and asked for credentials as I made my way into the building, but the roadies I passed were too intent on their tasks to be worrying about anything else.

The hammer of a snare drum was bouncing off the walls as I went in. It seemed all the more shockingly loud for being on its own: no bass, no toms, only snare beats every half second. The auditorium was a big rectangular standing area surrounded on three sides by a gallery level. It made me think of a venue for something brutal, like cage fighting. This was probably down to a twisted fear that in a few hours, psychologically speaking, I might be the one being torn apart in front of a baying crowd.

As I came up the ramp I saw people and activity all around, familiar faces concentrated upon their tasks: plugging in leads, fussing over kit like mums over children. Everybody else was already here, which was about the size of it: from my point of view, in Savage Earth Heart everybody else always had been already here.

I got a few waves and nods, but not a lot of hail and hello. I realised I might have been *on schedule* – I had told Jan that I could get here from Shetland in a day – but that wasn't quite the same as *on time*.

I saw Scott, the bass player, no longer the runt of the litter since I became an official member rather than just a session player. I saw Damien, hunched over a pedal board, a guitar pack transmitter partly shadowing a couple of inches of high-quality bum cleavage. And of course I saw Rory, pounding away on the drum riser.

I didn't yet see the star of the show, but I knew she must be around.

A bearded guy in a Nine Inch Nails T-shirt bounded up, the end of a lead folded over multiple times and gripped in his left hand. The face-fuzz looked daft on him: the lengthy whiskers seemed pasted on. He began speaking without introducing himself, a stream of techno-babble. I took in almost none of it and hoped it wasn't important.

I wasn't sure whether I was supposed to know who he was: venue staff or one of the road crew, I couldn't tell. I felt anxious, like I'd been off school and missed lessons. Everybody else seemed to know who each other were and what they were meant to be about.

I felt like an impostor and kept expecting to be told that my being here was a mistake, which was made worse by the fact that the person who had requested my presence was nowhere to be seen. And in truth, my great fear was that she would be the one who would demand to know what the hell I thought I was doing here. I never knew where I stood with Heike from day to day and sometimes hour to hour.

I had been amazed when the producer phoned and asked me to come in for some session work on the new Savage Earth Heart album. I thought it was someone from the orchestra winding me up, because I had taken some flak after I was heard playing along to *The Venal Tribe* in my hotel room. I went as far as getting the guy to hold while I Googled the recording studio he claimed to be calling from and checked the number that was showing up on my handset.

I was a little star-struck the first time I met her, and worried that I'd be all thumbs when it came to playing. Luckily the pressure of trying to please my mum served me well, and I really killed it that day. I remember being delighted with my performance, and then disappointed that Heike said so little about it, detached behind the soundproof glass of the mixing booth. All I got out of her throughout the sessions was technical stuff: give us another run-through; give us more of that; give us less of this. We barely spoke beyond the professional; in fact, we were seldom in the same room.

So it was another big surprise when she asked me to join the band outright: not just for the forthcoming tour, but as a fully fledged member. I didn't need to be asked twice, thinking she must have been running the rule over me in ways I didn't appreciate during the album sessions. I expected our relationship to take on a different footing after that, but I can't say that it did, really.

From then on we were in the same room, at least, hammering away for hours at a time in a rehearsal space down by the Clyde in preparation for the live shows. But at the end of those days Heike just seemed to disappear, hardly ever coming for drinks or a bite with the rest of us. She always had somewhere she needed to be: meetings with Mairi, the band's manager, meetings with the label, media interviews, photo shoots. I wondered whether she was subtly laying down a dividing line between herself and the rest of us, as though to emphasise that we were only her backing band.

Maybe that was what was going on during set-up here in Bristol: the minions scurrying around, making everything ready before their queen graced them with her presence.

I only needed a glimpse of her, maybe a nod or a wave: just

something that would make me feel I was in the right place, because nothing else was doing that so far.

I got shouted at to knock off tuning up because it was interfering with something else on the console. Then I got shouted at again because I had gone off in a worried daydream and didn't realise I was being addressed when the sound engineer actually needed me to play.

And all the while, Rory was providing an unsettling backbeat to my discomfort, testing the mics on each part of his kit.

I'd spoken to our drummer even less than I'd spoken to Heike. He made me a little nervy. Scared, even: like of a dog, where you're not sure if it's because you don't know the animal or because your instinct is rightly telling you to beware. In all the time we'd been rehearsing, I don't think his words to me were in double figures. He rarely came to the pub, and when he did he sat away from me.

It had struck me on one such night that maybe he'd been pals with Maxi, the band's original fiddler. Yeah, that thought made for a cosy evening.

At some point Rory finally stopped hitting things, though only because the sound engineer was asking him something.

'No, I told you,' he grunted irritably in reply. 'I don't want to hear any fucking fiddle.'

At least nobody in the audience would be bearing a grudge about the appearance of a new violin player, like they might if we were a metal band who had swapped out a legendary guitarist. There was only one member of this group that wasn't replaceable. The band had been praised for its musicianship and for developing a distinct sound, but we were under no illusions: Savage Earth Heart was Heike Gunn.

Everybody understood that. Most of all Heike.

The young guy with the mis-beard returned and attached an instrumental mic to my fiddle.

I nearly jumped when I first drew the bow: I had never heard it make such a loud noise, reverberating around the empty hall. I got a brief thrill of power, followed by a less pleasant awareness of how amplified and obvious it would be if I got anything wrong.

At first it sounded like I was playing my fiddle inside a giant biscuit tin, but as the engineer altered a few settings it gradually became warmer until I was enjoying the sound and the volume so much that I had to be shouted at again to knock it off. I was yet to learn that this part of the soundcheck was always very stop-start, full of double-backs and minor adjustments.

It often sounded just fine to me, only for him to alter it again, sometimes for the worse, other times for an improvement I could not have anticipated.

'Don't worry about it,' he said, noting my frown in response to him deciding on a final setting that seemed rougher than the last. 'We're not happy until you're not happy.'

I was so intent upon the process that I hadn't noticed Heike appear on stage, a few feet to my left.

Since last I saw her, only a few days ago, she had dyed her hair pink in a startling change from her trademark cream-blonde, and had straightened it to wear down rather than in its familiar tight curls. When I say pink, I don't mean bright, screaming pink. It was kind of a half-arsed, mixed-colours-in-the-washing-machine pink. I didn't get it. It looked like she had been going for Hayley Williams and picked up the wrong bottle. That wasn't Heike, though. If her hair was a specific colour, that style, that length, it was for a reason.

She gave me a quick smile and nod, then turned her attention back to Angus, the guitar roadie and the one guy I knew was definitely on *our* crew, as he had been at most of the rehearsals. She crouched down with him in front of her pedalboard, instantly focused on her preparations. I caught a glimpse of that letter H she had tattooed on the inside of her right arm, which reminded me that I was the only person in the band – maybe even the only person in the building – who didn't have ink.

I had half-hoped she'd bound over and welcome me, say she was pleased I had made it, maybe ask about the funeral.

I ticked myself off for being so needy. She had a lot of responsibilities, and there wasn't time for hand-holding and making sure I fitted in. It was a soundcheck, for God's sake. We were all busy.

Still, I felt myself become determined to make her glad I was here, and ensure she had a wider smile for me before the show was over.

After a period I guessed was possibly longer than our scheduled set, everybody was happy enough with the set-up to try running through a few songs. I was almost bursting with my need to actually play something, but the first number only kicked off more tinkering. Heike seemed unsatisfied with just about everything.

The whole soundcheck broke down for about half an hour while she fussed over her guitar and vocal levels. Two of the guys nipped out for a fag, while I took the opportunity to speak to the one person to whom I could admit I was terrified.

I wandered off to the wings, crouched down against a wall and fumbled for my phone.

'My hands are trembling,' I told Keith. 'I can barely grip my bow.'

'Don't be daft, Mon,' he replied, his tone patient and reassuring. 'You've done this a million times, and with *proper* musicians.'

'These *are* proper musicians.'

'You know what I mean. You're used to playing at a higher level than anybody else on that stage.'

'I'm not used to playing in front of this kind of crowd.'

'And that's why you shouldn't worry. Nobody in that audience is going to notice if you get a note wrong, not like at an orchestra recital full of trained ears. The fans will all be half cut. Plus, the only thing they'll really be paying attention to is the singer.'

He was right about that much. There was little doubt that she knew it too, hence my waiting and waiting for Heike to decide she was happy with the sound.

When we were through, the support act barely had time to soundcheck before the doors opened, and they didn't look too pleased about it. They had been hovering outside in the loading bay the whole time, smoking and waiting for the all-clear.

I heard Damien try to smooth it over with their singer.

'Sorry mate, we're always like this the first night. Bigger venue than we're used to. We'll take half the time tomorrow, you'll see.'

I noted the 'we', when it was obvious to everybody that Heike had been the one drawing things out. I didn't know whether Damien was being loyal or protective, or whether he was just aware that it was best to stop things becoming personal.

'Yeah, no worries,' the singer replied, giving Damien a pat on the shoulder as he left, but as soon as our guitarist was gone, he resumed his moaning.

'One spawny hit off the back of a fucking Yank TV show and she thinks she's Lady Gaga,' he spat.

'Yep,' replied their keyboard player. 'Gonna be a long fucking tour.'

One of them glanced across as though just noticing I was there. He looked away again, unperturbed. I realised that as they had been outside during our run-through they didn't know who I was.

It made me feel oddly powerful for a moment, like I enjoyed the gift of invisibility and now had a secret I could use. Then I realised that they'd suss who I was soon enough. Great. I would already be feeling awkward about it before it became mutual, and we still had twelve dates with these guys.

'Steady, lads,' said a voice, gruff and firm but not aggressive. It belonged to a burly middle-aged bloke in a Def Leppard T-shirt, spinning a roll of tape around his index finger.

'Don't let your emotions run wild and give you a false impression. None of you know Miss Heike yet.'

'Yeah, okay, but—' the singer responded, still too angry to be apologetic.

'She's a complex young woman,' Def Leppard went on forcefully. 'Now, I appreciate she might have got your backs up a little tonight, but I promise you lads, by the end of the tour . . . you're gonna fucking *despise* her.'

He said this last part quietly, through his teeth, glancing briefly at me as he spoke. He knew I was there and he knew who I was, or at least that I was in the band, but very clearly he didn't care.

It was like he was sending me a warning: I just couldn't work out whether it was about Heike or about himself.

What Happens on Tour

Mairi had arranged for the band to meet Parlabane at their regular rehearsal space, a low-rise warren of soundproofed rooms off the Broomielaw, in the shadow of the Kingston Bridge. From the number of flight cases lining the walls and floors of the place, it looked like there were several bands at work today. He was pretty sure he passed Joe Rattray of Admiral Fallow in the corridor, and his inner fanboy wished he had the luxury of just hanging around and listening at a few doors.

Instead, he would be listening to lies and evasion.

He was expecting four of them: Scott Hastie, the bass player; Damien Lowe, lead guitar; Rory Friel, drummer; and Monica the violinist. He was also expecting them to be late, and they didn't disappoint. Mairi didn't show up on time either, leaving him to sit in the reception area like a spare tool. He tried not to dwell on the fact that he was currently in possession of the biggest showbiz scoop in the country but bound by what few principles he had left not to share it. Reflexively, as was the modern custom whenever one had a minimum of thirty seconds to kill, he got out his phone, but he wasn't checking Twitter or firing up Angry Birds. These days Parlabane's idle-hands temptation was to ring Sarah on the off chance that one of these times she'd pick up.

They'd be a little tentative and awkward at first, but they'd have news to discuss as they hadn't spoken in so long. Small talk, little details about what they'd each been up to. That would lead to more solicitous enquiries, rekindling familiar interest in each other's thoughts and feelings. Soon enough they'd be talking like they used to and she might start asking herself if this didn't mean things were better: that maybe all they'd needed was a break.

It went to voicemail after a few rings. He didn't leave a message: that would betray that he had no pretext for calling.

Three of them pitched up at the same time, piling out of a cab. It was the three males, Damien paying the driver while the other two lingered on the pavement, making no move towards the building. Parlabane read the dynamic right away: Damien was in charge, and they weren't proceeding without the reassurance of his presence. He'd probably been the one who rounded the others up so that they made it here at all.

Mairi called just as they were sauntering through the car park.

'Your flight late?' he asked.

'Yes, sorry. Boarded on time, then there was a problem on the runway, so my phone's been off. Are they there?'

'Just arrived. The guys, anyway.'

'No Monica?'

'Not so far.'

'Shit.'

She didn't sound surprised.

'Problem?'

'I've left her messages telling her the when and where, but she hasn't called me back.'

'She's blanking you?'

'Maybe.'

'Any idea why?'

'I think she might be in the huff. She called me on the tour a couple of times and I gave her short shrift. She was being needy when I didn't have time to indulge her, and I thought learning to toughen up would be more valuable to her in the long term. I'm guessing this is payback.'

Or maybe she had reasons why she didn't want to talk about what had happened in Germany, especially not to a journalist.

For one thing, there were the pictures Mairi had referred to, his laptop screen having filled up with nothing else simply by using 'Savage Earth Heart' as a search string. Clearly relations between the *Tatler* cover's two warrior women were likely to have been strained in the wake of this intrusion, and another few seconds' browsing illustrated the extent of the fallout plume. Monica Halcrow had been engaged to one Keith Jamieson when she set off on tour, but it was safe to say she was free and single by the time she returned home.

Parlabane had been planning to interview them all together as a group and then one by one. He knew they would be particularly guarded during the latter exercise, but he wanted to suss the group dynamics, the body language, who responded to what, the subtle signals that might betray fault lines and allegiances. The absence of the one other female in the line-up was going to alter those dynamics immeasurably.

He listened to their chatter and found it disarming to observe how young they seemed, apart from Damien, who was like the veteran footballer brought in to steady a team of raw and inexperienced talent. The rest were in their early- to mid-twenties, which made it seem incredible that they could be on their third album. That was until he remembered how far *he* had come by that age, once upon a time.

He recalled that Sarah had thought he was in his mid-thirties when they first met. He had actually just turned twenty-seven. He had joked that his career up until then gave a new meaning to the term 'tough paper round', but it didn't help that he was not long off a plane from Los Angeles, his jet lag accentuated by having spent some of the intervening time in police custody.

Looking back, it was perhaps the first signal that she saw someone else whenever she looked at him. She had certainly endeavoured to shape and modify him thereafter, so perhaps there was an idealised image that she always had in mind. If he ever had a son, that would be one of the most valuable pieces of advice he could impart: beware the woman who sees you as a work in progress.

'How's Jack?'

'Let me show you the blueprints.'

If he ever had a son. He still caught himself speculating like that. There had been a time when it had seemed like an eventuality he didn't need to hurry towards. Then, just like that, it became something he had to accept was never going to happen.

'So, a successful tour,' Parlabane said to them. 'Sold-out shows all across Europe. Hit single playing everywhere, new album, *Smuggler's Soul*, ready for release. Sounds like days of wine and roses. You guys must feel like your ship's come in and you're living the dream. Or at least, that's what everybody will assume. I'm guessing the reality feels less glam and more knackering, would I be right?'

He was laying down his markers, letting them know he wasn't here to do a puff piece and inviting them to talk about the day-to-day.

'More beer and vomit than wine and roses,' Scott suggested with a self-conscious grin, identifying himself as the joker in the pack.

'And if our ship came in,' added Rory with a little more steel in his tone, 'then its journey was fuelled by several years of slog and sacrifice.'

This was where he wanted this to go: not the encores and the plaudits, but the toil, the grudges, the divisions and the resentments.

'Wait, you're saying it isn't all first-class travel and topless groupies peeling grapes?'

'I'm not going to whine about it,' Rory replied. 'It's the best job in the world. But it's not the easiest job in the world. We've all come a long way to get here.'

'Aye,' agreed Scott. 'Damien especially: they hadn't even invented the electric guitar when he was in his first band.'

Damien laughed indulgently. Parlabane saw an act of solidarity rather than a genuine response to what had to be a very long-running and probably decreasingly funny joke.

'Rory's right, though,' he said. 'It's been a long journey and the results of our hard work are all there to be seen and heard. We're amazingly proud of *Smuggler's Soul*: it's an album you could have played us five years ago and we'd never have believed we were capable of producing it. I mean, it's a way more layered sound than its predecessors: less raw, but not less bold. It's more confident. More polished.'

'Aye, polished like a coffee table,' said Scott, laughing.

Damien clouted him gently on the back of the head. Parlabane looked for a hint that there had been divisions over a shift towards the mainstream, but there was nothing: no hint that Scott had a serious point beneath his joke nor that Damien was annoyed by his indiscretion. Clearly they had talked about what the critics and the fans might say.

'It's more commercial than before,' Damien admitted, 'but that's been more about us learning what we're capable of. These soaring, sweeping soundscapes aren't something you can do after a few jam sessions.'

Parlabane quickly sussed that Damien had assumed the PR role. Even if he believed this journalist was offering a vent for their gripes and a chance to talk about life at the coalface, he was determined to finesse Parlabane's impression of the band. He was talking everything up and steering the conversation away from dangerous areas.

Parlabane's job was to steer them right back there.

'I suppose the other thing that must have affected your sound is the replacement of Alistair Maxwell with Monica Halcrow. Has that been a smooth transition?'

Rory and Scott said nothing, conspicuously deferring to Damien. The pause only lasted half a second, but it was enough.

'Well, Monica's been a breath of fresh air,' Damien responded, clutching at a cliché to fill the gap while he thought of what he ought to say.

'Literally,' added Scott, 'considering how much Maxi used to smoke.'

'Maxi was a big part of Savage Earth Heart getting where we are today,' Damien went on, his efforts to manage the message extending to the band's history now. 'But Monica's a class apart. She's schooled in both classical and traditional music, and she's managed to bridge both styles within our new sound.'

'It can't have been easy for her, though,' Parlabane suggested. 'First-ever tour, wee quiet girl from Shetland dragged around half of Europe. How did you all get along?'

'She's not that quiet,' said Scott. ''Specially if you're through the wall from her room.'

Rory tried to stifle a smirk. Damien shook his head and gave Parlabane an apologetic grin, as if to say: 'What can you do?'

'So did she come out . . . of her shell?' he suggested.

'Touring is a very demanding business, physically and mentally,' Damien said, back in the role of spokesman and thus charged with speaking while saying as little as possible.

Parlabane was happy to let him get on with it. He had spent more than twenty years interviewing people who thought they were telling him nothing. Consequently he was adept at seeing the shapes cast by the shadows where they were determined no light would fall. And if that didn't work, there was always the hacking and burglary route.

'Monica handled it well,' Damien went on. 'I think it helped both her and Heike to have another woman around. They were pretty close.'

Damien seemed to be leaving it there, then evidently decided not to ignore the elephant.

'Things got a bit strained for a while after the photos, but what would you expect? They were all pals again soon enough. She realised it was just collateral damage from the press's obsession with Heike.'

'And does that collateral damage not get to the rest of you sometimes too?'

'I've thought about lamping a few photographers,' Rory admitted. 'Just to remind them that if they want to get to her, they have to go through us first.'

Damien nodded sagely at this, Parlabane unable to miss the warning that was being aimed at him.

'I get that you'd need to be as tight a unit off stage as you are on it,' he acknowledged. 'But do you ever feel you don't get your dues when the press makes it all about Heike? I don't mean are you envious; I mean, is it frustrating that the media are obsessed with her for reasons that have nothing to do with your music?'

'Aye,' said Rory. 'That's another reason I want to lamp the photographers.'

'They're not there because Heike's a singer,' said Scott, finally sounding sincere. 'They're not even there because they see her as a person. They're just interested in the next episode of "Heike the media persona", like it's her *band* that's the sideshow.'

'We have to take the rough with the smooth, though,' added Damien, Parlabane taking quiet note of his use of the collective rather than the personal, like he was reminding the others of the official position. 'As a band, the exposure we're enjoying is undeniably greater because of Heike's profile. That's why we have to tolerate the media's intrusions, but also why we do what we can to protect Heike from their excesses.'

Yes, Parlabane wondered, but did you all know that was what you were signing up for?

Heike Gunn was big news, fast becoming one of Britain's most iconic musical figures. Too fast, Parlabane might have said. Being perfectly honest, before Mairi engaged his services and made her revelation, he would have regarded Heike Gunn going missing as a source of welcome relief from her ubiquity.

It wasn't that she was over-exposed so much as *where* she was exposed. Her opinion – which she never seemed shy of giving – was solicited and splashed across the media on every subject, from fracking to twerking. A couple of years back, Savage Earth Heart were a moderately successful indie band (and one Parlabane admired), but nobody in the press thought that two highly regarded albums were a sound basis to go seeking Heike Gunn's opinion on the pressing issues of the day. Then, shortly after 'Do It to Julia' became a worldwide hit – more than a year after being thoroughly ignored upon its initial release – suddenly she was an expert on everything from the environment to international relations. However, one song wasn't enough to make anybody a superstar, even one given the considerable helping hand of being featured during a season-defining moment in a hit TV show.

The sad truth was that if Heike was four feet tall with a hump, she might still sell a few records, but she wouldn't have the media chasing her all over Europe. She was attractive, she was stylish and she knew how to sell a carefully constructed image of herself. She courted controversy, baited the tabloids with an alacrity bordering on the reckless and she knew how to make any given story about her.

And, of course, there was the issue of her father. Ramsay Gunn had been among the most influential Scottish artists of his generation, one of those Bowie-like figures who always seemed to be tapping into a cultural seam before anyone else even noticed it. He had lived and worked in California in the late sixties, and was said to have been present at the birth of the modern green movement. He painted cover art for prog-rock classics in London in the early seventies, then pre-dated punk's own rejection of the same when he lit out on an ultra-realism period, immersing himself in an almost documentary style of painting, from African war zones to the theatres of European leftist terrorism.

Coming on the back of this, of course, he spent the late seventies and early eighties in West Berlin, but returned to his native Islay before the Wall fell, in order to raise his German-born daughter.

It was said that Heike was born to be a cultural icon, but from what Parlabane had discovered about her upbringing, she wasn't exactly groomed for the spotlight. Nothing was in the public domain about her mother, who had died in Heike's infancy, resulting in Ramsay's retreat to the island of his own youth and a more contemplative period of landscape work. He had raised his daughter largely on his own, a succession of muses, female artists and hippy flakes fulfilling motherly duties to highly varying degrees, according to the gossip.

'On the whole, I think she's played her hand well,' Parlabane suggested. 'She's used the exposure to give herself a platform. But don't you ever worry she's riding a tiger?'

'You worry, sure,' said Scott. 'She's my big cousin, for God's sake. But on the other hand, Heike's smarter than the tabloids. They think they know what she's about, but Heike's always one step ahead of where you think.'

Rory let out a chuckle.

'Yeah. I'll never forget the *Sun* calling her a hypocrite for backing the No More Page Three campaign when she had done what they called topless modelling. She had posed nude for a painting by a woman who had won the fucking Turner Prize, and the result was hardly spank-bank material.'

'It would be like wanking to a Picasso,' Scott said.

'The media claim she wants to have her cake and eat it,' said Damien, once again grabbing the reins. 'They say she's partly selling her music on her image, while at the same time condemning sexism in the media. It's impossible to describe just how much they don't get it. And it's not about an image: it's about who and what Heike is. There's a million beautiful women out there, a million singers, a million songwriters. It's about the whole package. It's that unquantifiable but unmistakable thing: star quality. Whatever it is, we all know Heike's got it. She's touched by magic, and everybody wants some of the stardust to sprinkle on them.'

When the last of his interviews was over, Mairi was waiting for him in the reception area, sipping a coffee she must have bought from the greasy spoon he'd passed on the way in.

'Well?' she asked expectantly. 'Did you find out anything?'

'Yeah. That they're all lying.'

'What?'

'By omission, at least. I've been speaking to them for two hours, and in all that time, nobody told me one thing that wasn't already in the public domain. On a certain level it's pretty impressive. It takes a degree of concentration to filter out anything, even an innocuous detail, that might have come from your own memory rather than reportage.'

'Like I said, what happens on tour . . . So what's next?'

'I'm not sure yet. I should talk to the road crew: they might be a little less guarded.'

Mairi looked confused.

'But what about the band? Is there not more you can find out from them?'

'Your ground rules make it kind of tricky. I could press harder if they knew Heike was missing, but you don't want that. I'll have to come back to them when I've got more information from elsewhere. Right now I've got no leverage.'

Confusion was giving way to undisguised disappointment. Parlabane didn't know what she was expecting, but he hadn't delivered it.

'No leverage? Don't you have other means of finding out what they might know?'

'Like what?' he asked, adding an admonitory sternness to his tone.

'I thought you were the kind of guy who would stop at nothing to get to the story.'

'For one thing, I'm not allowed to *tell* the story, so maybe that's taking my edge off. But that aside, these days I stop at the stuff that's liable to get me the jail.'

'I just thought . . .'

Mairi sighed.

This was when he realised why she hired him.

'You just thought what? That I could maybe hack their phones or pull some black-arts shit you heard about during the Coulson and Brooks trial?'

'But you said it yourself: it wouldn't be for publication, and there's someone missing who I'm worried about. Wouldn't the end justify the means?'

Parlabane laughed. He couldn't help himself. He thought about the blueprints, the modifications Sarah had been so determined to make. She had been the driving force in getting him to clean up his act, to cut out the practices that were going to see him 'end up dead or in prison again', as she often put it. And he had done so, more or less. That was the biggest irony about how he had been hung out to dry by some of his former employers: he had long since stopped doing most of the things he was being scapegoated for.

He wasn't the same man any more, but whoever he'd become, it seemed Sarah didn't think much of that bloke either. Or maybe it was just that *he* didn't think much of that bloke. He couldn't blame Sarah for not loving someone who didn't much like himself.

Now it appeared the only gig he could get was working for somebody who thought they had hired the old Parlabane. Unfor-

44

tunately, he wasn't coming back. He had tried being his former self again: that was how he'd ended up with Pine and Mitchell up his arse.

'Have you heard of the Westercruik Inquiry?' he asked her, realising he'd probably been mistaken in his assumption the other day that she must have done.

'Vaguely. Remind me.'

'It's looking into the Anthony Mead scandal. The MoD leaks. The "intelligence services conspiracy" story that turned out to be the biggest riddie for a UK newspaper since the Hitler diaries.'

'Oh, yeah. Something about a stolen laptop that was actually bait to find the source of the leaks. I realise it must have turned up the heat on journalists, but this isn't state secrets I'm asking you to—'

'I'm Alec Forman,' he interrupted. 'I was the one who hacked the laptop. I've got the Met all over me trying to find out how it came to be in my possession. So not only am I a busted flush, but even if I'm a very good boy I'm going to be doing very well to stay out of the clink.'

'Alec Forman? I thought your pseudonym was John Lapsley.'

'Needed a new one. It's an anagram of *roman à clef*. John Lapsley's gone. I'm sorry, Mairi. I'm not the guy who found out the truth about Donald, any more than I'm the guy who used to come round your parents' house when I was seventeen.'

Mairi said nothing for a few moments, then emitted a small tut.

'Pity,' she said. 'I quite liked both of those. I'll take what I can get, though.'

'I know the feeling.'

Our Thing

The period after the soundcheck felt like an eternity of waiting. I knew I would have to learn to occupy myself, somehow make use of the time, as it was going to happen every night we performed. Practice would be one option, but I didn't feel like even touching my violin until I was ready to take the stage.

We dined together; or rather we sat down to food together. I barely ate anything for fear of not keeping it down.

I felt very alone in the dressing room. I sat at one end of the mirrored wall, conscious of not being entitled to join any particular conversation.

Heike was sitting on her own too, thumbing through a book, though not really reading it. She kept looking at the clock.

I had spoken to her, but only when she asked if I was okay and I answered yes. She seemed distant yet focused; just not focused on the here and now.

Nobody was saying much, in fact. Rory was silently nodding his head to whatever was playing in his headphones. Damien was normally the one geeing everybody up, but even he was quiet.

Scott came back in for the third or fourth time. I wondered whether he had a nervous bladder, as it was a worry of mine to find myself mid-performance and in dire need. Heike looked at him harshly.

'Just a fag, I swear,' he replied with a chuckle, as though amused by whatever was in this unspoken accusation. She gave him a sour look, but I couldn't suss why.

Every time he opened the door I could hear the support band on stage. I felt I ought to go and watch them, as a distraction or maybe out of politeness and for the sake of future relations, but I didn't want to catch a glimpse of the hall yet, either from the stage or the floor. I knew it would make me worse, and quite possibly make me puke.

That was when I realised everybody else was just as on edge as me.

Nobody was on solid ground here. This was a bigger venue than they had ever played, and was not even the biggest on the UK schedule. This tour was a major step for the band. It was nights like this that would make people fans for life, or go home thinking, Yeah *The Venal Tribe* is a decent album, but they're shite live.

I was suddenly all the more conscious of what the others had already put into this, while I had been dropped in at the last minute. Sure, I had played on every track on the new album, but nobody was coming tonight because of that. It made it all the more crucial that I did nothing to jeopardise their success. I had to play well, and I had to look like I belonged. I knew I was capable of the first. Right then the second felt more of a stretch.

Finally, after that endless wait in the dressing room, we got our cue, almost running on to the stage, where suddenly time accelerated.

I have literally no memory of the first three, maybe four numbers. Nothing. It's like someone wiped the tape, seriously. First thing I recall from the set was realising that my eyes were closed. I mean, yes, sometimes I do play with my eyes closed, but it seemed I had them shut tight for most of those opening songs. I only became aware of this during 'Zoo Child', when I sensed someone shoot past me and blinked them open in surprise. It was like I had been practising alone and then suddenly found myself transported on to that stage in front of a packed hall.

It was Scott who had almost bumped into me. He gave me a funny grin of acknowledgement, opening his eyes comically wide to make the point. I guessed then that it was actually me who had almost bumped into Scott, so I must have been moving around more than I realised.

With my eyes open, I stayed relatively still for the next few songs, hiding from the spotlights by keeping closer to the wings stage right. But then it was time for 'Dark Station', when there was no hiding place. It was just me and Heike on stage, fiddle and acoustic guitar, a stripped-back sound for a haunting, desolate song, rallying at the end with a defiant cry of hope.

During the intro, without the thunder of drums at my back and with nothing else coming through the monitors in front, I could hear not just the murmur of the crowd, but could make out individual voices. Then when Heike opened her mouth, her lips almost kissing the microphone, I could hear hundreds of other voices sing along. She let them take a final repeat of the chorus, dropping out her guitar so that I was the only accompaniment to the crowd. It was literally spine-tingling: I felt like there was static thrilling through me; that if anyone touched me we would both be electrocuted.

I was supposed to segue into 'A Square of Captured Light', but completely forgot. I think it was for the best: Heike looked quite shaken to hear her words sung back to her by so many people, and she needed the moment that was given her by the cheers and applause. There were tears in her eyes, though only I was close enough to see them.

Something passed between us right then: an understanding, a responsibility, a trust. I might have seen something I wasn't supposed to, but she expected me to keep it to myself.

The applause began to die, and I launched us into the more upbeat 'Smuggler's Soul'. That's when things really got strange.

As per the album version, it starts with guitar and violin beneath Heike's vocal on the first verse, while the rest of the band quietly file back into position, exploding as one into the chorus.

We were five on stage again, but it was like Heike and I were still a separate unit in the midst of the others. I stayed next to her centre stage, and as the song built towards its long outro, we started dancing around each other.

Most of the time, I sit down to play, as that's how I'll be throughout an orchestral performance. Sometimes when I'm playing alone I'll stand, but it's like I'm in the naughty corner. I retreat inside myself, and anyway there's never much space on the stages I'm used to.

But on that night I found myself birling about like I was possessed.

The others gave us space as Heike and I spun around each other, approaching and retreating, then dancing back-to-back while below us the audience were screaming in approval.

Suddenly we flew apart on the first beat of a new bar, Heike skipping to the front and thrashing away at her strings before a swell of bodies rushing to be near her.

I found myself heading in the opposite direction, towards the back, and I leaped onto the drum riser, facing Rory. It was a surge of energy, I guess.

He looked astonished, then reacted with aggression on the drums, as if I had invaded his turf and he was trying to drive me out. I came back at him, looking him in the eye as I worked the bow furiously. It was like we were in combat, feeding off each other's energy and fuelling an ever rising level of performance.

He went to the floor tom to start a roll, swinging around as if he was about to throw the thing, then whiplashed back for a cymbal crash. His taut muscle drove wood against the brass like it was meant to kill, and sweat flew from his arms. It sprayed against my face, and instead of grossing me out, well . . . I'm embarrassed to write it even for myself.

We locked into each other's stares again and I felt this surge of aggression that shocked me. I don't know where it came from and I don't even know if I wanted him sexually or I wanted to hurt him. What's for certain is that if someone had teleported us away somewhere in that moment, I'd have launched myself at him, tearing clothes, scratching, biting, like an animal, primal.

I have never felt so alive, and I've never felt so afraid. It was one of the most disturbing and exhilarating experiences I have ever had: to be frightened of myself.

Just as suddenly as it began, the show was over. I remember the journey back to the dressing room as though it was a tunnel with a moving walkway. I was aware of voices, laughter, arms around shoulders. I had never felt so close to a group of people, so much a part of something amazing, and yet another side of me wanted to be alone, given space to deal with my emotions.

I think I must have been standing there looking a little dazed, because Damien was so soft-spoken and delicate with me. He gave me a bottle of beer and said nothing for a while as we both drank. Saying nothing seemed like the best way of expressing what we had just experienced.

Then finally he spoke.

'You felt it, didn't you?' he asked. He didn't wait for my reply. 'That's why we do this. That's why we put in the hours we do and why we put up with all each other's shite. Because only together can we make *that* happen. Hold on to the feeling, because it's the thought of having it again that's going to pull you through when the going gets rough. And believe me, you've no idea how rough it can get.'

Heike stopped talking to Scott and came over and hugged me. She was drenched in sweat, which was when I realised I was too. Heike's sweat smelled fresh, like she had been out running. There were other smells in there too: body spray and shampoo. I breathed them in and didn't want her to let go.

When she did she told me: 'You were amazing.'

I wanted to say 'you were too' but was tongue-tied.

Over her shoulder I saw Rory, leaning against the wall. He glanced back, raising his bottle in salute. He had a smile on his face, calm and unreadable; not that it would stop me from reading things into it. I had the most vivid fear that he knew what had gone through my mind. I knew this was daft, but the moment had been intense enough to make me believe some very strange things were possible.

A voice in my head told me to phone Keith. I needed to centre myself, or maybe ground myself was more like it, given the electrified sensations I had experienced on the stage.

I reached inside my jacket for my phone, but something stopped me as I swiped the handset awake. When I'd called after orchestra shows, I'd wanted to tell Keith all about it, to share my experience. This time I had been driven by a fearful instinct to place myself back outside of this.

Holding the phone in my hand, I realised I didn't want to do that. I didn't want to share it with him. He wasn't part of this, and nobody who wasn't part of this could understand it.

I put the phone back in my pocket, downed what remained in my bottle and picked up another, clinking it against one Scott was holding up.

Loyalty

As he walked towards his car, Parlabane heard a voice call for him to wait. He turned to see Damien striding across from a huddle of musicians who had gathered outside for a smoke.

If he hadn't looked up his details online, Parlabane wouldn't have guessed him even close to his late thirties. It wasn't just how he dressed, but something about his manner that seemed buoyant, optimistic. Maybe that was how he'd managed to carve out one more chance at the big time after already having had a couple of near misses.

He looked rather serious right now, though.

'I just wanted to check,' Damien said. 'Did I hear you say you were interviewing Heike for this piece as well?'

He was looking Parlabane in the eye, crows' feet around the edges of an intense gaze that betrayed his true years. They also betrayed that Parlabane was being closely scrutinised.

'That's right. Monica as well, though I gather she's maybe not the best disposed towards my profession.'

Damien ignored this attempt to divert the focus.

'When you meeting Heike?'

Interesting.

'Mairi's still working out the fine details, to be honest. I need to file before you guys head to the US, so it's not urgent, but sooner would be better. Maybe you could put a word in, say I don't bite. When are *you* seeing her?'

'I'm not sure,' he replied, poker-faced.

Damien knew something was up, and was curious as to what Parlabane might know, but couldn't probe for fear of giving anything away.

Parlabane had been looking for a weak spot in the façade

Damien was shoring up, and he was pretty sure he'd just found it.

'You used to be in Discolite, didn't you?' Parlabane asked, pretending this had spontaneously occurred to him.

Damien nodded.

'The whole time in there, I was trying to work out why I knew your face. I saw you guys play the Kelvin University Union.'

The guitarist couldn't help but smile.

'We were practically the house band for a while. Never quite found an audience beyond Glasgow, unfortunately. It might well have been our final gig that you saw.'

'Well, I liked you, for what it's worth.'

Damien's gaze remained intent, perhaps asking himself what a guy Parlabane's age had been doing at the student union back then, and coming upon a genuine recognition of his own.

'Hang on, you were . . . We played the inauguration ball – were you not the rector or something?'

'In another life. And I only won the election by default. I'm nobody's idea of a figurehead.'

'You were an investigative reporter, though, were you not? As opposed to a music journalist.'

He said it with just an edge of accusation. That's right, pal: follow the breadcrumbs.

'I go where the work is,' Parlabane replied, choosing his words with precise ambiguity.

Damien reflected on this, then glanced towards the rehearsal suite.

'How do you know Mairi?'

'We go way back. Known her since my teens.'

Damien nodded, getting the picture.

Parlabane knew he could take a risk here. This was the experienced head Mairi described as the glue that held the band together, but Parlabane also recognised that Damien was the one he could most trust to keep quiet about his suspicions. This band was the ship Damien must have thought had long since sailed without him, so he was going to do nothing that would take her into choppy waters.

'Mairi's having trouble getting hold of Heike,' Parlabane said, dropping his voice a fraction. 'She's starting to get a wee bit worried, just between you and me.'

Damien's silence said plenty, his lack of surprise blethering unguardedly too.

'When did you last speak to her? Berlin maybe?'

Still he said nothing, and still his silence spoke volumes.

'I'm wondering if there was something on her mind. New album due out, this huge US tour coming up . . . That's a lot of pressure. How did she seem when you last saw her?'

'She was fine. Normal.'

Parlabane nodded, like he understood.

'You know, loyalty isn't always what you think,' he said. 'Telling me the truth doesn't make you a grass.'

Damien's cheeks flushed a little as he weighed this up. They both knew he was lying now; all that remained was whether he would keep up the charade.

'She was pretty withdrawn,' he admitted.

'In Berlin?'

'Before that. After Rostock. I've never seen her like it: so distant, her mind somewhere else – away from the music, I mean. Normally, no matter what else is going down, Heike's still a pro. I've never seen her so disengaged. I put it down to running out of steam towards the end of the tour. Things were pretty fraught after the photos.'

'I can imagine.'

'I tried to engineer a bit of a clear-the-air tête-à-tête between the girls in Rostock, but I guess it backfired. Heike was dealing with it better than Monica at that point, which is what you'd expect, but after that it was the other way around.'

'It seems disproportionate from the outside, but I suppose when you're on tour and living on top of each other, you can start to feel besieged.'

Parlabane was trying to seem sympathetic, but really he was fishing. He just wanted to keep the conversation going, to see where Damien might take it. He was looking for what he called a satellite: a significant outlier that had stuck in the guitarist's mind for reasons not immediately obvious even to himself.

He listened to Damien talk about the pressures of life on tour, and the stresses Heike in particular had to endure, not merely of being the main attraction, but from being one of only two women in the party. That was when he spotted it.

'I suppose in terms of other women there were also the merch girls: they were on the bus a couple of times, though that wasn't exactly all sisters together. Heike had a problem with them being there, in fact, but that was way before we got to Germany.'

'Merch girls?'

'Merchandising staff. I think they worked for Bad Candy.'

Pen Portraits

I could hear raised voices as soon as I opened the door. I was returning from a café on Westgate Road with two heaving cardboard trays, having volunteered to get us all something a bit more appetising than yet another round of instant coffees before we started the soundcheck. All had been calm when I left, although everybody was a little stiff and cranky after getting stuck in a motorway tailback for an hour en route to Newcastle.

I say voices plural, but mostly it was Heike's that was carrying; the responses low male mumbling. Heike had quite a register. She didn't have to shout for it to be loud and forceful, the kind of tone you could feel vibrating your chest.

'We haven't even soundchecked yet,' she was blasting. 'We've barely set up. There's two miles of cable still rolled up and guitars sitting there needing strings.'

'Christ's sake, it's only a wee bit of ching,' came the response. Sounded like Scott. 'Need something to perk us up after that fucking bus journey.'

I approached, feeling like I used to when my parents were arguing and they'd seen me in the doorway, so there was no option to sneak away and pretend I hadn't heard.

Heike was facing down Scott, the bass player, and Angus, the guitar tech, both of whom were stood with their heads bowed like guilty schoolboys. The others were waiting awkwardly, wishing they could be somewhere else until the aggro was over. Rory looked even more uncomfortable than the rest, which made me wonder whether he had been about to join in before teacher arrived and caught them at it.

The scene was one we had seen before: Heike overreacting to something she couldn't control and which, as far as everybody else was concerned, didn't matter.

'Only,' she stressed. 'Only. Does that word not ring any alarm bells about your perspective? It's a class-A drug. Enough to get you a night in the cells if someone wanted to throw a spanner in our works. And where did you get it?'

She rounded on Dean, the head of the road crew, and the one I had heard mouthing off about her to the support act in Bristol.

'Did you sell them it? Is dealing your sideline this tour, or do you only specialise in flesh?'

'We're all fucking adults here,' he said. 'You're their lead singer, not their fucking mother.'

He walked away, not staying for the scolding like the others.

'I know they're adults,' Heike said to his retreating back before directing her next words at Scott and Angus. 'I just thought you were professionals too. You need something to get you through a *soundcheck*? Are you kidding me?'

'All right,' Scott said, 'no, I don't *need* it, but it was *there*, and—'

'This is how it starts, Scott. Maybe you tell yourself you just want something to celebrate with after the show, or to keep the buzz going when you come off stage. Soon it becomes the thing you're looking forward to and the show's the thing between it and you. I've seen this before. We *all* have.'

And with that, she walked away, stomping off outside leaving us all to stare at each other awkwardly for a few moments before Damien geed everybody up to get themselves back to work.

So, basically, just another day on tour with Savage Earth Heart.

You'd be amazed what you can learn about people when you're around them every waking hour for the best part of a fortnight.

Such as, bugger all.

Don't get me wrong, I found out a lot about their habits, moods, what they ate, sleeping patterns, grooming regimes and even OS preferences, but very little of any real substance. This was, of course, because they were mostly men. I try not to generalise, so I'll acknowledge that statistically speaking, this was a very limited sample, but my data suggested that men can talk all day about music, movies, books, TV, sport, science, politics, religion and even clothes, but almost never about themselves: their families, their upbringing, their relationships, their ambitions.

Heike put it more bluntly when she said that men talk about their feelings like they talk about their periods.

As for who these people really were, I found out more in ten minutes on my laptop than from several days sharing a coach, a dressing room and several hotels. It felt a bit creepy, to be honest, looking up websites to investigate the people I was travelling with, as suggested by the fact that I only did it in my own room. Was that daft? I wouldn't have felt at all conflicted about doing it if I had just been a fan of Savage Earth Heart, but now I knew these people, it seemed a bit stalkery. However, the whole issue was that I *didn't* know these people.

It was a jolt to see my name listed on the band's Wikipedia page. Worse, the words hyperlinked to some Royal Scottish National Orchestra and National Youth Orchestra pages, where there lurked some truly embarrassing photos from my earlier years, just waiting to be discovered by the curious. Seriously, I'd have felt less squirmy knowing nude selfies had been hacked and posted (not, I should stress, that I have ever taken any nude selfies).

Scott had been in the band from the start, and it turned out he was Heike's cousin. She had taught him to play guitar when he came to stay with her on Islay one summer, according to one of the few articles that made much mention of anyone other than Ms Gunn. I was envious of the instant advantage this gave him: even of the fact that her big-cousin status meant she was constantly on his case.

I found out that Damien was thirty-nine, which was at least twelve years older than I thought. I could still see why I had assumed that, though. He was naturally young, always positive and energetic, by far the least cynical person with regard to his outlook on music, which was even more surprising when I read that he had been around the block a few times. I knew Heike looked up to him due to his greater experience, and I wished I could be calm and impressive around her like he was.

I learned that Rory was divorced, which was some going for a guy not long turned twenty-five. I was unsure how this made me feel, especially after all the remarks I had heard about being already engaged at twenty-two (even if we hadn't set a date yet). 'That's awful young, is it not?' people would ask, implying I was making a mistake, or at least hadn't given myself time to consider all my options.

Rory had worked as a secondary-school physics teacher until the sudden success of the second album meant he could concentrate full-time on the band. A bit embarrassingly, I also sussed that he had nothing specifically against fiddle players. It was at our Cardiff soundcheck, when the engineer asked me what I wanted in my monitor mix, that it dawned on me that this was what Rory had been talking about when he said he 'didn't want to hear any fucking fiddle'. It would have been nice to be able to say that I told him about this and we shared a laugh over my hilarious misunderstanding, but despite learning that he didn't hate my guts, I felt even more awkward around him after whatever weird mojo had passed between us up on that drum riser.

I still wasn't particularly comfortable around any of my bandmates, to be honest. Heike was the one it was easiest to learn about, but it also felt the weirdest to be reading up on her online, when surely I could simply walk up and ask her about herself. But that was the problem, wasn't it? I didn't feel like I *could* simply walk up and ask her. It didn't seem appropriate.

I noticed that a lot of articles described Heike as a siren, usually preceded by 'sultry'. It was one of those tabloid terms they applied to just about every female vocalist, interchangeable with 'songstress' or 'diva'. Like with the law of the stopped clock, in Heike's case the word 'siren' was more accurate than any of the newspapers truly realised.

People were drawn to her, almost hypnotically. I've heard folk talk nonsense about star quality, claiming instantly forgettable wannabes have it and thereby diluting whatever meaning it might have. Maybe someday scientists will be able to pinpoint what it is about certain people that makes them shine a little brighter and dazzle the rest of us, but for now, I can only say that Heike had something about her that made you want to be in her presence, touched by her grace.

She was aware of it too, but not in the way you might think. Maybe it was fairer to say she was wary of it: as though this siren feared that if you came too close, *she* might be the one drawn to her doom. Or maybe she was just scared of all the attention she got.

That's why asking direct questions about her life was right out, though it did mean that on the rare occasions when she shared something it felt all the more precious. That I alone had seen her tears on stage at Bristol that night felt like a secret treasure.

I wondered whether she liked being in this male-dominated company because she could hide there, where nobody was likely to ask her anything truly personal. We all wanted to get nearer to her, wanted in different ways to please her, but the trick was for her not to notice you were doing it, for you not to be caught *trying* to please her. It was like that childhood game where you all sneak up on someone with her back turned, trying to see how close you could get before she spun round and chased you all away.

Any time I felt we had made a connection, either she'd start avoiding me soon after or she'd find a way to make things awkward between us, like criticising my playing or changing the set to drop a number with a violin solo.

Not all sailors were vulnerable to the siren song, it must be said: such as Dean. His less charitable take on her was that she was 'another fucking spoiled diva who's got used to people sucking up to her all the time and as a result she thinks she can treat everyone like shit'.

I heard him mutter something about officers and enlisted men with regard to her attitude to the road crew, but from what I could see, nobody was given special consideration when Heike was on the warpath. In fact, if anybody got it worse than the rest, it was probably Damien, despite always being the soothing voice whenever tempers threatened to flare. Maybe it was actually *because* he was such a calming influence that she knew it was safe to take out her frustrations on him. Sometimes it was like she was goading him to finally lose it with her, and the less he bit, the angrier she became, which may well have been Damien's way of winning the battle of wills.

He was definitely spot-on with what he'd told me backstage after the opening night. No matter what had gone down before, all of it was forgotten when we took the stage.

Forgiven, I'm not so sure.

Not Spam

As Parlabane saw it, NDA or no, the only way to proceed with this investigation was to act as though it was any other story. He didn't know what kind of nonsense Mairi's head was full of regarding phone hacking and other shady practices, but twenty-odd years of experience had taught him that real journalism was all about good sources, even (and perhaps especially) when they might seem, to other eyes, unlikely ones.

He wasn't being polite when he told Mairi he liked Savage Earth Heart, and it was more than a matter of merely being one of the mainstream millions who had been bludgeoned into submission by the ubiquity of 'Do It to Julia' last year. He had followed their progress with the faintly proprietorial interest of one who had been aware of the band since the earliest days, but this wasn't down to his visionary judgement or ear for future talent. Rather, it was that the band had been brought to his attention by a friend who had been the recording engineer on their first three-track release.

Cameron Scott ran a recording studio just off Love Street in Paisley, a place that had initially made its money from cutting demos for aspiring new bands. It built a reputation for making even the most rough-and-ready outfits sound polished, and thus Scottsound Studios had become a well-trodden step on the ladder for a lot of Scottish artists.

One of them had been Savage Earth Heart, whose debut EP, *Salt Sting*, was passed on to Parlabane with uncharacteristic insistence by the man who recorded it, backed up by the assurance that 'this lassie's a bit special'. It was the sort of evangelical recommendation that one might recall as involving a CD being thrust eagerly into one's hands, except that the man passing it on could never be described as doing anything that sounded quite so energetic.

Parlabane was looking for him right now in a busy café near Gilmour Street Station, though not looking that hard, as his guest was almost always late. Then he realised that the guy grinning at him from two tables away was the man he was searching for, if not quite the man he was expecting to find.

His hair was neatly trimmed and he was wearing a shirt. Clearly, something had gone very wrong with the world. It was like Prince Charles turning up as a goth. No wonder he didn't recognise him: Parlabane realised he had never seen quite so much of his face before.

'Spammy. What the fuck?'

He was giggling with disproportionate amusement at Parlabane's surprise, almost like he had only done it to see the response it would get.

'You like it? I'm thinking of robbing some places and maybe murdering a few folk. Seriously, it's like I'm fuckin' invisible.'

Parlabane hadn't seen him in more than a year, and given all that had happened in the intervening time, he felt an unexpected urge to hug the guy. He resisted, however, realising that it was simply an instinct to cling on to someone who represented the warmer certainties of the past.

Plus, you just didn't hug Spammy. Apart from the fact that he wasn't a hugging kind of bloke, there was the physical consideration too. He was an assembly of the hardest, sharpest and boniest limbs Parlabane had ever had the misfortune to collide with. Even the slightest accidental contact with him could leave you feeling as though you had fallen against a metal structure wrapped in a sheet. Seriously, the guy was like Wolverine, if Wolverine had smoked weed fourteen hours straight every day for ten years.

'What happened?' Parlabane asked.

Spammy grinned again, sheepish.

'Met a lassie. Three months now. Seriously punching above my weight. Keep thinking the spell's gaunny wear off and she'll walk in one day and see this dozy plamf standing there, but until then I'm lapping up every moment.'

'Wow,' he responded, taking a much-needed seat.

A girl. That certainly explained everything, though he couldn't help but worry: was Spammy someone's work in progress? What the hell, even if he was, the boy seemed deliriously happy. Parlabane tried not to hate him for it.

'Plus it was beginning to come through grey in places. Checked the mirror one morning and realised I was starting to look like a badger.'

A waitress came by and they placed their orders, their divergent choices reassuring Parlabane that his friend had not been completely transformed. Meals such as this had always given a different meaning to the compound 'brunch', in as much as it was lunchtime for Parlabane and breakfast for Spammy.

'So, to what do I owe the honour?' Spammy asked.

'It's to do with Savage Earth Heart. Launched on the path to global domination from Scottsound Studios.'

Spammy responded with a near-conspiratorial grin.

'Aye, tell't you Heike Gunn was bound for glory. She just had a quality about her, what they used to call the x-factor, before that dye-job wank-hammock Cowell debased the term for ever.'

'As I recall, you engineered their first single.'

'Engineered it? *I* fuckin' produced it. I know that's not what it says on the sleeve, but it's what happened.'

'Who's credited in the notes?'

'It says "Produced by Alistair Maxwell", the only document on Earth where you're gaunny see that phrase, because he's "produced" fuck-all else. He didnae know what he was doing, but Heike looked up to him at the time.'

'Not a fan?'

'He was a cunt. A talented cunt, grant you, but a cunt. Actually, maybe more of a fud than a cunt, if you know what I'm saying.'

'Sure,' said Parlabane, who really didn't. This was just how Spammy spoke: not everything made sense, but it was wiser to let him maintain his flow than to ask for an explanation, as that only sucked you deeper into the vortex of Spammy-logic.

'He'd played with a lot of people; I mean, gie him his due, he was well quoted, but in his own mind he was some kind of national fucking treasure. I think he had Heike convinced she was his "discovery". He was never getting away with that for long, though: the lassie had too good a conceit of herself.'

'Egotistical? Manipulative?'

'You say that like it's a bad thing. She was all right with me, but you need to be a bit of a selfish, pig-heided nightmare if you want to make music that sounds like *you* imagine it, and not some supermarket-ambience Mumford and Sons shite.'

'And did her bandmates understand that?'

'Fuck knows, mate. I couldnae care less as long as they did what they were tell't and naebody cried all over my mixing desk.'

'What did you make of them?' Parlabane asked, intending to compare impressions.

Spammy shrugged.

'They were all right. Wee Scott, the bass player: he's Heike's cousin. Think he used to have bother from the local young team growing up; noo they all turn up cadging places on the guest list. Fair play to him. He was quite shy. Liked a toke, him and Angus, the guitar roadie. Angus dealt a wee bit. Always had a line on a supply. Good gear,' Spammy remembered with a wistful smile, wiping up some egg yolk with a slice of fried bread.

Parlabane recalled his astonishment when Spammy gave up weed, a pragmatic development of the smoking ban. It had proven to be a temporary aberration, but he wondered about how things stood now, given the new girlfriend, the shorn locks and the shirt that didn't even look slept in.

'Damien never touched it,' Spammy reflected. 'Wouldnae do anything if he thought it might affect how he played. Honestly, if the guy thought having too many hand-shandies detracted from his picking, he'd just have bought looser jeans for his swelling balls. All about the music, that boy.'

'And what about the drummer?'

Spammy responded with a baffled expression, like he didn't understand the question.

'He was a fuckin' drummer,' he said with a hint of exasperation. 'What else do you need to know?'

'Fair enough.'

'I got on fine with all of them, to be honest,' Spammy went on, lathering Tabasco sauce on to the mass of haggis and black pudding he had been patiently combining with the edge of his fork. 'Apart from Maxi, that is. Things got a bit strained with him because he could kid on to everybody else that he knew what he was doing, but he was acutely aware that I knew he was busking it. Ungrateful bastard, given how much I saved him from himself. You should have heard some of the things he was considering to give the impression he was full of bright ideas.'

'Like what?' Parlabane asked, intrigued.

'He brought in a saw player at one point. A fuckin' saw player. Daft fud had been listening to Mercury Rev or something. Maxi came out with some pish about wanting sounds that were elemental. I'm thinking, Away outside and record the fuckin' wind, then. But no, he's for a saw player. This fudnugget fronts up: a professional saw player. It says it on his card. Who the fuck is a professional saw player?'

Spammy shook his head and scooped a forkful of the haggis/ pudding/Tabasco abomination into his mouth. He looked like his professional sensibilities still remained affronted these five years later.

'So I take it the saw-playing never made the final mix?'

'Final mix? I never even pressed Record on the cunt. I'd have given him a fair shout if he hadnae taken himself so seriously. How can you take yourself so seriously when you wobble a fuckin' saw and call yourself a musician? Anyway, it didnae end well. Bit of an atmo, you know?'

Spammy's grin told Parlabane that, however it had ended, it had been by his design and to his liking.

'What happened?'

'Saw Boy finished doing his piece and he asked if we wanted him to do anything else. I says, aye, could you take a centimetre aff the bottom of that door there that keeps sticking on the new carpet? Cunt went mental.'

Parlabane did well not to spit his coffee all over his hamburger. He might have shorn his locks, but he wasn't Samson unmanned. Spammy was still Spammy. Parlabane could have sat listening to him all day, a reassuring reminder of better times. He had a job to do, though, and there was something else he needed the gen on.

'What can you tell me about Bad Candy?'

Spammy fixed him with an evaluating gaze. He had known Parlabane long enough to be aware he usually had an agenda, and he had clearly arrived at it.

'The tour promoters? Their star's on the rise, I know that much. They've come a long way and they're not really Bad Candy any more. Well, they are in some ways,' he added.

Parlabane wasn't sure whether he was being teasingly vague or whether this was just a result of the way Spammy's brain ordered the information.

'Not the same how?'

'They were a British promoter, but they got gobbled up by a big German company. The Germans liked the handle, though, so they changed the name of their *own* firm. Sounded more rock 'n' roll than whatever the hell they were called, not to mention more international.'

'They're not just promoting in Germany, then, I take it.'

'Naw. Economies of scale and all that. Bands can tour all over Europe with Bad Candy running the whole thing. Record companies love it: keeps things simple, and instead of negotiating with fifty different wankers you're only negotiating with one super-wanker.'

'What do the bands think of it?'

Spammy shrugged.

'Bands don't give a fuck what company's name is on the tickets as long as there's a crowd to play to. Plus, instead of staying in dodgy B&Bs they'll be in corporate chain hotels that Bad Candy have done a deal with. It's not about the bands so much these days, though.'

'Who is it about?'

'Exhibitions and conferences. The German firm always had a finger in that, and now it's the major part of their business.'

'Makes sense. Presumably they're often dealing with the same venues.'

'Gotta be less bother as well. I'd imagine you cannae get many folk trying tae stage-dive at a catering-industry expo. But I'm guessing that seeing it's you who's asking, it's not because you're thinking of buying shares.'

'Well, if I was, I'd be remiss not to look at the whole picture. Is there dirt?'

Spammy gave him an arch look, like Parlabane was at it.

'It's the music business, and they're called Bad Candy, for fuck's sake.'

'I don't like to judge. What have you heard?'

Spammy reached for the Tabasco again, further dousing what remained of his breakfast.

'Bad Candy was started by Brian Crossan, who had been a roadie and a tour manager going back to the seventies. The rumour was – and by rumour I mean one of those cast-iron facts that folk are inexplicably coy about mentioning – that he was also a serious drug dealer. The word was that you could always get gear on a Bad Candy tour, but you could only get it through the road crews. Nobody else got to supply the bands and the after-parties. Strictly in-house.'

'How does that work if a band has their own roadies?'

'Another reason the record companies like them: Bad Candy supply their own personnel, which keeps down the payroll at the band's end. Obviously, a band's gaunny have a trusted guitar tech and a sound engineer, maybe a lighting guy, but the tour managers, the drivers and the basic box-humpers are all Bad Candy permanent staff.'

'And that staff controls drug sales to the musicians on their tours?'

'That's how it was before the Germans came in and it all went corporate.'

'So it's cleaned up now?'

'Are you daft? It's bigger than ever, just the suits don't know or don't care. They've a squeaky-clean corporate image, but the guys in the shiny offices won't have a clue what's happening out on the road.'

'Sounds like they'd have a ready-made distribution network: Europe-wide, several tours out at any given time, buses and trucks criss-crossing.'

'Don't forget there's the exhibitions as well now,' Spammy reminded him. 'You know how many folk turn up to an expo in Frankfurt or Milan? I'm not even talking about punters, but exhibitors, tech staff, IT. That's a lot of folk looking for a wee boost to keep them peppy, or a come-down after a hard day's kiddin' on they like people.'

'Bad Candy right enough.'

'I think they call it hiding in plain sight. Never used to think that would actually work as a strategy, but see since I got this haircut?'

Musical Differences

I was having breakfast in the hotel with Heike and Angus, just enjoying the company at that time of the morning. I was an early riser and was used to eating on my own as the only other person ever up by then was Rory, who usually went out running.

I was grateful for the distraction of having someone else at the table, but worried they might read something into my expression and ask what was up. Before they arrived, I had just come off the phone to Keith, having caught him in the car on his way to work.

'I looked into flights,' I told him. 'There's one gets into Manchester about seven. We're not on-stage until nine, so you'd be in plenty of time for the show. Then there's one at ten-thirty the following morning, so you'd only need to take the one morning off.'

Before Newcastle, we had played two nights in Glasgow then one in Aberdeen. Keith didn't come to any of them. We were used to not seeing each other for a couple of weeks at a time, but we were running out of chances before I went to Europe for the best part of a month.

He worked in the oil industry, based in Aberdeen, but his job regularly took him back to Shetland, which was mostly where we met up these days. Sometimes he would come down to Glasgow over a weekend, but he preferred it if I travelled up, because he didn't have to share me with so many people, he said. What he meant was share me with people who weren't his friends, as it wasn't like he got me to himself when we went back to Shetland.

The day before we played Aberdeen, he called to say he had been sent to Sullom Voe and would be struggling to get back over to the mainland in time for the gig.

It couldn't be helped, but he had already missed the Glasgow shows because he had work in Aberdeen the next morning. I was pretty sure that some of the people at the Barrowlands gigs had driven further than he'd have needed to, and would be driving back home afterwards. Maybe at the time he hadn't thought it was important as he'd be coming to the Aberdeen show, but when he then got sent to Shetland I started to wonder how hard he had tried to get out of it.

'I'm sorry, Mon. I just learned that we've got the Norwegians coming in at lunchtime that day.'

'You'd still be back in time. The flight gets in at eleven forty-five, and then it's only—'

'I can't risk a delay. Besides, I need to prep for the meeting.'

'You could do that on the plane. Come on, this is the last chance for us to see each other before I'm away for weeks.'

'And whose fault is that?'

'It's nobody's *fault*,' I replied, a bit rattled that he was making this about blame. 'I don't make the tour schedules.'

'No, but it's your choice to go off with that band for weeks at a time.'

With that band. That was how he always put it.

'This is my career, Keith.'

'Yeah, and this is mine.'

There was a horrible silence after that, part mutual sulk and part stand-off to see who would concede some ground. I saw Heike and Angus come into the room.

'Well, I guess I'll call you,' I said.

'Yeah,' was the extent of his reply.

I put on a smile as the others sat down, hoping that any hint of tears would just look like me being bleary-eyed.

I hadn't expected anybody to show until departure time because it had been a late one the night before. The Newcastle hotel had a few Savage Earth Heart fans on their staff, and they kept the bar open for what turned into an after-show party.

In Angus's case, I guessed that he hadn't been to bed and was probably buying a few extra hours with coke before napping on the coach. Heike was either unaware of this or choosing not to make an issue of it today. She seemed a little distracted over her coffee and pastries, her eyes looking over my shoulder all the time, like when you're talking to someone and they're permanently scoping for someone more interesting or important.

Suddenly she got up from the table and arrowed for the door, like a hawk that had just spotted its prey.

I glanced at Angus, who rolled his eyes: here we go again.

She was gone by the time I turned around, so I didn't see what had attracted her attention, but I could hear her voice. Conscious of being in a hotel lobby, she wasn't doling out the hairdryer treatment, so I couldn't make out what she was saying. Her tone was controlled but definitely terse.

A few moments later I saw Rory make his way into the dining room, his cheeks flushed with a combination of embarrassment and anger. He had enjoyed a lucky escape yesterday, but not today. Heike raised the volume enough for me to make out her last words; in fact, I think she intended them for as wide an audience as possible.

'You know, if you want even younger, there's people Dean can put you in touch with once we get over to the Continent.'

She didn't come back for the rest of her breakfast. Heike, I was coming to learn, believed strongly in the impact of a dramatic exit.

Rory made a direct line for the coffee machine and returned with what looked like a quadruple espresso in a teacup. He sat down with us, in the seat next to Heike's, and began chewing glumly on a bread roll.

I desperately hoped Angus would ask what that was about, but didn't feel it was my place to do so myself. Angus said nothing, though what was unsaid was pretty loud.

Eventually Rory decided we deserved an explanation; either that or he just wanted to unload.

'Fucking ambushed on my way through the lobby,' he muttered. 'It's not on. It's none of her fucking business.'

He took a mouthful of coffee, while nobody asked *what* was none of her business. Again, nobody asked it pretty loud, and I thought, For Christ's sake, Angus, aren't you curious? Don't you care?

71

'She's on my case about the girl I took to my room. Poor lassie was barely out the door when the H-bomb went off. I just hope she didn't look back.'

I remembered Rory being with two young girls in the bar and vaguely recalled him snogging one around the time my eyes were closing.

'The wee blonde one?' Angus asked.

Hooray! A bloody question!

'No, her pal. The blonde one went home about half-twelve.'

'So why's Heike kicking off?'

'She's ripping into me for the girl being too young. She was eighteen and we're in Newcastle, for fuck's sake. That's the local equivalent of thirty-five.'

Angus managed a laugh, but Rory's joke couldn't disguise the annoyance he was feeling.

Rory took another sip of espresso.

'All right, she might have been seventeen,' he admitted, 'I didn't ask to see her ID, but neither did the bar staff. So what's it to do with Heike?'

Angus looked pained.

'This isn't about you, though, is it?' he said.

Rory sighed and shook his head.

'No, I guess not.'

Who it *was* about no one said, but I could tell they weren't only referring to Heike. There was a flavour of 'not in front of the children' about their reticence, like they were sparing rather than excluding me.

I'd had enough of it, though.

'Sorry, for those of us who missed the first two seasons, can you bring me up to speed? Who are we talking about?'

Glances were exchanged, like they were wondering what to do. I don't know if the problem was that I didn't have clearance for this intelligence or just that a girl was messing with the man rules. But they understood that there was no way out.

'Maxi,' Angus said.

So that was it. The ghost at the feast: the person nobody

ever talked about, especially around me. Maxi: Alistair Maxwell, Savage Earth Heart's original fiddle player. I think I must have known this subconsciously, hence my remark about the first two seasons.

'What about him?'

They shared another of those troubled male glances, though mostly it was Angus I could see, and he was the one truly on the spot, as he apparently knew a lot more about it.

'He and Heike were an item, once upon a time. Way back. Before the band, even, but the fallout had a long half-life.'

A too-long pause to take this in and a look of confusion betrayed me.

'What?' Angus asked.

'Nothing. I just—'

'Thought she was gay?'

'Well, I'm sure I read . . .'

'What, you disappointed?' Rory asked, a little too knowingly for my liking. 'Don't worry: you could still be in there.'

'As far as I know, she is,' Angus said. 'But these things are never simple.'

'Hell of a thing to have on your sexual CV,' Rory added. 'Turned Heike Gunn to the muff side. No wonder Maxi flings it about.'

'Flings what about?'

'His dick. Last tour, he was nailing anything that didn't struggle, and I'm the one taking the grief for it.'

Angus nodded.

'He was shagging like it was the Olympic trials,' he confirmed. 'Heike took it sore every time she saw him going off to his room with yet another young girl.'

'Or girls.'

'We weren't in these nice big hotels then, either. Some of the places, you could hear everything. Maybe Heike thought he was waving it in her face or something, I don't know. It was two or three years since they'd been together, but you know Heike: in her mind, everything's about her.'

'So she fired him for *that*?'

73

'No,' Angus answered. 'She fired him because he was turning into a liability.'

'I think "fucking nightmare" is the term you're looking for,' Rory added. 'You'd never expect it would be the fiddle player who became a rock cliché, but that's how it was.'

'Safe to say Maxi became less interested in the music than in the lifestyle that went with it,' Angus said, his understatedness lending it all the more weight given he was only awake right now thanks to the cocaine in his system.

'Less interested?' Rory went on. 'That's putting it mildly. Towards the end, the only occasion you could say he left it all out there on the stage was the time he puked on it. He was wrecked all the time, late for every rehearsal, too pissed to play half the gigs he did turn up to and pouring most of his energies into making sure he was sorted for gear and sorted for girls. I mean, I once drove down to fucking Nottingham on a Sunday for a show, knowing I'd be driving home again overnight and going straight to work as I'd school in the morning, and that cunt . . .'

He let it go there, shaking his head like he couldn't believe he was still getting angry about it all this time later.

'That's why she was ripping into me and Scott yesterday,' Angus explained. 'She was chewing us out to make herself feel better about the fact that she never chewed Maxi out back then. She was too intimidated by him to do anything until it was too late.'

Rory finished his espresso, looking a little calmer by the time he'd swallowed it.

'To be fair to Heike, I think she's feeling a lot of pressure,' I suggested. 'She must be stressed out at the possibility of anything going wrong now, when there's so much at stake.'

'Aye, well, the stress comes as part of a tidy package,' Angus replied, sounding less than sympathetic. 'I wouldn't mind that pressure if it came with the same salary and benefits. All that money she's got, she can pay for some therapy once the tour's over.'

'Or she could lighten up a bit and stop finding pointless wee conflicts everywhere,' said Rory.

'Why didn't Mairi do something about Maxi?' I asked, wondering what the manager's role had been in all this. 'Or was she not managing you then?'

'No, it was a guy called Jake Duggan,' Rory said. 'And the problem was he was a mate of Maxi's: that's how he ended up managing the band. Plus, he didn't come on tour with us. Oh, and he was a useless arsehole. Shouldn't discount that as a factor.'

'But what about the tour manager? Was it Jan?'

Angus and Rory exchanged another of their uncomfortable looks.

'Yeah, it was Jan,' Angus said, getting up from the table. 'But he didn't really see band politics as his remit.'

There was more, I could tell, but I wouldn't be getting it.

Angus yawned and stretched, then stuck a muffin in his jacket.

'Sorry, chaps,' he said. 'I need to go and check out of the room I haven't actually been into.'

I assumed Rory would be heading out too when he stood also, but he had the teacup in his hand. He went off to get even more espresso from the machine, asking if I wanted anything. There was still tea in my pot, so I shook my head. To be honest, I was struggling to speak as I was a bit anxious that he was planning to stay.

Looking around the empty room, it dawned on me that with Heike having just chewed his arse, he might be feeling short on allies, particularly on the female side. If that was the case, he'd better drop the leery innuendo and pretend he was back in front of his physics class.

'You're right,' Rory said, sitting back down. 'She *is* feeling the pressure. And Angus is too focused on the money to see what's going on here. After "Do It to Julia" became such a hit, it would have been very easy for Heike to relaunch herself as a solo artist. The record company would have been far happier with a pretty young female to market rather than a pretty young female and a bunch of hairy-arsed musos. But she knew we had all played our part, and she's not the kind of person who would ditch us when opportunity knocked. She's been loyal to us, and I guess she's entitled to ask plenty in return.'

'Plus, if it goes wrong, she's got the most to lose,' I said.

'See, that's the crux,' he stated. 'We've *all* got a lot to lose. If this goes breests-up, I'll be back teaching disinterested weans instead of touring the world and rubbing shoulders with rock stars. That's why there's got to be a line drawn between meeting reasonable standards of professionalism and pandering to somebody who's losing her sense of perspective. The danger here is that if we go along with any demand Heike makes purely because we all want to stay on board the showbiz express, we could end up creating a monster.'

He had another sip of espresso. I hoped he had managed some sleep after his controversial tryst, as there was no way he'd be catching forty winks on the bus having necked that much caffeine.

'Christ, listen to myself,' he said. 'Getting as bad as Heike for overdramatising. I'm just a wee bit raging about getting painted like I'm Jimmy Savile purely because I got lucky last night.'

As far as I was aware, Rory had got lucky quite a few nights on this tour, and I guessed luck had very little to do with it. He struck me as a smooth and accomplished operator: he had an eye for the kind of girl who might respond, and as the singer put it on a track Damien was playing on the bus the other day, he knew how to ask the question more than one way.

He was attractive: he looked younger than he was, friendly and uncomplicated. Whether the girl from last night was seventeen or eighteen, she probably thought he was closer to her age than was the case. I didn't think he was deliberately misleading her to get what he was after. If a girl was interested, Rory shouldn't have to show his ID any more than he should be asking to check hers.

'It just tends to be younger girls that are interested in me,' he explained. 'I think older women must assume I'm younger than I really am, or think I'll be immature. It was murder at work, because I was a teacher who looked barely older than some of the pupils, and a few of the lassies got really flirty with me.'

I had seen this exact same thing happen when I was in fifth year, girls in my class toying with a young maths teacher. They started to sense the power they had, but didn't yet understand it. They meant him no harm, but they didn't give much thought to what they were putting him through.

'That must have been tricky. One lapse in judgement and you're on the front page of the *Daily Record*.'

'Yep. And older women thinking I'm immature? I've been through trial by fire and come out the other side. Which is why it's nice to be off the leash. Now, if some nubile seventeen-year-old wants to throw herself at me I have no reason not to oblige.'

So she *was* seventeen.

I wondered about him being already divorced, and if he had had trouble keeping it in his pants.

'You were married, weren't you?'

I knew he wouldn't like me bringing this up, but he had been sounding a little too pleased with himself.

He nodded, eyeing me, wary that I had just declared I wasn't going to be one of the lads over this.

'Too young,' he said. 'A lucky escape for both of us.'

'Did you cheat on her?'

He looked at me as though I had no right to ask, then seemed to realise that, like it or not, his sex life was already on the table.

'It was more the wanting to that told me it wasn't going to work. It was painful, but I'm glad I ended it before I really hurt her. I am still very fond of her, but . . .'

He sighed.

'We were close growing up. Known each other since we were kids. Kind of childhood sweethearts. Then bang, one day you're an adult and you realise your perspective has changed. The future doesn't look the same as it did when you were seventeen and making plans: the horizon just became so much wider, you know? And they suddenly seemed such very small plans.'

I poured myself more tea. I didn't want it, but I needed to busy myself with something while Rory was looking so intently at me, silently asking if I understood.

'She wanted kids, suburbia, visits to Ikea on a Saturday afternoon. She would have been entirely content to live in this neat wee capsule and leave the world outside completely unexplored. Do you know what I mean?'

I knew fine what he meant.

I was disappointed but not surprised by Keith changing his mind about flying down for the Manchester show. I was starting to believe that he wanted to deny my being in the band was happening, so actually turning up to watch me play would have messed that up completely. Any time he called me before the tour kicked off, he kept referring to rehearsals as session work, like something casual and temporary.

'*It's your choice to go off with that band for weeks at a time,*' he had said.

I wasn't *with* that band. I was *in* that band. A band that were big news, but Keith seemed to be blanking them out.

He had happily come to plenty of my orchestral performances, usually in the comfortable company of proud relatives. Our families had been friends for generations.

Keith and I were close growing up. Known each other since we were kids.

Kind of childhood sweethearts.

Police Presence

Hiding in plain sight was the only camouflage Parlabane still had available to him.

One of the reasons the golden rule never to let yourself become the story was particularly applicable to investigative reporters was that it didn't serve to be recognisable. For him, that ship had long since sailed, something he had tacitly acknowledged when he accepted the nomination to be rector of a university. He had already become the story several times before that, not least when he ended up in jail, so his days of playing the undercover reporter were done long before his picture was splashed across all those front pages gleefully reporting a rival title's embarrassment.

He had grown more conscious of being recognised: signals that he'd have previously ignored as insignificant or coincidental could now reasonably be interpreted as evidence that someone was quietly taking an interest in him. Consequently, he had developed a sharper awareness of when he was being watched, and this had kicked in as he took the train back from meeting Spammy in Paisley.

He wasn't just being watched, in fact. He was being followed.

He had noticed the guy in the nondescript grey suit as he stood on the platform at Gilmour Street. He hadn't quite gone so far as to write 'COP' across his forehead with a Sharpie, but the signs were legible if you knew what to look for. The way the suit hung on him, for one thing: there were people who looked natural in a suit and people who looked conspicuously constrained by it, forced into the thing by diktat. Cops, in Parlabane's experience, tended towards the latter: proper cops anyway. The ones who looked most comfortable in a suit were also likely to be most comfortable behind a desk.

Merely spotting a cop, of course, didn't mean he was under

surveillance. The clincher was spotting the inevitable second one, who emerged from behind a pillar as the train pulled in, stepping on to the carriage one in front.

Parlabane pretended he didn't notice, blithely staring out of the window and checking his phone during the short journey to Central. Partly for confirmation and partly for his own amusement, he strode out of the station via the Hope Street exit, the opposite direction from his intended next destination. This meant that when he saw them again at Queen Street Station, having looped around to get there, he had subtly let them know he was on to them.

This was no great triumph, any more than he could congratulate himself on having made them back in Paisley. These guys were here because of Westercruik, and he was only seeing them because they wanted him to. It was just a little reminder that the eyes of the law were still very much upon him, a bit of passive intimidation intended to make him contemplate the simple action that would make it all go away.

They followed him on to the next train too, though as he was going back to Edinburgh, they should probably have bought their tickets at an advance saver rate. Nonetheless, he still had a final twist for them, as he had one more meeting scheduled that day. He couldn't exactly call it a 'fuck you'; more a flicking the Vicky.

He got off at Haymarket rather than staying on to Waverley as they'd have perhaps expected, then walked the short distance to the Police Scotland offices at Torphichen Place. If nothing else, at least it would confuse the buggers.

He was there because he still had at least one friend on the force, though he wished he'd made a point of getting in touch sooner upon his return from London. It wouldn't sound quite so sincere to say he'd missed her if the first time he showed up, it was cap-in-hand.

Jenny Dalziel came down to the lobby to greet him, and he was surprised when she pulled him into a hug, particularly in front of fellow officers. He was also surprised by the level of affection in it. It was as though he had forgotten there were still a few folk

80

out there who liked him, but that was what mass vilification did to a person. It was a lot easier to be thick-skinned when you still had people whose judgement you respected applying balm to your wounds.

'It's great to see you, Jenny,' he told her, worried for a moment that he was going to fill up.

She led him to her office. He had met her when she was a young suede-headed and sharp-tongued Detective Constable. Nobody called her Jenny any more. She was Jennifer in most of the circles she now moved in, and in this building she was generally addressed as 'ma'am'.

'Thanks for seeing me at such short notice,' he said.

'It's not that short. Soon as I heard you were back in town I knew the clock was running on you turning up and asking me for a solid.'

Yeah, there it was.

'I'm sorry I didn't get in touch sooner. I've been back in town a few weeks, but I've been keeping my head down. I kind of assumed people wouldn't be in a hurry to meet up with me and my big bag of awkward.'

Jenny slid into her seat behind an impressively large but intimidatingly cluttered desk, gesturing for him to pull up a chair opposite.

'Given your position,' he went on, 'I didn't think it would have done you many favours to be seen fraternising with me. That's why I'm all the more grateful for you fitting me in.'

Jenny fixed him with a steely look.

'Self-pity isn't a good fit on you, Scoop. You were always sexier when you were being an arrogant wee prick.'

There was once a time when he'd have replied with a remark about her *never* finding him sexy because she only had eyes for his wife. There would be none of that today, for any number of reasons.

Jenny was as striking as ever, growing into her elevated new role as much as he felt he had shrunk from his old self.

'You're looking very well,' he said.

'Still would?' she asked, her tone gently mocking.

He felt himself blush.

'That's what I thought. Nae luck. You're still one Y chromosome over the limit.'

'Not to mention that it would be cheating,' he observed. 'For one of us anyway.'

Jenny gave him a sad little laugh.

'Yeah,' she said softly. 'What happened there?'

Jeez, women just came right out and asked this stuff, didn't they?

'Nothing I can summarise,' he replied, and he'd given it some thought, aware people such as Jenny were likely to ask. 'Even if I tried, it would be like a time-lapse photo sequence of a process that was so gradual and incremental that we didn't realise it was happening until it was so far on as to be irreversible.'

'I'm sorry, Jack. I know you've been through the wringer.'

'How about you?' he asked, keen to hear all was well and hoping to Christ she wasn't about to tell him her relationship was falling apart as well. 'Maggie still . . .?'

Jenny nodded, an uncertain smile on her face: the smile of someone who was happy to report good news but knew she couldn't take anything for granted.

'Still in the clear. Due another follow-up in a couple of months, but so far so good. Apart from being one tit down on the whole deal.'

Parlabane laughed, though he wasn't sure it was appropriate. Actually, he knew it wasn't, but that was why Jenny said it. God, he'd missed this woman.

'So what can I do for you?' she asked. 'Is it about getting these Met wankers off your back, because that's out of my jurisdiction.'

'No. Had two of them follow me here today, though, as it happens. Can you lift them for stalking?'

''Fraid not. Anything else?'

'Yes. It's concerning Heike Gunn. You know who that is?'

'What are you insinuating?' Jenny fired back, mock-defensive. 'Dykey Heikey? Did you come to me with this just because I'm a lesbian? Watch your step or I'll slap you with an order to attend a four-week awareness-training course.'

'She's missing,' Parlabane told her, feeling a bit of a dick at having to bring down the serious.

Jenny's features sharpened.

'How missing is missing?'

'Missing enough for her manager to have hired me to look into it, but not missing enough for anybody to be allowed to know. It's very delicate.'

'What do you need from me?'

'Apart from your silence, I was wondering if you could get the Border Agency to confirm whether she re-entered the UK. She was last seen in Berlin, and I'd like to at least know which haystack I'm looking in.'

Jenny wrote something down on a notepad.

'I'll see what I can do.'

'Thanks, Jenny. I really appreciate it.'

'There's a quid pro quo,' she told him. 'I could actually use your help in locating a missing person myself.'

'Who's that?'

'Jack Parlabane. If you see him, tell him there's a sad-sack miserable bastard going around using his name.'

Warrior Women

Heike was dressed in Roman battle gear, complete with helmet and breastplate, her legs bare beneath a red knee-length tunic, her feet criss-crossed by the leather straps of her sandals. In her right hand she held a microphone stand like a spear, an acoustic guitar at her left side instead of a shield.

We were standing in the main courtyard of the British Museum in Bloomsbury, Heike between two Roman columns while the photographer and his staff adjusted collapsible reflectors, umbrellas, lighting stands and flashes. Hair and make-up artists buzzed around Heike, never quite happy with what they were seeing.

I was sitting a few feet away on a folding stool, my violin in its case at my feet, wondering why Heike had asked me to bring it. I was only supposed to be here for company and moral support. She didn't look like she needed that, as she was confident in the spotlight, but she had seemed a bit nervy in the cab over, so maybe she was good at putting a calm face on it. The shoot was for *Tatler*, for God's sake. I'd have been in bits.

Heike had natural grace. There was no other word for it. She didn't have supermodel looks, but there was just something pleasing about her face, a timelessness, I guess, that made it easy to picture her in any era. Maybe that was what the photographer had seen when he came up with the concept for the shoot. It was obvious from the way they were talking that he had worked with Heike in the past, or at least had met her before. His name was Steff Kennedy. I had heard of him, but for some reason thought he would be English or American. It turned out he was from Motherwell.

He snapped away at her for about ten minutes, then got his assistants to start moving kit again. He and Heike spoke quietly, almost conspiratorially to one another, then I noticed him glancing towards me. Maybe I was to play now: I couldn't see what that would add to the shoot, but what did I know? Besides, one of his team was videoing the whole thing for their website.

'We think you should be in the shot,' Heike announced.

I thought she was messing with me, then I glanced at Steff and saw that he was totally sincere; worse than that, determined. He was about six foot seven with long hair, and beneath the Roman columns he looked like a warrior or a pagan god. Either way, I wasn't sure I could defy him. I felt horribly trapped.

'Don't be daft,' I said weakly.

'No, seriously,' Heike insisted. 'Steff thinks it will be more dynamic to have both of us.'

'But I'm not good in front of a camera. Trust me, I'll ruin the shot.'

'You've got more than you give yourself credit for, and you're only going to see that once you get to look through someone else's eyes. Besides, I already did the interview, and half of it was about you joining the band, about how it's changed us to have two women at the heart of things. The magazine really wants both of us in the spread.'

I made a face, but I could see one of Steff's assistants already holding up a costume and gesturing me towards the changing area they had set up using stands and drapes.

'Just give it a shot. Come on, if you can get up on a stage in front of two thousand people, you can pose for a photo.'

That sounded like an okay comparison, as long as you ignored that it would be seen by ten times that number, and that wasn't even including the internet. I was thinking to myself, I didn't sign up for this, when I realised that I actually had, by joining the band. I just hadn't thought it through.

Steff's assistant handed me a tunic that looked like it was made of thousands of leather scales, and a headpiece she called a khepresh. I thought for a moment whether these were from the museum, worrying about damaging them. Then I noticed the scales weren't real leather and kicked myself for being stupid: like they'd be letting us play dressing up with priceless archaeological artefacts.

I stripped to my underwear and put the tunic on, grateful that it sat high and tight around my shoulders. I didn't think a visible bra strap would be acceptable and I really didn't fancy what this thing would do to bare nipples.

I stepped out barefoot, feeling a bit of a lemon, and the hair and make-up girls promptly sat me back down as they got to work. Heike took a seat beside me, while Steff got busy taking light readings and moving gear around.

'Couldnae see this working with your last fiddle player,' he said.

'No, he wasn't as pretty as Monica,' Heike replied. It sounded like a deflection.

'Or as obliging,' Steff said, batting it back but looking at me with a smile.

'Yeah, I heard he wasn't the most reliable,' I offered. I felt I was on the spot and expected to make some kind of a response.

There was a sudden alertness to Heike's face, like she needed to be on guard.

'What else did you hear?'

I felt guilty about what I knew, like I had been caught snooping into something personal that was none of my business. This was daft, though: I was in the band. If that meant I was dressing like an Egyptian charioteer, then it also meant that Maxi *was* my business. But I didn't want to seem coy, or leave Heike wondering how much I really knew.

'I heard about the last tour,' I said. 'I also heard that you and he were once, you know, a thing.'

She raised her eyebrows and allowed herself a small smile.

'A thing. That's as good a description as any.'

I thought she was going to leave it there, but I was rewarded for fessing up. Either that, or Heike needed to share.

'I got to know him when I moved to Glasgow from Islay, when I first became involved in the music scene. He was a few years older and he knew everybody. He'd played with so many bands. I really looked up to him. I was totally thrilled when we started to play together: it felt like a kind of endorsement, you know?'

86

I wanted to nod, but the make-up girl was working around my eyes and I didn't think moving my head was a wise idea.

'Oh yeah,' I said instead. 'I can relate. There was this quite experienced singer who took an interest in me. At first I was flattered, but next thing I knew I was dressed up like a haddy outside a museum.'

Heike gave me the finger.

'I'm reaching out to you here,' she said, feigning a huff.

'I know. And I do know what you mean.'

'So you'll appreciate, I was a bit doe-eyed over him at first, and that impression stayed with me. It swayed my judgement for a long time: I saw the guy I initially looked up to rather than the one who was in front of me. I learned a lot from him, and I don't mean in a "bitter experience" way.'

'Musically?'

'Yeah. My songwriting definitely improved from working with him. We wrote a few things together. This was before Savage Earth Heart, though: that stuff's all mine.'

'Did I read that you were with him in your first band too?'

Heike looked upwards, a weirdly innocent smile on her face, like the sun had just come out.

'No, my first band was actually with Angus, back on Islay.'

'Angus? The guitar roadie?'

'Yeah. We were in the same class at school. We wrote some songs together as well. Angus is actually a really interesting songwriter, but . . .'

She frowned, then shook her head sadly.

'Wasted potential,' she said. 'He never had the conviction to put in the hours.'

She reached across and took hold of my hand. I think it was the first time we had touched that way, and I started ever so slightly, wondering what she was doing. She ran her fingers along the tips of mine.

'I bet those were like leather by the time you were about twelve,' she said.

'Ten,' I countered.

'Me too. I practised every hour I had. Later than I should, in fact, as my dad wasn't always the most responsible about telling me to go to bed because I'd school in the morning. Bohemian arty types – what can you do?'

I got what she was saying.

'But not Angus?'

'No. He could play guitar well enough but he was as likely to be playing video games or chasing the lassies. Scott, on the other hand: he was a man with a mission once I showed him his first chords.'

'He's your cousin, yeah?'

'That's right. He grew up in a really rough scheme. Came to stay with us for the whole summer holidays one year, because there had been trouble with gangs where he lived. Serious trouble: stabbings and the lot. The wee man just seemed so delighted with the sounds he could make: like he couldn't believe it was coming from him. I think it gave him a glimpse of things that he thought weren't possible, doors he'd assumed were closed.'

The regret she felt about Angus was matched by happiness at how her cousin had turned out. I could easily appreciate then her dismay at finding them both doing coke before rehearsals. It wasn't all about Maxi.

She was back to talking about him now, though.

'I felt like a bit of an idiot when Maxi broke things off. He made me feel like a daft wee lassie, or a bloody groupie who didn't realise her time was up and the next girl was waiting. Part of me was determined to show him I was more than that, and I sometimes wonder if I kept him in my band as much for those reasons as for his playing. It sounds nuts, but it seemed important to me to prove myself to him.'

'No, I get that,' I said, though I didn't admit that it wasn't from any personal experience. I bluffed on, hoping *Gossip Girl* hadn't lied to me. 'You want guys to know they're the one who's not bloody worthy. But they never see that, do they?'

'No kidding. No matter how things went for me and for the band, I think Maxi still saw me as a daft wee lassie who looked up to him. That's why I wasn't very effective at reining in his behaviour. Until I sacked him,' she added.

'I bet that felt good.'

'It felt awful, actually. Nothing satisfying or vindicating about it. Now, imagining his face the day "Do It to Julia" broke the *Billboard* top ten?' Heike grinned. '*That* felt good.'

The make-up artist finally decided she was happy with her work and showed me a mirror. I gasped with such an intake of breath that I was lucky there were no flies going past, or even small birds. I looked like some Egyptian princess, and if I didn't know I was looking in a mirror I wouldn't have recognised myself.

It was strangely empowering; or maybe liberating is more accurate. I was able to throw myself into the shoot without any self-consciousness (or at least the usual quantity of self-consciousness) as I felt like I was playing a part.

Steff directed us to prowl around each other like gladiators. Heike repeated her shield and spear poses while I used my bow like its archery namesake, threatening to fire my violin like a giant arrow. I decided this was just wrong, as well as likely to damage both, so switched to gripping them like my own sword and shield. He got us to snarl at one another, which lasted for about twenty seconds before we broke down hopelessly into giggles. Once we had recovered, he stuck to directing still poses, all of them with us holding the instruments like weapons.

As Steff took my arms and posed me like a doll, dressed as I was in this second costume they *just happened* to have brought along, I wondered about Heike's insistence that I bring my fiddle.

I went through about a dozen cleansing wipes getting all the gunk off my face, then nipped behind the screens and got changed back into my own clothes, which felt really light after the weight of the faux leather. When I emerged, Heike was excitedly beckoning me across to where Steff's laptop sat on a table.

Steff was scrolling through uploads from the shoot, the images startling in their vivid detail. I was standing feet from where they'd been taken, but they seemed to belong in another, more glamorous world.

'She looks brilliant,' Heike said, to everyone and no one in particular. 'Doesn't she look brilliant?'

She sounded delighted, like she'd forgotten that she was the main subject of the shoot. It reminded me of my mother's excited pleasure whenever I did something she felt proud of.

Steff's hand paused.

'Oh, this is the shot,' he said, taking his fingers away from the keyboard. 'This. Is. The. Shot. That is a front cover right there.'

The image showed me balanced on one knee, thrusting my bow like it was a sword, my chin held high and my khepresh level, like I was drawn in profile on the inside of a pyramid. Heike stood above me with her head thrown back, her spine bent in a graceful arc and her microphone stand held almost perpendicular to the ground behind her. She looked like she had just been mortally wounded by me or that she was ready to unleash a killer blow.

I had to admit she was right. We both looked pretty amazing. I mean, I didn't look anything like me, but maybe that's why I looked so good.

As Heike purred over the picture, I spotted an email printout among Steff's gear, on top of a press release about the forthcoming album. It was his brief from someone at the magazine, and it was headed, alongside the date and appointed start time, 'British Museum: Savage Earth Heart's warrior women.'

The email was from yesterday, before Heike's interview, so the concept for the shoot could not have come out of her talk with the journalist. It was confirmation, if I still needed any, that it had always been Heike's plan that we be photographed together. I guessed her earlier quiet chat with Steff was her telling him that she would have to reel me in gently.

I had been played, manipulated, yet all I could feel was a silent, secret gratitude. She had brought out something in me I didn't know was there, shown me a version of myself I could never have imagined.

She had known it was there, though. She had seen it clearly, and was now delighted to see it revealed in high definition.

Oil and Metal

There are certain undignified and downright embarrassing items that, when people are younger, they never for a moment envisage they will one day have in their possession: items such as pile ointment, nose-hair trimmers and, in Parlabane's case, an all-access pass for a Prelude to the Slaughter gig at Manchester Apollo. A couple of days ago, he'd have imagined himself buying tickets for a Lostprophets reunion concert before he contemplated going anywhere near a venue hosting this shower, but as fate would have it, several of the Bad Candy crew who had worked the Savage Earth Heart tour were now on the road with this Cornish death-metal atrocity.

Mairi had sorted him out with a pass so that he could get close to the crew, but his cover for being there was that he was interviewing the band, something Mairi had also cleared with their press office. She had initially suggested he pretend he was writing a piece about what it was like to be a roadie, but Parlabane explained to her that this would merely make them more guarded about the image of themselves they wished to put across. In his experience, people on the fringes of something were more likely to let a few candid details slip if they believed he was interested in someone else.

Naturally, this conversation had taken place before he learned which band the crew were now out with.

Parlabane watched them assemble the centrepiece of Prelude to the Slaughter's stage set: a twelve-foot plastic statue of a vertically thrusting guitar neck with two large-breasted naked women wrapped around it like pole-dancers. It was staggering to believe these same personnel had been setting up for Heike Gunn to sing 'Dark Station' a couple of weeks back. He wondered which suited their personal aesthetic more.

91

The tour manager was a Dutchman called Jan Rademaker, but Parlabane hadn't encountered him yet. Who he had gotten a truck-load of, however, was Dean Irons, a pot-bellied and foghorn-voiced uber-roadie who looked like he had been given his first Marshall amp to lug around as a toddler, instead of a pull-along doggy. Parlabane's first impression upon meeting him had been 'helmet', but he reined in his instincts and reserved judgement until he had heard what the guy had to say, whereupon he revised his verdict to 'utter helmet'.

Also among the crew was Angus Campbell, Savage Earth Heart's guitar roadie. Parlabane had expressed his surprise that he should be squeezing in a twelve-date UK tour with another band before heading out to the US, but Mairi said he needed the money.

'Isn't Savage Earth Heart a full-time gig?' he had asked.

'It is these days,' Mairi replied. 'But Bad Candy tours had been his bread and butter up until recently. He's still on their roster, and I guess if there's paid work going he'd rather be earning than taking a break. That's Angus for you.'

'Workaholic?'

'No,' she had laughed. 'He's a natural-born waster who can't hold on to money.'

Spammy had fondly mentioned Angus always having good gear on him, and from one look at the guy he could picture the two of them getting on. They were definitely from the same tribe, though Spammy had always been good with his cash, as well as deceptively diligent about the things that engaged him. Angus, it seemed, was industrious too, albeit out of self-created necessity.

He had first shuffled into view wheeling a huge flight case, his face obscured by the straggly brown hair that hung down over it as he bent his shoulder to the task.

'Here he comes,' announced Dean with a cackle. 'Fresh from getting his balls back.'

Insufferable as he found him, Parlabane nonetheless had to pretend to be amused by Dean in order to keep him talking, in the hope that the sludgy river of sexist indiscretion and UKIP-level prejudice would give up a nugget of gold.

'How so?' Parlabane asked.

'Been out with Savage Earth Heart around Europe, ain't we? Angus here is their guitar tech. Has to be on his best behaviour for Queen Heike.'

Angus responded with a bashful if indulgent grin, the kind that knew he had to take his lumps or it would only be revisited all the more.

'Is she a bit of a ball-breaker, then?'

Dean suddenly put on a butter-wouldn't-melt expression.

'I won't hear a word said against her,' he replied with exaggerated sincerity, inviting laughter from his colleagues.

Angus, Parlabane noted, did not join in.

'Bit of a buttoned-down kind of tour, was it?'

Dean gave him a sly but nonetheless self-congratulatory look.

'There's always good times to be had, if you know where to look: specially on the Continent. Just gotta be discreet,' he added, tapping his nose.

Parlabane mimicked the gesture, then amended it to running a finger beneath his nostrils.

Dean grinned approvingly, responding in kind then altering his own gesture to a horizontally thrusting middle finger.

'All manner of fun,' Dean said.

'Just among the road dogs, or did the band party a bit too?'

Dean gave a dirty laugh.

'Ooh, when I think of the self-righteous image she likes to give them. Gotta love her for it. She likes to keep everybody on a tight rein, and she's perfectly happy as long as she thinks it's so. Fucking amazing what she doesn't realise is going on right under her nose.'

'Like what?'

It proved an inopportune moment for Jan Rademaker to show up, striding from the wings clutching an iPad and making haste towards where Parlabane was standing.

'You must be Jack Parlabane,' he said loudly, offering his hand to shake. 'Mairi Lafferty told me you wanted to talk about the Savage Earth Heart tour.'

This had the immediate effect of shutting Dean up, the roadie giving Parlabane a slightly suspicious look before wandering off to help a colleague heft a monitor. Given the swiftness with which Dean abandoned the conversation and busied himself elsewhere, Parlabane couldn't help but wonder whether this had been Jan's intention. Did he really need to mention Mairi's name?

'Let's go someplace a little more private, where we can talk,' he suggested, a slight raise of his brow communicating that he knew what they had to talk about was best not shared.

He led Parlabane to the dressing rooms, where Prelude to the Slaughter's various leather garments were laid out in waiting for the band's later arrival.

Maybe it was the traces of Dutch in his otherwise Americanised accent, but to Parlabane the guy seemed more porn business than music business. There was something slinky about him, but that wasn't necessarily a criticism, particularly in this game. Some people were good at their jobs because their very oiliness was what prevented those around them grating against one another.

'Mairi told me you're looking for Heike,' Jan said, grabbing a bottle of water from a crate on the floor and sitting on the dressing table that ran the length of a mirrored wall on one side. 'So I take it she still hasn't been in touch.'

'Unfortunately not. You were the last person to speak to her, is that right?' Parlabane asked, deliberately getting it wrong.

'Yeah,' Jan replied, then seemed to give himself a shake. 'No. I mean, I just *told* everybody I spoke to her, so that I could keep the situation quiet. As far as I know, Monica was the last person to *actually* speak to her.'

'Why did you lie? I mean, how could you have known she wouldn't walk in the door of the venue two minutes after you just told everybody she'd flown home sick?'

Parlabane expected him to bridle at the implied accusation, but he seemed phlegmatic.

'It was a judgement call,' he said with a shrug. 'Part of the job. I'm paid to be the one who ends up looking like a lying asshole now and again. Something wasn't right, though, I could tell. I mean, its rock 'n' roll, people don't always keep to their schedules, but Heike would never miss a soundcheck, and if she did, she'd call to let me know what was up, you know?'

'Was there anything else that maybe tipped your judgement? I mean, were you concerned about Heike's state of mind?'

'I'm always concerned about Heike's state of mind. I don't mean I'm always worried about it, but I'm monitoring it. People think the job of tour manager is all about arguing with venue staff and making sure everybody gets paid, but above all else it's to keep the show on the road. When it comes to a band like Savage Earth Heart, Heike's state of mind is priority number one. No show without Punch, as you say here in England.'

'And did you have any specific concerns in the run-up to Berlin?'

'Of course. You know about the photos, right?'

'Yeah.'

'That made things pretty tense for a while. I thought we had ridden the bump, though. But then Heike was a little off-form in Hamburg, and I just thought she was running out of steam. It happens.'

'Was there anything else that caused tensions on the tour?'

'Not that I can think of. I try very hard not to let molehills become mountains, so maybe I'm guilty of playing things down sometimes – it's how I roll when I'm having to deal with a lot of conflicting egos – but Savage Earth Heart are an easy ride compared to some.'

'I've not heard many people say dealing with Heike is an easy ride.'

Jan rolled his eyes, as though caught between discretion and a need for honesty under these circumstances.

'There's only one of her, though,' he said.

'I heard there was an incident on the tour bus, something about her falling out with some merchandising girls?'

Jan looked blank for a moment, then shook his head and gave a wry chuckle.

'Just a misunderstanding. I don't really remember the details: you know, the he said, she said. Or she said, she said, in this case. It was nothing, though.'

'Okay,' Parlabane replied, choosing not to probe further.

Damien had told him what happened, so he knew Jan had been at the heart of an incident that held up their bus for over an hour and had involved the police.

Sometimes the most valuable thing you're going to learn from someone is merely the fact that they're lying to you, and it's all the more valuable if they think you're buying it.

Warning Signs

'I can't believe what you just got me to do,' I told Heike.

We were sitting in a café off Seven Dials, having walked down from Bloomsbury. Steff had volunteered one of his assistants to transport our instruments to Brixton in a cab, as Heike had wanted to take a walk around the shops, but we needed fuel first.

'I believe there are a lot more ways you could surprise yourself, Monica.'

'I was always going to be in the shoot, though, wasn't I?' I asked, eyeing her over my gingerbread latte. 'That was your plan.'

I thought she would maybe smile and acknowledge 'you got me', but instead she looked serious, challenging, even.

'If I had just wanted a fiddle player, there's a lot of good ones out there. After I binned Maxi, I saw quite a few, and at the time, I'll admit, I was only looking for somebody to fill a gap and play his parts live. I considered a change of sound for the third album, maybe no violin at all. But when I saw you play – and I mean saw, not just heard – I saw someone who could bring a lot more to the band than Maxi ever did. That's why I asked you to join.'

'You didn't ask me if I wanted to be part of a photoshoot for *Tatler*, though,' I said, trying to make it sound easy-going.

'I knew you'd be intimidated by the prospect, so I saved you the prospect bit. I also knew you'd come alive in front of the camera. And I was right on both counts, wasn't I?'

'Yeah,' I admitted. 'I'd have been terrified. I'm too much of a wee mouse to go flaunting myself like that. The costume helped, and the make-up. It's easier when you're playing a part, not being yourself.'

'I think you're actually playing a part when you think you're being yourself,' Heike said. 'The wee mouse is the part you've always thought was appropriate to play for the people you've been around growing up. It's what was expected of you, but that doesn't mean it's what's inside. I think the real you is ready to emerge.'

After coffee, Heike took me down to Long Acre, literally leading me by the arm.

'When I first moved to Glasgow,'she said 'I used to spend hours wandering around the shops: Buchanan Galleries, Princes Square, Fraser's and the like. Just looking at stuff, with no means or intention to buy. "Glimmering", I used to call it, but not any more.'

'Why not?'

'Because these days I have the means *and* the intention to buy. Come on.'

We traipsed in and out of shops, dallying in some for Heike to try things on, while in other places she'd turn on her heel only a couple of seconds after entering. It was like she was shopping by instinct, and knew straight away when she was on barren ground.

Heike was favouring skirts and dresses on stage on this tour, a change from the jeans and white denim jacket people most often associated with her. She had bought a couple of tops and a skirt, and she still seemed unsatisfied, like some deeper need had not been met.

Then suddenly she pulled us both towards the dark rear of an exclusive-looking boutique in a pedestrianised lane off Covent Garden. It was the type of shop where assistants would come up to me and ask 'Can I help you?' in a way that clearly meant 'What do you think you're doing in our shop, you extremely unhip poverton?'

But today I had cachet by the bucketload. I knew it was down to hipness by association, but I didn't care. I noticed one of the assistants checking Heike out, nudging her colleague and alerting her to who had just walked in to their store. They were trying to act cool about it, but every time I glanced their way I could tell their eyes had been on her.

I was seriously getting off on being the one she was with. Yeah, hip-chicks, she's in your store, but I'm in her band.

'Oh, yes. Absolutely,' Heike said, lifting a dress from a rail. She held it up to regard it, rather than draping it against herself, which should have been my first clue about who we were really shopping for here.

She insisted I hit the changing room, and I couldn't argue. After dressing up like an Egyptian warrior all morning, I knew making a fuss over trying on a frock would be self-indulgent, even if it wasn't a look I had a hope of carrying off.

As I stepped out of my jeans I noticed the price tag and almost jumped. Not as bad as when I had feared I was about to wear something of the original King Tut's, but we were still talking the best part of six hundred quid. Then I realised that this was my free pass, as Heike would surely understand that I couldn't spend that kind of money on anything, never mind a single garment.

Might as well enjoy dressing up one more time, I thought, and slipped it on.

It looked good. *I* looked good. Better than good, in fact: I even thought about taking a selfie in the changing-room mirror. It wasn't me, though. I could barely bring myself to wear it outside the cubicle in front of Heike and the staff, never mind in public.

Delicately, no doubt a picture of discomfort, and feeling really self-conscious, I stepped into view.

'Oh, Monica. That. Is. Stunning.'

'It's not really me,' I said apologetically.

'No, no, it's absolutely you. This is what I was talking about: there's a version of you that you don't allow yourself to see.'

I was worried this might be where she was taking it, but it was about to get much scarier than that.

'You should wear this on stage. You'd look amazing playing with this on. *We'd* look amazing. We'd absolutely bring the house down when we do that dance during "Smuggler's Soul". It's perfect for you: you like sleeveless things when you're playing.'

This was true: nothing to restrict the movements of my arms and shoulders. But we were talking about vests and halter tops.

'This isn't just sleeveless,' I said. 'It's almost completely backless. It would look daft with a bra strap across my back.'

As soon as the words were out, I knew I had made a mistake. From the moment I saw the dress I understood that it wasn't meant to be worn with a bra, which was part of the problem.

'You don't need a bra,' she said, like she knew I knew this.

I did, too. I'm not completely flat-chested, but I know I wear bras more for the sense of security they give me than for support.

I had to play my get-out-of-jail card.

'I can't afford it anyway,' I told her.

Another mistake, as it betrayed the fact that part of me would love to own it, even if it was only to wear in front of my bedroom mirror.

'So it'll be my gift,' she said.

On the surface it was a generous gesture, but I knew it was actually a dangerous moment. I thought of Rory's words about the price of going along with Heike's demands. She was exercising power, and the worst thing was: I couldn't resist her.

'Honestly, Heike, I can't let you do that. It's amazingly generous, but it would be a waste. I mean, if you can find a wood nymph whose other diaphanous dress is in the dry cleaner's, I'm sure she'd be very grateful.'

I tried to make light of it, and her grin told me I'd pulled it off, but I realised the remark had just amused her.

'I told you,' she said, taking the dress to the counter. 'I've got the means and the intention.'

She smiled and I told myself I ought to accept with good grace, but I couldn't help feeling that Heike wasn't giving something to me. She was taking something from me.

Heike had a radio interview to give before the soundcheck, so I carried on to Brixton alone, stopping at the hotel to put the dress in my room. I laid it out carefully on the bed before going to the loo, then hung it up in the wardrobe as soon as I came out of the bathroom. I was already feeling stressed every time I looked at it.

I had been mulling over Heike's words about the wee mouse being a part I played, and beginning to admit to myself that there might be some truth in there. But even if the real me was actually ready to emerge, it wasn't going to be in that dress in front of four thousand people.

I had a nosy around the hotel lobby and bar in case anyone else was hanging about, ready to leave, but there was nobody. I remembered Damien and Rory saying they were going to the Tate Modern and convincing a sceptical Scott that he would enjoy it if he tagged along.

I checked the time as I walked to the Tube. It was a little early, but I was anxious to get to the venue and check my fiddle had been dropped off safely.

It seemed strangely quiet as I entered the venue. Instead of the usual sounds of shouted instructions, squeaking castors, the dragging of stage skids and the buzz of the PA, I could hear only quiet laughter and voices speaking at conversational volume.

Angus noticed me first, bringing me to the attention of Dean with a nod. The chief roadie turned a bit shiftily, giving a smirky look to the others there. I was pretty sure he'd been doing a line: quite possibly all of them had. They were gathered around a transport cabinet for one of the amps like it was a table: Angus, Dean, Jan the tour manager and a fourth bloke, who still had his back to me.

'Oof, can we bribe you not to tell teacher?' Dean said, brushing a knuckle against his nose.

He was painting me as the proper little madam, as he always did. It bothered me more than usual today, after all I had been thinking about.

'It's *your* septum,' I said with a shrug. 'Did my fiddle get dropped off safe and sound?'

'Eh, yeah,' replied Angus. 'I'll just get it for you.'

At this, the fourth bloke finally turned around, casually, to face me.

'Ah, so you must be my replacement,' he said.

Alistair Maxwell was taller than the impression I had got from photographs and video clips. Perhaps it was a proportion thing, as he was broad across the shoulders and looked like he worked out.

(Though, to be honest, I often expect men I've never met to be smaller than they turn out, as I am five foot nine and used to many of them being shorter than me.) He looked younger than I was expecting too, especially after the tales of hard living I had heard. His hair was cropped shorter than in any of the photos and his beard was gone.

'How you finding life aboard the good ship Savage?'

He sounded friendly, but also mildly amused, and I got the impression he wanted to patronise me in front of the others. Clearly he was still pals with the road crew, and with Jan. So that maybe explained why the tour manager hadn't intervened when Maxi's behaviour was becoming a major problem.

I wondered who else in the band he was still close to, and why I should suddenly feel so threatened by it.

'Every day's a school day,' I replied. My first instinct was not to tell this guy anything, but I wasn't sure why.

'I saw some clips from the Glasgow shows on YouTube. Have to hand it to you, you're playing my stuff pretty well.'

His stuff. Fuck you.

'She's certainly a lot nicer to look at than you ever were,' said Dean with a gravelly chuckle.

Stay off my side, I thought, before sussing that a remark like that didn't mean Dean was *on* my side. It was tag-team patronising.

'And how are you getting along with she who must be obeyed?'

'If you mean Heike, I'm getting along just fine. We've just done a photoshoot together. For *Tatler*.'

I don't know why I came out with that. I was feeling prickly and defensive and I wanted something to throw back at him, but I regretted it as soon as it was out there. My instinct to tell him nothing had been the right one.

'Together, eh?' His eyes sparkled with calculation. 'And was that Heike's idea or the record company's? Never hurts the profile to get the girls out front and centre, but I can't see her wearing it if it was someone else's suggestion. And I *definitely* can't see her sharing the lens if it was someone else's suggestion.'

'I don't know whose idea it was,' I lied. 'Either Heike's or the photographer's. They wanted to advertise the fact that there's a new dynamic to the band.'

That being one without you, you smug dick.

'A new dynamic, that's sure true,' he said, like it was the understatement of the day. 'I suppose it can't have been easy for her, being the only girl, especially out on the road. And I know the way I conducted myself last time out certainly didn't help. It's no surprise Heike decided to redress the balance.'

'I think I was brought on board for more than my gender,' I said, giving a coldly polite smile, unsure if I should be calling him on being offensive or if this was precisely the response he was after.

'Oh, no, that's not what I was implying. I just meant that a tour as extensive as the one you're on could be a pretty gruelling ordeal. It's very important that everybody gets along. How are you finding it?'

'It's been fine,' I said, determined to give nothing more away.

'So far,' said Dean, who had wandered around behind me with an armful of cable. 'But she ain't even left Blighty yet. Whole new set of rules when we hit the Continent, ain't there?' he said to the others, cackling.

'Not at all,' said Jan, smiling at me but obviously in on whatever was being hinted at. 'We run a tight ship: no man – or woman – left behind.'

'Nah, we'll be gentle with this one,' said Dean, placing his hands on my shoulders and squeezing, not for the first time. I don't know what creeped me out more: that he did it like we were on familiar terms, even the first time; or that he did it despite us most definitely not being on familiar terms two weeks further on.

'She's a virgin,' he added, in case I wasn't quite uncomfortable enough. 'In terms of touring Europe, that is.'

It was all I could do not to shudder after he let go, though I don't know why I wanted to hide it.

Angus approached with my fiddle, so I hurried over to grab it, a pretext to scurry away to a quiet corner.

I took it out of the case and was giving it my usual borderline-OCD check (as I did any time it had been out of my keeping, or in anyone else's possession, even for five minutes) when I became aware of Maxi looming nearby.

'Don't mind Dean. He's just a bit . . . unreconstructed. But you're gonna need guys like him on your side. The world you're heading into, it's going to feel like a long way from Shetland.'

'I'm not some wide-eyed peasant girl just off the boat. I've lived in Glasgow nearly two years.'

'I'm only trying to give you some advice, from one who's been down the road before and not made the best job of it. Dean and his crew, those guys will look after you over there. They're not who you need to be wary of.'

'Well, if you mean pissed violinists puking on the stage, I think that will be less of an issue this time.'

He gave a small laugh and angled his head: touché. But it seemed what I'd said had left me open.

'From that deft wee deflection, I think it's clear we both know who I'm talking about. After everything I put her through, it's small wonder Heike went out and found herself a tame violinist, someone she can control.'

I was about to object, but once again found I was walking into his next barb.

'So I'm sure it will be plain sailing – as long as that's what you are. But if it turns out you're not, there could be stormy seas ahead. I'm just giving you fair warning: you don't need to go off the rails to end up on the wrong side of her.'

Retreat

The roadies were conspicuously blanking Parlabane when he emerged from backstage. Dean had evidently spread the word and his cover was blown, though the fact that they believed they had something to hide regarding the Savage Earth Heart European tour was significant in itself. There was also the substantial consolation that this probably meant he would no longer have to go through with the charade of interviewing the Four Horsemen of the Anal Prolapse.

Nonetheless, there was still one member of the crew he reckoned would talk to him. He found Angus near the wings, leaning over a trestle table upon which he had rested an effects pedalboard in its open case. He had a black box in his hand, some kind of diagnostic device that he was plugging into each of the pedals in turn.

He glanced sideways at Parlabane then back at the pedalboard, but didn't draw the same 'well *you* can fuck off' look the others had been pitching him.

'Angus, isn't it? Angus Campbell? I believe you know a good friend of mine: big Spammy.'

He called him Spammy rather than give his real name, in order to establish that he was more than merely an acquaintance. Parlabane generally didn't like playing the mutual friend card, as it left him hostage to whatever impression said friend might have given based on what he or she *really* thought of him. However, he was confident he'd have gotten a decent account out of Spammy – just providing his name had come up at all.

'I'm Jack, by the way. Parlabane.'

Angus paused what he was doing, some light having switched on in a diagnostic device inside his brain.

'Spammy's mate Jack. You're the guy . . .' He trailed off, either unable to elaborate or deciding it unnecessary.

'I'm the guy,' Parlabane replied.

Or at least he used to be.

'I thought you were here to interview Prelude. Now Dean's saying you're digging dirt on Savage Earth Heart.'

'I'm not here to dig dirt on anybody. Mairi asked me to look into something, and I'm trying to fly under the radar.'

Angus turned to face him.

'What has she got you looking into?'

Parlabane glanced around, making a show of checking that nobody was in earshot.

'What do *you* think I'm looking into?' he replied, looking the guitar tech square in the eye.

Angus thought about it, checking his surroundings like Parlabane had just done.

'Something's going on with Heike,' he ventured quietly. 'That's it, isn't it? She fucked off in Berlin and Mairi's worried she's bailing on the US tour.'

Parlabane said nothing, waiting to see how he reacted without being given confirmation.

'I knew it,' he went on. 'I've called her a few times and got no response.'

Okay, Parlabane thought, so now that's two who suspect something is wrong and care enough to be worried, and one who *knows* something is wrong but is lying.

He went through the same questions with Angus as he'd put to the other two. He got the same arm's-length impressions about how alienated she seemed in the days before her disappearance, but Angus knew nothing about the bus incident as he was riding in the truck at the time. No new information, basically. But then Angus said something he really wasn't expecting.

'How hard has anyone actually looked?' he asked.

Parlabane responded with an expression of confusion: if he was prepared to brave a Prelude to the Slaughter gig in Manchester, how much harder did Angus have in mind?

'I mean, I'm sure plenty of folk have tried calling her and no doubt Mairi's been round and chapped the door of Heike's flat, but this might not be what it looks like. There's more than one explanation for why nobody's getting a response from her mobile.'

Parlabane got it.

'She might be somewhere there's no reception.'

'We both grew up on Islay,' Angus told him. 'We were at school together. In our first band together: I taught her to play "Why Does It Always Rain on Me" during a wet playtime.'

He looked self-conscious telling Parlabane this, like a proud dad talking about how he taught his daughter to ride a bike, when these days she was competing in the Isle of Man TT.

'You know she never had a mum, right?' Angus asked, squinting as a rack of overhead lights got tested above him.

'I've read a little,' Parlabane replied. He thought of the vague and ambiguous accounts of Ramsay Gunn's relationships, the implications of the age differences and the fact that he was still living with a woman twenty years younger when he died at the age of seventy-one. 'Her dad had a series of . . . significant others,' he settled for.

'There was one woman Heike was close to, though, and stayed close to after her dad had moved on to the next. She wasn't one of Ramsay's arty types, she was a normal person. Her name is Flora Blacklock. She still lives on Islay, away up by Sanaigmore. I don't think even LinkedIn can spam you out there.'

'That's pretty remote, I take it?'

'Put it this way: if you leave her house and head west, the first pub you come to will be in Newfoundland.'

The Uninvited

The atmosphere was quite subdued as we filed backstage towards the dressing room. Heike wasn't with us, having been waylaid to give a brief to-camera interview for VH-1. All sweaty, her hair pasted either side of her face and her hands holding a bottle of water and a towel, she looked more like an athlete speaking after a race.

She hadn't come first tonight.

The final night of our UK tour at the famous Brixton Academy wasn't the triumph we had all been hoping for. I mean, we weren't bad, and the audience was happy enough that they'd got what they came for – i.e. to hear 'Do It to Julia' live (saved for last so that we always got called enthusiastically for an encore) – but the show never really caught fire.

We all knew why.

Heike had been noticeably down from the start: it wasn't for the first time, but we all knew there were nights when things took a while to get going. More significantly, she had dropped 'Smuggler's Soul' from the set at the last minute, which pissed everybody off as it was becoming the highlight of the show, the one we all really looked forward to playing. It was the set's secret weapon, the song that really built things up going into the second half: we'd strip everything down to just Heike and me for 'Dark Station', then boom, we'd pull the pin and rocket the tempo all the way down the home straight.

Heike refused to explain why she was dropping it and the guys knew it was useless to push the issue. They just put it down to another one of her power trips. I knew the reason, though, and was grateful they were in the dark.

It was because I didn't wear the dress.

I just couldn't. When I went back to my room and opened the wardrobe, there was no indecision, no internal debate. I just knew it wasn't happening.

I showed up back at Brixton in black jeans and a black sleeveless T-shirt. Admittedly this combo was even less colourful than usual, but I was running to what I knew, as I do in times of insecurity. And you better believe I had a bra on too.

Heike said nothing, but her face was a ten-minute rant. I was getting her schoolmarm treatment, as she'd done to others before me, but like all the worst teachers, she decided to punish the whole class.

Other than Heike, I was the last one back to the dressing room, not in any particular hurry to face my bandmates. They couldn't know about what had – or hadn't – happened tonight, but that didn't stop me feeling paranoid.

This wasn't helped by the sight of Maxi standing among the group. He was talking with Rory, and getting a sight more out of him than I ever had. Maxi was drinking from a bottle of mineral water, while everyone else was into the booze rider. Beers were being handed round, the body language less peppy than usual: consolation drinks rather than celebratory ones.

I heard Damien telling Scott it didn't matter.

'London audiences are always pish anyway. If we had to have an off night, this was the place. They're spoiled rotten down here. You can give them your all and they just stand there.' He mimed someone half-heartedly clapping, a dull look on his face. 'If you took them to the Barrowland, they'd fuckin' shite themselves.'

Scott laughed, then I saw the smile disappear from his face like a switch had been flipped.

Heike was standing in the doorway. I didn't recall seeing a large consignment of awkward written on the rider, but it had arrived now. The floor suddenly became very interesting to a lot of people. Nobody wanted to look at her. Nobody except Maxi.

'What is *he* doing here?' she demanded, taking in the whole room. Obviously she didn't have a single suspect in mind. Not everybody bore Maxi a grudge, then.

She saw the triple-A pass clipped to his jacket.

'Who gave him that?'

'He's just dropping by to say hi,' said Jan, though I wasn't sure if this was a confession.

'He's not part of this any more,' she said, refusing to address Maxi directly. 'He doesn't *belong* here.'

'Oh, come on, Heike,' Maxi responded. 'I don't think that's entirely true. I mean, you're what, *two* weeks into the tour? Going on past form, I'm guessing at this point I've got more friends in this room than you have.'

Heike said nothing. She was trying to remain steely but I could see the lump in her throat. That had hurt.

'Anyway, I had to make sure you got this.'

He pulled an envelope from his jacket and handed it to her.

Heike looked uncertainly at it, then ripped it open. There was a letter inside, a couple of paragraphs of text. She read whatever it said then stared at him in disbelief.

Maxi gazed back, unmoving, a hint of a smile at the corners of his mouth, like he couldn't quite hide it.

Heike bustled into the dressing room, grabbed her things and hurried out again. It wasn't like her other dramatic exits: no shouting, no slamming of doors – she just wanted to be away from here, and fast. She kept her head down the whole time, but I could see she was fighting tears. Fighting but losing.

'What was that?' Damien asked, confused more than anything.

'Unfinished business,' Maxi replied. 'Don't worry. It's nothing that will affect you guys, or the tour. Apart from getting you all some much-needed peace from Miss Crabbit-Knickers tonight.'

After she had gone, the tension disappeared like the room itself had sighed with relief. Maxi had definitely got that right. More beers were being opened. There was a sense of bonding I might find very valuable in the weeks to come. At the same time, I kept picturing Heike's flushed face, trying to hide her tears.

I thought of my conversation with Rory and wondered if a night in the doghouse might mean Heike learning a lesson, and at the right time as well. But I also found it hard to ignore a friend – for surely Heike was a friend – clearly suffering, and none of us could know why without reading that letter.

If I had known just how much was going to turn on that moment, in that decision, would I have chosen differently? I honestly don't know.

I began to get my things. It didn't go unnoticed.

'Don't go running after her,' Rory said. 'That's what she wants.'

'I'm not,' I lied. 'I'm just calling it a night.'

Maxi gave me a look, like he knew otherwise.

Tame violinist. Someone she can control. But if it turns out you're not . . .

I looked in vain for a taxi, before giving up after realising there were at least fifty people in my immediate environment attempting the same thing. I headed for the Tube, wondering whether Heike had been any more lucky.

I saw her as I came through the revolving door into the lobby of the hotel. She was walking from the bar, holding a bottle of Bowmore, and making for the lifts.

The doors pinged open as soon as she pressed the button, and she stepped inside. She had her head down as I approached, so I knew she wouldn't see me, and I didn't know her room number. I could phone, but it would be easier for her to cut me off.

I called out to her before the doors could close.

'Heike.'

She glanced up, looking surprised and a bit affronted, like I had burst in and caught her naked. I thought for a moment that she was going to let the doors close, or even reach for the button to shut them quicker. I felt myself isolated from everybody: blanked by Heike and missing out on the group therapy that was kicking off back in Brixton. I wondered if it was too late to rejoin the guys, walk back in with a smile and say: 'Fuck the early night, I'll sleep on the bus tomorrow.'

Instead Heike held the doors for me, one hand on the button, the other gripping her Islay malt.

111

'Do you want to slide my hangover down a few notches by helping me out with this?'

'I'll do my bit,' I said.

Whisky wasn't really my drink. I was more of a G&T girl, but there had been gatherings back home where it was the only thing on the table. Surely she hadn't seriously been planning to drink the lot?

I stayed where I was, wondering if a different venue might be more suitable now it wasn't drinks for one.

'Do you want to take it back to the bar?'

She glanced towards the revolving door.

'Don't know when that lot might come piling in.'

I wasn't sure how I felt about Heike inviting me back to her room, but maybe I was the one who had been doing the inviting. Where did I think this heart-to-heart was going to happen?

I stepped into the lift. It felt like an overt act.

Heike got two glasses from her bathroom and poured a huge measure into each on top of the little desk-cum-dressing table at the end of her bed. It being London, the room was cramped. Heike perched cross-legged on top of the duvet, while I sat a few feet away on the room's only other item of a furniture, a revolving chair.

She held up her glass rather joylessly for me to clink mine against.

'Thanks,' she said. 'I really appreciate this, under the circumstances. I'm not easy sometimes, I know that.'

I said nothing. No point in pretending it wasn't the case.

'What was the letter?' I asked. It seemed just as pointless to avoid the issue.

Heike took a mouthful of whisky and gulped it back. I could imagine it burning all the way down, but she never showed it. Maybe she had already swallowed something worse tonight.

'He's suing me.'

'What for?'

'He wants co-writing credits. I knew it was coming. My lawyer warned me that she'd had preliminary contact with Maxi's lawyer. She said it was a gambit: at best he's looking to get an arrangement fee and he's hoping I settle. It's kind of inevitable when you have a big hit like "Do It to Julia". People come out of the woodwork trying to get a piece.'

She took another drink, less this time, but still a lot more than a sip. I had some too, finding its warmth comforting as it ran down inside me.

'He's not just naming "Do It to Julia", though He's named six songs from across both albums, claiming they were based on songs we wrote together before. It's a means of strengthening his case: he names six songs, but Julia's the prize. That wasn't what upset me, though.'

She looked at me and swallowed, though there was no whisky in her mouth. Her eyes were tired, her face almost scared, vulnerable.

'He's named "Dark Station". He could have named any five songs to bolster his case, but the bastard is claiming he co-wrote "Dark Station".'

Her voice was steadier than I was expecting, making me think that maybe she was already cried out, but it faltered at the end. I didn't understand why.

'Do you know what that song means? What it's really about?'

I held my glass, wishing I could hide behind it. I knew what I *thought* it was about, but it didn't seem like the time to offer my own half-arsed analysis of a lyric that I had already once seen Heike tearful after singing.

'In Berlin, before the Wall came down, there were these underground stations where the trains wouldn't stop. Ghost stations, they called them. They were places where the lines ran through East Berlin: you could be there physically, you could pass through, but you couldn't ever get off.'

She took another drink and refilled her glass.

This was as much as I had understood: that the song was about never quite being able to connect with someone, no matter how close you got. Then I suddenly saw what had been in front of me so long, having played this number alongside this woman every evening for a fortnight.

113

'Your mother,' I said. 'She was from Berlin, wasn't she?' My words came out as a whisper, and sounded like a gasp.

'I never really knew her,' she said. 'That's what the song is about. She died when I was very young. I don't even know *how* young. My dad got together with her when he was living in West Berlin in the eighties. She was an artist too, but she was also a heroin addict. He took me away from her not long after I was born, and I don't think she put up a fight. He wouldn't tell me much about her, and now he's gone too.'

Heike was unable to speak then. She seemed determined not to cry, but it was touch and go.

'I'm sorry,' she said.

'No, not at all.'

'They say you don't miss what you never had, but . . .'

I thought she was about to break down, but instead she smiled in a way that I couldn't quite read.

'You're one of a tiny handful of people I've ever told this,' she said, looking me in the eye, both fragile and accusing. Like that first night in Bristol, she had found herself exposed in front of me, with no choice but to trust me with what she had revealed. But she had trusted others, and been betrayed.

'You told Maxi.'

Heike nodded, her expression cold, but her anger making her lip tremble.

'He listed "Dark Station" to hurt me. It's his revenge for me kicking him out of the band. This is something that's mine, mine alone. It's one of the few things in my life that makes me feel some connection to her, even though it's about *not* being able to connect. So when somebody makes a claim that it's half his, turns it into a commodity, turns it into a *battleground* . . .'

She was crying gently, as something in her seemed to give in. She looked helpless.

I moved off the seat and on to the edge of the bed. Heike leaned into me and let her head fall into my shoulder. I felt a wetness on my neck as her cheek brushed against it.

She wasn't sobbing. Her head just moved up and down softly

as she breathed, a perfect quiet falling upon the room, the outside world far, far away.

I knew Heike would make me pay for getting this close, but right then I didn't care. I felt the most perfect sense of calm inside, of serenity.

Then she raised her head and we looked into each other's eyes.

I don't know if I kissed her or she kissed me. I just know that it happened. It was soft, it was tender, and then it was over.

Heike pulled away with a look of shock and doubt, trembling.

'Oh, God, I am sorry. I am so sorry. Jesus, I wouldn't have thought there was a way I could contrive to make myself feel worse tonight.'

'Heike . . .'

'I just got caught up in the emotion. I was so touched that you were here for me, and this is how I . . .'

'Heike . . .'

'Jesus, I'm effectively your employer. It's like I'm your boss and I'm taking advantage of—'

'Heike,' I said again, this time taking her hand.

She was looking at me, still apologetic, even a bit scared.

'Forget about it,' I said. 'It happened. It's forgotten, okay?'

She bit her lip and wiped her eyes, recovering a little.

'Are you sure?'

'I'm sure.'

I poured us both another shot, trying to hide the fact that my hands were shaking.

'Hey, *Bridesmaids* is on the pay-per-view. Let's get tipsy and watch it together,' I suggested.

Because I didn't want to leave.

'Okay,' she said, with a little smile. 'As long as you're all right.'

'I'm fine.'

'You sure?'

'I told you. It's forgotten.'

But it wasn't forgotten. It *couldn't* be, because I didn't want to forget it, any more than I had wanted it to stop.

Elements

Heike Gunn's voice filled the inside of Parlabane's hire car as he drove through the Trossachs and on towards Kennacraig. He had the volume high and his foot to the floor on a clear morning, enjoying being behind the wheel for the first time in more than a year. It was crisp and still, Loch Fyne creating a spectacular if unnerving illusion: its placid surface reflected the image of the mountains, making it appear as though there was a dizzying plunge beneath the level of the road.

Sarah had liked Savage Earth Heart, probably more than he had. He could still remember her singing along to 'Western Pagodas' as they drove past distilleries on a weekend break to Speyside, though he had always been tempted to skip the next track, 'It Meant Nothing', as it unavoidably reminded both of them of the time she had a one-night stand with a colleague.

He missed her. Sometimes he would tell himself what he missed was the way it felt when they were together, that he only missed the woman she used to be. Maybe that was true, but it was hard not to think that they could both be those people again, that with a little luck and a bit less pressure they could get it right.

It felt good to be out here on the road, the scenery reminding him of pleasant things too long forgotten. When had he last been out here climbing? It had to be years. How did that happen? He used to love it, used to live for it, so much that when he was back from a trip he would see the city around him in three dimensions while everyone else lived in flatland. Time was, he couldn't look at a building without seeing toeholds, mapping out how he would scale the thing.

It was something they couldn't share, however. Sarah didn't like heights, and she got increasingly worried about what might happen to him when he was indulging what she saw as a pointlessly risky pursuit. There was also, he knew, a concern in her mind that the more adept he remained at climbing, the more tempted he might be to break into some office in search of evidence to stand up a story. This concern was not entirely groundless, he had to admit, but it wasn't a temptation he had actually succumbed to since the time it landed him in jail.

The music was beautifully clear, the hire car boasting a very beefy sound system. Mairi had given him an advance copy of the new album, which was her way of underlining what was at stake, as one listen told him that this was a band striding boldly up to the next level.

Smuggler's Soul was confident, mature and accomplished, if a little safe, suggesting the influence of big-label A&R. However, everything Parlabane knew about Heike Gunn gave the impression she was stubborn to the point of bloody-minded, so he didn't imagine this move to a stadium-baiting epic sound had constituted a surrender on her part, or even a compromise. She was thinking big. The question was, had she become spooked by just how big this was looking to get? Maybe she had decided she needed a bit of alone time: breathing rather than bailing.

As he examined the lyrics for clues to her state of mind, he was certain that these songs were not the work of someone who was starting to crack under pressure. Savage Earth Heart's third album wasn't quite a manifesto for world-domination, but it was the bold and confident work of someone who was aware the world was watching, and was happy to showcase her talent. Perhaps for that reason it was a little less personal, volunteering fewer candid insights into Heike's inner self and her vulnerabilities. It was outward-looking, optimistic and discernibly careerist.

Heike had unmistakably chosen the path to stardom, a path that would take her a very long way from Parlabane's destination. As he drove the lonely miles towards the ferry port at Kennacraig, he wondered whether she'd had second thoughts about where it might ultimately lead, and whether she could ever truly come home again. Did she look into her immediate future and fear she had created a monster? And was she scared that the monster was her?

Parlabane had never been to Islay, and had therefore never taken a ferry from Kennacraig either. The longer he drove, the less likely it seemed that such a place would turn out to exist. He kept thinking he must have wrongly programmed the sat-nav, as surely there ought to be a settlement nearby if he was approaching a port; a fishing village at least.

As the hire car snaked through the glens, there was a point when the looming landscape ceased to seem a vertical playground waiting to be explored and began instead to underline how remote and isolated Parlabane was. It was a transformation largely effected by the lingering presence of a black Audi in his rear-view mirror. It had been behind him since Inveraray, too far back for him to get a look at the driver but close enough that he was always in its sight. Parlabane attempted to salve his paranoid instincts with the logic that it was hardly the same as constantly seeing the same car behind him in a built-up area. When there was only one road, it didn't count as being followed: you were merely in front of another vehicle. However, those paranoid instincts had been on the money of late, and the prospect that this was another Met tail was at the optimistic end of his imaginings.

Parlabane had successfully hacked a laptop belonging to a senior figure at the MoD: that part was not so much in the public domain as in the 'embarrassingly public' domain. The Westercruik Inquiry was interested in ascertaining how he had acquired it, though that was small potatoes in the grander scheme. What was truly under investigation was corruption and collusion linking the MoD and the defence industry. They knew that the security failings required for it to have ultimately fallen into his hands would need to have been many and varied, and therefore if he gave up his source it may well be the first domino. Consequently, there had to be a lot of people getting nervous that Parlabane would crack: powerful, connected and ruthless people, all of whom would sleep better tonight if he happened to have a tragic accident out here in the middle of nowhere, with no witnesses.

The black Audi turned off at Tarbert, leaving him feeling less relieved than logic should have dictated. The car was gone, but the fears that it had unleashed were still loose in his head.

When he finally saw the sign for the turn-off, directing him down a narrow road with only the sight of water in the middle distance indicating a connection to maritime activities, he was half expecting to find a wizened old man with a wooden raft and a long pole. Instead he found a jetty and a building that advertised itself as the ferry terminal, but which more closely resembled a newsagent's or a building-site office.

As he parked in the queue and glimpsed movement in his rear-view, he was startled to spot the black Audi rolling slowly into line behind him. At last he got a close look at the occupant. He was male, mid-to-late forties, squat and jowly, sporting close-cropped grey hair and wearing a suit. Could be a cop, could be something else.

If he *was* a cop, what did these Met dicks think Parlabane was going to do? Bury the secret of the stolen laptop beneath a bronze-age cairn in the Hebrides?

And yet if he wasn't a cop . . .

Parlabane contrived to drop behind him once their cars were on board, waiting in his vehicle until he saw the guy exit the Audi. It was one of the advantages of having identified a tail that the bastard had to pretend to be oblivious of him, and this allowed Parlabane to surreptitiously snap his picture with his phone as the guy took a seat in the forward lounge. Another one to add to the polis gallery, and if he wasn't polis then it was good to have a documented image of whoever had been sent after him.

He decided he should go right up and make conversation, just to see how the guy reacted. More importantly, it would make the prick understand that there was a whole host of witnesses who could testify to having seen them talk, which might put a spoke in any grim plans he had.

Parlabane was about to make his move when the guy got up and headed for the bar. He followed at a short distance, but it was long enough for someone else to get in the queue between them.

Nonetheless, it wouldn't stop him making conversation as the guy left with his drink; indeed the more forced it appeared, the better.

Then he heard him order.

'I would like a black coffee, please.'

He spoke in a gravelly European accent, and unless UKIP's worst nightmares had come true and even the security forces were now overrun with immigrants, then he wasn't Parlabane's problem.

'First time to Islay?' the purser asked him.

'First visit,' he replied with a friendly chuckle. 'But not my first *taste* of it, yes?'

'You like the malts, then?'

He gave an eager laugh.

'I am on, how you say, a pilgrimage.'

Christ.

It was a timely reminder of how paranoia was a symptom of gross egotism and self-obsession. Yeah, like Parlabane was that important to the Westercruik Inquiry that they would send someone to follow him from Edinburgh to the Mull of Kintyre.

He drove off the boat at Port Askaig and headed south-east. He checked the time as he reached Bridgend, and felt amazed that he had been driving through Edinburgh only a few hours ago. It barely seemed like the same country, or indeed the same century. He drove past crisp white-painted houses, looking out to sea in little rows like they were huddled together for warmth. He saw tiny cemeteries, headstones counting in mere dozens rather than hundreds. Dry-stone dykes ran along single-track roads, often bereft of any markings. And every so often, he'd come over a hill or around a headland and see the black, triangular-topped towers of a distillery: western pagodas.

Parlabane thought of Heike's father Ramsay Gunn, who had been witness to so many scenes of uprising, turmoil and change around the world that he was like the zeitgeist's advance location scout, and yet had come back here, where it was easy to imagine time standing still. He must have felt that this was somewhere his daughter would be safe, a place of stability and certainties, but the one thing he hadn't been able to give her was a mother.

As he drove slowly along the single track, he could see white heads of surf rolling towards the shore. He recalled Angus's remark about the next pub west being in Canada, and thought of what he'd learned about the woman he was planning to doorstep.

Flora Blacklock was an Islay native who had been a champion solo sailor back in the eighties. This had led to her being the subject of a painting by Ramsay Gunn, as part of a series of portraits that depicted women triumphant over their corresponding elements: air, stone, fire and, in Flora's case, water. Of all his models and muses, it seemed she was the only one who had developed a lasting relationship with Ramsay's daughter.

It must have been difficult for her growing up, Parlabane thought: watching these women move in and out of her father's life, wondering why they didn't stay. Flora, at least, had never left the island.

The house was a low, L-shaped stone building in grounds that stretched back towards an inlet bay. He could see a sailing boat tied up at a jetty, and recognised it as the same vessel from the painting he'd seen online. These days Flora ran boat trips around the Hebrides for bird-watchers and other adventure-minded wild-life lovers, but these were advertised as leaving from Port Charlotte, so this wasn't her commercial vessel. Had she taught Heike some seacraft, he wondered. If so it would be the ideal way to drop off the radar. She could be anywhere from here to Shetland and there would be no way of tracing her.

The wind whipped at him as he climbed out of the car and walked towards what he couldn't decide was the front or back garden. As he passed through a gap between dry-stone dykes in lieu of a gate, he saw the woman he had come to speak to, striding from the house towards a flat-bed Toyota Land Cruiser. She tossed an armful of ropes into the back, then finally noticed him as she was slapping her hands together to dust them off.

She looked late-fifties, her silver hair tied back and tucked under a blue cap. She was dressed in jeans and a polo shirt revealing taut and wiry arms.

'Can I help you?' she asked, an openness in her tone suggesting

121

she actually would if she could. She regarded him with a smile of patient curiosity, like she was pretty sure he was in the wrong place but interested to know what had brought him here.

'Hi. You're Flora Blacklock, aren't you?'

'That's right,' she confirmed, dangling her car keys absent-mindedly in her right hand.

'My name is Jack Parlabane. I'm a journalist and I'm doing a feature on the band Savage Earth Heart. I realise this is a bit of a Hail Mary, but would you happen to know where I might find Heike Gunn?'

His heart leapt as he noticed she was nodding, but there was something apologetic about her smile that told him his celebration was premature.

'Yes. She's in America,' she said, her tone almost pitying that he could have failed to be aware of this. 'On tour.'

'No,' he corrected her, 'that's not for another couple of weeks.'

'Oh. I was sure she said June, but she must have meant the end of the month.'

He tried not to think about the distance he had travelled in order to hear this. The woman hadn't spoken to Heike in weeks. Still, she was one of the few people who might be able to offer some insight into the real woman behind the public persona, so the trip could yet prove worthwhile. He had to be delicate, though. It wouldn't do to worry the woman by letting her know Heike was missing, not least because it wouldn't be long in going public after that.

'Do you mind if I ask you a few questions?'

'Not at all,' she said. 'But I'm just on my way out. I've a boat down in Port Charlotte and I need to prep her for tomorrow. If you don't mind following me down the road we can talk while I work. That's unless you're any good with ropes, in which case you can make yourself useful.'

Parlabane got back in the hire car and trundled behind the Toyota, which he guessed she was driving slowly as a courtesy to his axles. Ironically the pace slowed further not long after they hit proper tarmac, as they got stuck behind a tractor. He noticed from the dashboard display that his Bluetooth-connected phone had recovered a signal, and as his car crawled along, the modern time-to-kill reflex prodded him in its usual way.

Call her.

He could see water less than half a mile away. He might only be two minutes from the port. It would be sod's law if this was the one time she picked up, when he didn't have long to talk. Then he thought that maybe sod's law could work *for* him, because if now was the one time she picked up, then at least they'd get to speak.

He tried not to dwell on how desperate that logic sounded as the ringing tone pulsed through the car's stereo. There was a familiar click as it diverted to voicemail: not even her voice either, just a standard network recording.

Fuck.

He grabbed a handful of ropes from the back of the flatbed and followed Flora aboard her tourist tub, the *Hecate*. She dumped her bundle on the foredeck and sat down on a bench, where she began cutting heavy-duty plastic tape into even lengths with a short-bladed knife.

'All these years Heike's been in the limelight,' she said brightly. 'And you're the first journalist ever to come and ask *me* about her.'

She spoke with an odd mixture of pride and disappointment.

'An untapped resource,' he replied.

'And all yours. So what would you like to know?'

'When did you last speak to her?' he asked.

'In the flesh or on the phone? She was last here for a couple of weeks just after Christmas, but the last time I spoke to her must have been, let me think, a few weeks back when the band were playing in Glasgow. I was supposed to travel down to see the show but I had a bad cold and couldn't face the trip. Why did you think she might be here, incidentally?'

'Eh, it was Angus Campbell who suggested it. I've been inter-viewing all the members of the band for a piece, but Heike's proving a little elusive. He said you and she were close, so if she was laying low before the American tour he thought this might be where I'd find her.'

'Angus. Yes. Not seen him in years. He couldn't wait to leave, to be honest. Always wanted to travel.'

She smiled at the thought, presumably picturing a younger version of the shaggy-headed road-dog. Then she sighed.

'I'm sorry he gave you a duff tip. Have you come far?'

'Edinburgh.'

'Oof. At least you got a dry day for it.'

She picked up another length of rope and began whittling at the frayed end of it with the knife. Her fingers were rough and callused, criss-crossed with a thousand nicks and scratches.

'I gather you've known Heike a long time.'

'Since she was a girl.'

'You must be very proud of what Heike's achieved.'

'Proud, aye. Though not surprised. She was always very strong-willed, and a grafter. They say hard work only beats talent when talent doesn't work hard, so she had the perfect combination to succeed. Young Angus not so much. It always bothered Heike that he never made the most of himself. He had the gifts: his father was a fine musician, great accordion player.'

'Heike's father must have been a high bar for her to measure herself against,' Parlabane suggested. 'I imagine that could easily have been intimidation as much as inspiration. Do you think that's why she went into music rather than art?'

He knew this was a bloody stupid question, but reckoned it would boost his music-journo cover to pose a query that indicated no understanding of the creative process.

'Och, that's the kind of thing you'd really have to ask Heike herself. I can recall with a fair degree of accuracy the things she did and said when she was nine years old, but as for what goes on inside her head, you might as well ask me about quantum theory.'

'So what was she like as a child? Was she precocious? Withdrawn? Huffy?'

'Robust,' Flora replied. 'On the outside, at least. She was sensitive, but she didn't like anyone to know. She preferred to put on a brave face than have anybody notice she wasn't indestructible.'

He was surprised by her candour. She really wasn't kidding about never having talked to a journalist before. Parlabane's phone buzzed on the bench beside him. He saw the name 'Jenny Dalziel' flash on the screen. He'd have to call her back. This woman was opening up to him and he couldn't let an interruption break the spell.

'Do you think that came from not having a mother around?'

'Undoubtedly. Heike never likes to lean on anybody: it's both a sign of strength and a sign of vulnerability. She doesn't like the idea of being dependent on anyone, and that definitely comes from the way she was raised. She likes to gives the impression she doesn't need anybody else, but anyone who has known Heike or even just paid attention to her songs would know that she's been looking for her mother all her life. I mean, that's hardly a scoop for you, is it?'

'And do you think she looked for her mother in you?'

Flora glanced out to sea for a moment, a wistful mixture of regret and affection in her face.

'Part of her may have, but I'm not sure she'd allow herself to find her. For the reasons I've just mentioned, she doesn't like anybody getting too close. I'm there for her, she knows that, but she still puts on the brave face even for me. I think that's why she's comfortable with the adulation of crowds, which would have other people scurrying for cover: me in particular. It's anonymous and impersonal, and she doesn't have to expose her real self to them.'

She picked up a length of tape and began wrapping it around the frayed end of a rope, goose-pimples on her arm as the breeze caught her skin.

'You worry about her being in the public eye, don't you?' he suggested. 'Everybody wanting a piece.'

'I think that's what the kids call "first-world problems", but sure. I mean, I don't worry about whether she can handle it. I worry about the cost to herself *of* handling it: of never letting the cracks show.'

His phone buzzed again, this time with a text. Jenny's words scrolled across the screen: 'Call me ASAP. Beyond urgent.'

Shit.

He apologised to Flora and walked towards the prow of the boat as the phone auto-dialled.

Jenny picked up after one ring.

'Where are you?' she asked.

'I'm on Islay. Looking for Ms Gunn.'

'Well, you're not going to find her there. According to the Border Agency, she never came back to the UK. But I was kinda hoping you were gonna say you're somewhere further than that.'

'How come?'

'You didn't get this from me, Scoop, but they're turning up the gas on Westercruik. I just heard from a strong source that the Met have sought a warrant for your arrest.'

Merchandise

I had one of those hangovers where you kind of see yourself from the outside, and it's really not pretty. We were in Bordeaux, with the bus for Barcelona leaving in about half an hour. I needed some air. I needed some coffee too, but I couldn't face the breakfast room. All it would take was the sight of a plate of someone else's food and I might spew.

All things considered, it probably wasn't the best time to take a call from Keith.

I had last spoken to him on the bus to Dover, the morning after Brixton. It had felt great to talk to him then, just to hear his voice. Part of me wanted to bail and run away, back to him, back to Shetland, back to normality. We talked like we hadn't done the whole UK tour, like two people who were really missing one another. He even hinted he might fly out to meet me on one of the European dates. I suggested a few destinations.

'Maybe I'll surprise you,' he said.

I knew he wouldn't, but that didn't matter so much: it made me feel closer just to hear him talk about it. Keith never did anything spontaneous. Okay, strictly speaking he had *once*, but the circumstances weren't something either of us liked to dwell on, and I wasn't sure if the definition of spontaneity stretched to things done during a massive loss of temper.

I think we both knew he wouldn't fly out, and he definitely wouldn't surprise me, but it was progress that we could have a bit of fun talking about it.

We had shared less of a cosy chat as I stood outside the hotel in Bordeaux.

His tone was off from the start: even the way he said 'Hi' told me he was feeling huffy.

'I was starting to think you'd lost your phone,' he said. 'You haven't called for days, and whenever I call you I get diverted to voicemail. Do you even switch the thing on?'

I wasn't in the best mood to be moaned at.

'Of course it's on: it's just I can't hear it while I'm doing a soundcheck or a show.'

'Yes, you told me, which is why it would make sense for you to be the one calling *me* now and again.'

'You don't like me phoning you at work. You've told me enough times you're not supposed to take personal calls.'

'Yes, but what's wrong with first thing, before I go in? Or lunchtime?'

'First thing? What, you mean like eight o'clock? I'm not on a school trip over here. I can't remember what eight o'clock looks like.'

'You're too busy living it up with that band to make time for a phone call?'

That band.

'Christ, Keith, don't act like a wean. It's not always easy, that's all I'm saying. It doesn't mean I'm not thinking about you.'

Except that I mostly wasn't.

'It's not easy for me either, wondering where you are and whether you're okay.'

'Well, you can always come out and see for yourself how I'm doing. Did you look into getting flights yet?'

I knew he hadn't. Part of me hated myself for using this against him, as by making it a big deal, it seemed even less likely he would do it.

'I'm having to stay on top of a lot of things at work. There's opportunities I have to make the most of right now because they won't come round again. I'm trying to lay down the foundations for a solid career, Monica.'

'And what do you think I'm doing?'

'I'm not sure you even know yourself.'

Yeah, cheers, Keith. Thanks for that. Self-doubt always goes really well with a stinking hangover, and this was the worst of what was fast becoming quite a collection. Every morning I told myself I'd stay on the soft stuff tonight, that I couldn't be hammering it after every show, especially with the schedule that was rolling out in front of us, and every night I decided: What the hell, I'm twenty-two and if this all falls apart I don't want to look back and think I didn't live while I had the chance.

Actually, I could have had an even more brutal hangover after Brixton. It should have been truly horrific, given how much neat whisky I drank, but it didn't work out like that. Sure, I felt a bit fragile on the bus to Dover, but the headache and the quease were weirdly anaesthetised by knowing just how much worse I *might* have felt.

I woke up in my own room, with little recollection of having got there from Heike's, and before the first sign of après-whisky could strike I was overwhelmed by this vast sense of relief at what hadn't happened. Between the overcharged emotions in that room and the malt, there was plenty to explain what did happen, and it was easy to imagine how I would have been feeling if things continued along that path. It wouldn't have been a hangover, it would have been an emotional holocaust.

Heike and I were okay after London. I think we both knew we couldn't pretend nothing had happened, but we also knew it didn't have to mean anything. Or at least it didn't have to mean everything. We were closer, I felt.

The French morning sun sent me limping for the shade, and I abandoned my thoughts of a walk around the block. I settled for sitting on the edge of a planter and sipping mineral water. The bus was in the car park and the driver had the engine running, but I wasn't cooping myself up in there until the last possible moment.

I looked around for Heike, which was when I realised that, on top of everything, I had slept in. I was supposed to have left two hours ago.

Shit.

Heike wouldn't be travelling with us that morning. She had gone on ahead by train to do an interview for Spanish TV. It had been a late change to the schedule, Jan only springing it on her yesterday evening, and he had asked if I wanted to go along to keep her company. It had sounded good at six o'clock yesterday evening, not so much twelve hours later when my alarm went off.

Oh well. She had ended up travelling alone after all, but at least going by rail she wouldn't have to spend another six hours on the bus. Whereas we'd be relying on the faulty air-con to save us all from heat exhaustion and death by fart poisoning.

And just what you need when you're feeling and looking as bad as I was is for a gaggle of sprightly and attractive girls to rock up and join your tour party.

They climbed out of two taxis in the car park, seven of them in matching T-shirts and hot pants, and queued up to collect matching rucksacks from the boots of the two vehicles. They looked made-up and manicured within an inch of their lives. Not a brain cell between them, I thought to myself in my admittedly grouchy, hungover condition. At first I assumed they were part of some kind of marketing or publicity operation, headed for the hotel, until I noticed Jan get out of the second taxi and pay both drivers. That was also when I noticed that the matching T-shirts all had the Savage Earth Heart logo.

'The hell is this?' Damien asked, bleary-eyed as he stepped from the lobby, chewing on a croissant. 'Are we on a reality show now?'

'Shh,' said Rory next to him, staring in disbelief. 'Don't make too much noise or you'll wake me up. I'm having this dream that seven porny-looking burds are getting onto our tour bus.'

Jan wandered over to where we were all stood in the shade, our bags at our feet.

'Everybody ready to hit the road?' he asked, like all the other stuff wasn't happening, and let's all pretend we see nothing please kthxbai.

'Ehm, what the hell?' I asked, as Heike wasn't here to do it.

Jan laughed self-consciously.

'Crazy rock 'n' roll, huh? These are the merchandising girls on the Serpent tour. It starts tonight in Barcelona, and as it is also being promoted by Bad Candy I've been asked to give them a lift.'

Jan over-enunciated when he was feeling uncomfortable, like he was playing the dumb foreigner: English is my second language, please don't give me a hard time.

'That's Serpent's merch team?' Damien asked. 'I'm in the wrong band.'

'Serpent are a big deal,' Jan said apologetically, not realising Damien wasn't serious. 'They are playing the Palau Sant Jordi: all arena venues.'

'So why are they all wearing Savage Earth Heart T-shirts?' I asked.

Jan shrugged.

'Kind of a favour for a favour. A lot of people will be looking at those T-shirts at the Palau, you know?'

I started to wonder how convenient it was that Heike wasn't here to witness this, but it wasn't my place to make a fuss. Plus I wasn't exactly feeling up for a fight. I just wanted to curl up and go back to sleep, but I'd settle for getting to Barcelona without being sick.

The new arrivals all piled on board and sat together towards the front. I got a closer look as I shuffled along the aisle, feeling self-conscious about keeping my shades on, but knowing I'd feel worse if they could see what I looked like without them. I felt really hacket.

At first I thought they looked early twenties, but seeing past the make-up I realised that was stretching it. More like late teens, the lot of them. They didn't say much, not even to each other: maybe they had been touring together even longer than us. They didn't look French or Spanish. I'd have said Eastern European, maybe Romanian or Bulgarian. I wondered how they'd ended up doing promotion work for a Scandinavian metal band on tour.

I did get off to sleep on the bus, but was woken when it got pulled over past Puigcerda on the Spanish side of the border. I had a horrible moment when I thought I'd lost my passport, before finding it under my bag on the seat, where it had fallen as I moved my book, laptop, purse and phone out of the way to look for it.

We all had to get off while the police checked our documents.

I noticed that Jan had a thick stack of passports, which he handed over while waving towards the merchandise girls. I didn't understand the Spanish he spoke to the cops, but he seemed cheery and relaxed. None of this was new to him. Or to the others, it turned out.

'The whole open borders thing doesn't really apply quite so much when you're in a band,' Damien explained, eyeing the two sniffer dogs that were so far being kept back on a leash. 'It's not so much random checks as a wee bonus if we cross a border and *don't* get stopped.'

'Maybe they think we're the mules for Serpent's stash,' suggested Scott. He was kidding, but his joke did make me worry where Dean was keeping his.

In the event, they gave us the all-clear and waved us on our way without the dogs getting involved.

'I think that was just to let us know they're watching,' Scott said.

I saw Jan standing by the door, collecting passports from our seven guests as they filed silently back on board.

Definitely, I thought. But watching what?

Holidays in the Sun

Parlabane stood looking out for Mairi in front of the Brandenburg Gate. She was running late, but at least he didn't need to worry that he was waiting for her in the wrong place. It wasn't as though there was another one just like it.

He gazed up at the quadriga and found it both beautiful and intimidating: a bit like Heike Gunn, to be honest. The goddess thundering forward on her chariot unavoidably brought to mind that image on the cover of *Tatler*.

She was Victoria, goddess of Victory, but was also interpreted to be Eirene, goddess of peace. Conquest and affirmation; contrition and reconciliation. These were the two sides to Heike's songs: the combative and crusading, ever ready to fight someone else's battles; and the gently ameliorative, seeking tender connection and offering a balm to emotional wounds. Which side, he wondered, had led her to become lost?

'Jack.'

He heard her voice and turned to see that Mairi had crept up behind him. She had flown in from London, he from Glasgow. She got in first, and had already headed out by the time he checked in to their hotel, so she'd texted him to meet up here.

She was carrying a Starbucks coffee, purchased from a place nearby on Unter den Linden.

Parlabane couldn't recall when he last bought one. Even after they had generously 'volunteered' to pay some tax, he had thought: No, fuck you for ever. And yet the sight of Mairi was a timely reminder that any such principled stance would always be an exercise in farting into thunder while the majority of folk remained blithely disengaged.

Mairi had a pair of sunglasses on top of her head, and was

dressed in linen trousers and a grey T-shirt that could easily have been a nondescript combo on most other women, but on her looked like it cost more than Parlabane's entire wardrobe. While his thoughts were turning to where he could get something cold down his neck, the coffee she was toting just seemed to further underline her natural cool.

He had come on foot, eschewing a taxi in order to get his bearings and establish a feel for the place. The hotel was on Tiergartenstrasse in the diplomatic quarter, all embassies and electronic security gates. It had inevitably turned his thoughts to Sir Anthony Mead and that honeytrap laptop, but he could put all that to the back of his mind for now. He wasn't sure how soon the Met were likely to be granted their warrant, but he'd left the country within only a few hours of speaking to Jenny.

Mairi stared at the jacket he had slung over his shoulder, an unnecessarily heavy-duty affair. Indeed, any jacket was a garment too far on a day like this.

'Yeah,' he confessed bashfully. 'For some reason, I thought it would be chilly.'

'It's June, Jack.'

'Too many Cold War movies, I guess. I need it to keep my stuff in, though.'

'Get yourself a man-bag.'

'I have my dignity.'

She looked him up and down, her verdict on his appearance indicating she was unconvinced by this last claim.

They made their way through the crowds of tour parties and proprietorially noisy gaggles of American teenagers, heading for the venue where Savage Earth Heart had failed to play the final night of their tour. It was a place called simply Palast, a two-thousand-capacity converted cinema just off Friedrichstrasse. The plan was to get talking to the venue staff and develop an objective version of events prior to Heike's disappearance. Parlabane wanted to hear about the show that did go ahead, as well as some first-hand accounts of the behaviour of both band and crew in the lead-up to Jan's announcement that the singer had a throat infection.

The place was shut. There was no show scheduled for that night, and no amount of ringing the doorbell or phoning the management office roused a response. They'd have to come back the next day.

'Let's got to the Brauereihallen,' Mairi suggested.

'I know almost no German, but that sounds enough like brewery hall as to strike me as a great idea.'

'It's where we made the video for "Zoo Child" – that's the next single. I came over for the shoot. Heike chose it because they played there on the last tour. I came over for that too. It's a big multi-use venue, different size halls for gigs and for clubs, chill-out spaces, decent food. I remember Heike was very keen on one of the bars: we'd hung out there before. We were there well into the night.'

'I thought you weren't managing them on the last tour.'

'I wasn't. But I knew what was in the wind and didn't think it would hurt my chances if I "just happened" to be in town towards the end of what I knew to have been a very trying period.'

Parlabane gave her a slightly chiding look.

Mairi shrugged, unabashed.

'Serendipity is often a one-way illusion that takes a hell of a lot of work and planning behind the scenes.'

'And people say I'm cynical.'

The Brauereihallen was busier than Parlabane would have expected for late afternoon, a very mixed crowd thronging its central concourse, a courtyard once open to the elements that was now enclosed by a glass ceiling. Scruffy student-looking types lustily drank beer from steins at long tables, while a middle-aged arty clientele quaffed white wine outside a small salon housing an exhibition of paintings.

Parlabane tried not to hate all of them, but it was a big ask. He felt like one lot represented his irretrievable past and the other his unavoidable future.

Mairi led him to a place away from both constituencies, into an enticingly gloomy cavern from which he could hear Foals thumping from the sound system. It was the kind of retreat where the ambience, the lighting and the music would make it difficult to discern whether the hands on the clock indicated ten past four in the afternoon or the morning.

Parlabane got the drinks in while Mairi went to the ladies. He carried them to a table bolted to a wall covered in a panoply of overlapping flyers that looked six layers deep in places. There were ads for forthcoming gigs, albums, art shows, poetry readings and club nights layering over posters for events past like a fresh fall of leaves. He scanned the names and logos as he took a first sip of his beer, almost choking on it when his eye alighted on a recently pinned-up sheet of A5.

At just that moment Mairi came hurrying towards the table, clutching a copy of the same notice that she must have found in the toilets. It showed a black-and-white photograph of Heike, a classic shot of her with the curly blonde crop and white denim jacket. Underneath were three lines of text, the top of which consisted of a single word in a large, bold font: 'VERMISST'.

The text meant little to either of them, apart from the name 'Heike Gunn' and the word 'Kontakt' next to a mobile phone number.

Mairi leaned over and snagged the attention of a waitress with a peace-sign tattoo on her neck, who was clearing glasses from an adjacent table.

'Can you tell me what this means?' she asked, pointing to the top line.

'Yes, of course,' she answered. 'It means "missing".'

Stolen Glances

Damien was right about touring. We played six dates in France, and from as much as I saw of it we could have been anywhere. The only sights we got to take in were through the bus windows, the only flavour of being somewhere different coming literally in the food.

And your day off will be in Gdansk, he had said, but so far there had been no days off. However, sometimes the schedule threw us a bone. We were playing two nights in Barcelona because the first one sold out so fast (technically it was the second one, the extra show being added to what would have been a free date after Bordeaux). There was no night off, but it meant a day without travelling, so we got some time to see the place.

A trip to the Nou Camp had been a big draw for most of the guys, even the ones who didn't like football. Heike and I opted for more cultural pursuits, taking a walk through the old town to the Museum of Contemporary Art. Heike talked knowledgeably and sometimes passionately about the exhibits, making comparisons to other artists I hadn't heard of. She wasn't just firing off references or spouting her manifesto: the way she discussed certain painters, it was like she was talking about family friends. Then I realised that she probably was. Her father was sometimes described as a reclusive individual, but he had been really well known in European art circles.

Whenever I thought I was getting to know Heike, something like this would make me realise I was kidding myself. She had grown up on a small Scottish island, like I had, but she came from another world. Sometimes when I looked at her it was as though she was a work of art herself: intriguing, provocative, beautiful, but closed off, protected by a wall of glass, something you could only glimpse or visit. She was something you could never have to your-self, something precious that would never truly be yours.

Just to underline this, as we browsed one of the exhibitions I noticed that one of our fellow visitors was spending more time looking at Heike than at the paintings. I was pretty sure I had seen her near the front at the show last night. She was about my age, her hair dyed a cream-porcelain blonde and styled to match Heike's before the start of the tour. Her denim jacket was a lot like the one Heike wore in the video for 'Dark Station'. Needy little clone, I thought. Why would you be trying so hard to be somebody else, somebody specific? Heike didn't seem to notice, or maybe she had become used to dealing with it by *pretending* not to notice.

'How did your TV thing go yesterday, by the way?' I asked her, as we sat down for a much-needed caffeine hit in a café along the road from the museum. I had avoided the subject up until now, still feeling awkward and embarrassed about sleeping in and standing her up.

'It didn't,' she replied. 'I had no sooner arrived at the station than I got a text from Jan saying sorry, but the producer had called to tell him it wasn't happening any more. I got a nice train ride out of it, I suppose, but I would have preferred the extra couple of hours in my bed.'

I wished I hadn't drunk so much in Bordeaux. I could have had her all to myself on that train, nothing to do but watch the country-side go by and talk for hours with no one there to interrupt.

'How was *your* journey?" she asked.

I thought about saying it was uneventful, but couldn't be sure she didn't already know something. That knowing look in her eye could have been still in reference to my hangover, but it could have been more than that.

I told her about the extra passengers, and my suspicion about Heike's hastily arranged TV interview, especially with it having been just as quickly cancelled.

'Hmm.' Heike sounded non-committal, like she was giving it some thought and trying not to jump to conclusions.

'These things do sometimes happen like that. Surely I'm not so scary that Jan feels he has to get me out of the way in case I object to him giving some girls a lift.'

'The deal was that they would be wearing those Savage Earth Heart T-shirts at the Serpent gig. Maybe he didn't think you'd be delighted about going down the T&A route of advertising.'

'No, I'm bloody not,' Heike said.

I took a nibble of my pastry, which was when I noticed that the girl from the gallery was sitting a few tables away, close to the door. She looked nervous, pulling at the sleeves of her jacket like she was cold.

'Don't stare,' I told her, 'but I think you've got a stalker.'

I gestured with my eyes at Heike's out-of-date doppelgänger.

Heike didn't turn her head; didn't even look.

'Yes, I spotted her. She was at the museum too.'

'I wasn't sure you'd noticed.'

'I was actually trying as hard as she was to steal glimpses without getting caught. I spotted her down the front last night. She seems familiar and it's doing my head in that I can't think from where.'

'The mirror, maybe?' I asked, unsure if Heike was winding me up.

'No, it's not that: it's her face. I can picture it with different hair. I've definitely seen her before.'

It bothered me that she was intrigued by this wannabe. Surely there were dozens just like her, nothing unique or even interesting about any of them.

Heike glanced across more noticeably.

'Maybe we should invite her to join us,' she suggested. 'Let her get a photo together, talk for a few minutes.'

'Are you serious?'

Heike smiled and stood up. As soon as she got to her feet, the girl by the door grabbed her bag and scurried away, looking spooked.

'Smart girl,' I said. 'Knows her mythology: it never works out well when the mortals get too close to the gods.'

Heike sat down again, staring through the window as the girl disappeared into the flow of pedestrians.

I wondered aloud whether we'd see her again tonight, but Heike wasn't listening.

I had seen her do this before. She had zoned out, her mind elsewhere; not having drifted, but instantly transported beyond the here and now. Back to her home planet, maybe.

'Gods and mortals,' she suddenly said, alert again, giving me an insistent look, as though I was holding back some answer she needed.

'What about them?'

'For a song. It fits with something I've been knocking around in my head, lyrically and musically. I have to work on it now. I need to play you what I've got, see where it goes when you bring in the fiddle.'

'All our stuff is at the venue,' I said.

'Where better? That place had great acoustics.'

And like that we were on our way, Heike dropping thirty euros on the table without bothering to ask for the bill.

Time could melt when we were playing like this. It was hypnotic, a strange state between meditation and intense concentration as we went over and over the same bars, reinforcing certain phrases, gradually evolving others. It was as though we were willing something into existence, but neither of us quite knew what it sounded like yet: we would only recognise it when we heard it.

We were alone in an empty theatre, the space around us making us feel weirdly enclosed, cocooned in this precious act, this coming-together. I had never felt so close to Heike, not even when I held her that night in London. Unlike then, I felt no anxiety, no tension. We both knew what we were about, drawing upon each other's sounds, pushing each other to reach connections we could not have happened upon alone.

It was better than playing to a crowd, because I didn't have to worry about how it sounded to anyone else, only to Heike. I didn't have to share her either: no other instrumentation, nobody else leading the beat, just two people who couldn't have this without each other.

After all of it, though, we still only had a rough sketch of what we were trying to achieve; a short, half-heard preview of a song.

It wound down naturally: there's a point where you just know that if you keep going, you will only be grinding gears. It was also the point where I became aware that I must have been ignoring my bladder for an hour.

I headed backstage to use the loo, but found the dressing-room door locked. As I went further down the corridor in search of another, I became aware of voices but no words. I heard low rumblings combined with giggly approval, and something else, emotionally heightened but weirdly muted.

I turned a corner and found myself at the open door to a cluttered office. I only saw what was inside for a moment, but it was more than enough: enough for the image to be imprinted in my mind, and enough to be seen myself.

I saw a young girl bent over a desk, naked, being screwed from behind by Dean the roadie, his horrible blotchy-white beer belly wobbling as he thrust. Standing at the other end of the table was the venue manager, a balding middle-aged guy whose name I never bothered catching. His dick was in the girl's mouth, her hand holding it at the base.

The guy had a beer in his hand. So did Dean. I'm pretty sure there was coke on the table as well. The venue manager had his back to me, but I was unable to avoid meeting the eyes of both Dean and the girl.

He winked at me. He actually winked at me. He was loving the fact that I had seen this, enjoying my discomfort. It was like he was drawing power from it. Everything I read in his expression made me sick, but none of it made me feel so bad as what I saw in the girl's.

I recalled Heike's look of affront by the hotel lift after Brixton: like I had walked in on her naked, at best intruding; at worst worming my way in.

This girl's eyes showed something simpler, bleaker, colder: she hated me for seeing this. She wasn't angry or upset. This was not just about embarrassment, about being seen naked or caught in the act. I had witnessed something she had a far deeper desire to conceal.

I had seen her shame.

Heike knew something was wrong as soon as she looked at me. I had taken some time in the toilets to compose myself, but it was going to take more than splashing some water on my face to hide what I felt.

I told her what I had seen, and as I did I couldn't help thinking this was exactly what Dean wanted.

Heike's reacted with distaste, but not surprise.

'You don't seem taken aback,' I said.

'It's not a first, safe to say. And I'm trying not to overreact or jump to conclusions. Not saying I'll manage, but I'm giving it a shot.'

She shrugged, though she was obviously disgusted.

'Unfortunately it's not unknown for silly wee girls to blow the crew in order to get tickets or a backstage pass. Can't see the groupie types putting out for access to us, though. I mean, I could understand if it was for Serpent . . .'

'I don't think that's what was going on here,' I said.

'Why not?'

'Well, I'm no expert, but I'd have thought the type you just described would be a bit more, I don't know, shameless. This didn't look like someone using sex to get where she wanted.'

Heike gave it some thought, then looked hard at me.

'Was she one of the girls from the bus?'

'I honestly couldn't say,' I told her, which was the truth. 'I only saw her for a second, and I didn't really see enough of the girls yesterday. I was sitting behind them most of the time. I wasn't at my sharpest either,' I admitted.

'Plus it must be hard to get a positive ID from a face that is largely obscured by cock,' she said acidly.

As we were making our way out of the theatre a little while later, we heard footsteps behind us in the corridor and saw the girl walking quickly towards the exit, head down. She tried to ignore us, avoiding my eye as she attempted to hurry past.

'Hey,' Heike said, waving an arm in a way that was impossible to miss. The girl did her best to pretend she had seen nothing. She had a look of alarm on her face like someone minding her own business who thought she was about to be mugged.

It was probably a long time since anybody had ignored Heike, and she was having none of it. She skipped ahead and barred the doorway, standing with her palms up.

The girl stood there helplessly, eyes darting left and right as though looking for options.

'Are you all right?' Heike asked. 'Is everything okay?'

'It's cool,' she replied, flashing an empty smile.

'What was going on back there?' Heike enquired, not in a disapproving way, more just interested.

The girl gave a coy shrug.

'Nothing. Just having a little fun. It's cool, okay?'

The words sounded rehearsed, like stock phrases. They came across almost as natural as the smile and shrug.

Heike stepped aside and let her out. She all but ran across the pavement to the road and jumped in a taxi.

'Well, you got a better look at her there,' she said expectantly.

'I still couldn't say. There were seven of them, and they were heavily made up. She did look Eastern European, though.'

'But you heard her, right?'

'I couldn't place her accent. I didn't hear them speak English yesterday.'

'That's not what I'm talking about. I mean you heard how she sounded.'

'Like she was acting,' I said.

Heike nodded severely.

'Like she was a fucking robot.'

Contact Lens

Parlabane stepped out from the noise of the bar into the covered thoroughfare at the hub of the Brauereihallen, where he called the number on the flyer.

He spoke briefly and guardedly to the woman who answered. They politely established that she spoke English, whereupon Parlabane told her he was ringing with regard to the missing girl, Heike Gunn.

'Do you have information about her?' the woman asked.

'Yes.'

'Thank you for calling. Please tell me what it is you know. It is very important.'

'I'd rather tell you in person,' he said.

Truth was, he wanted to know who else was looking for Heike, and it would be a lot easier to find out if the other party couldn't suddenly terminate the conversation by pressing a button on a handset.

'You do not live in Berlin?' she had deduced. 'You are a visitor?'

'That's right.'

'Okay. We can meet somewhere that is easy for you to find.'

'Now I feel like I'm *in* a Cold War movie,' Parlabane told Mairi, about ninety minutes later.

'How so?'

'I'm standing in Alexanderplatz beneath the World Clock, awaiting the arrival of an anonymous contact who will have to identify herself to me, but who doesn't know what I look like either, and our meeting is intended to facilitate a cagey exchange of information in which at least one party is seriously disguising his intentions.'

Admittedly, it wasn't quite swapping briefcases at a park bench in the Tiergarten, but it was enough to turn his thoughts to an era that was only a quarter-century gone and yet felt like it had taken place in a parallel world.

It had seemed a time of absolute political rigidity, an age in which activism felt like a religious observance: morally obliged, dutifully undertaken, but done so despite a constant nagging concern that it was ultimately futile, because nothing was going to change. Thatcher would be in power for ever; Nelson Mandela would never be freed; the Wall was never coming down.

Mairi underlined just how pleasingly wrong he had been.

'I've not seen many Cold War movies,' she observed, 'but I'm guessing their version of Alexanderplatz tends not to feature a host of Japanese teenagers spilling out of KFC toting Captain America plushies they've just bought at the Galeria Kaufhof.'

Parlabane strained to look through the crowd, past them, over them, scanning the faces streaming through the concourse and trying to picture what his contact would look like.

It seemed imperative to see her coming, to avert the vulnerability he felt in standing there waiting for a stranger to identify herself. He had nothing to go on, however: only the hope that he'd see someone who was visibly on the lookout as she approached. They'd only spoken for a few seconds and there was little he could gauge from a voice, especially with a foreign accent. She had sounded quite husky too, so she could be forty years old or she could be twenty-two with a forty-a-day habit.

He had his phone out and switched to camera, swiping the screen every so often to prevent it going to sleep. He knew he ought to alter the setting, but it only occurred to him to do so at times like these, when he had to have it ready to shoot and therefore couldn't go dicking around in the sub-menus.

'Do you photograph everybody you meet?' Mairi asked.

'If possible, yes.'

'Why?'

'Because although I've got a good memory for faces, flash memory is even better. More effective than any amount of adjectives too, if I'm trying to describe a person to somebody else.'

'Don't people object?'

'Not if they don't know I'm snapping them.'

'I'm guessing that's going to be tricky in this case, seeing as we don't have a clue who we're looking for.'

Parlabane fixed upon a tram that was slowing down, watching it deposit a dozen or so people about thirty yards from the World Clock. Then, when it moved off again, he suddenly spotted a face he recognised.

'Fuck me.'

'What?'

Parlabane didn't answer as he didn't want Mairi staring conspicuously at his subject. He raised the camera and focused, holding it so that it obscured his own face.

When the tram cleared his view his attention had been drawn to two men moving more purposefully than the rest of the crowd, striding towards the tramlines from the north side of the concourse. They were both white, both mid-forties, one close-cropped and jowly, the other tall and gaunt.

'Jack, what?' Mairi asked again.

'Look to your left,' he said, so she would look the wrong way and stop conspicuously searching the crowd for whoever he was aiming his phone at.

He was too late, though. The close-cropped one returned his gaze just as he snapped the pair of them in burst mode, taking six images with one shot.

Parlabane watched him become suddenly animated. He didn't stop, didn't point, but spoke urgently to his companion, then they both veered off hurriedly in different directions, neither making for the World Clock any longer.

'Oh shit.'

Mairi turned back to face him.

'Jack, would you tell me what the hell is it?'

'We need to go.'

'Why? What about our contact?'

'I think he just left. I must confess I often have that effect on people, but they've usually at least spoken to me first.'

146

'He? I thought you spoke to a woman.'

'I did, but I think she was just taking a message for her boss. Come on.'

Parlabane began walking, leading her towards the U-Bahn station. 'Who did you see?'

'It's not so much who I saw as where I've seen him before. There were two guys heading straight for us, and one of them was on the CalMac ferry to Islay two days ago.'

Tightrope

I phoned our manager, Mairi, when I went back to the hotel before the soundcheck. I wanted someone further up the chain to know about the incident backstage, and to find out what was with the merch girls.

I got fobbed off, even getting a dressing down: her way of warning me what was worth wasting her time with in future.

'It's not my concern what consenting adults get up to, Monica, no matter how distasteful either of us might happen to find it. You're not in the orchestra any more: you're going to see a lot worse than that if you're planning a career in this business. There's a reason they talk about sex, drugs and rock 'n' roll.'

She made me feel like a daft wee girl, and maybe she was right. I hadn't told Heike I was going to phone Mairi because I hadn't wanted her to know I was calling for help, so I guess deep down I knew I was being a bit pathetic. Heike's mind was soon on other things anyway.

I saw her doppelgänger in the crowd that night. Okay, truth is, I couldn't help looking for her: always a mistake. During a show you just see darkness out in the auditorium, catching the occasional glimpse of an individual as the lights sweep across the stage. If you start searching for a face in the crowd, eventually you start imagining it on every head that bobs in and out of view. Making it harder, more than one girl down the front was rocking the Heike signature cream-blonde look.

I thought I spotted her about a dozen times, then there she was for definite, stage left, having made her way to the front. She was singing along, almost in a trance. She knew every word. I suppose that wasn't a surprise.

More of a surprise was the fact that she showed up in Bilbao the next night. I wasn't looking for her then; in fact, by that point I had pretty much put her from my mind. It was Heike who drew her to my attention, giving me a weird grin halfway through 'It Meant Nothing' and indicating with a nod. There she was again, almost in the same spot as she'd found the night before, stage left, in a different city, four hundred miles away.

Heike seemed amused, maybe even flattered. She was used to this, I guess, but I was less sure about where the line was drawn between fandom and stalking. I thought it was just creepy: what kind of sad-act moulds her whole existence around an obsession with one person?

Heike had a word with Angus as she was changing guitars, and I saw him scuttle across the stage in front of our backline, leaning down to hand the girl something. To my annoyance I realised it was a backstage pass.

I couldn't understand why Heike wanted to do this, but on our way to the dressing room she said that what would only cost a little of her time, this girl might remember for ever. 'And if she's an obsessed nutter, it might help to see I'm as full of shit as anybody else.'

Whatever, I thought it was unnecessarily generous on Heike's part.

Looking back, I can see why some people say no good deed ever goes unpunished.

Right after a show Heike could be many different people, and it was difficult to predict which one you were going to get. As I knew, having all of that adulation, energy and passion flow into you for ninety minutes can have a dizzying effect. It was the feeling that Damien said made it all worthwhile, but we were only picking up sparks around the edges. Heike was the one earthing the whole supply.

The night Maxi turned up and served his writ it was that amazing high that contributed to her landing with such a crash.

She could be bubbly, chattily cheerful, like she would burst if she didn't share the goodwill that was gushing through her. She could be controlling and precious, the fawning of the audience tapping into her inner two-year-old. She could be clingy, needing the physical touch of her bandmates to maintain the closeness she'd had on stage, and she could be solitary, totally unapproachable, reliving every note in her head in a quiet corner with a beer or a shot of Islay malt.

That night she must have felt she had something to give, though maybe she knew there was something she could take too. She sat with the girl, whose name was Hannah, in a corner booth of the bodega we had gone to after the show. It was just around the corner from the hotel, spotted earlier by Scott who'd said it was late-opening and in staggering distance of our rooms. Heike sat basking in the glow of Hannah's worship, Hannah enjoying the fact of Heike's very being there.

She looked more comfortable than when I'd seen her in that café in Barcelona, but there was still something nervous about her. She kept tugging on the sleeves of her Heike-copy white jacket. I wondered if she self-harmed.

There were plenty of nights when Heike liked to hold court during the comedown from her performance, but here I saw her listen as much as talk, really intent upon what the girl was saying. What the hell could she be seeing in this person? I wondered.

Heike was good at faking it, though: when she wanted to, she could make your every word seem fascinating to her, so I knew this might be a performance for Hannah. I offered Heike an out: leaning into the booth I said I was heading back to the hotel and mentioned being back on the road in the morning. It was a cue to allow her to say she had better call it a night as well, but she didn't take it.

If anything, I was the one she seemed impatient to be rid of.

The next morning on the tour bus, Heike was ashen-faced, hiding behind sunglasses and getting into a seat with her headphones on to signal Do Not Disturb. As I was becoming quite the connoisseur of hangovers – other people's as well as my own – I recognised this as more than the consequences of overindulgence and not

150

enough sleep. She looked wounded. Actually, she looked exactly like I would have done the morning after Brixton if our kiss had not been abandoned so quickly.

I sat tapping my journal into my laptop in my usual disjointed way, in between bouts of staring out of the window at a landscape that was becoming more familiar but no less exotic.

About two hours into the trip Heike sat herself down opposite and took off her shades.

'Do you mind?' she asked. 'I need to talk.' Her initial courtesy was made moot by the insistence. It was strangely unnecessary, though, and I got the impression she felt she had some making-up to do. I couldn't work out why, but I was eager to find out.

Her eyes were heavy. She looked like she hadn't slept, and might have been crying.

'What's the script?'

'I think I've screwed up,' she said, before proceeding to fill me in on what had been a very late night with Hannah.

'I've spoken to plenty of hardcore fans and sympathetic critics over the years, but I've never encountered anyone who so *got* what I'm all about. I mean someone who truly connected with my music, and not just in a passive way.'

I admit I felt surprise and disappointment as I listened to this. Get over yourself, Monica, I thought. Heike was sharing something with me *now*.

'It was both humbling and, I don't know, *inspiring* to learn that my music has genuinely helped somebody: helped her understand herself, and deal with some of the things she's gone through. She said it felt at times like I had written these songs specifically for her to relate to, but it turns out that's because we have a lot in common.'

She glanced out of the bus window, biting her lower lip.

'Like what?' I said, intrigued more by what she might be about to admit about herself than what she had learned about Hannah.

'She lost her mother at a very early age too. She was two and a half. She has almost no memory of her, just fragments, impressions, and can't separate her own memories from the few bits and pieces told to her by people who actually knew her mother.'

151

'So I guess "Kaleidoscope" is on her playlist a lot,' I said, letting her know I had also understood the song. '"A Square of Captured Light" too.'

'Yeah. She said she even *has* actual Polaroids. Plural, so she's doing better than me on that score.'

'You only have one? I thought that song . . .'

Heike smiled sadly.

'One Polaroid photo. That's the only image I have of my mum.'

'Can I see it?' I asked.

'It's in my flat back in Glasgow. I never take it anywhere in case I lose it. I've got a photo of a photo, though.'

She pulled out her phone and tapped at the screen, then handed it to me, resting it on her palm like it was priceless. Having seen her toss the handset around at other times, I understood the near-ritual of this, and all that it meant.

I really felt for her as soon as I saw the picture, and a song I had played night after night took on so much more meaning. God, her mother looked so young, much younger than Heike was now. She couldn't have been more than twenty, if that; elfin-featured and delicate. I couldn't see a striking resemblance, but that was partly because of what truly moved me: there was so little detail for Heike to treasure. It wasn't a close-up head-and-shoulders shot. Her mother was standing several yards from the camera, next to a Litfass column, her hands pointing to one of the posters on it. I wondered if the poster had something to do with Heike's father, but there was no way of reading it. Her face must have been smaller than the end of my thumb, even on the original, and this was all she had.

'She's so young,' was all I could think to say.

Heike nodded, not wanting to go there.

'I did a lot better than Hannah in other ways. At least I had my dad: she never knew hers. She grew up in care homes and other institutions. I think there was abuse, but she didn't go into detail. She said that when she discovered my songs it meant every-thing not to feel so alone any more. I only wrote them to make sense of my own feelings, so it's amazing to discover how much they've meant to someone else.'

'I guess when you're writing something you never know who it's going to touch, or how deeply.'

'It wasn't just the stuff about our mothers. Normally I'd have been quite spooked by something like that, and I'd definitely be a bit wary of some stranger baring her soul and maybe thinking I had this vast significance in her life. It wasn't like that, though. I felt so comfortable in her company, so quickly at ease. What she said was so insightful: it was like we'd known each other for years. I don't think I'd ever felt anything like it.'

I felt another sharp pang of envy, but it was cut short by the very fact that we were having this conversation. Whatever else had gone on between them, their meeting hadn't ended well.

'So what went wrong?' I asked, before realising I already knew the answer. I suddenly saw the tightrope Heike had to walk whenever she felt a connection with someone, the tightrope on which she had temporarily lost her balance with me.

'I tried to kiss her,' she said, closing her eyes. 'I felt so close to her, there seemed to be so much chemistry, but it's as easy as it is perilous to misread the signs. I just thought, at least, that she must know *I'm* gay, so if she was sending me these sorts of signals . . .'

Heike stared out of the window again, biting a fingernail. She looked so vulnerable, such a contrast to the person who commanded the stage or stared out from album covers. It was just so horrible to watch her suffer. I wanted to hug her, let her feel some comfort, let her feel I was there for her, but that was the last thing that was going to happen, and possibly the worst thing I could do.

'What happened?' I asked, as there seemed to be more, but I felt slightly bad about asking. 'I mean, I can't begin to imagine what that felt like. I'm guessing awkward doesn't really cover it.'

'Awkward I can handle. I've dealt with it plenty of times before,' she added, deliberately looking me in the eye. 'I've retrieved more than a few misread situations, and I've been bloody generous when some bi-curious girl gets freaked and decides she's not so curious any more. But I never got the chance to smooth it with Hannah.'

'She bolted?'

'Like a startled deer. She said something like "No, this is wrong, I'm sorry," and hared off. I went after her, but when I hit the street, she had vanished.'

The bus ate up the miles, but there were a lot of miles to eat, and after looking out of the window with her headphones on for about an hour, Heike asked if I wouldn't mind working with her.

'I just need to get my head somewhere else for a few hours, and it's often the best way.'

I was delighted. Before going on tour with the band, I'd had visions of us all jamming to while away the journeys, and when such things failed to happen, I was secretly a bit embarrassed at having had such a notion.

The hours really did melt away once we took up where we'd left off in Barcelona: tinkering, repeating and improvising, each of us happy both to lead and to follow, the journey often taking us somewhere barely recognisable from our starting point. Most were dead ends, meaning we had to go back to where we started, but every so often we would play a sequence that excited us both, and caught glimpses of the song that was trying to be born.

The chord structure was becoming all but cemented; we'd practically ruled out all the possible wrong turns before we found the right path. Then I suggested Heike switch to arpeggios on alternate phrases and let me drive the melody.

She lit up like a flare, her energy warming me.

'That's perfect,' she said, explaining that the lyric she was working on was essentially an exchange between two parties, a god and a mortal, but the song was about how they were each more alike than the other assumed.

'The chords and the arpeggios are constructed of the same notes, but take different forms.'

I felt quite elated. The last hour dragged as we got caught in traffic, but the journey was ending in a far better place than it had begun. Heike was scribbling lyric notes, still tired but calmer, the angst of last night's encounter gone, or maybe turned into something else.

But Jan had noticed Heike's earlier manner and expressed his concern.

'You should try and grab a nap before soundcheck,' he suggested. 'And maybe I'll look into getting you a flight from Madrid to Milan on Friday instead of the bus.'

I was touched by his kindness, but then I guessed this was the sort of thing a tour manager had to be aware of. It wouldn't do to have the main attraction burned-out and exhausted with more than a dozen dates left to play. Then I remembered the last time Jan had arranged to spare Heike the bus journey, and wondered if we would have some extra passengers again.

Mind the Gap

They proceeded briskly but didn't run, Parlabane aware that doing so would only make them more conspicuous as they moved through the crowds and down inside the station.

'How can you be sure it was the same guy?' Mairi asked.

'I took his picture,' Parlabane explained, trying not to sound *too* vindicated.

Mairi rolled her eyes. He couldn't decide whether this was in disdain at his weirdness or in irritation that his weirdness had just proven justified.

They joined a short queue at a ticket machine, both of them rifling through their pockets for coins as they waited for the old punter at the front to finish his purchase. Parlabane was glancing over his shoulder, checking his six, and seriously thinking of offering the bloke some of his own change if it would get him moving.

'Why did you photograph him on Islay?' Mairi asked.

'It wasn't actually on Islay, it was on the ferry to Port Askaig. I thought he was a cop. He'd been following my car all the way from Inveraray. It's happened a few times recently: low-level harassment from the Westercruik Inquiry.'

Mairi collected their tickets from the machine and they rejoined the human flow through the entrance hall and down towards the U5 platforms.

'That's the business with the stolen laptop.'

'Yes,' Parlabane confirmed, unsure whether Mairi was taking the piss. There was something unnervingly guileless about the way she so succinctly referred to the situation that was currently ripping apart his career and might yet see him back in jail, making it sound trivial or incidental.

'So had you assumed he was a Brit?'

'Right up until I heard him talking on the ferry. I clocked the accent, and given he was asking somebody about distillery tours I assumed I'd read it all wrong. Sneaky bastard must have been trying to throw me off the scent, cover up the fact that he was following me.'

'Can I see?'

'Sure.'

Parlabane took out his phone and swiped through the gallery until it showed the image he had taken in the ferry's forward lounge. She took the phone in her left hand, pausing to punch their tickets at a validation post on the westbound platform.

Mairi looked at the shot from the ferry, then verified Parlabane's identification when she scrolled forward to the most recent pic.

'You photographed the receptionists at our hotel?' she asked with fading incredulity. 'The bellhop too?'

'That hotel was one of the last places Heike was seen. Somebody there might know something. I asked if they still had CCTV footage of the lobby from that time and the receptionist said she'd look into it.'

'Actually *look into it* look into it, or *yeah, that'll be right* look into it?'

'That remains to be seen. I was quite charming and tried not to come over as a goggle-eyed paranoid freak, but who knows what's in the eye of the beholder.'

An eastbound train rumbled into the station, a pale yellow lozenge cutting off his view of the opposite platform and its wall of glossy green tiles. The two tracks ran side by side in the centre, divided by a row of matching green-painted steel columns. Up above, the chamber was lit by parallel rows of semi-spheres, the bulbs of which he imagined must be a bugger to change. Underfoot was a black line of floor tiles two feet back from the edge, but he and Mairi seemed to be among the few treating it as an imaginary barrier. The locals were polite, though, it had to be said. The platform was fairly filling up, and in London he'd have been getting nudged forward at this point, black line or no black line.

'What if he *is* a cop?' Mairi said, handing him back the phone. 'I mean a German cop, looking for Heike.'

'He bailed the moment he realised I'd recognised him. Cops don't do that, especially if they're en route to hearing what someone with a phone-in tip might have to tell them about a missing person.'

Parlabane felt a hand on his back as the westbound train came clattering in from the tunnel. He assumed it was someone steadying themselves as the throng on the platform moved forward in response, but then he was driven sharply from behind and found himself tripping over a foot that had been placed in front of his own.

He sprawled headlong over the edge as the train bore down on him. There was no way to correct his balance, only air to push against. He heard Mairi scream, then her voice was lost in the sound of steel on steel and a shriek of brakes. Even as he tumbled, his mind was making calculations, too fast to be rendered in conscious thought. Decisions drove his limbs via altogether more ancient neural circuitry. There would be no time to climb back up. He needed a survival space. Unlike London or even Glasgow, there was no channel beneath the middle of the tracks, and thus no option to lie flat. Dead ahead, the eastbound train was only just beginning to move, so there was no route clear of the westbound track.

The central pillars. They were his only chance.

He sprung to his feet and righted himself side-on against one. The westbound train screeched to an emergency stop, the metal of its carriages inches from his face. Behind him, the accelerating eastbound service was so close it jetted air up his shirt. He was grateful for Sarah's years of insisting on healthy eating: a few too many haggis suppers and he'd have been getting spun and shredded right then.

He stared through the windows towards the platform from which he had fallen, looking for who had pushed him. His view was obscured by shocked faces staring back from inside the train, mere inches away. Beyond them was a further host of onlookers: curious,

158

frightened, anxious, confused. He wondered whether there was at least one who was disappointed.

'I just lost my balance,' Parlabane said.

They were sitting in a small office off the ticket hall, the station manager unwilling to let them leave until she had ascertained that he was unharmed and, more importantly, that the police had logged the incident and a proper investigation was under way.

Mairi was looking wan, her natural grace finally failing her after she had rushed around to the eastbound platform, breathless and slightly teary with shock. She hadn't seen what happened, and he wasn't filling her in just yet.

An irritatingly young and even more irritatingly handsome uniformed police officer was standing opposite, asking questions in slow but precise English.

'You were too close to the edge?' he enquired.

Parlabane wasn't sure whether there was a hint of accusation in this, or whether it was simply a projection of his own prejudices.

'The platform became very busy,' he answered. 'I think I moved forward a little without realising.'

Eventually the young cop seemed happy that he could consider the incident dealt with, though the station manager still appeared far from content. Her English wasn't great, but Parlabane guessed that wasn't the only reason she didn't seem satisfied with his answers. Accidents evidently weren't allowed on her watch, so she wanted a better explanation for what happened than he'd been able or willing to give her.

'Jeez, she was a bit intense,' Mairi said after the station manager had personally escorted them safely aboard a westbound U5 train. 'I think she must take it personally, like any accident impugns the integrity of her station-running protocols.'

'No,' Parlabane replied, 'she just couldn't see how my story added up. Which is understandable, seeing as it didn't.'

'How so?'

'Someone pushed me, Mairi. Hard. Deliberate. Unmistakable.'

She gaped, uncomprehending.

'Why did you tell them you tripped?'

'Because it's going to be a lot harder to find out what's happened to Heike if we've got the German police all over us. If I made an accusation, the first thing they'd do is look into why someone would want me dead. It will take them one phone call and about five minutes to discover that I am currently being investigated regarding my role in a possible conspiracy to steal secrets from the MoD. There might be an arrest warrant for me by now, but even if there isn't, from that moment on it will primarily be me the German cops are interested in. They'll be watching my every step, and I'm not very comfortable with that.'

'Are you comfortable with the fact that somebody just tried to kill you?'

'You'd be surprised,' he told her, grinning. 'There's a rather perverse side of me, to whom that part feels like coming home.'

'I'd heard you have a sick sense of humour. To be honest, I think the word "deranged" really sells it.'

'You have to look at the evidence dispassionately. At least this means we're on to something.'

'That part isn't reassuring,' she replied, folding her arms.

Parlabane let her simmer.

He hadn't told her the whole truth about why he didn't want to involve the cops, as it entailed the possibility that what had happened wasn't about Heike at all. As he was climbing back up on to the eastbound platform, his brain racing to analyse the impli-cations, it had occurred to him that Mairi's earlier suggestion that the thick-necked jowly bastard was a polisman might be right: just not a German one.

What if Bawjaws *was* following him, and it was nothing to do with Heike, but with the Anthony Mead business? It would be an effective cover for a British cop – or a British something darker – to pretend to be foreign on that ferry when he was concerned about having been made. Parlabane had dipped his toe in some very murky waters with that MoD thing, and he had no idea whose agendas he might have disturbed, or who might be moving against him.

Until he could at least find out what he was dealing with, it seemed wisest not to make himself the focus of a police investigation.

'So what do you suggest?' Mairi asked as the train arrived at Brandenburger Tor.

'I'd liked to get an ID on Bawjaws back there.'

'Where are you hoping to come by that?'

'Same place we got his secretary's phone number.'

Tall Poppies

The Valencia show that night felt special, maybe because I had feared Heike might be off-form and subdued. Her first few songs had borne this out before she came to life on 'Who Do You Want Me to Be', and started throwing everything into her performance. I used to think it was a song about coming out, but after what she had confided today I got that its darkly funny anxieties were saying something much more complicated. After that, she seemed to be pouring herself out into the microphone and into a joyous sweat-lashed thrashing of her chords.

I got the impression she was losing herself in the show, like she had set about losing herself in our work together on the bus, and had the sense that she was giving everything she had because what would be left over wasn't going to be worth much anyway. So it was no surprise when she headed straight back to the hotel and an early bed.

When I'd worked out the time difference I figured it wasn't too late to give Keith a call, and managed to catch him on what I intended to be the final try after several failures before the show.

'Monica!'

He sounded delighted to hear from me, energy and enthusiasm in his voice igniting the same in me.

'I hope it's not too late to call. We just got off stage.'

'No, I was really hoping you'd ring. I got a promotion.'

'That's brilliant.'

'I know. All those extra hours paid off. They're starting a new department to develop . . . well, never mind the technical stuff: they want me to head it up.'

'Fantastic. You must be really juiced.'

'I'm minted is what I am. This is going to be worth an extra

162

five grand a year basic, but it's the opportunity that matters. It's a platform for my personal career growth. We can really start planning for the future.'

'How about planning a holiday?' I said.

'Well, yeah, of course. With the promotion under my belt, I was thinking we could go to Thailand in the autumn, like you always said you wanted.'

'God, yes. That would be amazing.'

'It would give us the chance to take a step out of things and take stock, look to the long term. I've got real stability now.'

We spoke for ages, almost until my battery was out. I kept to myself the fact that the autumn dates he was talking about were already being pencilled in for more touring to build on the expected momentum around the new album.

The sound of his voice only made me realise how lonely I felt when I finally hung up, so I was in the mood for some company. I joined Scott, Damien and Angus for some late-night tapas, red wine and, for some, dangerously flowing Spanish brandy.

When I asked where Rory had got to, I got awkward looks and half-answers, suggesting another of his solitary pursuits that they assumed I would have a problem with. I wasn't judgemental towards Rory, I just couldn't help wondering why he didn't have any concerns about the desperate girls throwing themselves into one-night stands with him.

I was sitting on a banquette beside Damien, with Scott and Angus opposite. Damien ordered for everybody, talking comfortably and, as far as I could tell, flirtily in Spanish with the waitress. I wondered how he became so fluent.

A few bottles and a lot of dishes in, we went around the table on the subject of best and worst live acts we had seen. It had been Scott's suggestion, and he spoke with evangelical enthusiasm about Augustines before dumping a bucketload of scorn upon some *X-Factor* Live abomination he had been obliged to attend with his then girlfriend.

Angus cursorily praised Green Day but had considerably more enthusiasm for ripping into Chvrches.

'Fucking sell-out electropop shite. Two miserable cunts standing behind synths like it's the fuckin' eighties.'

His words were a bit slurred, and in his drunken bitterness I detected more than a hint of jealousy.

Damien held forth on the consistent merits of the Manic Street Preachers, but wouldn't choose a worst, resulting in serious protest.

He wasn't having it, though.

'Thing is, I've been down pretty low in this business. I know how much effort it takes to put on *any* show, and I know what depths you can plumb just to stay in the game, just to be playing. I mean, once upon a time, sure, there was almost nobody I didn't believe I was better than, or would one day *be* better than. But when this game teaches you humility, it doesn't pull its punches.'

'How low are you talking about?' I asked, now all the more anxious to avoid my own contribution, as I didn't feel I had yet earned the right to slag anybody off.

'I spent nine months playing in a show at a theme park here in Spain,' he answered. 'This hideous eighties and nineties hair-metal pastiche about vampires and zombies. Three performances a day in high season, inside a Mayan-themed amphitheatre with a bloody rollercoaster shaking the stage every three minutes. When I was in Discolite and The Descendants, it was a real buzz when a stranger recognised me. But at the theme park it was my biggest fear that somebody might come up and say: "Hey, last time I saw you, you were playing the Barrowlands."'

He was laughing as he spoke, but I could tell he was talking about his personal long dark night of the soul.

'It was a total brass neck, but it was a gig, the only way I could still get paid to play at that time. That's what I told myself anyway, but there comes a moment when you wonder whether there's more dignity in admitting it's all over. In my case it was playing in low season in front of nine people, four of whom left after ten minutes because their toddler got scared by the noise. I'd like to say I left at that point, but I hung on another three months.'

Bored of Damien's gloomy confession, Scott and Angus started pouring more venom on despised targets.

'How did you last nine months?' I asked Damien.

'There was a girl involved,' he said, turning a little in his seat to face me more directly. 'This dancer called Natasha, from St Petersburg. We were in the same show, and very much the same boat. We were both past thirty, and we both knew we were there on the way down. We were very close, but . . .'

He sighed, toying with a piece of bread, soaking up the last of the sauce from a dish of *patatas bravas*.

'Maxi got in touch and said he was in a new band that was looking for a lead guitarist. He told me Heike was something special. I had three days off and spent two of them getting over to Glasgow and back: horrible flight connection times because it was high season and everything was full. I was barely in town long enough for the session, or audition, as I suppose it was. It was long enough, though, for me anyway: one afternoon playing with Heike and I knew that was my ticket out for sure – if she wanted me.'

Damien tipped half his brandy into his mouth and let it sit there for a few moments before swallowing and inviting the burn.

'Maxi phoned me on my mobile at Luton, ninety minutes into a six-hour transit, told me I was in. The check-in wasn't even open for my next flight, so I just went to the desk and booked myself and my guitar on to the first plane back to Glasgow, and I was in Maxi's flat before my flight to Spain would even have taken off.'

'You never went back?'

He shook his head, an apologetic yet firm look on his face, like he knew I wouldn't approve but he'd make the same decision every time.

'Natasha knew why I was going to Glasgow, and what that meant. That's how it was between us. If I had come back we'd have gone on same as before, nothing said. I wish I could have taken her with me, but I guess we all wish we could rescue somebody. We both knew that if either of us got a chance of something better there would only ever be room on the lifeboat for one.'

Still unable to compete with how little sleep my bandmates could get by on, I left at around two, and was surprised to be joined on the short walk back to the hotel by Angus, of all people, normally one of the hardiest insomniacs in the party. He had seemed pretty hammered as he cackled over the table, so maybe he did actually know his limits. Had I downed what he'd skulled over the past few hours, I'd have vomited my own bodyweight.

The air must have sobered him up a little, as he seemed a bit less slurred of speech. But I was wary of him, as his mood was still pretty dark, and I found his archness even more unnerving because he normally came across as completely happy-go-lucky.

I had watched him early on in the evening, playing his solo opening set. He did it when the schedule permitted, which meant the opportunities were very much in Heike's gift. There was an obvious correlation between, for example, Heike catching him and Scott doing coke in Newcastle, and the soundcheck overrunning that night so that there was only time for the main support act once the house doors were open.

When he did play, he would run through five or six of his own songs with an acoustic guitar, a loop station and a stomp box. Building up the loops and rhythms, it could sound like there was a full band backing him by the time the vocals started, switching between registers impressively.

I had only managed to take in his performance a few times so far, but on each occasion I saw the charismatic player Heike had sparked off of back in their schooldays. It wasn't hard to see the scorn he had been pouring upon Chvrches as a way of deflecting his regrets at pissing his talent up the wall in his adolescence instead of honing it like Heike, Scott or even me.

He was humming something I recognised, and it took me a moment to work out that it was actually the song Heike and I had been jamming on the bus.

'Lightning in a bottle,' he said. 'That's what you're trying to do: catch lightning in a bottle.'

'Feels like that, yes,' I said, agreeing just to keep the peace.

'You can be brilliant and not get lucky, never catch the lightning. Or you can be super-lucky. One song on a fuckin' telly show and suddenly you're a fuckin' millionaire.'

He gave a tipsy laugh at this, but I sensed only resentment, and I was done putting up with his pissed self-loathing.

'Catch on to yourself,' I said. 'If that were true, then every song that got used on a TV show would make its singer a millionaire. It takes a special song to have the impact "Do It to Julia" had. It takes a special singer.'

'Oh, she's special. Nobody knows that better than me. I've been in the passenger seat for most of the journey. But I'm just trying to warn you: she's selfish and ruthless too.'

'I'll consider it noted,' I said, picking up pace now that the hotel's awning was in sight.

'You're not hearing me,' he insisted, grabbing me by the sleeve and stopping me on the spot. 'I'm telling you this because I've been where you were today. She's the most manipulative person on the planet, and it's when you think she's not manipulating you that you're truly in her control. She's like the fucking . . . morning sun,' he slabbered. 'She'll make you feel you're harnessing power you never knew you had, that you can be so much more than you thought. But in the end she'll take as much as she gives, and then she'll take some more. She'll steal from you. You think what you did today means you were writing together? Don't you think Maxi did the same thing – jamming, improvising, suggesting. Don't you think I did too?'

His eyes were wild, his words drunkenly overemphasised like they were a new gospel.

'Maxi says he's got something up his sleeve, says he's gaunny get his pound of flesh, but I don't know. Damien's been around the block, and he hitched his wagon to Heike because the minute he saw her, he knew she was a juggernaut. Heike will get wherever she wants to be, but she'll leave bodies in her wake.'

Lost Generation

The Brauereihallen had an altogether more vibrant feel about the place upon their return. It was just after nine and there was a gig in progress in one of the larger halls. Parlabane reckoned it must be the support band's rhythm section he could hear throbbing behind the heavy wooden doors, as there were dozens of people wearing the headline act's T-shirts still milling around in the covered concourse.

Mairi had made a few calls as they walked up Friedrichstrasse, getting someone back home to pave her way with the venue staff by vouching for her role as Savage Earth Heart's manager. Fortunately that distinction had currency here, the band having left the Brauereihallen a couple of years back on better terms than they had Palast.

Another factor in greasing the wheels and getting them both sorted out with passes was the fact that tonight's troubadours, Altar State, were being chaperoned around the Continent under the Bad Candy imprimatur.

Parlabane's intention was to get the venue staff and road crew to have a look at Bawjaws's photo, but Mairi insisted they stop for a bite to eat as she hadn't had anything since Starbucks.

'I had a Mississippi mud muffin,' she told him. 'Tastes exactly like it sounds. She mimicked a southern accent: '*Unleash your inner fat-ass, with a Mississippi mud muffin.* At the time I thought it would be weighing me down all day, but I'm glad I had it or I'd have faded ages ago.'

'Aye, if only they could cut out the fat as effectively as they cut out their tax liabilities,' he muttered.

Mairi ignored him and helped him order from a food stall. 'Helped' meaning she overruled his request for currywurst and chips, which he would have to confess he thought was the when-in-Berlin thing to order. He didn't know what it was actually going to entail.

'It's disgusting,' she assured him. 'Almost no natural ingredients.'

'You know, I thought it was one of the consolations of being separated that I wouldn't have my dining choices dictated by someone else's health obsessions.'

'This is not about health, it's about taste. If you want a giant sausage and chips, have a bratwurst or a paprikawurst if you like it spicy. Just don't have the currywurst. Trust me on this: it's like eating a sliced-up plastic dildo smeared in warm ketchup.'

'And you would know this how?'

She ignored that as well.

They found places at the end of a trestle table otherwise bustling with noisy adolescent Altar State fans. Mairi had ordered them both something called flammkuchen, which seemed to be a very thin German version of pizza. He caught a glimpse of what he deduced to be currywurst in front of one of the lads further down the table, and decided he'd dodged a bullet there. Or dodged a sliced-up dildo, anyway.

Their dining companions were cheerful and boisterous, and between the language barrier and the intent manner in which they were yelling all communication back and forth, the effect was to make Mairi and Parlabane's end of the table seem private and secluded.

Two girls in the middle of the group began singing one of Altar State's anthems, belting it across the table into each other's faces in accented and occasionally mistaken English.

Parlabane stole a glance at them and must have failed to disguise a baleful look, which Mairi homed in on.

'It's shite getting old, isn't it?' she said, almost but not quite nailing what had been depressing him. 'You see all these kids at gigs, and in your head you're still one of them. Then you go to the loo and catch sight of yourself in the mirror.'

'Aye, that's the trade-off: part of you feels younger for being there, and another part gets made to feel all the more ancient by being around all these . . . children. It's a price I'm willing to pay, though. I still love gigs: the smell of aftershave, perfume, make-up and spilled beer; plastic pint glasses flying; fashion calamities everywhere; and a group of incurable dreamers pouring their heart into every note up on the stage.'

Mairi had a wistful smile as she nodded her agreement.

'I love looking at the younger fans' faces whenever a band takes the stage,' she said, 'wondering if it's their first time seeing them, because I know what that felt like. It's the closest you can get to feeling it yourself again. It must be like being a mother on Christmas morning, when the wee ones come into the living room and see what's under the tree.'

Parlabane took a mouthful of beer, ostensibly to wash down the flammkuchen, but really to cover the fact that she had just zeroed in on the true source of his angst when he had looked at those teenagers losing themselves in their singalong.

Oh yeah, and throw in Christmas morning just to really stomp it into the carpet.

He had long since made his peace with never being twenty-one again, but he'd been almost as long in expectation of that vicarious thrill Mairi was describing. One day he was going to be taking his kids to a show, he used to think. Wouldn't matter who it was, how awful, how loud, he'd be happy about it. He had looked forward to being the old fart made to sit three rows away from junior and his mates even though he was the one driving them home after watching Slipknot or Korn or whoever. Christ, even Prelude to the Slaughter, and if he had a girl, One Direction or whichever vapid boyband was cool with that particular intake of nine-year-olds.

Fuck.

Sarah had cheated on him, and they got past it. It was a one-night thing, but it got very public, unavoidably humiliating. They got past it. It was only sex. They got past a lot of things, and he had assumed that anything that went wrong in a marriage was fixable.

Until they found out they couldn't have kids.

It seemed absurd that something they had managed perfectly well without for so many years could suddenly trump all other considerations now that they'd discovered it was unavailable. In that respect, this discovery appeared to be an injection of poison that went straight to the heart of their marriage, but only if you ignored the hidden untruth in the previous statement.

They *hadn't* managed perfectly well. Thus, this discovery was not an injection of poison but more like a trace agent that showed up how many fault lines were already running through their relationship, ready to crack. The thought of a child had been like an invisible glue, as though they both knew they were growing apart but they each secretly imagined a better future that would happen once the dynamic changed, when they became parents rather than just partners.

Lucky escape for the wean, anyway.

And what about Mairi, he wondered. What was in that look as she talked about what it must be like as a mother at Christmas? Was there sadness and regret hidden there? Not that he could detect. She had to be forty-two, so she couldn't be kidding herself that there was plenty of time left yet. Besides, she was already playing mummy to Savage Earth Heart and sundry other charges, and right now one of them was very late for her tea.

'Did you have any luck speaking to Monica yet?' he asked, aware that as mother hen she hadn't quite kept all her chicks in line.

Mairi frowned.

'Still nothing.'

'Quite a huff. Do you think she'd come out of it if we told her Heike is missing?'

'Undoubtedly. But there's a chicken-and-egg problem. I'm not leaving that kind of information on her voicemail.'

'Just how much did you upset her? I need the truth, Mairi.'

'Everything's out of proportion when you're Monica's age,' she said, a reply but not an answer.

The venue manager, a tall and rangy young bloke called Hannes, came over and sorted them out with backstage passes, but upon Mairi's instruction, they waited until Altar State were playing before venturing into any of the protected areas. The immediate run-up to the show was the worst time to ask anybody for a moment of their time, and they wouldn't win anybody's goodwill by getting in the way.

In the meantime they showed the image of Bawjaws to the bar staff, waiters, venue security and even the merchandising people. Mairi was the one who presented them with Parlabane's phone, so that he could watch their faces as they looked at the image. He wanted to note who even just thought they recognised this guy, as well as who appeared to recognise him but claimed they didn't.

He got barely a glimmer. It was a long, slow procession of furrowed brows and apologetic shakes of the head, though at least Mairi was getting better at pronouncing the German for 'Do you know this man?' as Hannes had taught her. Parlabane tried not to think about how the likelihood of them getting a bite was worsening with every blank response, because if Bawjaws showed up with any frequency in this place, his face would surely have rung a bell with someone by now.

With Altar State in full cyber-rock flow, they made their way backstage in Halle Vier, where it was a delicate matter of choosing their moment. In the narrow pit behind the crush barrier, security staff stood vigilantly attentive upon the audience: there would be no speaking to them right now. Ditto the sound and lighting engineers.

Others stood in the wings, less occupied than merely on standby. Mairi knew their roles, and who it was safest to disturb. Once again, nobody said they recognised Bawjaws, but this time there were two men who reacted to the image. Nothing dramatic, but there was a difference between the studied neutrality of their responses and the blankness he had been witnessing so far. Parlabane took note of who they were, and on a hunch made an enquiry of Hannes the next time he spotted him breezing past: permanently busy, lolloping in his stride, but somehow always able to spare a second.

Parlabane asked him to indicate who was venue staff and who was road crew. Then a brief blether to Altar State's guitar roadie established who else was on the band's permanent payroll.

That made it official: both of the guys pretending not to recognise Bawjaws worked for Bad Candy.

They watched the rest of the set from the floor rather than the wings so that they could show the image to a few more front-of-house personnel. They got more blanks, then waited by the sound desk after the encore while the staff ushered everybody else outside and the roadies immediately got busy taking the kit apart. Mairi showed the phone to the sound engineer, a bloke called Stan whom she seemed to vaguely know. Finally they got a hit, if not a positive ID.

'I've seen this guy,' Stan said, concentration etched on his face as he tried to place him.

'Here at the Brauereihallen?' Mairi asked.

'No. It was when I was out with Famous Blue Raincoats towards the end of last year. Saw him a couple of times. He was in Milan, and I think I saw him in Cologne as well, though it could have been Frankfurt.'

'Could he be with Bad Candy?' Parlabane asked.

'I don't know. I didn't see him at gigs: I saw him in hotels. There were always girls with him: young, very glam. I thought he was a Russian oligarch. Or a porn baron.'

They made their way back out to the covered courtyard, where a queue had already formed outside Halle Ein, inside which something called Club Clash was kicking off. The food stalls were still doing a brisk trade from those whose appetites had been worked up by a hard night's moshing, and by those grabbing a bite before hitting the club. Parlabane wondered how many beers were required to make currywurst seem like a good idea, and reckoned it was roughly the same as a doner kebab or a half-pizza supper.

He became aware of someone sidling up to them as they stood against a wall, trying to stay out of the way. Parlabane recognised him as one of the Bad Candy blokes who had reacted to the image but told them otherwise.

He had a concerned look: very serious, very sincere, and very much like someone who didn't want to be seen talking to them.

'This man you showed me,' he said, his accent local. 'I have a friend who may be able to identify him. Can I show her the phone?'

He held out his hand close to his side, keeping the gesture subtle, like a drugs hand-off.

'It will take two minutes,' he added.

'Can't you take me to her?'

'She is in a restricted area in Club Clash. It would take me longer to get you a pass than to just show her the phone.'

Parlabane eyed the waiting hand and shook his head.

'I'm sorry mate, but I'm not letting my phone out of my sight.'

The roadie's face darkened, incredulity mixed with offence.

'Hey, fuck you, I'm not a thief,' he said, before walking away in the huff.

'Well played, Jack,' said Mairi. 'Slick. Why didn't you just give him the phone? You know who he is: his name was on his laminate. Karl something. It's not like he could steal it and act as though nothing happened.'

'Well, actually, that's precisely what he could do. And I don't care if I know his name. Would you hand over your phone just like that?'

'My whole life is on this phone,' she admitted, by way of conceding the point. 'My existence runs on iOS.'

A few moments later Karl reappeared, still acting like he was concerned about who might be watching.

'Hey, I'm sorry,' he said quietly. 'I overreacted. I wouldn't hand over my phone to a stranger either. It's just, you make an offer to help, you don't expect to get it back in your face, yeah?'

'Sorry. No offence intended,' Parlabane replied.

'Why don't you Bluetooth me the photo,' he suggested, producing his own phone.

'Sure thing.'

'We really appreciate it,' Mairi added.

Parlabane transferred the image of Bawjaws and as soon as it appeared on his screen Karl hastened off in the direction of Club Clash.

They remained against the wall, waiting patiently as Karl's estimated two minutes crept up closer to twelve.

'Just so we're clear,' Parlabane said, 'we're now about eight minutes past the point at which I'd have started to worry had I handed that guy my phone.'

'Wait a minute: you're getting in an "I told you so", even though we didn't take the course of action you disagreed with?'

'I'm just saying.'

Mairi stared at him a moment, then nodded to herself.

'Separated, aren't you, you and your wife?'

'What's that got to do with . . .'

'I'm just saying.'

Karl finally returned before it could further degenerate. His face was darkly purposeful.

Result.

'She knows who this is.'

They waited for him to give them a name, but none was forthcoming. Parlabane realised Karl wasn't here to relay the information.

'So are you going to take us to her now?' he asked.

Karl shook his head, briefly but intractably.

'She will talk to you, but not here. Not where people know her. She says this guy is very bad news. She wants to meet somewhere less public.'

'Where, then?' Mairi asked.

Karl handed over a piece of paper with an address written on it.

'Where Bodestrasse meets Am Lustgarten,' he said. 'In front of the Alte Nationalgalerie.'

Mairi sighed, doing little to suppress her exasperation.

'When?' she asked. 'Please tell me tomorrow *morning*, at least.'

'She said one hour. And she will only speak with you,' he added, indicating Mairi. 'No men. You wait for her where she said, on one of the curved benches. If she sees anyone else she walks away.'

Face in the Crowd

After the Lisbon show I stayed on stage as the crew and venue staff stripped the place around me. I loved the venue so much I didn't want to leave. The acoustics were beautiful, even our foldback wedges sounding pretty good. The Coliseu dos Recreios was how I imagined a Viennese or Parisian opera house would be, the kind of place I grew up dreaming of playing.

'Do It to Julia' had been really successful in Portugal, thanks to a dance remix by Iz-Ma, one of the country's biggest DJs. The show wasn't a sell-out, but Jan said that it would have been if downstairs had been an all-seated audience. By leaving it clear for standing, the capacity went up to four thousand, but Jan assured us that ticket sales weren't far off that anyway.

I gazed out at the auditorium, listening to the crash of plastic glasses being swept across the wooden floor. It was a sound familiar to this part of my evenings, and it always surprised me how loud it was, emphasising the emptiness once the audience was gone.

I heard my name and looked up to see Heike coming towards me looking anxious and impatient. She had her phone in her hand, holding it like it was weighing her down.

'I got a text from Hannah,' she said.

She handed me the phone, like she couldn't bring herself to read it aloud.

Heike, I'm so sorry I ran out on you like that. It wasn't what it looked like. You have to let me explain. Can you meet me in Madrid? I'll be at the Museo Reina Sofia from four. I know you're playing the Palacio Siroco – it's only five minutes away. Please be there, it's really important we talk.
Hannah

'Well, that's good news, right?' I said, but she seemed reluctant to see it like that.

'Maybe. Would you mind coming with me? I'm feeling a bit vulnerable about this and I could do with some moral support.'

'Sure. I've got your back,' I told her, though I was already wondering at what point the role of wing-woman would transform into that of gooseberry.

The bus got us into Madrid before three, about six hours after setting off from Lisbon. We weren't due on stage until ten, so the soundcheck was scheduled for five. The museum was a short walk from the hotel, though a glance at the map showed that the 'five minutes' of Hannah's text must have meant a car ride. On foot it was a good twenty minutes away along Ronda de Atocha, and it was hot.

The Museo towered above us as we walked towards it, the exterior scary-looking and industrial. It turned out that this was because we were approaching from the rear, though the front wasn't much more welcoming. It was like a well-maintained prison.

Heike had said almost nothing all the way there. I don't think I'd ever seen her this nervous, not even last night, before singing to nearly four thousand people. When she went on-stage she always appeared calm, even impatiently eager to play, but there was still a real apprehension about her if you looked closely: an edge, which she fed off. We all did. Anybody who ever says they're not nervous about going on stage is either lying or about to give a phoned-in apology of a performance.

This Hannah was obviously some girl. I wondered what Heike saw in her that I didn't, and then I remembered: herself.

I had felt a pang of jealousy when I first saw the text and realised she was back in the picture. Then I remembered I was the one Heike had come to for support, on something so intimate, so personal. This was trust, and I would do anything to prove myself worthy of it.

We strode into a covered courtyard where modern and traditional architecture seemed locked in a battle to swallow each other. Light poured through plunging grey wells in a huge red ceiling, beneath which more big red plates and grilles faced off against massive older walls of pale stone. I was getting a queasy claustrophobic feeling about being here, despite the vastness of the space. I'd have hated to walk through it alone.

The great concourse was full of people, as though it were a town square. Heike was craning her neck, almost walking on tiptoe as she peered over the faces for the one she wanted.

We both saw Hannah at the same time, standing against the pale stone at the far end, searching the crowd as eagerly as Heike had been doing, then waving when she saw us. She still seemed distracted by her surroundings, though, glancing anxiously everywhere as if there was someone else she was looking for.

Or, as it turned out, someone else she had seen.

We were maybe fifty feet away when they seemed to sweep in from nowhere, like undercover cops during a raid. There were two of them, burly men in grey business suits, one of them squat, shaven-headed and jowly, the other tall and muscular with jet-black, obviously dyed hair.

Hannah looked like she was trying to appeal to them, but whatever she said cut no ice as they began escorting her away. She didn't struggle or cry out, just let herself be led, glancing back once towards Heike with longing and regret.

'What the hell just happened?' Heike asked, looking at me in outrage.

I opened my mouth uselessly, then followed Heike as she started off in pursuit.

The shaven-headed one must have noticed, because he stopped and turned, pushing his companion towards us while he kept Hannah moving away.

The giant thug blocked our path with a huge beefy hand, like a traffic cop. There were rings on each of his thick sausage fingers; rings and scars.

'Where are you taking our friend?' Heike asked him.

He gave a tiny but firm shake of the head. Over his shoulder, Hannah was disappearing around the corner and out of sight.

178

'Anezka is not your friend. She *our* friend, okay? You stay away.'

'Her name is Hannah,' Heike insisted. 'I need to speak to her.'

He gave her a sneering grin, amused by what she had said.

'You want time with Anezka, we can make arrangement, but you pay, okay? You pay, same everybody else.'

I stared into his hard red face. He didn't look Spanish, and he didn't sound it either.

I'd have said Eastern European, maybe Romanian or Bulgarian.

Tourists

The taxi dropped them off in front of the Humboldt Box, a structure that more closely resembled a video games console than the video games console it was currently whoring itself out to advertise. Its vertical proportion and futuristic design could not have been more of a contrast with the classicism of the Berliner Dom and the Altes Museum across the street on Museumsinsel, and its gaudy lighting shone like a warning beacon in comparison to the gloom that was enveloping the site of their destination.

'Do you think if she'd put her mind to it she could have maybe chosen somewhere a bit creepier?' Mairi asked, as they walked through the Lustgarten and deeper into shadow. There was no moon, and the street lighting around the museums was both sparse and dim, possibly due to the building works that seemed to be enveloping the island.

Parlabane knew it wasn't just the darkness that was spooking her. He felt dwarfed by the scale of the architecture, and there was an august gravity about the place that probably seemed reassuringly timeless during the day, but felt desolately unmodern at night. Great old buildings, witness to history, but coldly indifferent to it too.

'I hear you,' he agreed. 'Never thought I'd be grateful for the sight of two dozen American teenagers in backpacks, but if a busload pitched up right now, that would be just dandy.'

It was about to get worse, because they had to split up. After what had happened earlier Parlabane wasn't ready to take a faceless stranger at her word by staying away from the rendezvous, but Karl had only stipulated that she would walk if she *saw* anyone else.

She wouldn't see him.

They had got there early for precisely this purpose. Parlabane raced ahead towards the Alte Nationalgalerie, climbing the left of the twin staircases. When he reached the first platform, where the staircase returned, he found the second flight barred off by steel gates. They were only shoulder height, so he all but vaulted them with a practised move, then ascended to where a huge statue of a man on horseback towered above the apex, looking south across the Lustgarten.

Parlabane didn't need the bronze equestrian's elevation to find a vantage point, tucking himself in against the wall and peeking over the balustrade. From here, he had a view of Mairi sitting as instructed on one of the semi-circular stone benches, but more importantly he could see all of the approaches beyond the covered walkway that ran around the square. Am Lustgarten was dead ahead, leading back towards the main road, perpendicular to Bodestrasse, which ran east–west, crossing both channels of the Spree. The route from the east was closed to cars due to construction work, which meant that anyone approaching on foot would be obscured by plastic sheeting until they reached the corner of the walkway.

Parlabane glanced up and saw that he was crouched at the metal feet of a robed woman clutching a cross like she thought someone might steal it. Christ, even the statues seemed on edge.

His phone vibrated in his pocket, giving him a jolt. Mairi.

'Speak to me,' she said quietly. 'I'm getting freaked out. Starting to get what you meant about a Cold War movie: waiting on a bloody bench at midnight.'

'It's not midnight, it's only half-eleven.'

'Thanks. That makes me feel so much better. Can you see anything yet?'

'No, but stay on the line. I'll give you a commentary as soon as there's anything to comment on.'

Parlabane squinted through the gloom, peering out towards the light beyond. Trees blocked the view to the left of the cathedral, while off to the right, his sight of the road was partially obscured by blue pipes erupting from the ground in front of the covered walkway, a surreal parody of its Roman columns. They routed water to and from the building works, snaking around the island like a

181

partially exposed vascular system that broke the surface in places then plunged out of sight elsewhere. The building work cutting off Bodestrasse was effectively making a horseshoe of the road, with the section of it that ran between the Altes and Neues museums hidden from view.

Fast access in and out by car, out of sight of the main road, low lights, trees, pipes, columns. It suddenly struck Parlabane that if he had been asked to come up with an ideal spot for a hit or an abduction he'd have been pushed to do better than this.

'You know what I don't like about this?' he said into his phone.

'No, what?'

'Absolutely everything. I say we walk. Right now.'

'But if this girl can tell us who that guy was, it . . .'

'Mairi, we've seen this picture already today. The Cold War movie. Us waiting for information from a girl we've never seen, who isn't coming, because . . . Oh shit.'

'What.'

'Mairi, get out of there. Now.'

They appeared at the same time, a carefully synchronised operation. Parlabane saw two men running from the pedestrian-only bridge to the east, emerging from the cover of the building works at the same time as a black Audi came speeding in from the west. Mairi got up and began to run towards Am Lustgarten, and would have been caught in a pincer movement had it not been that the pincers weren't there to close in on her.

The two men on foot did not divert from their course as she made her exit. They were heading towards the museum steps, sprinting across the grass only yards from where Mairi was escaping.

Eejit. He realised he had been wrong-footed by a simple bluff. The instruction had been to isolate Mairi, knowing that Parlabane would be close by, his vigilance entirely concentrated on her safety. It was him they really wanted, and he'd cornered himself for them. Bastards had probably been close by the whole time, watching him take position.

They didn't have him yet, however.

His two pursuers began to diverge as they approached, intending to take one staircase each so that both routes down were blocked. One had dark hair pulled back in a ponytail and was wearing a white vest, all the better to show off his muscles. The other was dressed all in black, his peroxide crop reminding Parlabane of Spike, Joss Whedon's punk-refugee vampire.

They both looked younger than him, as well as taller, better built and undoubtedly more schooled in the noble art of punching fuck out of people. Nonetheless, younger didn't necessarily mean faster or fitter, and Parlabane was highly schooled in the arguably less noble art of running away.

He raced back down the top flight and vaulted over the gates on to the return landing. As he swung his feet clear of the steel bars he could hear Spike's footfalls thumping on the stone just yards away. The thought of them thumping on his ribcage gave his heels that extra spring. He scrambled over the balustrade and on to the little ledge on the other side of it. From there it was a drop of ten or twelve feet, which he reduced by draping down and finding toeholds to take his weight before that last freefall.

He spun around in the air and landed with a practised crouch, bending his knees like a suspension system. After a tiny moment's recovery time, he was sprinting away from the foot of the wall towards the covered walkway where it turned the corner at the rear of the Neues Museum. He had never been here before, but from the map he'd looked at on his phone back at the Brauereihallen, he recalled that there was a narrow channel between the Neues and the Pergamon. This led to a pedestrian bridge across the Spree and off the island.

He stole a glance back, mindful of the car that had been approaching when he first told Mairi to run. The bollards meant it couldn't come into the courtyard, but he had been expecting it to have disgorged more personnel to chase him down. That he couldn't see any was not reassuring. They could have headed around the other side of the Neues Museum in anticipation of precisely the route he was planning.

There was a worse explanation, which was that they could be busy bundling Mairi into the Audi. If your target was likely to be a tricky capture, why not nab his companion for leverage?

Spike hadn't fancied the jump from the balustrade, and was only just rounding the staircase as Parlabane reached the corner. He didn't seem to be going flat out, so maybe he wasn't so fit and the stairs had knocked the wind out of him.

Or maybe he'd been to Museumsinsel recently.

Parlabane rounded the corner and discovered he'd been running towards a dead end. The passage was blocked beyond the entrance to the Pergamon museum, tall wooden panels bolted into place to mask off more building works. They looked too high for him to scramble a purchase on the top. Short of finding a ladder, the only way out of here was back the way he'd come.

But as always, Parlabane's perspective took in more than one vertical plane. Back the way he'd come didn't necessarily mean retracing his steps. Against the rear wall of the Neues Museum the twin rows of broad Roman columns gave way to a single line of temporary modern beams. These were thin rectangular structures, sheathed in plywood to a height of two metres, holding up a concrete roof that extended halfway out across the passage.

A quick haul to the top of that got him one third of the way in half a second. The next part would be tougher, and the final bit a real high-stakes test of whether he was still cut out for this shit.

A glance to the side showed still no sight of Spike, though he could hear his footsteps, advancing at a brisk walking pace. No need to run when your prey is cornered. Spike was preserving his breath for the bit he did best: the punching fuck out of people part.

Parlabane whipped off his belt and looped it around the column. He pushed away with his feet and gripped the makeshift climbing strap with both hands. He recalled getting screamed at by his mother when she caught him doing something similar up a telegraph pole when he was about nine.

'You'll end up killing yourself,' she had warned him.

He reached the top as his pursuer stomped around the corner. He was out of the guy's reach but far from in the clear, and it would all be moot if it turned out his muscles weren't the only guns Spike was packing.

Parlabane threw his left arm on to the overhang and dangled by just that for a moment as the tension in the belt was lost. This was when he found out whether it would still be worth a trip back to those Highland rockfaces, and more immediately whether he would have the option.

The fingers on his right hand found purchase and he hauled himself over the edge. He silently thanked Sarah for the years of nagging that had kept him on the right side of the algorithms governing workouts and haggis suppers; specifically their corresponding relationships with weight and upper-body strength.

He had a look towards the wooden fence. It was too far to clear with a running jump, and anyway he couldn't see where he'd be landing on the other side. Even if he didn't impale himself on the end of a rebar strip, the fall from this height would easily break his legs. There was only one way to go, and it was a bloody long way.

He sprinted along the edge of the walkway's roof, reluctant to test whether the glass covering the stone slabs would bear his full running weight. Down below he heard urgent shouts back and forth in German. He wished he spoke it. Maybe these guys had more idea than he did as to where and how he was planning to get down from this thing.

He thought of those blue pipes on Bodestrasse. The ones rising up were feeding a horizontal tube running parallel to the walkway. The problem was, he didn't have the head start for getting down that he had enjoyed for the ascent. Plus there was still the issue of the black Audi, which he could see parked behind the Altes Museum. Wherever he chose to come down, they'd be waiting for him.

Unless, that was, he came down somewhere they couldn't wait.

He kept running, his pursuers doggedly following below. They still appeared to be in no particular hurry, content to keep him in sight in the knowledge that he was stuck up there. Then their voices became more urgent and their pace picked up as they realised that he wasn't as contained as they assumed.

On the far side of the square there was a high security gate

185

running from the walkway to the outer wall of the Alte Nationalgalerie. The walkway extended just a little past this, where it abutted a low, curved building right on the edge of the river.

He scurried towards it, seeing the fud in the ponytail fumble hopelessly at the locked barrier.

'Aye. There's your dinner,' he muttered to himself

Parlabane ran along the roof of the curved stone structure. It looked like some kind of admin office for the rest of the island. It was too small to be another gallery, but unfortunately too high for him to drape down from. Fortunately, there was yet more building work in progress on the other side of the security barrier, a steel shipping container only a short drop beneath.

From there he had to navigate a maze of construction machinery, skips, pallets of building materials and treacherously steep-sided excavations. He used his phone as a torch so as not to have escaped these bastards only to kill himself down a pile shaft.

He stopped to catch his breath and to consider his course. He was conscious that his pursuers might have a better knowledge than he did of where this building site would allow him to emerge. He had to find an exit that they didn't anticipate.

A railway line ran above and to his right, creating a narrow channel between its high walls and the back of the gallery. He was wondering whether there was a way up to it when the phone buzzed in his hand.

The screen told him it was Mairi, her face smiling up at him from his palm. He had snapped it in the kitchen of her flat in Hoxton the day she hired him, one picture he *had* asked permission to take. She looked composed and confident, and he really hoped that was how she would sound when he pressed Answer.

I wasn't Mairi who spoke. It was a male voice, guttural and low. Jowly.

Bawjaws.

'I have your woman.'

'I think you'll find she's her own woman, slabberchops,' he replied, anger putting steel in his voice where otherwise it would be tremulous.

'So you do not care about her. I am mistaken.'

'The relevant point here is that *you* sure as shit don't care about her, so why don't we cut to the cum-shot. It's me you're interested in, so I'm guessing you'd like to trade.'

'You are very correct, Mister—'

'How about you tell me your name first.'

'You can call me Boris.'

'I could call you Fudnugget as well, but I'm guessing that's not your real name either.'

Boris let this slide.

'If you want her back, you come to Rosa-Luxemburg-Platz. Be there in—'

'No. I don't know where that is, and I'm not walking into an ambush.'

'This is not a negotiation,' Boris told him testily.

'Yes it is. You've been chasing me all over this city for hours like I stole your briefcase or something, so let's not pretend you're the only one holding what the other wants.'

'Where, then?'

'Somewhere public, where I can see you coming and I can see that she's okay.'

'I only want to talk.'

'We're talking now. What is it you want to know? Where is Heike Gunn? Afraid I can't help you with that one. Why are you looking for her anyway?'

Parlabane didn't expect to get a useful answer, but he was buying a moment to think. He needed to come up with somewhere he knew, so that he had some idea of the environment he would be walking into.

'I am not looking for her,' Boris replied. 'Perhaps you should learn some German.'

Parlabane didn't catch his meaning, though he had been feeling faintly embarrassed at the fact that most of the Berliners he spoke to had been at least competent in English, while just about the only fragment he had absorbed of their mother tongue was their all-purpose hail and farewell greeting, *Tschüss*.

187

'How about we meet at the Sony Centre, Potsdamer Platz?' Boris suggested. 'Ideal for tourists,' he added witheringly.

Parlabane was still thinking of a rendezvous point that would give him a chance of at least ensuring Mairi got away. Unfortunately, as his time spent in this city could be measured in hours, that didn't make for much of a list.

There was one place on it that leaped to mind, though.

'The Hauptbahnhof,' he said, having switched to the U-Bahn there after taking a train in from Schönefeld airport. 'I want to be able to see her get on a train and away from you.'

Bawjaws thought about it, then agreed rather quicker than Parlabane would have liked.

'Okay. Hauptbahnhof.'

'I'll meet you in the main hall, ground level, at the entrance with the horse statue outside.'

Parlabane was thinking he could raise the alarm with the station staff as soon as Mairi was brought in under visible duress. Unfortunately Boris wasn't having it.

'You are right that this is a negotiation, but you are not negotiating with an idiot.'

'So what's your counter-offer?'

'You take a train from Friedrichstrasse. It will arrive on platform sixteen, where we will be waiting. I do not know in which car you arrive, so when I see you on the platform I release your woman. She can get on the train before it leaves. She goes free, you come to us.'

'Okay. I get off the train, she gets on it. Alone,' Parlabane added.

'Alone, yes. But let this be clear: if you try to get back on the train, or if you run before it leaves, someone will get on the train with her, and he will cut her open before she can call for help. After that, we will catch you anyway. You understand?'

'Yes, I understand,' Parlabane replied. 'Your English is very good,' he added acidly, then hung up.

It wasn't exactly a zinger of a comeback, but from what he had seen of the main station earlier that day, he reckoned he just might be able to conjure up a better one.

Travel Agency

We had just finished soundchecking when Jan stepped out from the back of the stage, shimmying between Rory's keyboard stand and Damien's amp rack with a self-satisfied look that told me his friend Charlie was in the wings. He was holding a white A4 envelope and heading for where Heike and I stood, a winning smile on his chops.

'Hey, my superstar ladies. Air Jan has got you both seats on a flight to Milan tomorrow, so some extra time in bed, a break from the bus, and an extra day in Milan while we break our journey in Nice, okay?'

He opened the envelope and handed us each a printout with flight details and a booking reference for online check-in.

'What about us?' Rory asked.

Jan slapped him playfully on the shoulder.

'You're not pretty enough. You're pretty, Rory, but the cut-off is very high.'

I felt quite self-conscious right then, wondering if this might not cause resentment. That was until I remembered to ask myself why Heike needed a companion to take a short flight and spend one extra night in Milan. My gender was the deciding factor here: it just wasn't for the reasons Rory thought.

Heike was gazing in my direction, holding the printout like it was court evidence. Neither of us was buying this.

Without a word, we both headed for the ladies' toilets, where we knew there would be no one else in earshot.

'He bought me a train ticket to Barcelona for a non-existent interview,' she said. 'And now I'm flying to Milan because I'm tired?'

'I was booked on that train to Barcelona too. I slept in because

I was hungover. I wasn't meant to be on the bus that day. Neither of us were supposed to see those girls.'

'Because they're hookers,' Heike said. 'And Jan knew I'd cause trouble about it.'

'But how could he know the guys wouldn't object?'

'The guys wouldn't know what they were looking at any more than you did at the time. He says they're merch girls, who's going to argue? Even if the guys did think something was off, he knew they wouldn't be sufficiently empowered or inclined to rock the boat. Safe to say that these days I'm both.'

'Why wouldn't you have bought that they were merch girls?'

'Maybe I would, but Jan wasn't taking any chances. There were hookers servicing that wanker Dean and some of the Bad Candy road crew on previous tours. It was particularly bad when we went round Europe supporting Pale Strangers. That band were fucking sleazebags. I kicked up a stink, but nobody really cared what I had to say.'

'Could this be bigger than just a few prostitutes?' I asked her.

'Bigger how?'

'Bordeaux to Barcelona. Madrid to Milan. Those journeys were international. There haven't been any merch girls on any of our city-to-city trips.'

'No, you're right. And you said Jan was holding their passports? I'm starting to wonder whether a rock band's tour bus wouldn't be the perfect cover for trafficking girls around Europe.'

Heike gave me a steely look, which I met in kind. In that moment we formed an alliance.

'I think I'll be setting an alarm to catch that early bus tomorrow morning,' she said. 'How about you?'

I folded the piece of paper Jan had given me and ripped it in two.

Down in the U-Bahnhof at Midnight

Friedrichstrasse station was quiet, though the platform did fill up a little more the longer he waited. It was after twelve, and he guessed the frequency of the trains had dropped significantly. This meant the Hauptbahnhof, one stop ahead, would be quiet too, and there would be no element of doubt as to which train he was arriving on.

Parlabane chose a position roughly halfway along the platform, augmenting his memories of the Hauptbahnhof from earlier that day with images he was able to search on his phone. It was like an exploded diagram: spaces and surfaces, shapes and angles vivid and open. Escalators zigzagged between floors, cylindrical glass lift shafts punched through concrete, vast grids of glass glistened from the office buildings bracketing the central concourse, while columns, girders and suspension cables proudly advertised their roles. Getting off his train from the airport, he had considered it an adult version of a children's soft-play area. Tonight, however, he profoundly appreciated that this was going to be very hard play.

As the train rolled into Friedrichstrasse, he took care in choosing where he boarded. Halfway along the platform at Friedrichstrasse didn't necessarily correspond to precisely halfway along the platform at the Hauptbahnhof, but he could move back or forth along the carriage as required.

As the train pulled out, an announcement reminded him that his destination was only one stop away. Parlabane didn't know how long it would take, only that he could have done with it being longer. He didn't feel ready, but how could he? He tried not to think about what might be happening to him or to Mairi within the hour if he didn't pull this off, though just a glimpse was enough to sharpen his instincts. He could only afford one outcome here.

He felt the train slow as it glided into Hauptbahnhof. His brain began rapidly taking in and analysing information, consciously and at a more primal level. Platform sixteen was sparsely populated, so it was easy to identify Boris and his team from the narrowing distance. He had men positioned at the tops of both sets of escalators, the man himself next to the first of the cylindrical lift shafts. That's where Mairi was: held behind the glass until he stepped from the train and made himself visible.

Her face was anxious, fearful. Their eyes met as the train passed, and he gave her a wink. He hoped he looked more confident than he felt, and that it came off as a cocksure gesture rather than a nervous twitch.

She looked puzzled. He'd settle for that. It was an improvement on terror and borderline despair.

He had estimated pretty well. His carriage was going to stop fairly close to where platform sixteen overhung the central concourse, which stretched towards a towering arch of glass above the northern entrance two floors below. He chose the far-away door, putting him closer to the second lift. Mairi was about thirty yards distant, inside the other one.

Parlabane let all the other passengers get out first, then waited just a little longer. He wanted to limit the time between showing himself and the train departing again, denying them the chance and the temptation to improvise.

He strode forward, making eye contact with Boris, who stepped aside to let Mairi out of the lift, accompanied by Spike. Mairi gazed towards Parlabane, her expression a mix of helplessness and apology, as though this was somehow her fault.

Parlabane nodded towards the open doors, urging her to comply. She looked away and disappeared inside.

Spike stayed right at the doors. He was now wearing a jacket over his black T-shirt. He looked to Parlabane and briefly opened it to show why. A blade glinted inside: short, stubby and doubtless razor sharp. It was the kind of knife with which he could quickly and repeatedly stab someone using a minimum of conspicuous action.

The doors hadn't begun to close, but already Boris's men were making their move. The guy with the ponytail was approaching from the lifts, while from the escalators Parlabane could see another one striding towards him. He was troll-like, both facially and in build, resembling a squat and steroid-pumped Michael Gove. It was a truly horrible vision, but on the plus side, it would make it a lot easier if Parlabane ended up having to punch the guy really hard in the face. Indeed, remembering to stop and run off would be the main hazard.

The doors closed and the train began to pull away. Parlabane urged it to hurry, to speed up. Boris's men were each less than fifteen yards away and closing, Spike joining the hunt now that Mairi was out of the equation.

He glimpsed Mairi's face one last time as her carriage passed, the train picking up speed. He just wasn't sure it was picking it up fast enough.

Ten yards. Eight.

The rearmost carriage whipped past him, and suddenly his path was clear. It just wasn't clear to his reception committee, though perhaps it should have been: the fuckers had forced him on to the rails once already today.

Parlabane leaped down from the platform and across the tracks, taking care to hurdle the third rail. There was a narrow concrete pathway on the far side. Horizontal steel railings ran along it, affording a clear view down towards the main concourse. He could still feel the floor beneath him vibrate as the train departed.

Parlabane vaulted over the rails and climbed on to a girder extending away from the platform. He gripped a steel shaft forming a giant window frame in the office towers that bookended the hall. Passengers wandered obliviously beneath him. It was too high to jump.

He checked his footing and hopped down on to a suspended departure board. It wobbled and lurched under his weight, but it held. A second later he had draped down on to solid concrete.

He glanced back to see Gove-Troll careering down the escalator. Above him, Ponytail was clambering over the railings.

Parlabane sprinted for the broad staircase that descended to ground level. He slalomed two drunks in Bayern tops then gripped the handrail as he took the steps ten at a time. There were more Bayern fans towards the bottom, four abreast on the stairs, arms around each other's shoulders.

Scheisse.

He vaulted over the barrier on to the up escalator, catching his ankle on the moving handrail. Glass and steel spun around him as he tumbled to the deck in a tangle of limbs. He'd rattled his head on the edge of a stair too. Blood was running into his right eye, closing it. Through his left he could see Gove-Troll bounding towards the top of the staircase as the escalator took him back up

He climbed to his feet again and stomped down the rising stairs. A few seconds later he was on mercifully unmoving ground, the wall of glass ahead of him. His thigh muscles screamed at him as he sprinted towards the doors.

He barrelled through them and out into the warm air. Across the concrete he could see a taxi rank. Mercifully there was a cab waiting, and the driver wasn't even outside having a fag with his mates.

Less mercifully, the driver locked the doors as he tried to get in. He babbled something Parlabane didn't understand, then gestured to his face. He remembered he was bleeding. The guy thought he was a nutter, or at least that he was going to bleed all over his seats.

Back at the station entrance, Gove-Troll was bustling through another clutch of Bayern fans at the doors.

'Please,' he begged, pulling on the handle. 'I was attacked. Look.'

The driver glanced towards the station, then suddenly unlocked the doors.

Parlabane sprawled across the back seat as the car pulled away.

'FC Hollywood,' the driver said with distaste.

Parlabane watched Gove-Troll pull up as he realised his quarry was fled, Spike almost crashing into him from the back. They stared in impotent frustration at the departing taxi.

Tschüss.

He took out his phone and dialled Mairi, clenching a fist in elated relief when she answered.

International Incident

We didn't need to wait for the bus to encounter more of Jan's 'merch girls'. I was fairly sure I saw several of them draping themselves over a bunch of suits in the hotel bar when we came back from the gig that night. We were staying in some corporate place, but neither girls nor suits looked like delegates at a conference. These guys were high-end: expensively dressed and cordoned off in a private area of the bar by their own personal security. The girls were dressed to look like they belonged in such high-rolling company, but I couldn't help thinking the designer outfits just made them look even younger and less plausible. One of them was definitely the girl from backstage in Barcelona. I caught her pretending just a bit too hard not to have seen me.

I'd no idea till how late the merch girls were entertaining the boardroom bawbags, but they were up bright and early the next morning, which was obviously dress-down Friday. There were seven of them sitting in the lobby, all back in their Savage Earth Heart T-shirts, and toting their matching rucksacks.

Heike and I stood close by with our own luggage, determined to really bring the awkward when Jan fronted up.

We watched him wander across the hotel lobby, bleary-eyed and yawning. He woke up pretty fast when he took in what was in front of him, and made a few rapid and troubling calculations.

'Ladies, what are you doing?' he asked, in fake puzzlement. 'Did you forget about the plane? It doesn't leave until three, yeah?'

'I think the bigger question is what are *they* doing?' Heike replied.

'Serpent have already played Milan and Nice,' I told him, returning his fake confusion. 'I checked their tour schedule on my phone. Or are the girls connecting to a flight to Oslo?'

Jan glanced around and upwards for a flustered few moments,

like there might be answers printed on the ceiling. It must have been hard to think of an explanation while channelling so much effort into hiding how pissed off he was at both of us.

'They're bound for a trade fair at the Fiera Milano,' he said. 'Bad Candy have a marketing and promo operation these days. They'll be working a stand for . . . I think a software company. Video games, you know?'

'Is the video game also called Savage Earth Heart?' Heike asked witheringly, indicating the T-shirts.

'It's cross-promotion,' I answered for him, to show we knew he was full of shit.

'Listen,' he said. 'This is not what you think.'

'What do we think?' Heike asked him.

'I'm just saying, it's complicated. Very complicated. Over my head, yeah? Just stay out of it.'

'How can I stay out of it? I'm sharing a bus with it.'

'And that's your choice, okay? I got you plane tickets.'

'Yeah, you did. Why was that?'

Jan didn't have an answer, but truth was he didn't need one. Now that we all knew he was lying to us, it still left the more problematic issue of what we could do about it.

He found out south of Perpignan.

French police pulled the bus over into a lay-by short of a pedestrian footbridge over the autoroute. Unlike before, this wasn't a random check, and it wasn't because we were a rock band who might have drugs. Heike had looked up the authorities on her mobile, ringing them from a payphone when we stopped at a services area north of Girona, so that the call couldn't be traced to her.

They weren't immigration, simply two uniformed cops responding to a despatch resultant of Heike's call, and checking whether there was something in need of further investigation.

Both officers boarded the bus and asked to see everybody's identification. That was when Jan found out that something was very wrong. He went into his bag to retrieve the girls' passports, but they weren't there. Heike had stolen them a couple of hours into the journey, while he was catching up on the sleep he didn't get the night before. The merch girls were dozing as well, and I wondered if any of them had been the one keeping our tour manager awake.

It was satisfying to watch him scramble and rummage, no doubt wondering if the whole lot might be sitting on a lobby table back in Madrid. But our pleasure only lasted until we saw the panic that was starting to appear on the faces of our guest passengers. They were looking towards him, then frantically checking their own bags as it dawned on them their documentation was not in Jan's possession. They looked ashen despite the make-up, and a few were in tears.

One of them wasn't panicking, though. She was pointing. So not all of them had been asleep, and this latest development must have helped her explain what she maybe only *thought* she had seen.

Before Jan could do anything, Heike held up the passports in her right hand, her left gesturing to him to stay back. One of the police officers stepped purposefully past Jan and reached out to take the documents.

Holding them back, Heike asked whether he spoke English. When he confirmed that he did, she told him she suspected the girls were here under duress and being taken en masse, possibly against their will.

'I took their passports from his bag,' she said, indicating Jan. 'He was holding all of them.'

The cop talked quietly with his colleague, then called a name from the first passport he opened: Sabina Dumitrescu. Anxious-looking and tearful, the girl put her hand up and was asked to accompany them outside.

I could see them question her through the window, the cop with the passports holding hers up and occasionally pointing back towards the bus. The girl was shaking her head, speaking quickly and firmly.

After a few minutes they sent her back inside and called another name: Radka Danchev. It was the girl I had seen in Barcelona, who had hidden her shame behind the mask of, as Heike described it, a fucking robot. Again I saw head-shaking, animated gesticulation and quite a lot of anger. This time she was the one pointing towards the bus, with what I took to be accusation.

I saw Jan glance towards us, sitting on the edge of his seat with his feet in the aisle. I expected him to be angry but he just seemed worried. You bloody well should be, I thought as I watched the policemen climb back on board, their faces much more grim than before.

It was huckling time.

As they walked up the aisle towards Jan, I suddenly wondered what this might mean for the Milan show, and for the rest of the tour. But then they continued past him and instead ordered Heike to follow them outside.

Only a few minutes later she was making her way back to her seat, her face flushed and her eyes filling with tears of anger and humiliation.

Some of the girls were glaring at her. One called her 'a fucking stupid bitch'. Others just looked shaken, not quite ready to feel relief until the bus was definitely back under way.

I didn't ask what had been said. She didn't look ready to share.

Jan went outside with the cops, talking with them longer than anyone else had. From his body language I was able to predict that the interruption was coming to a halt. Half of Jan's job was about smoothing over awkward situations, and even with his back to me I could tell he was doing what he did best.

It was all smiles and handshakes before he came back on board and the cops strolled back to their car. I could imagine how it played out at the end: all a big misunderstanding, temperamental rock-star stuff, crazy chicks having a falling-out. Apologies for your troubles, officers, but have a thought for the shit *I've* got to put up with.

What I didn't understand was why the girls handed their passports back to Jan as soon as we were back on the road. Why, if they were being forced, would they lie to the cops when there was a chance to get their documents and escape? And if they weren't being forced, why did they all look so afraid when the cops boarded the bus and their passports were found to be missing?

Very little was said after that. Heike stared out of the window for the rest of the journey, occasionally glancing ahead towards where our extra passengers sat with their backs to her.

We reached Nice around eight in the evening, Jan returning from reception with the news that they only had one room free, so Heike and I would have to share. He claimed he had been assured over the phone that two rooms were available, but I thought he was lying and had booked us a twin on purpose: we weren't supposed to be here, and he was underlining the fact. Neither of us had started complaining about the twin before he was explaining the situation, so I filed that one under 'protesting too much'.

He hadn't said anything about Perpignan, and I thought he was just going to act like it hadn't happened, to keep things friendly. Then, as he handed Heike the keycard for our room he glanced in either direction as though checking for eavesdroppers, and spoke quietly but firmly.

'That was a very stupid thing you did, okay? Very stupid. You have no idea what you are messing with. Stay out of this, or you'll get people hurt. You understand me?'

I felt something grip me from my stomach to the ends of my fingers. I thought about the fear in the faces of the girls on the bus, and understood why they hadn't taken the chance to run. They knew who would come looking for them.

Late-Night Movies

There was a taxi stopped in front of the hotel as Parlabane's cab pulled in behind it. He could make out Mairi in the back seat, handing the driver his fare. He'd spoken to her on the phone only a few minutes earlier, but he still felt a rush at seeing her in the flesh, back here safe and sound.

She noticed him as he climbed out of the beige Mercedes and came running forward, almost bowling him over as she flung her arms around him and clung on. They stayed like that for a long time, saying nothing. She needed this, he understood, but he was feeling conspicuous being out here in the street. He had to break it off. (Yeah, that's why.)

'We need to get inside,' he said. 'Out of sight.'

'Of course,' she replied. 'I'm just so glad you're okay.'

'Bit of late-night parkour, always good for the cardiovascular system.'

She took a seat in the lobby. Now that she was under decent light he could see she'd been crying but was putting a brave face on it, like she didn't want him to see how scared she'd been. He felt ultra-protective of her, and not merely because she'd just been thrown in at the deep end. There was something else driving it, perhaps to do with the fact that she was Donald's sister and he didn't want to let his late friend down. Or maybe it was that she was Donald's *wee* sister, which made her seem more vulnerable.

(Donald's trendy wee sister whom he had always secretly fancied.)

'Is this . . . normal for you?' she asked. 'I mean . . .' She held up her hands, like she couldn't begin to describe what had just happened.

'Well, some days I'm mostly on the phone. But it would be true to say that my idea of journalism can be a little idiosyncratic. I don't crib from press releases. Things might have gone a lot smoother with my wife if I had.'

(Ex-wife.)

Mairi looked puzzled.

'It's not like you're the one who brought this down on us, Jack. It was me who dragged *you* into this.'

'Yeah, but Sarah might say that if you'd dragged someone *else* into it the situation might not have escalated quite so drastically. She claims I've got a habit of finding dangerous situations and effortlessly making them worse.'

'That doesn't sound fair to me.'

'Well, you definitely can't say I don't know how to show a girl a good time. We had drinks, went out to dinner, took in some museums, saw a gig, met some interesting new people. To be honest, I don't know how I'm going to top it on the second date.'

Mairi laughed, and he felt relieved to see her smile. But then she looked rather serious again.

'Is that what this was? A date?'

And suddenly there was one last danger to negotiate tonight.

Parlabane took a moment to choose his response.

'This was work,' he replied.

Mairi let out a tiny laugh, as if to say 'good answer', but it was clear that a good answer in this instance wasn't the same as the right answer, or even the wrong one. It was a way of avoiding the question.

Before she could point this out, he posed her a more pertinent one.

'While you were in the car, did you notice anything or overhear anything that might give us a clue?'

'Afraid not. It was all in German. Actually, that's wrong: I don't know what language it was in. Something Slavic, maybe, or Russian. I'm pretty sure I heard the name Boris.'

'That's what he told me his name was, but I suspect it's a pseudonym. Did he say *anything* in English? He must have asked you some questions.'

Mairi shook her head.

'All the time I was expecting him to, and I was terrified about not being able to answer, or being able to answer but not wanting to tell him the truth. But he didn't ask me a thing. Just prodded away at his iPad. I'd have thought he would at least ask who I was or what I wanted, but it was like I didn't exist: I was leverage and nothing more.'

'An iPad,' Parlabane mused. 'Did you get a swatch at the screen?'

'The odd glimpse, but he was in the front seat and he had it angled away most of the time. It must have had some important stuff on it, though, because he was keying in a password every time he woke it up, and it went to sleep if it was idle for about twenty seconds.'

They went to the desk to ask for their room keys, which were attached to metal lozenges the size and weight of a cosh, thus encouraging guests to comply with the hotel's request not to take them off the premises. The hotel was in a weathered townhouse, with heavy doors on every landing to keep out draughts from the stairwells, and old-school locks on the bedroom doors rather than modern card-swipes.

Parlabane missed proper locks, from a criminal connoisseur's perspective. There were easy enough ways to fool a card-reader or bypass a code, but there was something altogether more satisfying and accomplished about successfully picking the old metal tumblers.

The bloke on the desk was called Ralf according to the name badge. He went to the pigeonholes and promptly turned around, clutching a thin slip of paper. There was a message.

'Mr Parlabane?' he enquired.

Parlabane felt himself stiffen. Nobody but Mairi knew he was here.

'Yes?'

'Ah, good. My colleague said you had requested to view our CCTV files. She is gone home now, but she enquired with Florian, our head of security, and it appears he kept the tapes from the day you asked about as there was a minor incident. I can show you.'

Ralf beckoned them behind the desk, where a door led into the back office. The lobby was deserted, and Parlabane guessed the guy was only too happy to indulge them in order to break the monotony of his nightshift.

'Here,' he said, and directed them to a computer monitor.

Ralf woke up the screen with a mouse and showed them silent footage of the lobby. It was from the day that Heike disappeared, according to the date-stamp. The time was 12:41, not long after Monica said she had last spoken to Heike.

There was a male figure sitting on one of the couches where Parlabane and Mairi had just been talking. He was facing the door, his back to the camera.

'He is there a long time,' Ralf said. 'More than an hour before this.'

Heike Gunn came barrelling through the lobby, head down, purposeful and hurried in her gait. The man got up and strode out to block her path. There was no audio, but it was clear that he was laying into her: lots of finger-pointing and aggressive body language. Not a lot of 'I' statements, Parlabane reckoned.

He couldn't say Heike gave as good as she got, as it looked like one-way verbal traffic, but her demeanour suggested any time he wanted to go fuck himself would be fine by her. Eventually she did speak, at which point he *really* kicked off, prompting the security guard to hurry over and intervene. Heike let loose a parting salvo as he was physically removed from her path, and shook her head like she really didn't have time for this.

Mairi was staring at the screen with a look of intense concentration.

'Do you recognise him?' Parlabane asked hopefully.

'He's familiar. I'm just trying to place where from.'

'He is on this file also,' Ralf said. 'Florian kept all of these in case there was a complaint arising from the incident. This is from the night before.'

Mairi gaped as they watched more soundless footage featuring the same man as in the first tape. This time he was talking to Monica Halcrow. It didn't appear to be going any better for the guy, as he looked both crestfallen and pissed off by the time Monica got up and walked away.

'That's Keith,' Mairi said. 'Monica's fiancé. Ex-fiancé, I should say.'

'Ex because Heike Gunn led his betrothed astray,' Parlabane observed. 'And now it turns out he's the last person to have seen her before she disappeared.'

'I don't follow how this fits in with what happened tonight,' Mairi said. 'It seems to be getting more complicated all the time.'

'Or maybe it just got a lot simpler.'

Exposure

I remember the first time Keith saw me naked; or part of me at least. Actually it was my right breast, but there was something symbolic about it that felt more like a rite of passage than when we were both finally in the altogether.

It was at his parents' house on a Thursday morning before Christmas when we were both in sixth year. I had stayed overnight, which was often the case on weekends, but as the last day of term had been the Wednesday, it felt like a Saturday morning. The only difference was, there was nobody else around. Keith's parents were at work and his sister Ailish was staying over at a friend's place, which meant I got her bed.

He brought me a cup of tea and a slice of toast just after nine. I had blissfully slept in while people were showering, eating and getting ready for work. Keith sat on the edge of the bed and chatted as I ate. We talked about our plans for the holidays, by which we mainly meant lazing around watching DVDs and stuffing our faces.

I remember that the weather was horrible, rain pelting against the windows like it was determined to get in. It made me feel all the more cosy behind the double-glazed windows, with the central heating blasting out warmth from a radiator that Ailish always kept turned up to max.

We started kissing and I felt so comfortable as I lay there, so snug, so secure and so cherished. When Keith cupped my left breast, which was as far as we usually went, I undid some buttons on my pyjama top and pulled it away from my shoulder.

I'll never forget the look we shared: he was a bit surprised, a bit unsure if I was definitely okay with this, and, of course, more than bloody delighted. I smiled to reassure him, and his gaze fell slowly upon my breast, happy in the moment but not staring. We both giggled, then he started kissing my neck really slowly. I knew where he was going, and must admit some impatience to know what it would feel like, but I loved the fact that he took his time.

When he finally kissed my nipple, my heart was beating so hard I thought it was going to bounce his lips from my chest. It was scary in a good way.

The next day, he wrote me a letter about it, describing it from his point of view, and telling me what it had meant to him. I thought that was just the sweetest thing. His letter also said this didn't mean he was making any assumptions about what was next, and especially how soon.

What was next was not soon, but neither did it feel like there was a hurry. It was a gradual process, and every step felt like a gift, though not from me to him. It felt like something both given and received by each of us. And like that first morning, it always felt scary in a good way. We were tapping into something sacred and ancient; something innocent too, and yet exciting for an edge we were skirting, a fear of the forbidden.

Each step brought us closer as a couple: and I don't mean through the actual removal of the next material barrier – my nightie, my bra, my pair of M&S undies – but through the bond of trust that deepened with every line we crossed.

To let someone see you naked is to give them a special privilege, like showing a secret self. So it has to be at your own deciding, and that decision must be a free one.

Why am I saying this?

Thankfully, the reason is not as obvious as it might have been.

We didn't hang around in Nice. The bus set off at nine the next morning. Heike got a lot of resentful looks as she boarded, and on another day it might have been funny to see so many people in Savage Earth Heart T-shirts giving her the stink eye.

'They stuck to their script,' she had told me the night before, just as I was about to close my eyes in search of sleep. 'The girls who got taken off the bus said they were part of the tour, hired by Bad Candy's marketing division, and of course fucking Jan had the accreditations to prove it.'

Heike had told me this only once the lights were out. When she said the next part I understood why.

'They also told the cops that I had pulled this whole stunt because I'm a dyke who was pissed off that they had all rebuffed my advances.'

I couldn't see her face but from her voice I knew she was crying.

On this final leg, there were no incidents around the French–Italian border, and we made it to our hotel in Milan around the end of lunchtime.

Having once heard some been-there-seen-it-done-it idiot colleague of Keith's slag off Milan as a grim industrial place, I was ready for somewhere that at its best would look like Birmingham on a sunny day. Instead, within half an hour of dumping my bag in my room, I was at a pavement café with Heike, Scott and Damien, sipping cappuccinos while beautiful people cruised up and down the broad boulevard on Piaggio scooters.

A group of locals came up and asked if they could have their photo taken with us. We obliged and signed autographs. They seemed so thrilled, bursting with disbelieving happiness at this chance meeting and probably posting on Facebook within minutes. It was a nice reminder of why we were in this. The sun was warm and the architecture all around me was captivating. In a few hours' time I would be playing to a sell-out crowd at Alcatraz, performing with a band that was getting more electrifying with every show. Life was looking pretty good.

Then I heard the chime of a text pinging into my phone, and a few seconds later everything was poisoned.

My phone didn't recognise who it was from, listing only a number. The text just said:

Stay out of our business and we stay out of yours.

With the sender anonymous and the message so vague, I thought it might have been sent by accident. Then I noticed there was an image attached. I tapped to download, my curiosity overcoming my caution at the possible roaming charges. It was my last act in a cosseted world where the price of an image was measured in pounds or euros.

My phone screen showed a photograph of me naked, stepping out of the shower in what I recognised as the bathroom I had shared with Heike last night.

I felt my face flush and my stomach tighten; confusion, anger, fear and disbelief threatening to overwhelm me. How was this possible?

Even as I looked in horror at the image I heard a chime from another of the three phones on the table. I watched as, almost in slow motion, Heike reached for it.

I wanted to stop her, wanted to tell her not to look, but I felt paralysed. It was like I was separated from the scene behind thick glass. Even if I could find my voice, I couldn't warn her without letting the others know why.

I watched the same horror wash over her, the same shock. She glanced towards me and noticed I was mirroring her expression and her pose, my phone suddenly held like it had become a grenade. A whole conversation took place in one wordless moment between us. We were both under siege but we had to pretend all was normal until we could get away from Scott and Damien.

Somehow I forced down the rest of my coffee, but it tasted of nothing. I felt like the sun had dimmed, the colours faded, the buildings closed in.

We ditched the guys and climbed into a cab, saying we were going to look at shoes, then as soon as they were out of sight, told the driver to take us to the venue.

'That Dutch bastard was behind this,' Heike hissed, keeping her voice low despite the driver appearing to speak no English. 'He booked us into the same room and we only got one keycard. He must have used the other to get in and plant a miniature camera. Christ, I feel like I might throw up.'

So did I, but weirdly the cab ride helped settle my stomach. As the driver sped along inches behind other cars, through gaps in the traffic, the tension stopped the churning sensation threatening to make me puke.

We found Jan outside, overseeing the unloading of our gear from the truck. He gave us a relaxed smile and assured us it was going to be a great show tonight, as this was a fantastic venue. His complete lack of interest in why we had pitched up at two in the afternoon wasn't quite a signed confession, but it definitely didn't stand him in good stead when he claimed afterwards to know nothing about the naked photos.

To be honest, his denials were so half-hearted it was clear he was just observing formalities by not cutting straight to the chase. He was fed up carrying out a phoney war.

'So now you get why I tried to keep you out of this?' he asked. 'These are not people you can cross.'

'Keep us out of it? You put a fucking camera in our bathroom.'

'No, I didn't. Absolutely not.'

'You had a keycard. You only gave us one.'

He had the decency to look conflicted at least, but only, it transpired, because he was protecting someone else.

'I was told to get the keycard. I didn't know what they were going to do.'

'Who did you give it to?' Heike demanded.

'One of the girls,' he admitted tiredly.

'What, and she happened to have a miniature spy camera on her that she could hide in our bathroom?' I asked.

'What can I say? She's a hooker. This isn't James Bond shit any more. These things are the size of a lipstick, plug into a USB port. For all I know, all these girls could be carrying them: record every trick in case the footage is useful.'

'Utter bitch. I was trying to help them. Which one was it?'

'I won't say. It's not her fault. She was just doing what she was told, same as me. You brought this on yourself, Heike. You made everybody nervous. Somebody must have reported back what you pulled on the bus yesterday.'

'Reported back to who? Why were you holding their passports? Why did they lie to the cops?'

'Because they're fucking *scared*,' Jan replied, exasperated. 'Okay? They do as they're told. This is not about me.'

'What, you're not seeing a slice of the action?' Heike asked.

'Yes, of course. I get paid. Everybody gets paid. Margins are tight on a tour. They ask me to do them a favour, they make it worth my while to say yes. But mainly I say yes because I don't want to find out what happens if I say no.'

'And that includes saying yes when they tell you to steal a key to our *bedroom*? They filmed us naked, Jan. They could release these images on the web and they'd be everywhere in no time, irretrievable, out there for ever.'

He hung his head, finding it difficult to look long at either of us.

'Those pictures are just a warning, okay?' he said, digging deep to find an even tone. 'They don't want to use them. They just want you to stay out of their shit. And believe me, there's plenty more they can do. These people could end this whole tour right now. They have connections. Suddenly every venue has a power cut, or plumbing problems. You want things to run smooth? Stay out of their shit.'

'And how deep is their shit, Jan? Prostitution? Human traffic? White slavery?'

Jan stood up straight at last, meeting Heike's eye. I got the feeling he'd weathered the worst of it and knew she was done.

'You don't like that these girls are hookers?' he shrugged. 'That's for you to decide. But in this business, we all got to swallow some shit to keep the show on the road, okay? It's up to you, Heike. You want to be a martyr, nobody's stopping you. You want to be a rock star, then you don't get to be a fucking saint too. It's your choice.'

Temptations

Parlabane stood outside Mairi's room, hoping the coffee and pastries he'd brought would make up for waking her. She hadn't shown up at the time they'd agreed and wasn't answering her mobile, so he'd figured she was still out cold, and unlikely to rally without caffeine.

She answered the door in a fluffy white dressing gown, towelling her damp hair with her right hand as he proffered his humble offering.

'Thought you might need breakfast.'

Parlabane followed her into the room. It smelled of shampoo, moisturiser and body-spray. He wanted to drink it in: his nose hadn't been assailed by such feminine scents in a long time. He took a seat on a low couch beneath the window, placing the bag down on a glass table and opening it to reveal the goodies inside.

Mairi took a sip from the polystyrene cup.

'Not your preferred Starbucks, I'm afraid. Had to settle for a family-run and tax-paying German bakery down the street.'

'You're a life-saver,' she said, then seemed to catch herself. 'Kind of need to recalibrate my scale on that, I guess.'

'I've been thinking about the Brauereihallen,' Parlabane told her. 'That roadie, Karl: I reckon he went off and called Boris the moment we started showing people the photo. He wanted my phone. The rendezvous at Museumsinsel was Plan B, after he had told Boris I wouldn't hand it over.'

'Why would he want your phone?'

'This all kicked off after I took his photo on Alexanderplatz. I snapped him on the Islay ferry, and I might not have been as surreptitious about it as I previously assumed.'

'Why would having proof that he'd been to Islay be something he'd go to extreme lengths to destroy?'

'I don't know. What's even more confusing is that when we spoke on the phone last night I asked why he was looking for Heike. He said, "I'm not." At the time I assumed he was stone-walling me, but what if he was telling the truth, in his own twisted way?'

'Like how?'

Mairi blanched as she answered her own question.

'He isn't looking for her because he knows where she is.'

Parlabane nodded, opting not to mention the further possibility that he wasn't looking for her because he knew she was dead.

'Karl lied to us last night, but he wasn't the only one. There was another member of the road crew who recognised the photo, I'm sure, and neither he nor Karl were on Altar State's core crew.'

'They work for Bad Candy,' Mairi stated, reaching for another pastry.

Her dressing gown flapped open slightly, and in that fraction of a second Parlabane was waylaid by a moment of déjà vu. He recalled another morning long ago, in the flat in Maybury Square, Sarah in a dressing gown that had similarly billowed as she leaned down into a low cupboard. He had been trying to be professional and detached up until that point, trying to keep his mind away from how attractive he found Sarah, and that moment had breached the dam and let it all flood in.

This time he just about managed to avert his gaze. However, the instincts it stirred sparked a further connection.

'Bad Candy crews have a rep for moving drugs,' he said. 'They run their own trade across the whole tour network. But remember what Damien told us about the merch girls: what if Bad Candy's roadies aren't just supplying bad candy these days?'

As though responding to the sleaze factor that had been intro-duced, Mairi pulled the cord tighter on her gown.

'Stan,' she said. 'Altar State's sound engineer: he told us he had seen Boris with groups of girls in hotels, like he was a porn baron.'

'Yeah,' Parlabane remembered. 'And he said this was in Milan and either Cologne or Frankfurt. Those are all big expo towns, and that's the bread and butter for Bad Candy these days. I'm betting Boris has a close connection to a certain concert and exhibition logistics firm.'

Mairi hurried across to the dressing table and lifted her iPad, quickly keying something into the touchscreen. She nodded approvingly at what it displayed.

'Bad Candy have an office in Berlin,' she told him. 'Rosenthaler Strasse.'

'Where's that?'

Mairi worked the screen again, calling up a map.

'Right here,' she pointed. 'Five minutes' walk from Alexanderplatz.'

'It's a short jaunt from Rosa-Luxemburg-Platz too,' Parlabane observed.

'Why, what's there?'

'It was Boris's first choice for last night's prisoner exchange.'

He got to his feet.

'Okay, I'm going to leave you to get ready. Take your time: I need to do a bit of an inventory, work out what tools I'm going to need.'

'Tools? For what?'

'Journalism,' he replied, feeling a glint forming in his eye for the first time in months. 'Of the kind that we as a fair-minded and respectable nation no longer consider acceptable.'

Defiance

I was brooding upstairs in my room after the soundcheck when I heard a knock at my door. I had been sitting there on the edge of the bed for I don't know how long. I couldn't remember feeling more in need of a shower, but I was afraid to have one.

I had looked up surveillance hardware on the internet, which was probably a mistake. It turned out you could get pinhole cameras everywhere, and they were tiny, often disguised and worryingly cheap.

I removed every loose object from the bathroom but it still had so many suspicious possibilities. What was on the other side of that mirror? Were those screws really screws? Was every hole in that fixed showerhead there to spray water?

I checked the spyhole – an aperture ten times the size of the cameras available for twenty quid on the web – and was relieved to see that it was Heike who was waiting in the corridor.

'I just came to say how sorry I am for dragging you into all this,' she said, stepping into my room. 'I was so caught up in what had happened that I forgot there was collateral damage. I brought this down on both of us, and I apologise.'

'You've nothing to apologise for. Let's not forget who the bastards are here. Besides, it can't be collateral damage if I'm a willing participant.'

She liked that, though it sounded braver and a lot more defiant than I actually felt.

'Still, it was my crusade, and I feel terrible about what's happened to you. I just want you to know it's finished now.'

I was relieved to hear this. One of my worst fears as I sat there mulling it over was that Heike would do something self-destructive in her rage. I had no doubt at all regarding Jan's claims that these were dangerous people.

She looked tired and beaten. I wouldn't exaggerate and say that we had aged over the past few hours, but we did both look like we'd been up all night.

Heike sat on a swivel chair in the corner, clasping her arms around her shins and rocking slightly. She could only have looked more defensive if she'd tucked her head between her knees and thrown a blanket over herself.

'It happened to both of us,' I reminded her. 'You were trying to help those girls. Don't apologise for that.'

Heike looked at the carpet, a scared and pale version of herself.

'Yeah, well, that's just it, isn't it? I think the real reason I'm feeling guilty is that Jan named my price. I hate him for that, but I hate myself more for the choice he knew I'd make.'

I thought about Heike's words while I occupied myself with ironing my trousers and top for the show, forty-eight hours stuffed into my luggage not having done them any favours. I felt guilty about the relief I had experienced, but this quickly turned to anger. We had nothing to feel guilty about.

Heike was wrong. Jan hadn't given her a choice: he just dressed it up to look like one. These bastards were holding all the cards. If she dug her heels in, she could ruin her own career, not to mention both our reputations, and still not make a dent in whatever was going on here.

Unlike Heike, I wasn't going to hate myself over what had happened to us. I didn't have any going spare, as all the hate I had was going to those who deserved it.

I hated the way they had used our bodies against us. I hated that they'd made me paranoid about undressing in my own bathroom. I hated that they had caused me to feel disgust at my own body, and I really fucking hated that they had made me want to go out on stage tonight in a baggy jumper and possibly a duffel coat.

I had to put the iron down before I threw it through the window. My anger was so great I couldn't articulate it beyond the two words pounding like a rhythm in my head, repeating themselves over and over.

Fuck them. Fuck them. Fuck them.

Whoever they were, fuck them.

I went into the bathroom, turned on the shower and stripped off, but not before looking out something totally different to wear tonight.

I turned up at the venue in my usual attire, the dress Heike bought me in London carefully tucked into my bag. I got changed at the last minute, hanging back out of her sight as we waited to go on-stage.

Heike strode out to the mic and began strumming the intro to the opener, 'Western Pagodas', her gaze lost in the black. She was more nervous than usual, sure of nothing right then, her thoughts no doubt as dark and shapeless as the crowd. I came in on the second phrase, stepping further downstage than I normally did at that point, catching the edge of her vision.

She missed an up-strum in her surprise when she saw me, then gave me the best grin. There was gratitude in her smile, an acknowledgement of our solidarity. In between phrases, she turned to me and mouthed 'Wow'. New energy lifted both of us as the rest of the band took up the song. It was going to be a great show despite everything we had been through today: we had just determined that, without saying a word.

I wasn't wearing the dress just to please Heike, and I think she understood as much. I was wearing it for both us, but I was wearing it for me first and foremost. I was wearing it because I knew I was going to feel naked out there tonight anyway. I was wearing it because there were men who wanted me to be scared and ashamed.

I was wearing it because fuck them.

Afterwards, I knew I should have been physically and emotionally exhausted, but when Heike said 'Let's go dancing,' I found I'd got wings from somewhere. The last thing I wanted was to lie in my hotel room and go to sleep.

We didn't dance, though. We were happy to just sit there together, listening to the music, sipping our beers, watching the beautiful strangers all around us, holding hands out of sight beneath the table.

I couldn't say whether Heike reached to mine or I to hers; maybe they just kind of brushed halfway, hanging accidentally-deliberately in the space between us. What's for sure is that once we touched we stayed in contact, our fingers slowly intertwining as though we were both afraid the other might recoil.

Hacking Inquiry

They checked into a hotel almost directly across from the building where Bad Candy had their Berlin bureau on the second floor. Mairi had not been enamoured of this suggestion.

'He's going to have people out looking for us,' she protested, 'and you want to move into a place on his doorstep?'

'The fact that he's going to be intently looking out for us is also the reason he won't notice that we're actually looking at him. Besides, we can't stay where we are.'

'Why not?'

'Like you said, they're going to be looking for us, and I think they might have inside information. Ask yourself: was it a coincidence that Boris just happened to be behind me on the road to Kennacraig? It's possible, but if somebody on a Bad Candy crew tipped him off after we were asking questions at the Altar State gig, then the same could have happened when I went to the Manchester Apollo. I went there because Prelude to the Slaughter had largely the same crew as the Savage tour – including the tour manager.'

'Jan,' she said, her tone indicating that it wouldn't tremble the foundations of her beliefs if Parlabane suggested there was something iffy about the guy.

'He lied to me,' Parlabane said. 'Made out he knew nothing about the incident on the bus. He was the one holding the fucking passports.'

'He's also the one who made the "judgement call" to cancel the show,' Mairi reminded him. 'I reckon he knew for sure that Heike wasn't coming.'

'If they're out looking for us and they know why we're here, it's not a leap to think that the first hotel they'll try is the one Savage Earth Heart were booked into when Heike disappeared.'

Mairi needed less than a second to take in the implications. 'I'll start packing.'

'Not quite yet,' he had told her, before producing some of the purchases he'd made while she was getting dressed.

They spent an hour dyeing Parlabane's hair black, unrecognisable from the dirty-blond that was these days mixed with increasingly liberal sprinklings of grey. Not wishing to impose similar levels of sacrifice upon Mairi, he had bought her a wig.

'I look like Julia Roberts early on in *Pretty Woman*,' she observed, tucking stray strands of her own black hair beneath the peroxide bob he'd got on Kurfürstendamm.

'I can't think of any circumstances in which that could be a bad thing.'

'How about circumstances in which I'm booting you in the nadgers for saying I look good as a whore?'

The new hotel might be across the road from Bad Candy's offices, but it was sufficiently further down the street that neither of their rooms afforded a direct line of sight. Mairi's window did have a good view of the building's main entrance, so she was given the more straightforward task of watching that. Two sharp eyes and her iPhone's camera were going to be sufficient. Parlabane's posting was more problematic.

Mairi had seemed positively disturbed by some of the equipment he had brought along, laying it out on her bed as he briefed her on his planned surveillance.

'It looks more like you're planning to break into somewhere than photograph it.'

'Don't be daft,' he told her, eliciting a look of relief. '*That* stuff's still in my room.'

Parlabane had found the service door to the hotel's roof via a narrow stairwell adjacent to the lifts on the top floor. The door was locked but happily not alarmed. It was a pop-lock, a flimsy affair intended to prevent unauthorised access by curious or dis-oriented hotel guests. It took longer to get the picks in and out of his carry-case than it did to open the thing.

From there he had walked on soft feet to the adjoining building, where he had to make a short climb as it was four or five feet taller than its neighbour. On the plus side, the greater angle of elevation meant that he was extremely unlikely to be spotted by anyone who happened to be looking out of the window over at Bad Candy.

He was on the roof of an office building on Rosenthaler Strasse, his Nikon SLR perched on a Gorillapod that was gripping a ventilation pipe like some kind of futuristic parasite.

He had patiently panned back and forth for the first half hour, looking for but not finding that jowly face. Parlabane familiarised himself with what he could see of the layout, determining where the bureau's windows began and ended. Tour posters decorating the walls verified that he was at least looking at the right place, but whether Boris actually worked there was a question that a whole day's surveillance may not answer. The guy might merely have contacts here, such as the bloke who'd been with him on Alexanderplatz, who, come to think of it, Parlabane hadn't seen since. Or Boris could be based here, but spend most of his time out of the office, not to mention out of the city.

Then Mairi made an excited announcement through the Bluetooth earpiece he was wearing. They had an open channel of peer-to-peer communication as his phone was still connected to the hotel's Wi-Fi network.

Their target had just walked down the street and in through the front door.

Parlabane picked him up a couple of minutes later, striding to his seat. He had a room to himself, so he was a few rungs up the food chain from the folk two windows along, who appeared to spend all their time chained to their desks and talking on the phone. Boris made and took a lot of calls too, but mostly on his mobile rather than the landline. He tapped away at the keyboard in front of his monitor, but was just as busy on the iPad. This he kept in a leather satchel, an over-the-shoulder number like Mairi had suggested Parlabane consider in warmer weather.

He had been there for two hours, and was grateful that they were doing this in June rather than February. The time passed quicker than most people would imagine. He entered an almost meditative state, calmly centred upon his subject, or upon the empty room his subject vacated whenever he got up from his desk.

Parlabane corrected the focus by the tiniest of increments, each micro-twist of the lens having an exaggerated effect when the zoom was at this magnitude. He could see Boris sitting at his desk, a spreadsheet open on his monitor. It wasn't his PC Parlabane was interested in, however.

He snapped away intently every time the iPad bobbed into view. There was no way he'd get the code at that distance – not from fingers on a touchscreen with the digits rendered as black circles – but he needed to be sure of the background wallpaper, lock screen and, of course, which build Boris was using.

Mairi's voice sounded in his ear again.

'He's on the move.'

Parlabane watched him through a pair of compact field glasses, safe to risk while the sun was behind him and there was no danger of a give-away twinkle alerting Boris to the voyeur above. He reappeared after a few minutes, clutching a paper bag and a large coffee.

'Shit.'

'What?' Mairi asked.

'Well, there's good news and bad news. The good news is that there's got to be some highly sensitive stuff on Boris's iPad. He's got a PC on his desk, so I'm guessing that's for official Bad Candy business, while the Apple slab is for Boris's business.'

'And what's the bad news?'

'He doesn't let it out of his sight: didn't even leave it on his desk to go down the street for a snack.'

'Not to mention that it password-locks after about twenty seconds,' Mairi added. 'Guess we can forget about finding out what's on it, then.'

'Oh, I didn't say *that* . . .'

Postcards from Another Life

We worked together for hours as the bus wound its way to Zagreb, the time disappearing once again as our attention stayed so intently focused. When we stopped at a services area near Trieste, it came as a jolt, as though we could have been anywhere and were surprised to discover ourselves on this vehicle and not in a studio or rehearsal space. It was the same song as had been taking shape since Barcelona, and now bore the title I had suggested in that café by the museum: 'Gods and Mortals'. Heike's lyrics were still only fragments, gradually coming together as the music took shape. Mostly she would hum the vocal part, getting a feel for the metre.

I played in two contrasting styles: smooth and low, under the assured voice of the god; then high and staccato to suggest the nervous, trembling human. What's weird is that I don't remember consciously deciding to do this. It just evolved out of the process, like there were things I instinctively understood about what Heike wanted, ways I could only play because I was playing with her.

We're catching lightning in a bottle, I thought. Then I remembered where I had heard the phrase.

'She'll make you feel you're harnessing power you never knew you had, that you can be so much more than you thought. But in the end she'll take as much as she gives, and then she'll take some more.'

I wondered, Should I get it out there, in the open? Should I ask Heike, Are we writing this song together?

But I couldn't. It felt like it would corrupt the chemistry that was making this happen. If she said yes, it might seem like I was being protective or needy, or worse, insulting her by implying I thought she was as dishonest as Maxi's lawsuit said she was. But most of all, I was afraid of what would change if she told me no.

That night I made sure to watch Angus do his opening set.

The venue was a club called Mocvara, a claustrophobic little joint compared to some of our grander recent gigs, and with a punkier crowd than we normally attracted. Heike had got the measure of the place during the soundcheck and swapped in a couple of more upbeat numbers to replace the mellow and stripped-down 'Square of Captured Light' and 'It Meant Nothing'. We were still doing 'Dark Station', but she wanted to build up more momentum before we got there.

Under the circumstances, I thought Angus had a thankless task going out there alone, while the place was just beginning to fill and the audience were more interested in getting a few rounds in. But he looked like he didn't care whether there was even one person listening. He was playing for himself.

To be honest, I was paying closer attention than before because I was listening out for similarities between his songs and Heike's. I couldn't help myself, even though I knew it was like staring at clouds: soon enough you start to recognise shapes as your mind finds patterns. Every so often I'd hear a chord change or phrasing that seemed familiar, but if I'd been listening for similarities with any other singer I'm sure I'd have heard them there too. Anyway, I had no idea when these songs were even written.

Then Angus announced a song as one he and Heike had come up with together when they were both fifteen, and its chord structure was definitely a pre-echo of 'Western Pagodas'. It was like an early sketch for a great painting: one was a much more accomplished piece, but the other did form a vital stage in its creation.

To me, the big difference was that Angus might have helped draw the sketch, but he could never have painted the picture.

Between the soundcheck and the show itself, Heike changed her hair. She turned up with her head shaved to maybe a number three, and dyed back to her cream-blonde. It looked like a DIY job, which I supposed made it all the more punkish. It seemed a radical step for the sake of one gig, so I guessed there was more to it than that. The change reminded me that I never did find out what her

straggly pink look had meant, and I wondered if this return symbol-
ised something as well.

Two days later, I stumbled upon the answer to both.

We were in Berlin, but not for an official part of the tour. We
were shooting a video for 'Zoo Child' at a venue called the
Brauereihallen. Heike had raved about playing there on previous
tours, but it was unfortunately too small to cope with the demand
this time. We were slated to play the much larger Palast instead
at the end of the tour, with both nights long since sold out. The
Brauereihallen was, however, the perfect size for shooting a fake
live performance in front of a packed crowd, whose enthusiasm
never wilted despite hearing 'Zoo Child' about twenty-five times
straight. As a thank-you to the volunteers, and as part of a deal
with the venue, we were going to play a free and unadvertised set
later on.

Mairi, our manager, had flown in to make sure everything was
all right with the shoot. In her world, making sure a video got
safely into the can was obviously more worthy of her hands-on
attention than the actual welfare of band personnel on tour. She
would only be here for a night, then she was back off to London.
Heike was always going on about what a mover and shaker Mairi
was. All I saw was a middle-aged woman dressing ten years too
young who was obsessed with the bottom line.

The director needed the full band for most of the shoot, then
Heike stayed on alone for close-ups.

It was obvious she was going to be there a while, and though
I'd have liked to stay and keep her company, Mairi was hanging
around, talking business and generally acting territorial.

I went out for a walk along Friedrichstrasse instead. I spotted
a bookshop and went inside in search of postcards. It was a habit
I had got into after passing through so many exotic cities with
little chance to take them in. Sometimes I would send them to
my mum or to Keith, but I always kept at least one for myself.
The part of me that worried 'this may never happen again' wanted
to be able to thumb through these yellowed and faded treasures
when I was ninety. Sometimes I found them in cafés or newsagents,

but bookshops were the best place if you wanted something more than the iconic or outright clichéd.

I found the rack in a quiet corner near the guidebooks, my attention immediately drawn to a selection of old-fashioned cinema lobby cards and miniature movie posters. I thumbed through postcards of German-language ads for familiar cult films – *Pulp Fiction*, *Eraserhead*, *Betty Blue*, *The City of Lost Children* – then I gasped. I was staring at an image of a vibrant young girl posed in the street, her hair dyed a pinky-red. It was a movie still, not a poster: there was no text on the front, so you were supposed to recognise what it was, like the shot of Uma Thurman as Mia Wallace right next to it.

I flipped it over and read the name: *Christiane F.* I hadn't heard of it.

I took the card and showed it to the woman at the till, asking if she knew this movie. Maybe she didn't speak much English, as she came out from the counter and led me to the back of the shop and a tall cabinet of DVDs. She ran a finger across the spines two shelves from the top and then handed me a case. The cover showed the same girl, but this image wasn't one for decorating your bedroom. She sat slumped against what looked like a toilet wall, her pink hair draped either side of the home-made tourniquet she was using to shoot up.

The title read *Christiane F: Wir Kinder vom Bahnhof Zoo.*

'You can select English subtitles,' the woman said, proving she did speak English after all.

'Can you tell me what this means?' I asked, pointing to the title.

'It means "We Children of Zoo Station". You don't know this movie?'

Zoo Child. How had I missed this? I started running the lyrics through my head, hearing them anew. It was a song about junkies, and I had never thought it was any more significant than that.

'No. I have a friend who is . . . interested in it.'

'It was a big deal when I was growing up: we all watched it a dozen times on videocassette. It was based on a book by some journalists published in the late seventies, a true story. This girl, Christiane, became a heroin addict when she was just thirteen.'

I could think of only one reason why Heike had adopted this look. I recalled the Polaroid of her mother, looking so young; maybe even younger than I had supposed.

'Thirteen. Jesus.'

'It's more shocking than that: she became a prostitute to pay for her habit. Nor was she unique. She had friends younger than her who were turning tricks, and friends younger than her who died. Bahnhof Zoo was the heart of a big heroin scene, big prostitution scene too. In the old days it was the main station, before they built their big new Hauptbahnhof.'

I realised how stupid I'd been not to see it sooner.

Now I understood why Heike had been on her crusade. I knew why she had shaved her hair back and dyed it blonde again too. To her mind, Jan had offered her a choice, and she had chosen rock star. She could no longer make her tribute to Christiane F, someone whom she probably knew more about than her real mother.

Because of her accent, I thought the woman had said 'old days'. She'd said 'Wall days'.

Zoo Station.

Dark Station.

Berlin.

Crack Paraphernalia

'Let me just run through my script again,' Mairi said as they neared the pharmacy.

'You'll be fine,' Parlabane assured her. 'It'll sound more natural if you're not word-perfect.'

'Yeah, but I'm scared I'll forget the major details. My father's feeling ill back at our hotel and he's forgotten his heart medicine – was that it?'

'Precisely. And the stuff he normally takes is . . .?'

'Fruzamode.'

'Close enough. Furosemide. They'll know what you're talking about.'

'But will they give me it over the counter?'

'They will if you're convincingly gormless, and I have to say I've every faith in you on that score.'

'Why ever would somebody try to push you under a train, Jack?'

His mobile rang, cutting off Mairi's chance for procrastination. He beckoned her to head off inside, indicating that he had to take this call, which was no lie.

'I need it in Mac iOS 7,' Parlabane told the caller.

'It shouldn't take too long to port,' came the reply, relayed in a modified female sat-nav voice. It would be quite an understatement to observe that the speaker was protective of his identity. 'There's already an iOS 5 version for the first-gen iPad.'

'Yeah, but the crucial part is it has to be in German.'

'I know someone who can translate.'

'No, it can't be a translation: it has to be the precise German wording on the interface.'

'Understood. When do you want it? At a pinch I could probably manage Friday, long as nothing comes up the rest of this week.'

'I need it by tomorrow lunchtime.'

'You never disappoint, Jack.'

'Just make sure you don't either.'

He disconnected the call and glanced through the window. The pharmacist was holding out a small white cardboard box and Mairi was nodding with anxious gratitude.

It was on.

They stayed in that night, cautiously opting to remain inconspicuous and to reap the benefits of an early bed after the previous evening's trials and exertions. They dined together in the hotel's small and cosy restaurant, Mairi remaining wigged up as a precaution, the large windows affording passers-by a clear view of the diners from the street. She insisted Parlabane reciprocate by wearing the glasses he had bought for further obscuring his face the next day.

'In a certain light you look like Colin Firth,' she told him. 'That being the light you get in the abyssal plains under the ocean, where the angler fish hang out.'

'Thanks. Now that we're into the cloak-and-dagger stuff, I'm thinking your blonde-wig look is more Kate Mara in *Shooter*.'

'Kate O'Mara? I hope this was an eighties crush you're harking back to, and you don't mean I look like her now. She's dead.'

'Wrong one. No O. Just Mara. And let's not talk about eighties crushes.'

Shit. That had slipped out, like an in-joke he had momentarily forgotten she wasn't party to.

'Why not?' she asked, swooping on it with a falcon's speed and alacrity.

'If I told you, we'd be talking about it.'

He managed to conceal the specific nature of his embarrassment, selling her the notion that this was merely a general area of cringe.

'Okay,' she conceded. 'So let's talk about cloak and dagger. This Westercruik business you're being investigated for. Let me get this straight: there's this laptop that belonged to Sir Crusty Tofftrouser.'

'Sir Anthony Mead.'

'Right. And you, shall we say, acquired it by undisclosed means.'

'I didn't say I stole it.'

'Okay, you didn't steal it.'

'I didn't say I didn't steal it.'

'Jesus,' she laughed, her spoon splashing down into her soup. 'Regardless, however you came by it, it had top-secret MoD stuff on it, right?'

'I thought it did, anyway.'

'Like what?'

'Evidence of a false-flag conspiracy, though that's putting it rather broadly. It doesn't matter, because that's not what was on there. It was a trap. The conspiracy thing was just the bait.'

'But presumably the laptop was password-protected? Military-level encryption.'

'Of course. Yes. If something's too easy to access, it's not convincing enough to make good bait.'

'So you broke the encryption? You can *do* that?'

'No. But the software encryption level doesn't matter because it still comes down to the meatware: ultimately any security measure is hostage to the intelligence and integrity of the human being setting a password. In the UK, that frequently means over-privileged and extremely over-promoted Etonian fuckwits like Sir Anthony Mead.'

'What, was his password his mother's maiden name or something? Is that why he's under investigation? Oh no, that's right: he had an affair. Did he tell it to his mistress? I read that she was being investigated as well.'

Parlabane shook his head.

'Westercruik is a hydra, with all of its heads looking in different places. They're trying to find out who's a leak and who's just a liability. I was suckered in and used like a plaque-disclosing tablet to show up what's rotten. They know what I did, but they're still lost as to how.'

He swallowed, finishing off a scallop.

'People always concentrate on the wrong areas when they're trying to work out how a trick is done. They've got theories that I broke into Mead's home, or that I broke into his mistress's place, that I used blackmail, that I hacked their mobiles, that I placed hidden recording devices. It's none of the above.'

'And would I be right in assuming you're not going to tell *me* how you did it, sitting here over dinner.'

Parlabane nodded.

'You would indeed. I'm going to tell you tomorrow, when we crack Boris's iPad using the same method.'

She Sells Sanctuary

There was a ghost at the feast that evening: Maxi showed up in the hotel bar as Heike and Mairi returned from the shoot. It was all the more unsettling him being here in Berlin, where Heike must have felt she'd left him far behind.

'The curse of fucking easyJet,' she muttered to me.

But she was wrong. This time, instead of a writ, he claimed to be bearing gifts, though my old Latin teacher could tell you that wasn't a guarantee of good intentions. Maxi was here, he said, because he was playing in Muse's expanded tour line-up and they were at the Arena Berlin tonight. As we were in town as well we were all invited to an after-show party they were throwing.

God, don't ever make an enemy of this guy, I thought, aware of the sleekit way he had just undermined Heike. Not only had he set her off balance by pitching up before the show, but he had blown a dog-whistle to call everyone away from any plans she might have had for later. And to hurt her even more, he had subtly underlined the fact that hers wasn't the biggest band in town that night. (If you wanted to give the knife a twist, we were not even the biggest *British* band.)

A selfish part of me was happy, though. I knew Heike would retreat away from him, and I was the natural sanctuary. Everyone else would go to the party, and I would get her to myself.

I wore the dress again. I had gone back to being comfortably covered in Zagreb, but the Brauereihallen, with its mix of the industrial and the classical, had a kind of steampunk elegance that complemented my costume, so I wore it for the video. Heike hadn't asked me to: it just seemed right. I felt I was playing a part on stage, same as I'd done during the *Tatler* photoshoot. Later on, though, during the free show, I was wearing it for her.

When we played 'Smuggler's Soul' Heike and I threw ourselves into our dance with abandon, a true connection isolating us from everyone else on stage, our alliance celebrating its own survival.

As I had predicted, she said she didn't fancy the Muse after-show. Heike asked me quietly if I'd like to come with her to a place she knew, saying she'd understand if I wanted to go with Mairi and the guys.

'I'm sure it'll be a great party,' she said.

'So am I,' I replied. 'And the best thing about it is that we'll know where everyone else will be: and where they *won't*.'

She smiled almost shyly, understanding what I was hinting at.

'Oh, that wasn't going to be a problem tonight,' she said, though I didn't follow why.

We took a cab to a place called Frauen Frei, which turned out to be a bar rather than a club. It had a mellow late-night vibe, low lights and slow jazz. It looked like somewhere we could talk.

Heike went to the bar to get us some drinks, and when she put them down she found that I had placed a *Christiane F* postcard on the table.

She nodded, saying nothing, maybe not able to at that point, as her eyes were brimming. I reached out my left hand and she took it in her right, resting both in her lap.

Heike took a sip from her bottle, blinking away tears. She gave a self-mocking smile, rolling her eyes to heaven, or maybe just to her hair.

'You worked it out? When?'

'I only found this today, in a bookshop. I'd never heard of it before.'

'You're too young. So am I, really. I dyed my hair because . . . I don't know. A gesture of affinity or something. Whatever it was, it didn't feel right after Milan.'

She ran a hand over her blonde hair.

'This is just as much of a gesture of affinity. Symbolises the fact that I'm a whore too.'

I took a drink of my beer as it let me swallow back my instinctive response. Having had time to think it over, I decided to say it anyway. If I couldn't tell her what I thought, what I felt, then I was kidding myself about what was going on here.

'Bollocks. Catch on to yourself, Heike. You're living the dream.'

Her eyes opened wide in surprise, then she started laughing.

'Thanks,' she said.

'What for?'

'Bursting that bubble. Calling me on my bullshit.'

'You're welcome. It's true, though. You're a role model, a heroine. You can do a lot more good that way than, you know . . .'

I didn't need to elaborate.

'*Your* star is on the rise too,' she said with a grin. 'I looked online, and half the shots from our Milan show are of you in that dress. The *Tatler* cover will be out soon too. You're on your way to bona fide rock chick status.'

'Yeah, so treat me right or I'm going solo, bitch.'

'Hey, don't get ahead of yourself. You had any Twitter rape threats? Because believe me, you're nobody in this business unless you're getting those.'

'No, but if I wanted to boost my profile, I know some guys who could leak some nudie pictures of me.'

Even as it was passing my lips, I couldn't believe I was saying that.

Heike gasped, but it was out of delight. We both broke down in hysterics, the threat of the photos finally disempowered by my joking about them.

When we had both recovered she took a long, slow drink of her beer, looking me in the eye as she did so. She put the bottle down on the table and sat up straight, ready to make a pronouncement.

'I want to kiss you,' she said, her tone matter of fact, almost businesslike.

She held up a hand before I could say anything.

'Just to be clear, I'm not making a pass, I'm making a statement, so no need to panic. I just want you to know that it's how you make me feel. Consider it, I don't know, a compliment. A way of saying, if things were different . . . You know?'

I squeezed her hand, holding her gaze.

'I won't run away,' I said.

A moment passed in silence, her eyes slightly scared.

I leaned into her and we kissed: softly, as though there was something fragile here that we both needed to protect.

When I opened my eyes again I felt suddenly conscious of my surroundings, afraid of who might have been looking on. A scan of the bar showed only women, which was when I realised what this place was, and what Heike had meant when she said the guys weren't going to be a problem.

I shed my fears and gave in to a longer kiss, losing myself in Heike's touch, reassured there were no unwelcome eyes upon us here. She had taken us to a place where we couldn't be more private, where we couldn't be more safe.

And where, it turned out, we couldn't be more wrong.

Tablet Recipe

At around two-thirty in the afternoon, Parlabane was buzzed into the building across from the hotel, and made his way up the stairs to the Bad Candy Berlin office. He carried a cardboard eggbox-style tray bearing four coffees, a box of twelve mini-doughnuts and his very own man-bag. He was all tricked out for subterfuge.

Mairi had chosen the bag, and had picked out the rest of his outfit too. He didn't merely need different clothes from the ones Boris had previously seen him in, but an altogether different look. The alacrity with which she had seized upon this task on Kurfürstendamm suggested that she considered such a transformation to be a pressing need even without the requirement for disguise.

'There's no way he's going to recognise you now that you look like a person who's been shopping in the twenty-first century,' she told him.

He had to admit that the clothes she had chosen looked a lot better on him than his usual wardrobe, but he couldn't shake a childhood echo of being dressed by his mother for a family occasion.

He reached the half-landing just short of his destination and took a moment to get his game face on. He was on edge, but in a way he liked. A way he had missed.

'Final check before going in,' he said quietly.

'Fine this end. Are you getting me okay?'

'Loud and clear.'

Mairi's voice was a little shaky. It was a timely reminder that he had somebody riding shotgun on this venture, someone who wasn't going to be getting off on the adrenaline buzz. They said the thrill for the gambler was not what he might win, but what he might lose. Mairi's stake in this was different, and he didn't want her to be watching through her fingers.

She was positioned on the roof where he had perched yesterday, monitoring the office through his field glasses. She had eyes on Boris, and it was her task to give Parlabane a running commentary of all that was happening outside his own line of sight.

For the first time in his life he was grateful to all those twats who had Bluetooth earpieces clamped to their lugs while going about their daily business, such as queuing at the bank or pushing a trolley round Tesco. It made him look less suspicious to have one attached right then, though he had refrained from sharing his belief that the duds Mairi had chosen also lent themselves to the authenticity of his new image as the type of guy who would go around wearing such a device.

A woman met him at the front door. She was tall, smiling and smartly turned out: definitely more from the boardroom and convention centre side of Bad Candy than the box-humping and unblocking a tour-bus toilet end of the business.

'I'm Helena Koenig, we spoke on the phone.'

Parlabane was working on the principle that Boris and his associates' clandestine enterprise was like a parasitic organism attached to Bad Candy, and that any such parasite was inextricably reliant upon its host. Mairi had called up her friend Charlene, who worked for Altar State's record label, and got her to contact Bad Candy's publicity department, telling them that there was a journalist writing a major piece on how a tour is put together, top to bottom.

Parlabane knew that Bad Candy's corporate PR people would be on the blower to the Berlin bureau immediately, instructing them to extend all courtesy regardless of the short notice, and so it had proved. Helena Koenig had phoned him within an hour of Mairi's initial call to Charlene, saying he should feel free to drop by. Parlabane said he'd be there as soon as he finished up the interview he was working on right then, which was his cover for the fact that he wasn't going to make a move until they verified that Boris had shown up for work.

Parlabane put down his cardboard tray on the reception desk so that he could shake the hand Helena was politely extending.

'Alec Forman,' he said.

'Lots of coffee,' she observed.

'Yeah, I find that if you're interrupting people's work, they're more forgiving if you at least buy them a latte. You want one?'

'No, I just had lunch, but I'll see who else might like one and I'll introduce you to everybody.'

'Actually, before you do that, do you mind giving me your Wi-Fi password?' He showed her the iPad that was sitting snugly inside his man-bag, another of this morning's Ku'damm purchases. 'I have some files I need to send.'

'Oh, no problem.'

Helena went behind the desk and handed him a laminated card with the code on it. He was keying it into the iPad when he heard Mairi's voice in his ear.

'He's on the move.'

A moment later, Boris emerged from his office off the hall.

Helena spoke to him in German as he approached. He gave Parlabane a cursory glance, not flickering a hint of recognition, which was gratifying. Less so was the fact that he grumbled something in reply to Helena and headed for the door, his iPad-bearing satchel slung over his shoulder.

Shit.

At least she hadn't offered him a coffee. It had been Parlabane's intention to have only one left by the time he introduced himself to Boris, one he would doctor to give a little more kick than just caffeine.

'Who was that?' Parlabane asked.

'That's Bodo Hoefner. He is in charge of logistical support. Bodo is the one who guarantees the show stays on the road by making sure our personnel always have whatever they need.'

No kidding.

'He's an ex-cop, so he's just the man to keep everybody in line,' she added with a chuckle.

Interesting.

'He has been very helpful in our expansion into eastern territories, as he has connections throughout the Balkans and Black Sea countries. He'll be able to tell you more about it himself: he's popped out for a cigarette.'

Helena introduced Parlabane to the desk jockeys, who dismayingly claimed all of the drinks and proceeded to fall upon the mini-doughnuts until the box was empty. Parlabane then sat and listened with one ear as they discussed their operations. With his other he was taking in Mairi's progress report on their target, whom it turned out had gone to the bakery for a coffee and a sandwich to enjoy with his fag.

Bugger. Talk about no battle plan surviving first contact with the enemy: ten minutes in and it was already falling apart. He still had three more mini-doughnuts secreted away in his man-bag, coated in an extra-special frosting, but Bodo was tucking into a late lunch downstairs.

'He's on his way back up,' Mairi warned. This gave Parlabane sufficient notice to wrap up his present discussion, apparently just in time for his next subject to come walking in the door.

A few minutes later (and upon Helena's insistence, no doubt enforced by authority from further up the corporate chain) Parlabane was sitting four feet from Bodo Hoefner, the man who had been hunting him for days. He felt a tingle of fear buzzing like an old fluorescent tube somewhere inside him. On a rooftop across the street Mairi was looking on in terrified silence.

Bodo hadn't seen him close up, as far as he knew, and was looking for a scruffily dressed man with blond/grey hair and no glasses. He was also, Parlabane assumed, looking for someone Scottish. Since walking into the office Parlabane had been conversing in his best generic, non-regional English tones, but the extent to which this was part of his disguise depended on how easy it was for a non-native speaker to notice the difference. Bodo had actually only heard Parlabane speak briefly on the phone two nights ago, though everything else he knew would have identified him as Scottish: the Savage Earth Heart connection, the Islay sighting and whatever that sleazeball Jan had told him.

Bodo gave no indication of recognising him. He barely looked at him, in fact, keen to discharge whatever duty he had agreed with Helena and then discharge this inconvenience from his office as soon as possible.

Parlabane had transferred the mini-doughnuts from his bag to the box and placed it on the edge of Bodo's desk. It sat with the lid hinged back towards Parlabane so that it was obvious they were being offered to his host. They twinkled invitingly, sugar mixed with the special extra frosting he had sprinkled on. The bastard proceeded to give them a damn good ignoring.

He talked about Bad Candy's logistics operations in impressive English, telling Parlabane little he couldn't have found on the company's website or a press release. Bodo knew he couldn't be unhelpful, but he also knew he ought not to be interesting or memorable: he did not want to be the story here. He prattled on, speaking without saying anything specific to himself, and all the time the only thing going through Parlabane's mind was, Just eat a fucking doughnut you monkfish-looking cunt.

Eventually it was clear that Bodo had decided time was up. He placed his hands together and asked if there was anything else, in a tone that suggested they both knew his visitor would be seriously pushing it if he said yes.

As he stood up Parlabane stole a glance at the satchel, tucked under the desk next to Bodo's right foot. It looked like it might be as close as he was going to get.

He thanked Bodo for his courtesy, their eyes meeting close up for the first time. There was a flicker there now, he was sure, and he felt the fluorescent tube start to thrum, warming up the flight reflex. The moment passed, however, and Parlabane walked out, leaving the doughnuts on the desk next to his digital voice recorder, the latter giving him a pretext to return once more before he finally left Bad Candy.

Mairi spoke as he stepped back into the corridor. Her voice was breathy and tremulous.

'I've got good news and bad news.'

'Fire away,' he replied quietly.

'The good news is he just scarfed two doughnuts in one gulp. The bad news is that he made a phone call the second you left the room.'

'Mobile or landline?'

'Mobile.'

'Shit.'

'I'm worried he made you. You should get out of there.'

'I only need a little more time. The clock is ticking on him now.'

'It might be ticking on you too.'

Helena strode along from the main office, asking if he'd got everything he needed.

'Not quite,' he answered.

Parlabane asked if he could take some pictures of the place and the staff for the article. He needed a plausible excuse to hang around, and given that these people must have witnessed a photographer at work before, they would surely understand that time had just entered a new realm of elasticity.

He was taking roughly his twenty-fifth 'pretend I'm not here' shot of everyone getting on with their work when Mairi gave him the news he'd been waiting for.

'He just shot up from his desk and sprinted for the door.'

Finally.

'Would you excuse me,' he said to Helena. 'I realise I've left my digital recorder in the other office. I'll only be a moment.'

Parlabane hurried along the corridor, the urgency of his pace hopefully conveying merely his keenness to retrieve his device. Somewhere ahead of him he heard a door bang as a body thundered through. It was the sound of Bodo being assailed by a need to urinate like he'd drunk ten pints of Pilsner and then walked past a waterfall on a cold winter's night. He'd be in there a minute at least, though Parlabane couldn't count on wash time. Bodo might not be the kind of guy who worried too much about germs.

Mairi had been less than impressed when he outlined his strategy.

'Given all the rumours and the accusations about you, I was kind of expecting that your plan for sneaking into his office and stealing his iPad would be a bit more ingenious than simply waiting for the guy to go to the toilet.'

Admittedly it didn't sound very impressive when she put it that way, but there was a little more to it than her description allowed. For one thing, he had to make sure that Bodo *went* to the toilet, and that Parlabane was free to make his move when that happened. This was not something he could leave to chance during the brief window he had: the guy could be in the office all afternoon and not hit the loo. But an even greater consideration was the possibility that Bodo was so protective of his iPad that he didn't leave it even to go for a slash, perhaps slinging his satchel over his shoulder and taking it with him every time.

Thus Parlabane had to engineer in Bodo a need to pee so sudden and severe that it would cast all other considerations aside; an urgency that could let nothing slow his path to a urinal in the brief few seconds he had left before he knew he would be pissing like a horse inside his trousers.

He had remembered Sarah telling him about an experiment she did as a medical undergraduate. Everyone in the group was given an identical white pill: one third were placebos, one third were a mild diuretic and one third were furosemide. They all had to pee into bottles, and at the end of the class they were to measure their urine output. Sarah knew very quickly that she'd been given the furosemide, as its effect on healthy kidneys was dramatic to the point of terrifying.

Once Bodo ate those doughnuts it was only a matter of time before he had to go, and with the seal broken he'd be going pretty regularly for the rest of the afternoon.

Parlabane slipped into Bodo's office and crouched behind the desk, relieved to note that the satchel was still where he'd last seen it. He slid out Bodo's iPad and removed it from its smart-case, swiftly replacing it with the iPad he'd bought that morning. He popped his prize inside the man-bag and headed for the door, pausing briefly to pick up his digital recorder and to give Mairi a big thumbs-up through the window.

'That, Miss Lafferty,' he said, 'was international-level piss-ripping.'

The tone of Mairi's response didn't suggest she was quite sharing his elation.

241

'Jack, a black Audi just pulled up in front of the building, and two of the guys from the other night are getting out of it.'

'Christ.'

His mind raced through contingencies. They wouldn't go hauling him out of the office as Bodo had an image to maintain in front of his Bad Candy colleagues, but they'd be lying in wait, perhaps in the stairwell. He should have checked the building layout. He'd have to head up to find an exit, along the roof and down through another building. He would also need to ensure they saw him when he hit the street, so that he could lead them away from this neighbourhood before doubling back.

'Okay, I'm going to have to improvise an exit strategy,' he said, as he spotted Bodo coming back around the corner from the gents' toilet.

'No, you won't,' Mairi told him. 'I made the last bit up. You were just sounding way too pleased with yourself.'

Public Interest

I was in a bit of a dream for most of the next day and night. I felt totally disconnected at times, alternating with stomach-churning confusion when I remembered what was waiting for me back in the real world where I had a fiancé.

We travelled to Salzburg and played a place called Rockhouse, which looked like a cubist sculpture on the outside, but on the inside was like a giant subway tunnel. From the stage, we could have been playing the Arches under Central Station back in Glasgow.

Throughout the journey, the soundcheck and the show, I felt strangely isolated from everyone but Heike, the closeness to her undermined by a sense of loneliness. I was caught between worrying about what might happen between us after the gig, and worrying that nothing would. I treasured every smile we shared, every glance that was meant only for me, then fretted that everyone else could read what was going on, that our seemingly subtle intimacies were obvious to anyone outside our circle of two.

I kept changing my mind as to whether I would be relieved if what happened in Berlin was never repeated, or whether I would feel I had lost something really precious.

As it turned out, we didn't get much time alone anyway, all of us gathering around one huge and groaning table of food in a busy café bar. With it getting late, Heike moved round to sit beside me and squeezed my hand under the table out of sight. It felt both exhilaratingly secret and disappointingly quick. With thumping music covering our conversation, she leaned close and spoke what were supposed to be words of reassurance, but they couldn't have been more ambiguous.

'You're worried about where this is going,' she said. 'But it doesn't have to go anywhere. There's no pressure. This is just now. It's whatever you want it to be. Don't worry about the future until you have to. As the boys are fond of saying, what happens on tour stays on tour.'

I was woken up by the phone: not my mobile, but the landline by my bed. My first instinct was that I must have overslept and Jan was putting a call through hotel reception. That, or somebody had dialled the wrong room.

I drowsily managed a 'Hello' into the handset, resting my elbow on the pillow.

An English female voice replied down the line, over the hubbub of a busy office in the background.

'Hello, Monica? Hi, this is Petra Collins at the *Daily Mail*. I was wondering if you could speak to me a little about your relationship with Heike Gunn.'

I fumbled for a light switch, the heavy curtains keeping the room in darkness.

'Ehm, I'm sorry,' I said, stifling a yawn, 'but I can't talk about the band unless it's been cleared through the record company press office.'

This wasn't actually true, but it was what Damien told me to say if I ever didn't want to answer a journalist's questions.

'Well, it's not your musical relationship with Ms Gunn that I'm interested in. I was wondering if you could tell me a little about your personal relationship with her.'

I shuffled my way into a sitting position, my shoulders against the headboard.

'It's still a matter for the press office. You need to ask for our publicist, Tanya Gallach—'

'It's just that we've got photographs of you and Heike kissing in a lesbian bar in Berlin. They're already live on our website, but I'm working on some background for tomorrow's print edition. The person who took them said you were in a clinch for quite some time – twenty minutes on and off – so I'm asking if you've any comment. Is this an affair that has blossomed on tour, or were

244

the two of you an item before? Is this why she brought you into the band?'

I felt like the walls around me were about to collapse, or that I had been suddenly cut adrift on this bed in the middle of a raging flood. I went to hang up but dropped the handset because my hands were like rubber all of a sudden. It bumped off the night-stand and dangled by the cord, spinning slowly. I could still hear the journalist's voice, tinny and distant.

'What do the other members of the group think about it? Has it caused any tensions?'

I replaced the handset at the second attempt, then scrambled across to my laptop, my heart thumping and my fingers trembling as I waited for it to boot and the browser to launch.

They're already live on our website. The most-visited newspaper website in the world.

The lead item was a piece about immigration. I scrolled down, seeing nothing, then spotted the link on the infamous 'sidebar of shame', to the right of the main story. It was just a thumbnail, but even at that size I recognised us both.

The link took me to the showbiz section, where they had posted two photos of Heike and me at our table: us sitting close together, face-to-face; then us locked in a kiss. A further link took me to eight more: two sequences shot from different angles. One had been taken through the window, using a zoom lens, and the other was from inside the bar, possibly snapped with a phone.

I sat staring with my hands on my cheeks, physically shuddering, my breathing becoming deeper until I was starting to hyper-ventilate.

A pitiless voice asked me how I couldn't have seen this coming.

I had somehow convinced myself we were in a world of our own. Our tour was the land of do-as-you-please, but now I could see I had grown donkey ears. Yesterday my biggest concern had been that someone in the band would pick up on our secret, but I hadn't worried about the outside world, other than what this meant when the tour was over and I had to go back to reality.

I thought we were invisible, far from home: out of sight, out of mind. What happens on tour stays on tour.

Oh God.

The old saying about tomorrow's chip wrappers didn't work any more. Now that these pictures were out there, they were out there for ever.

My mum was going to see these. *Keith* was going to see these. This realisation plunged me to a new level of despair.

Keith. My fiancé. I thought of how happy he sounded, telling me about his promotion, our talk of a holiday in Thailand, his cosy plans for the future. He was completely oblivious to all this. It was going to hit him like a train. There was no way he could understand this. There was no way he could forgive this.

I thought of how long I'd known him, everything we'd shared, everything we assumed we'd share in future. How certain it had all seemed.

All of it had fallen apart in a matter of seconds.

I don't know how long I sat there, numb and paralysed. I was only roused from my trance by a knock at the door, to which I wouldn't have responded had it not been accompanied by Heike's voice.

I zombie-walked across the room and let her in. She was dressed in black trousers and a loose-fitting blouse, which she always wore to travel. It was only as I took this in that I realised I was still in only the T-shirt I'd worn to bed, my feet bare on the carpet.

From her expression there was no need to ask if she knew.

I wandered back to the edge of the bed, a couple of feet from where my laptop sat on the dresser. The screensaver had long since kicked in: rain on a window, droplets running down the screen and distorting the display. To my eyes, they looked like tears streaking the images that stared out from the website.

I couldn't find anything to say. I just sat there, glancing from the laptop to where Heike stood, and felt totally helpless.

She folded her arms across her chest.

'The bus is scheduled to be leaving in about five minutes,' she said. 'You need to get your shit together.'

Her tone was businesslike, the terse side of neutral. There was no warmth in it at all.

I got the impression I had done something wrong; or at least hadn't done anything right.

I had expected her to act as she had done when we both got the nude pictures on our phones: concerned, angry and sorry for dragging me into this. Instead she seemed distant and severe, like I was a problem employee who needed to be dealt with. I had the definite sense that whereas the nude photos had pulled us together, this had driven us apart.

'I can't go out there,' I told her, grabbing uselessly at the bottom of my T-shirt, like I could stretch it down to my ankles. I wanted to pull a sheet over my head. 'I can't face them. Not if they've found out like *this*.'

Heike grabbed my pull-along and flipped it open, chucking me a pair of jeans.

'Aye, so, welcome to my world, Monica,' she said, rattling the space-bar on my laptop and bringing the images back into perfect focus. 'This says you live there now too, I'm afraid. There's no escape and no hiding place, so the sooner you get out there the sooner you can start getting used to it.'

I fought tears, feeling like a wee girl being scolded by her unsympathetic mum.

'I can't *live there*,' I protested. 'I can't do this.'

Heike all but manhandled me into the bathroom with a roll of her eyes. There was no compassion, only impatience. I didn't understand what I could have done to make her react this way, for her not to see that I was in way over my head and in danger of drowning.

'Yes you can. I hate to use the expression, but you're just going to have to man up, because this is going to get a shitload worse before there's any glimmer of it getting better.'

She sure got that right.

I sat on the bus unable to look at anybody. Damien had patted my shoulder as I went past, the gesture enough to push me over the edge into more crying. I also briefly caught Rory's eye. He had looked sympathetic and sheepish, but all I could think about was the time I heard him talk about images of Heike and her lovers being lodged in people's 'spank banks'.

This was a special kind of hell.

I turned towards the window, feeling awful and looking every bit of it too. Occasionally we'd pass a building tall enough for the shadow to turn the bus window into a cloudy mirror. My face was teary and swollen, and my sojourn in catatonia had cost me the chance of a shower and the opportunity to even wash my hair.

My phone started to ring about twenty minutes into the journey. Keith.

I just couldn't answer. How could I speak to him?

I was trying to think if there was any way I could spin this. The Scottish catch-all excuse of being a bit pissed wasn't going to cover it. What did that leave? 'It's not what it looks like.' Well, it looks like we're kissing in a women-only lesbian bar.

I pressed ignore. Thirty seconds later he was ringing again.

Heike was right: there was no hiding place, but I just wasn't ready yet. I switched my phone off completely.

I wondered why she was being so remote, why this wasn't us against the world, but something I needed to get over instead. Man up, she had said. My distress obviously meant a lot less to her than her own anger, which seemed so unfair. But was it?

I kept thinking how it wasn't my fault, and that was true, but maybe there was a difference between blame and responsibility.

I remembered that Heike had been living like this for a long time: ever since 'Do It to Julia' had brought her to mainstream attention. Once the tabloids found out that the outspoken and glamorous singer behind this international hit was gay, they had been all over her life. They even made the mistaken assumption, mainly from the title, that the song had some kind of lesbian message. As Heike put it: 'You can't expect the subliterate cockwombles on the *Daily Heil* showbiz and gossip desks to have read Orwell.'

It was a song about human weakness, and how we shouldn't judge each other too harshly for it: pretty much the antithesis of the British tabloids' stock-in-trade.

They had doorstepped Heike, offered money to her girlfriends for kiss-and-tell stories, but no one had come forward. There had been art before, but they never had an angle. Even Heike snogging a member of her band wasn't enough to get these pictures promoted from the website to the paper. For that, they needed a story, and I felt my stomach drop again as I realised I had given them one.

I had a fiancé.

They might not be aware of that, though. What would anybody at a tabloid know about an obscure fiddler who had only properly joined the band a few months back? By way of answer, I asked myself instead how hard it would be to find out. One call to my mum would do it.

Oh God. The thought of sleazy hacks calling up my mum – of me bringing this to her door – was almost impossible to take. How could something as tender as a few kisses cause so much hurt?

I switched on my phone and called home. It was engaged. Before I could try again, it buzzed with an incoming call. Keith.

I thought of Heike's words from the hotel.

This was where I lived now. I had to do this.

I pressed answer.

'Keith,' I said, my voice dry.

'Monica. Where are you?'

His voice was hollow and distant, and it was nothing to do with the signal.

'Outside Salzburg. On my way to Zurich.'

His question seemed absurd, my answer irrelevant. It was like we were practising for a conversation, not yet ready to really talk.

'I got a call from a reporter. A woman from the *Daily Mail*.'

Probably the same woman who had called me. If I hadn't been so spineless, I could have phoned him right away to warn him.

'I'm so sorry. Keith, you have to believe me, I—'

He talked over me. It was like he hadn't heard me, like he was in a state of numb shock.

'She made out like she was doing a general piece on you as a musician. She asked me about us. I told her I'd known you since we were kids. I told her we were getting married.'

I could feel tears run down my face as I held the phone to my cheek. I had done this to him. That sneaky cow of a reporter had conned him, but I had done this.

I expected him to be angry. Instead he just sounded hurt, his voice weak, his words confused and defeated.

He had more questions than accusations, and they were the questions of someone who already knew that the answers wouldn't help.

This was just as well, as I didn't have any.

'Why did I have to find out like this?'

'Have you any idea how humiliated I am?'

'How am I going to face people?'

'How long has this been going on?'

'Is this why you joined the band?'

'Have you always had these feelings, for women?'

'Are you sleeping with her?'

'Are you in love with her?'

I had nothing to give him, other than apologies, which I knew were worthless.

'It just happened,' was as much of an explanation as I could manage.

I was about to add that 'it meant nothing', but caught myself.

It was the title of Heike's song about betrayal, one that nailed how this statement was never true.

It didn't mean nothing. It meant I didn't love him.

If I loved him, I wouldn't have been in that bar telling Heike: 'I won't run away.' I'd have thanked her, said I understood, accepted it as a compliment, a sign of a strong and treasured friendship. But I didn't. I kissed her. That meant everything.

I knew there was no making this right, even if he'd let me, even if he wanted me to. The girl who left to go on this tour was never coming back. The girl he had become engaged to didn't exist any more.

Flesh Trade

Mairi opened her bedroom door and flung her arms around him before he could even step inside, let alone castigate her for almost giving him a coronary.

'What's that for?'

'I'm so glad you're back safe.'

'And I'd be safe with clean underpants if you hadn't had your wee joke.'

'I'm sorry,' she told him, closing the door. 'It's just, I lived and died a hundred times watching you over there, sitting a few feet from the guy, and you seemed perfectly comfortable, to the point of smug. I mean, I know you were the one with your head in the noose, but . . .'

'I understand. Any football manager will tell you it's hell to be watching from the sidelines, kicking every ball in your head. And if I seemed pleased with myself, it was purely relief at having got away with it.'

'You haven't got away with it yet,' she cautioned. 'When will we know if it's worked?'

He tried very, very hard not to look self-satisfied.

'It worked five minutes ago. I received the code before I even made it down the stairs.'

He held up Bodo's iPad, already unlocked and the security disabled.

'It's a simple act of legerdemain,' he had told Mairi a few hours back as he installed the software on to his newly purchased iPad. 'It worked with Anthony Mead and it will work with Boris too. What's crucial is that the wallpaper is the same, and so are any icons partially overlapped by the password interface. The hardest part with Mead was precisely matching the make and model of laptop, right down to the stickers detailing the spec. That's not a problem with something as standardised and generic as an iPad, especially when you're swapping it into the same case.'

'So you swapped Mead's laptop for one of your own?'

'Kind of. In Mead's case he was under the impression it had been lost and then found.'

'But the important thing is that he thought it was the same machine.'

'Correct. This software fakes a sleep or hibernation mode: it can even imitate the boot sequence if you want it to look like the device has been off altogether. Then it presents the user with the usual familiar password screen in order to log on properly. The user keys in his password, but it tells him it's incorrect. He keys it again, helpfully giving us confirmation, but it's never going to let him in because that would give the game away. Meantime this programme logs the passwords that were input and immediately sends them to an email account I can access from my phone. The real beauty of it is that he won't know anything is wrong until he's given us what we need.'

Mairi ran a finger almost reverently across the screen, like she had never seen a data tablet before.

'All right,' she said, turning to face him. 'You're entitled to look pretty chuffed with yourself now.'

She was looking into his eyes, their faces only inches apart. The smell of her was all around him, and the warmth of her body seemed so close that in his mind he could already feel it pressed against him. He understood that if he moved forward slightly, if he gave even the merest inclination of his head, they would kiss.

He knew it was what she wanted. He wanted it too, but there was something, still, that wouldn't let him.

'I think we should hold off on the self-congratulation until we've seen whether it tells us anything useful,' he said, turning his gaze to the iPad.

Mairi sighed, venting a frustration that he didn't flatter himself by interpreting as being entirely about what had almost just happened.

'I need to get out of this place,' she said. 'I feel like I've been cooped up in this hotel for days. I need air, I need space.'

Parlabane refrained from pointing out that she had just spent the past few hours outdoors, albeit on a roof. He understood what she was feeling. The tension of not only the last few hours but the last few days was making her feel trapped.

'What do you have in mind?'

'Dinner. And a view of something other than that place across the road.'

They booked a taxi from reception, in order to minimise their on-street exposure. Having gone to such efforts of disguise and subterfuge, Parlabane anticipated the twisted irony of Bodo walking out of his building just in time to recognise Mairi and his recent visitor standing on the pavement opposite, trying to hail a cab.

The taxi turned up after a couple of minutes and they hurried across the pavement, heads down like it was raining.

Mairi gave the driver their destination, while Parlabane was getting busy with the fruit of his day's labours. He had already changed the operating system language to English for ease of navigating through the architecture, though that wasn't going to help in making sense of Bodo's files.

'What's German for needle?' he asked.

'I don't know. Why?'

'In case I happen upon it inside this digital haystack.'

Parlabane scrolled through Bodo's emails, scanning principally for names, as they were the same in any language. Most were to his primary address at the Bad Candy domain, but roughly a third were addressed to an alias account. Parlabane separated them so that each account displayed in a separate window, concentrating first on the unofficial business.

'Oops,' he said pointedly, directing Mairi's gaze towards the screen.

'What am I looking for?'

'Something familiar.'

She stared at the iPad, Parlabane taking a moment to look at her while her attention was so intently fixed on the screen. The taxi glided towards Unter den Linden, passing the Humboldt Box on the left and Museumsinsel on the right. He recalled stealing such glances back in another age. She was no less beguiling now, and yet seemed no less forbidden to him. He just couldn't work out why.

'Jan,' she stated, spotting it. 'This is his email address. But this is Bad Candy business: from what I can gather, it's something to do with truck hire for Prelude to the Slaughter's gigs in Poland next month. Why oops?'

Parlabane pointed to the other window.

'Because he's forgotten to switch log-ins when he sent this email to Bodo's other account. This proves he's in on whatever else is going on. A whole raft of this correspondence could well be from him, when he's remembered to use his own unofficial account.'

'Yeah. Just wish we had the first clue what they're chatting about.'

The taxi dropped them off at the Reichstag. Mairi had expressed her intention to dine somewhere that was in marked contrast to last night's rather cloistered repast. It was after six and neither of them had eaten anything substantial since breakfast. They made their way up to the Käfer restaurant, on the roof alongside Norman Foster's gigantic glass dome.

Parlabane didn't appreciate how hungry he was until the food was presented to him, wolfing down mouthfuls with an undignified haste that was further exacerbated by his impatience to turn his attention back to the iPad.

It felt like a perfect tableau of why all his relationships were ultimately doomed: a spectacular setting, a beautiful meal, an ideal companion, and him unable to truly appreciate any of those things as his focus was fixed upon an object he had just stolen so that he could work out why somebody had been trying to kill him.

On the plus side, he was at least getting somewhere with that.

'There's an email here in English,' he reported. 'Looks like it must have been the common language for an exchange with a Danish guy who doesn't speak German.'

254

'Danish?'

'Yeah. Bodo appears to be chartering a boat. Tomorrow, in fact. From Esbjerg.'

'Anything else in English? Or Spanish? I speak a bit of that.'

'Not so far. That's why I'm switching my efforts to the non-textual.'

'Images? Do you reckon Bodo and his people may have had a hand in tipping off whoever took those *Daily Mail* pictures?'

'It's possible. The video shoot and the free gig were both at the Brauereihallen, so it wouldn't be a stretch for some Bad Candy apparatchik to have been tailing them that night.'

'I think those photos are another reason Monica's not best pleased with me,' Mairi confessed.

'How so?'

'She called me up when they went viral, like she thought there was something I could do about it. I could have been more sympathetic, I guess, but I was angry about the situation myself. I had warned her when she joined the band: romantic relationships between band members on tour are a crawling horror. She told me I had nothing to worry about when it came to her: she was happily engaged. I guess reminding her of that conversation wasn't the most sensitive thing I could have done at that point.'

Parlabane ran a search for images and video files, hoping that Bodo's browser cache wasn't about to reveal a scat-porn fetish that would have him spewing up his dinner.

It didn't, but what it did disclose was no less sickening.

'Look at this,' he said, placing the iPad on the table where they could both see it.

The search had thrown up a number of similarly posed head-and-shoulder shots of girls, distinct from the hundreds of other thumbnails that had inevitably populated the results. Parlabane had gone to the file location on a random sample and been repeatedly taken to the same document.

'It's a database,' he said. 'Dozens of girls, each with a profile and several other fields. These numbers could be earnings – or debts.'

'Jesus,' Mairi said. 'Ages. Physical measurements. I don't want to even speculate as to what some of these other statistics might be. And that looks like . . . Oh my God.'

'What?'

'This stuff at the bottom of each profile. It's in German, but I think I know what it is. I used to work in marketing, and this looks like feedback analysis data. We used a programme that collated . . .'

Mairi put her hand over her mouth. For a moment he thought she was going to gag. Her expression suggested it was still possible.

'Collated what?' he asked, bracing himself.

'Satisfaction surveys.'

She pushed her plate to the side, like she could no longer bear to look at the food still sitting there, far less eat it.

'I'm starting to wish I'd spiked his doughnut with something that would make him piss blood.'

'Much as I'd agree, it wouldn't help us any,' Mairi replied, her voice slightly dry from bitterness. 'This is nightmarish stuff, but I still don't see how it links to Heike.'

'Only insofar as it proves she was on the money regards what was really going on with the merchandising girls. Maybe the bus incident wasn't her final attempt to throw a spanner in the works.'

Mairi stared at him across the table, wide-eyed and almost accusatory.

'Are you saying he could have *killed* her, for getting in the way of his business?'

Parlabane knew he couldn't sugar-coat this. She had to understand what they might be dealing with.

'He had someone throw me under a train just for taking his photograph. I think we might need to prepare ourselves for the worst.'

Mairi put her hands to her temples, elbows on the table like her head suddenly weighed too much. It couldn't have been the first time that this possibility had struck her, but that fine membrane between the hypothetical and the genuinely probable had finally ruptured.

'Oh Jesus.'

Her eyes were filling up.

'I've been kidding myself, haven't I? Thinking I'm on some kind of adventure here with you, that's going to end with us finding Heike safe and sound after some, I don't know, silly misunderstanding; or us snatching her from the clutches of Eurotrash gangsters and laughing about it in a couple of months' time backstage in LA. We're looking for a dead person, aren't we?'

'Not yet,' Parlabane told her.

He picked up the iPad again and closed the database, taking him back to the search results. He scrolled down the page some more, in case anything else leaped out at him. There was months' worth of browsing data cached here, every last thumbnail, banner and logo on any site Bodo had visited. To narrow the sample he navigated to the folder where the database was stored, which was when he spotted two video files in there, their icons showing no preview images because they had been recorded in some non-native format.

He launched the clip, filling the screen with a grainy image it took him a moment to recognise as a shower curtain. The colour was rather washed-out and drab, but he could make out the horizontal line that denoted the rim of a bath, and to the left a vertical line that had to be the edge of an open door. There was an object in the foreground, dark and blurry, bleeding out of the right of the frame. It could have been a bag or a bottle. Immediately it told him what he was looking at. This was hidden-camera footage.

'I think I've found something,' he said.

He placed the tablet back on the table between them, feeling the hairs on his neck stand up in anticipation of what he might be about to witness. His hand hovered over the screen, ready to shut the thing down. There was a waitress standing a few tables away, her next destination unclear, but it wasn't only *her* eyes he was on standby to spare.

'What is this?' Mairi asked.

'Secret filming. A planted device.'

'Planted where?'

Mairi had no sooner asked than the image became brighter and sharper as a light was switched on in the previously gloomy bathroom. A figure passed in front of the camera, back to the viewer, leaning behind the curtain to start the shower running before undressing.

It was a woman, but they didn't see her face because she stepped behind the curtain without turning around. They saw enough, though: dyed pink hair.

'Heike,' Mairi gasped.

She grabbed the iPad and ran her finger along the slider, forwarding the footage to the point when the subject emerged, facing the camera. It was Heike Gunn all right: standing upright and naked as she wrapped a towel around her head.

'Somebody hid a camera in her hotel bathroom,' she said. 'Somebody working for these creeps. Fucking Jan.'

Mairi went to close the player but Parlabane stayed her hand. 'There's a second file. I need to know what else it shows.'

Mairi launched it then slid her finger along the play-line, causing a series of thumbnails to flash below the main display. Parlabane glimpsed another woman climbing in and out of a shower.

'It's Monica. The bastards snuck a camera into her bathroom too.'

'This is the same bathroom,' Parlabane corrected, indicating the blurred object to the right that proved the camera hadn't moved. 'They must have been sharing.'

'No,' Mairi insisted. 'Heike's contract guarantees she has her own room.'

'Well, leaving aside the more prurient explanations, I think we can deduce which hotel this came from. Damien said that Heike and Monica had to share a room when they insisted on taking the bus to Milan rather than flying. This would have been the same day as the incident with the merchandise girls.'

Parlabane picked up the iPad again and ran a search for files made or modified on the same day as the two videos. The results took him to several enhanced screen-captures from each clip: naked stills of both Heike and Monica.

Mairi quickly grabbed the iPad to close the images as she noticed the previously hovering waitress move more deliberately towards their table.

'Is everything all right?' the waitress asked, casting an eye over the rather abandoned-looking dishes.

'Yes, it's fine,' Mairi replied, that very British assurance offered identically to waiting staff amid dining circumstances ranging from culinary perfection to having been served oven-baked jobbie on a vomit and snotter compote.

'Can I bring you something . . . different?'

'No, just the bill,' Mairi replied perfunctorily.

'Was there something wrong with the food?'

'No, we have to be somewhere else.'

'I will bring it immediately.'

She was as good as her word, zipping back and forth from the desk in a matter of seconds.

'I really do have to be somewhere else,' Mairi told Parlabane. 'I need to be on my feet. My mind's going around in circles.'

'At least we've come to the right place,' he suggested, indicating the dome that lay a short distance across the rooftop. 'Or do you need air?'

'No, that seems like the ideal spot for the way I feel.'

Discord

When we reached Zurich I couldn't wait to get off the bus, like stepping out into the fresh air would put an end to the suffocating tension and insecurity. Instead, those feelings ramped up the moment my feet hit concrete, as there were reporters waiting for us outside the hotel. There were four of them, all of whom came charging forward as we approached the hotel doors, like monsters in a video game. There was no stealth, just this automatic bounding into action that would have been funny had it been happening to anyone else.

Watching them do this on TV, I had always wondered why they shouted their questions at people who were never going to answer, even if they could make out a single query from the hubbub. But right then, I understood. A part of me wanted to stop and say something, anything, just so that the shouting would stop and the pressure of ignoring them could ease.

'Heike, how long have you and Monica been having this affair?'

'Is it causing any tensions within the band?'

'Monica, what does your fiancé think about this?'

'Have you always swung both ways?'

It was one of the few occasions I was ever grateful for having Dean around. He and his crew created a human cordon and let us get to the reception desk, holding back the reporters while hotel security got their act together to chuck them out. Still they peered expectantly through the lobby's floor-to-ceiling window. They were like predatory animals at the zoo: they'd pick our bones clean if it wasn't for the security glass. Journalists really were the scum of the earth.

Jan put a hand on Heike's shoulder as she waited at reception for the slick-haired man behind the desk to give us a key. His touch was delicate and polite; he had long since lost privileges for anything familiar.

'Everybody okay?' he asked. 'I mean, we're still good for tonight, yeah?'

He was worried Heike was going to pull out of the show, something I had been secretly hoping for all day. I tried and failed to stop myself looking expectantly at her, and she noticed.

'Absolutely,' she said.

She seemed almost offended at the idea.

'It would take more than this to knock us off our game,' she added, sending a hard glance my way in case I missed who the message was really aimed at.

The hacks were gone when we came back downstairs to head for the soundcheck, but only because they were waiting for us outside the gig; photographers too.

It was a place called Kaufleuten, a kind of super-venue combining a restaurant, bar and several club spaces as well as the large hall where we were playing. It had entrances and awnings along three sides of a grand six-storey building, but at this time of day they knew to lay their ambush at the double door where our truck was parked.

'I'll deal with this,' Heike said.

I feared she would go off into an ill-advised harangue, but instead she struck a pose beneath an awning, making it look like a catwalk entrance. She had her game face on as they gathered on the other side of a gold rope, the photographers snapping and the hacks baying their same questions.

Heike didn't answer any of them, but with a cold smile thanked them insincerely for their 'sudden interest in music none of you gave a fuck about forty-eight hours ago'.

They barely looked at me as I hurried inside between Damien and Rory, the only two members of the band who were taller than me.

Scott allowed himself a wry smile as he watched her in action.

'Taking one for the team,' Damien said.

'Aye,' Scott agreed. 'Though I suppose the silver lining is we'll get plenty of press just in time for the new single coming out.'

Just changing one note can alter the sound of a chord or even the sense of a whole phrase. Major can become minor, harmony discord.

With Scott's words, the events of the past days suddenly played back in my head and became totally different.

Nobody knew where we were going that night in Berlin, only Heike.

I saw her leading me into the bar, choosing from half a dozen empty tables the one right in front of that big window. I saw her sit up straight and look me in the eye; heard her say, 'I want to kiss you.'

The first single was out next week, a few weeks ahead of the new album. It was called 'Stolen Glances'. Can anybody think of a good image to illustrate that? You know, for promotional purposes? How about a lesbian clinch between two band members? Would that get us some play?

I heard Angus's drunken warning, the one I didn't listen to:

It's when you think she's not manipulating you that you're truly in her control.

I thought of her supposedly significant dyed-pink hair, changed back to cream blonde in time for a video shoot.

She had planned this. She had made it all happen.

Heike will get wherever she wants to be, but she'll leave bodies in her wake.

I had seen her this morning in Salzburg, throwing clothes at me from my suitcase. She was coldly pragmatic, treating me like a problem rather than a friend in trouble, my meltdown an irritation she couldn't afford to indulge. I had served my purpose. Man up, she told me.

Finally, it was Dean's voice I heard:

By the end of the tour . . . you're gonna fucking despise her.

Manifest Destiny

Detective Superintendent Catherine McLeod looked at her notes again and grimaced as the car descended an off-ramp from the new M74 extension.

Her driver clocked her expression as they came to a halt at a set of traffic lights.

'What?' Beano asked.

'I'm thinking this could be the jurisdictional nightmare they teach cops about for decades to come.'

They took a right turn beneath the flyover, heading into a light-industrial zone. Beano drove them past a printworks and an insurance firm's sprawling car-repair depot, then turned into a horseshoe layout of low-rise units at the far end of the estate. A uniform waved them through, past a plastic cordon beyond which all of the premises sat closed for business, their owners and employees forming a human avenue on the other side of the tapes.

The reason for their temporary eviction sat taking up most of the available parking space. It was a flatbed lorry bearing a burgundy-coloured shipping container, the rear of which was slightly ajar, guarded by another uniformed officer.

Beano killed the engine and they both stepped out into the light drizzle.

'What is it this outfit imports again?' she asked him.

'Old fridges. Soviet-era relics. These guys recondition them, give them a paint job and then flog them to over-remunerated wankers in London as a conversation piece for their kitchen.'

The lorry driver was sitting inside the premises he'd been delivering to, bearing the resigned look of someone who knew he wasn't going anywhere for a while. Catherine could tell it hadn't been him who had made the discovery. Rather, there was another bloke sitting nearby who had *the face*. He was the one who had gone inside the container with a pallet-lifter and been confronted with a sight he'd never forget.

It was a scary prospect for Catherine too, but not because there was a corpse involved. That was hardly enough to require a Detective Superintendent to come down and oversee matters. No, the reason this had the potential to turn into the nightmare she'd alluded to was that the container had been dispatched from Kiev, road-freighted all the way through Poland to Hamburg, shipped overseas to Grimsby and finally opened here in Glasgow, where the contents were discovered to be one item over the manifest.

Beano had a determined look as he climbed the ramp that ascended to the rear of the truck. She wasn't sure whether the previously squeamish younger officer was getting better at dealing with this or just better at hiding it.

The uniform at the container's split door stepped aside and held it open for them, telling them where they'd find what they were here for. Catherine didn't recognise him. He looked bored and faintly resentful, like nobody at Tulliallan had told him about all the tedious standing-about stuff during his training.

They stepped inside the container.

The body was lying in a narrow channel between two rows of towering fridges, like upright steel coffins forming an oddly respectful guard of honour. The girl was face down with her head turned to one side, like she was sleeping. She wore a pair of tight black jeans and a white denim jacket, her hair a creamy blonde crop. It was instantly familiar, but Catherine couldn't quite place where from. Someone on a DVD box set she and her husband had been watching, perhaps.

There was dried blood like a shadow on the floor around the body's middle. What they could see of her face was grey, a hollow mask, smeared with more dried blood. Even her mother wouldn't recognise her. She had been dead a few days.

'Let me check for some ID,' Beano volunteered, stepping ahead of Catherine and crouching down in the tight passage. God love him, she thought. If only they all tried as hard as him.

'Whoa,' he said, flipping open the denim jacket. 'Check this.'

Catherine saw an adhesive patch stuck on the inside of the garment, flush with the seams about an inch from the buttons, positioned so that it could be quickly flashed at whoever needed to see it. She saw the letters AAA: access all areas. Beneath that, she could read the name of the venue and, more significantly, the name of the band.

Instead of searching her pockets as Catherine expected, Beano reached for her right sleeve. He rolled it up carefully but urgently, revealing the letter H tattooed on the inside of the corpse's forearm.

'Oh Jesus,' he said, his tone indicating a specific fear confirmed. 'Boss, I think this is Heike Gunn.'

Downward Spiral

They showed the security guard their passes and he waved them on through. They had registered downstairs on the way in, Parlabane remarking that it was the first time he had needed to give his passport details before being admitted to a restaurant.

'To be fair, I'd feel more nervous if they'd wanted to check my blood group and my organ-donor card.'

They began to ascend the spiral walkway that wound its way around the inside of the glass walls atop the German parliament. The crowds were light, but they nonetheless felt part of a never-ending procession, like ants on Escher's Möbius strip. Sound carried in the strangest way, like it was the world's biggest whispering gallery; consequently passers-by spoke in quiet tones, and yet voices would suddenly meet Parlabane's ears, their words incomprehensible and their sources impossible to discern. He hoped it was doing something for Mairi's clarity, because to him it was like being inside the mind of a crazy person.

She seemed deep in thought, working harder to digest what her brain had taken in over dinner than the modest quantity her body had ingested. They had made it almost to the top before she finally spoke, yanking Parlabane back from his own reverie as he stared out towards the Hauptbahnhof.

'If somehow Jan – or somebody else – managed to secretly film Heike and Monica having a shower, I'm surprised it's not already all over the internet. There would be money in it. Unless they figured there was more money to be had from *threatening* to put it on the internet. Was he using this stuff to blackmail Heike, do you reckon?'

'Perhaps,' he answered, 'though maybe not for money. I think it would more likely be used as leverage. If you ask me, this was a warning to mind her own business.'

'Which again makes me wonder why the images never got released, because if Heike heeded a warning to mind her own business it would be the first time. She's never been one to back down from a fight, even when it seems the sensible thing to do.'

'There's another factor here, though,' Parlabane suggested. 'They didn't just film her: they filmed Monica too. Maybe that explains why she *did* back down. Nobody else in the band seems to know about these pictures, or has mentioned any other incidents on the tour, apart from the *Daily Mail* photos that did hit the internet.'

'Knowing Heike, she might have backed down to protect Monica, but she wouldn't have let it go entirely. She must have found some other way to piss them off. The big question is what.'

Mairi glanced down at the iPad.

'There's got to be something else on that thing,' she said.

Parlabane swallowed back any number of comments about how he'd rather have been sitting down and sifting through it than wending his way around the inside of a giant snow-globe. What made it easier to stay his tongue was the understanding that the tablet was unlikely to yield anything further without the help of a translator. Such a person wouldn't be difficult to procure, but finding one who had no contextual questions about whose iPad it was and how Parlabane happened to be in possession of it might prove more challenging.

He became aware of a sudden brief squall of sound, its origin confused by having bounced around the cupola before reaching his ears. He heard a squeak of shoes upon the smooth floor, accompanied by what sounded like a voice raised in guarded indignation and another in either gruff apology or dismissal. Parlabane glanced through the glass barrier and very quickly identified the source about four loops below on the opposite side, conspicuous because several other people were staring at them as they glared up-ramp at whoever had presumably barrelled past them.

He had to lean over the rim to spot the source of their ire.

'Fuck.'

He saw three of them: Bodo, Gove-Troll and Spike, whom he knew could be carrying that nasty little stubby blade he'd flashed at the Hauptbahnhof. The two goons were gazing up and around – which was presumably why they'd clattered into somebody – while Bodo marched close behind with at least one eye on his phone.

'What?' Mairi asked, making to lean forward.

Parlabane held her back and led them both closer to the outside wall.

'It's Bodo and his little Bodites. They know we're here.'

'How?'

'I don't know, I disabled all the iPad's tracking services. But . . .'

Mairi glanced desperately up, down, left and right. Bodo and his men were ascending the ramp, the only path up or down. She looked suddenly wan and Parlabane was concerned that she might either pass out or just throw up.

'They won't try anything violent in here,' he said. 'There's armed police and you need to confirm your ID to get in. But if they get to us we'll have to hand over the iPad, and if they tell the cops we've stolen it we're seriously fucked.'

'What do we do? There's no way past them.'

'Don't be so sure. You stay in good shape, don't you?'

'I work out, yes, but I don't fancy my chances at British Bulldog against these guys. Not in Louboutins, anyway.'

Parlabane began to take off his jacket.

'There's another reason I never go out without my wearable handbag, as you put it.'

He unfastened the stud on a concealed flap in the lining of the maligned garment and began swiftly feeding out its contents like a magician pulling linked hankies from his sleeve.

'What the hell is that?'

'Climbing rope. Ultra-lightweight, extra-strong, neoprene core. I don't leave home without it. Not since I had to improvise a substitute a few years back.'

The aluminium railing was tight to the top of the glass barrier. There was nowhere to secure a loop. Instead he slipped the end of the cord around one of the arching support spars that held up the structure. He took a breath and concentrated on calming himself as his fingers worked the line into a knot: haste was imperative, hurry a hazard.

With the line secure, he stopped to give a smile and a friendly wave to the tourists who were starting to take an interest in what he might be up to, deploying the internationally reliable cloaking strategy for potentially suspicious activity in a public place: that of demonstrably drawing attention to oneself. For some reason it seemed to reassure people that there was nothing going on that ought to concern them. He had further found that gesturing to onlookers that they were welcome to help out or join in didn't merely render himself invisible, but temporarily erased their memory of what they had seen.

He glanced down and tracked the progress of Bodo and his boys. They were roughly two loops down, and he was pretty sure they'd seen their targets. Parlabane gripped the line in a folded-up bunch, ready to drop it over the edge on the outside of the walkway, between the ramp and the glass.

'You expect me to climb down this thing?' Mairi asked, her face more than hinting that she lacked faith in her ability to execute this manoeuvre.

'To *slide* down it, yes. It's that or big hugs with Bodo. It's also now or never.'

She glanced at the cord folded up into a bunch in his fist.

'It'll burn the skin off my hands.'

'Not if you take the weight on your foot,' he demonstrated, dangling a short length to the floor. 'You just wrap your expensive red soles around it and the tension will let you glide down easy.'

'That would only work if the bottom end was tight too,' she pointed out.

'And in two seconds it will be.'

Parlabane tossed the line over the edge and rolled inconspicuously after it like he was climbing into bed. He slid down, gripping the cord between his feet, keeping his eyes on the inside of the spiral as he descended. The curvature swung him in towards the outer rim of the level below, where he kicked off again gently, the cool glass of the dome a few feet from his shoulders.

He trapped the cord tightly between his feet to brake, and landed softly on the walkway, now two levels beneath Mairi. Above him, at roughly three o'clock, Bodo and his crew were closing in on her. They didn't notice his stunt as he'd timed it so that they had just passed on the level below when he dropped the cord. They'd notice Mairi, however, if she didn't hurry. They were approaching the point in their ascent where they'd have direct line of sight.

Parlabane looked up, beckoning her silently with a wave of the hand and an urgent expression. He had the cord looped around his leg and foot, anchoring it with his weight but ready to pay out whatever slack she needed. Like every bit of progress in climbing, this was all about making the commitment. Once she had done that, sheer instinct would take over, though this might well result in minor flaying. It depended on whether she heeded his advice, and whether she valued her palms more than her designer shoes.

Parlabane had to stifle a gasp as Mairi suddenly launched herself over the side, her flailing legs tangling desperately around the rope as she swung in the air. This flurry of movement drew the notice of their pursuers, but they were on the other side of the dome, at the furthest point away. They realised what was going on, Gove-Troll pointing towards Mairi as she dangled between levels and Spike staring directly at Parlabane.

She was holding too tight, gripping with her hands and her feet in a petrified clench.

Shit. Shit. Shit.

He could get out of here with the iPad: he had a head start of about a hundred and fifty metres. He couldn't leave, though, not while she was literally left hanging.

Suddenly she slackened her grip; Parlabane couldn't tell whether with her hands or feet or both. She fell too fast, plummeting almost a full level then grasping the cord again in panic. It only slowed her for a moment as she let out a muffled shriek. She'd burned her hands then loosened her grip again in reflexive response.

She fell again, another sickening lurch. Parlabane felt it as though he were the one falling.

She squeezed tighter with her feet, sending one shoe tumbling down into the void. The resulting jolt caused her to lose all grip with her hands and sent her tipping head first.

Parlabane thrust himself as far over the barrier as his balance allowed. He'd have been too late were it not that she had clasped her legs together as she plunged, slowing her just enough for him to grasp her flailing hands.

He eased her to terra firma as onlookers gawped in delighted astonishment, some of them applauding. He was pretty sure a girl was filming it too. It would be on YouTube within hours. He didn't begrudge her the hits.

'You do this shit for fun?' Mairi asked with sharp accusation, gazing at her trembling fingers. There were livid marks on both her palms.

'There isn't usually someone chasing me,' he replied, glancing upwards. 'You okay to run?'

She whipped off her surviving Louboutin and dropped it on the floor. 'Faster than ever in my life.'

She wasn't kidding either. Parlabane could barely keep up.

On the levels above, he glimpsed Spike sprinting and weaving, calling to people to get out of the way, while Gove-Troll was showing judgement comparable to his lookalike inasmuch as he believed the strength of his own determination meant far more than any amount of contrary evidence. Instead of hurrying down, he was continuing up, with the intention of also descending the rope, undeterred by the laws of spatial geometry that dictated he'd have to travel almost as far to the start of this shortcut as Spike would have covered to reach its endpoint.

Bodo, for his part, seemed worryingly unhurried, still glancing at his phone as he lumbered back down the slope.

Parlabane thought he knew why as he and Mairi approached the end of the spiral. He could see two police officers preparing to bar the exit, perhaps having witnessed at least part of their acrobatic display. He felt his pace slow involuntarily, but Mairi didn't skip a beat. She hurtled towards them and went into an impressively histrionic faux-meltdown, grabbing one of them by both hands.

'Oh, thank God, thank God. Do you speak English? There are men chasing us, do you see? They said they would kill us. Please stop them. They keep saying we stole something from them, but we've never seen them before. We're just tourists. Please help us.'

The cops took a look backwards and clocked what had to be the two most conspicuously henchman-looking fuckers they'd ever seen. Spike was stomping around the dome at full-pelt, all muscle and aggression. Meantime Gove-Troll had looped the cord around his leg once too many and found himself briefly swinging upside down before face-planting quite magnificently at the feet of two shrieking Japanese tourists.

Yeah, those guys were going to be busy a while, Parlabane decided.

He and Mairi walked briskly but without conspicuous hurry to the lifts, and a few minutes later they were outside, flagging down a cab on Ebertstrasse.

Falling bodies

I suppose it was inevitable I would do something desperate.

I'd never been so angry in my life, never felt such a sense of betrayal and hostility.

At the soundcheck in Zurich, Heike was focused and professional, going about her preparations like nothing was wrong. I steeled myself and walked over to where she stood. I couldn't bring myself to speak at first, just stood and looked her in the eyes.

'What?' she asked crossly.

'You did this,' I somehow found the words to say.

'I did what?'

'The photos. They were a set-up.'

She screwed up her face in confusion; too obvious confusion, as far as I was concerned.

'What are you talking about?'

'You think I'm fucking stupid, Heike? You used me. You did it to promote the new single.'

'I *used* you? To . . .?'

Her expression was overly horrified, a pantomime of disbelief and distaste. Then she threw back my own words from Berlin, words that had bonded us then, but which could only be meant to drive us apart now.

'*Catch on to yourself*, Monica,' she said, shaking her head like I was insane.

But she didn't deny anything.

Heike and I literally didn't speak for days after that. Previously I would have thought this impossible, given the way we were living, working and travelling, but we managed it. We played Munich, Frankfurt, Cologne and Amsterdam without a word passing between us; the first two without even making eye contact. We were two grown adults in a huff that lasted thousands of miles and several cities. Did this mean I had truly earned my rock 'n' roll wings?

I had read about band members not speaking throughout entire tours and dismissed it as music-biz mythology, but now I understood not only how it could happen, but how it could be necessary: how it could be the only way a tour might still work.

What amazed me was that the audience had no idea, as long as the music still sounded good. It's easy to smile at the crowd, easy to look like you're all happy to be up there together.

We weren't playing 'Smuggler's Soul' any longer, as though that needed to be said. But I found my own treasured places within the show, and Heike understood at some level that she still ought to let me express myself.

The hardest part – for both of us, I'm sure – was playing 'Dark Station'. The song represented all we had shared, the vulnerability Heike had allowed me to see, the trust that had existed between us. It was just the two of us on stage, standing within the pool of a single spotlight, but we were never more closed off to each other than during those four minutes. We put up our own invisible Berlin Wall to protect ourselves from each other.

Truth was, for a long time I couldn't even look at her without my hackles rising, as all I could see was her deceit: her face rising to kiss mine and her face mugging for photographers in Zurich after telling me to man up.

She wasn't offering any olive branches, never mind an apology.

In fact, it seemed nobody was in much of a mood to build bridges.

I kept checking the *Daily Mail* website, though I knew I shouldn't, like picking a scab. I don't know what I was looking for: it was just an insecure instinct to know what else was being said about me. And, like picking a scab, it only made things worse.

'Fiancé Keith Dumps Lesbian Love-Cheat Monica' ran the headline.

So this time I was the one who learned about a major development in my own relationship via the press rather than first-hand.

Keith had gone from shock and hurt to anger and recrimination, pouring his heart out to the same sleekit bint who had so ruthlessly bodyslammed him earlier.

Speaking from his home in Aberdeen, heartbroken Keith Jamieson (23) said that his engagement was over, and there was little doubt where he laid the blame.

'I don't know who Monica is any more,' he told us. 'Heike Gunn has turned her head, made her into someone else. Monica's never been the same since she met her. Heike's a selfish and manipulative person who just takes what she wants because she can. I could see that from the moment I met her.'

The spurned oil worker didn't hold back in his tirade against the Islay-born songstress.

'She's a spoiled diva who's grown up being told she's special all the time because her dad was some artist, and she's come to believe her own hype. She doesn't care whose lives she ruins. If Monica can't see that, then she deserves what's coming, because she'll get used up and spat out. I just want her to know that I won't be here to pick up the pieces.'

Every word stung, feeling his pain and his anger.

I also winced with recognition, seeing the ugly side of Keith so exposed. Keith wasn't exactly combustible, but when he did get tipped over the edge it could result in a complete loss of control, whichever straw had broken the camel's back. A couple of years ago he had ended up in the cells for the night after getting into a fight with a guy in a pub in Lerwick. We had been going through a bad patch, and to be honest I *was* flirting with the bloke, because it was nice to be chatted up at a time when I was feeling taken for granted.

Keith didn't attack him or anything: it could have all been easily resolved if the guy hadn't been a dick about it. There was unnecessary aggression on both sides, which is why it happened, but the point is that Keith was taking out his frustrations with me on someone else.

All the horrible things he said to the press about Heike were him expressing his hurt and rage at me. But maybe it was fair that she took the abuse, as it was the price she paid for the whole world getting to know that 'Stolen Glances' would be available on iTunes and Amazon from the following Monday.

I felt more and more isolated and insecure. I chatted plenty to the guys, but only as people who worked in the same place and had to get along; it felt like they were more colleagues than friends. The atmosphere was too awful. Plus they were wary about talking to either of us one on one, in case they were perceived to be taking sides. Add to that my general awkwardness about them (not to mention a few million others) thinking me and Heike were lovers and I was one very lonely violinist.

During the shows I found myself hopping up on to Rory's drum riser, or jigging with Scott or Damien during certain numbers. It took me a while to see myself from the outside and realise how much I was flaunting my heterosexuality. Or maybe I just needed to look and to feel like I belonged.

I was an emotional car crash, a disaster waiting to happen, and in Cologne it finally did.

Kölsch was involved, but that wasn't the most potent thing. Spending an hour in the hotel bar after the show watching Heike bill and coo with some fangirl didn't help, though I think that deep down the process was already in motion by that point.

I might have caught on to the reasons behind my antics with Scott and Damien, but it was something else that kept bringing me back to Rory. The weird chemistry between us on stage had not gone from my mind during my relationship with Heike: just lain hidden. I had been wary of it before, perhaps even afraid of it, but since Zurich I had been thinking about it, pushing it where before I'd have held back.

That night in the bar, I felt unstable, my emotions, desires and insecurities all mixed up. I was lonely, angry, scared, regretful, resentful, betrayed, undervalued, rejected. I needed someone to tell me everything was okay. I needed someone to tell me *I* was okay.

I saw Rory get up from the table and say he was calling it a

276

night. I gave him a head start of a few seconds then announced I was following suit. I caught up to him as the lift doors opened, and was kissing him by the time they closed. We hadn't even spoken: it was like he knew my intentions from the way I looked at him. But then, Rory was very adept at recognising such intentions. He spent most nights scanning whatever room he was in for exactly those signals.

On this night I was the one who had homed in on what I knew to be a sure thing.

The next morning I woke up with a dawning horror as I remembered where I was and what I had done. Several times, and in a dozen different ways.

I scrambled unsteadily to the bathroom, my head throbbing, fearing I was going to be sick. Unfortunately I was denied this small mercy. Everything horrible that was inside me was there to stay.

At the very least I hoped I could get my clothes on and leave before Rory woke up, but he stirred as I came out of the loo. He didn't seem too comfortable with the situation either. The atmosphere was so thick with awkward you'd have needed breathing apparatus to get from one end of the room to the other.

We hadn't spoken last night in the lift and we'd barely spoken during everything that happened after that. Now we really, really weren't speaking. We knew we had nothing to say to each other, and that we both wanted to be in different places.

As I gathered my things I realised why Rory had all but blanked me on those first nights out with the band after rehearsals. It wasn't because he'd been pals with Maxi, or because he'd anything against me. It was because I was spoken for. No point wasting effort on a girl who wasn't available.

That's the kind of guy he was. And I had just shagged him. The chemistry between us was simply lust with nothing beyond it, no fascination with each other's personality and presence.

By contrast, I had wanted to be in Heike's company constantly, like I was pulled in by gravity. I had thought about her all the time, wondered what she was thinking, felt something radiate inside me when we shared a smile. I had been drawn to her for reasons and by things that seemed to make gender incidental. When we kissed, there had been an innocence to it, like a kiss was everything in and of itself. It was not a prelude or an overture: I hadn't thought beyond it, about what it might lead to. In that sense it had reminded me of a time when that was how it felt with Keith.

I missed her, and I wondered if, beneath all the anger and the sulks, she missed me too.

Unfortunately, our chances of making up were not helped when she saw me leaving Rory's room. As soon as I stepped into the corridor a door opened across the hall, and there she was. She'd been in 307, Rory in 304. What were the bloody odds. She left it ajar just long enough to ensure I knew she had seen me, then closed it again.

As I stood there with my hair a mess and in serious need of a shower, I heard the sound of a TV from 305: someone watching CNN. It wasn't loud, but I could make out every word, which was when I realised the sound insulation was non-existent.

We had been really noisy, and Heike would have heard it all. She must have been waiting for me to come out so that she could communicate this. She had an expression of what I took to be disdain, but at the time my own feelings clouded my reading.

Looking back, I realised she mostly looked hurt.

As always, it was Damien who started the healing efforts, as he was concerned that the wall of ice on stage was detracting from the overall impact of the shows.

'You two need to sort this out,' he said to me on the bus to Dortmund.

You two, he said, but he wasn't talking to both of us. Heike was sitting a couple of rows forward, headphones on. I took this to mean he wanted me to make the first move.

'You think *I* should apologise?' I asked, keeping my voice down in case Heike's iPod wasn't playing as loud as I thought. 'Ask *her* to apologise.'

Way to go, Mon. Very mature.

'It's not about who's to blame. It's about moving on. It's about what's best for the band.'

'Heike finds it kind of difficult to tell between what's best for the band and what's best for Heike. That's why she started kissing me for the cameras just to help boost "Stolen Glances".'

Damien's face crumpled.

'Wait, you're saying that's what this is all about? That you think Heike had something to do with the press catching you two . . .'

'How the hell else do you think it happened?' I asked him.

'No idea, but I can tell you for sure Heike would never do that. Are you kidding me? Sell herself to the press? To the *Daily Heil*?'

'You never know how mercenary you can be until the choice is put in front of you, Damien. Do you remember telling me about a lifeboat with only room for one?'

He looked wounded and I felt shitty for what I'd said, but it was out there now, and I felt the point needed to be made.

Damien sighed.

'I've known Heike a lot longer than you, Monica. I know what she is and isn't capable of. She can be selfish, arrogant, controlling, careerist and the most infuriatingly bloody-minded person on the planet. But what goes along with it all is that she is utterly brazen when she's in the wrong: full, over-compensating defiance as it gets harder and harder for her to back down.'

'So you're saying I just have to ride it out? That I'm only making it worse by expecting her to apologise for what she's done?'

'No. Because that's not what's going on here. Heike isn't acting brazen: she's in the huff, and that only happens when somebody's hurt her feelings. It only happens when *she's* the one who's been wronged.'

It took a few seconds for logic to defuse my emotions, and even then I couldn't quite get the importance of what Damien was telling me. Kind of like you can't quite make out the rock wall in front of you is actually a mountain because it's so huge.

Oh.

Dear.

God.

How do you say sorry for that?

The short answer is you can't. Not to Heike.

Nothing I said made a dent, and I could understand why. I was the one she had trusted most, the one she had opened up to. I was the one she had taken risks on, taken risks for.

I was the one she had kissed, then I'd called her Judas for it. She would never forgive me.

Last Days of the Disappeared

She did speak to me a couple of times after I admitted my mistake, or more like talked *at* me, laying down what she was dealing with. I think it was part of my punishment that she was going to outline how much she was hurting but not let me do anything to help.

The last time I spoke with her in any depth was in Rostock, after we had played a club called Moya. It was an intimate venue, a place where the crowd really went for it, and where there seemed to be an unspoken gratitude for us having come beyond the usual cities of the German circuit. The owner told me the crowds in Hamburg and Munich would never understand what it meant to watch a band rock out up here on the Baltic 'because they never grew up listening to DDR radio'.

The show felt special. We all came off stage on a high, and I thought that maybe the ice was melting. Heike and I found ourselves together alone in a chill-out area, quite possibly engineered by our colleagues. I thought it might be the first glimmer of a new beginning. Instead all I saw was the beginning of the end.

There was almost nothing she said that didn't worry me about her mental state.

'We'll be in Berlin in two days,' she told me blankly. 'It was my request that we finish up the European tour there. I was delighted when the first night sold out and we added another. I had it in my head as a secret kind of homecoming. Now it seems like the closer we get, the more I just feel dread.'

'Why?' I asked, pleasantly surprised that she might be confiding in me again about her mum.

'Because of what's coming after.'

She meant the launch of the third album and the US tour.

'We'll blow them away,' I said, undercutting my bravado with a self-conscious smile. It was my way of letting her know I shared her anxiety but believed that we had what it took.

It didn't penetrate. I'm not sure anything would. I'm not sure she was even listening.

'I don't think I'm capable of holding all this together. I'm not sure I can keep being the person everybody else needs me to be. I don't even know what I'm more afraid of: success or failure. You think what the press did to us last week was tough? This is early days. They've only just noticed me. Once this album is out there, with all that big-label machinery pushing it forward, the person I used to be will be gone for ever, buried under the masks and costumes of the persona I'll need to inhabit.'

She took a sip from her glass. She was on whisky again, rather than beer. Bad sign. She'd bought a whole bottle of it from the bar.

'Everyone thinks I know exactly where I'm going, and that I'd do anything to get there. The truth is I'm lost, and I'm not even the one driving this thing. Do you know who Richey James Edwards was?'

A few months ago, no would have been the answer, but I'd been on a non-stop crash-course in rock history through living around Damien.

'The guy from the Manic Street Preachers who went missing,' I said.

'They were about to embark on a big US tour in support of their third album. The first track is called "Yes", and it's all about how you have to sell yourself in this business, become someone you're not. He couldn't face it.'

She stared into her drink: Bowmore, distilled on Islay, a long way from the world she found herself in now.

'Part of me wants to disappear. Walk away on the verge of this album's release and never be seen again. Let a myth grow up around me instead: the real version can only disappoint.'

Her words made me remember other late-night conversations we'd had on this tour, and I began to wonder if I'd heard what she was really telling me.

'Did you know that suicide rates actually go down during times of war and crisis?' she had said to me in Zagreb. We were talking about the Balkan conflict of the early nineties, about what some of the people we had met that day might have seen and done. I should have realised that Heike was really talking about herself.

'Some people create chaos around themselves, make their lives seemingly impossible, and we ask ourselves why. The truth is that they do it because they need the outside world to reflect what's going on inside their heads. War and crisis does that for them. Suddenly, for once, the world makes sense.

'It's why I'm addicted to this,' she went on, meaning her music, her lifestyle, the band, touring. 'Even though it's chaotic and out of control and it threatens to overwhelm me, I need it, and I'm afraid of what would happen if I didn't have it any more.'

She poured herself another worryingly big measure of malt and swigged back about a third of it in one go. It must have burned, but there were harder things to swallow.

'We're already booked to play Letterman, did you know that?'

I didn't. And now that she'd told me, I was already crapping myself.

'I'm on the verge of this massive exposure, this major break-through, and I just feel adrift. I'm not sure I can face what's in front of me, but I do know that once I've had it, losing it again would be unbearable.'

Looking back, that's when I should have said, 'Catch on to yourself, Heike.' I didn't feel such a thing was any more my right. I didn't think she would listen, and I was cowardly, afraid she'd kick off or even storm out.

That was when I failed her, because maybe that was my cue. Maybe she needed me to risk her anger because I cared enough to do so. Maybe that would have made things different. Maybe she'd have let me in again.

Maybe she'd still today be here.

Zero Option

Mairi told the driver the name of their hotel, but Parlabane advised her to alter the destination.

'We can't go back there until we're sure we're not being observed.'

'How can we be sure? I was pretty bloody sure when we jumped in that last cab, and then they appeared inside the dome. How the hell did they find us?'

Parlabane thought of Bodo's nonchalant lack of urgency, seeming as interested in his phone as he was in his quarry.

He swiped the iPad to waken it, looking for a list of all active programs.

'Remember you said there had to be something else on this thing? Well, I suspect there is: a secondary tracking app. Talk about belt and braces: he *really* didn't want this thing stolen. His default Find My iPad app was essentially functioning as a decoy, because it's the first thing a thief would disable.'

'Can you disable this other one?'

'No. I can't even switch the iPad off: the tracking app must be designed to keep it running.'

'So throw it out the window.'

'Not yet. I want to copy the database, Bodo's emails and the hotel room hidden-camera files to an iFlash drive.'

'Then we need to get underground,' Mairi said, instructing the driver to hang a left on Friedrichstrasse and take them to the U-Bahn station.

They ran down the stairs to the U6 line, Mairi stepping carefully in her bare feet.

Parlabane glanced at the progress of the transfer to his memory stick as they waited on the platform. It was getting there, but taking far longer than it should, given the sizes of the files. Something else was draining resources and busying the memory.

Mairi was staring in consternation at her phone.

'What are you doing?' he asked.

'Checking my location. Successfully, I'm afraid. We're not deep enough. If I can get a GPS signal down here, then so can that thing.'

'We need to keep moving. I just need a little more time.'

They boarded the first train, heading south, both of them casting anxious glances back along the platform until the doors closed.

Parlabane took a seat and returned his attention to the iPad. He didn't like what he saw. The transfer was complete, but he now knew what had been slowing it down.

'I think we just got proof positive that there *is* something else on here that Bodo doesn't want us to see. The problem is that he's taken the zero option now that he knows for sure who's got it. The tracking app is going into emergency mode and performing a remote wipe of the files. In a little while the only thing it will leave running is the shell of the OS and anything it needs to keep sending out its GPS signature.'

'Did you copy the files you need?'

'Yes.'

'So let's get off at the next stop and leave it on the train.'

'Two more stops,' he countered, frantically navigating through folders.

'Are you suicidal?'

'The app is deleting automatically, so at least Bodo hasn't been able to specify what gets wiped first. There might still be time to find something else.'

'Like what?'

He didn't know. Almost everything on it was in German, so there was no way of knowing what terms to search for, never mind knowing what files were worth copying before the digital axe fell. He had to triage rapidly. The only material worth the effort of saving right now would be files in English: anything German was a stab in the dark. Files were being annihilated by the millisecond

285

and he didn't want the last thing he salvaged to turn out to be Bodo's iTunes playlist.

'I need search terms,' he said. 'Words that might quickly identify that a file or part of a document is in English.'

'You mean like "the" or "and"?'

'Too general. We'd get a load of EULAs and manuals.'

Mairi sighed in exasperation.

'Well, how about searching for Heike Gunn? Or would that be too obvious?'

Parlabane gawped.

'I'd slap myself on the forehead but I need both hands to type.'

He keyed in the words and hit return, holding his breath as he awaited the response. About a dozen results filled the window, referencing emails in Bodo's legit Bad Candy account. He scrolled down, hoping to find one from the alias account, but he found a more conspicuous outlier: a text file named 'MHTB'. He pasted a copy onto the iFlash drive, then opened the original.

The screen filled with text.

I will always associate the sound of the fiddle with my grand-father.

It was the sound I heard whenever I went to his house, and whenever he came over to ours. I mean, it wasn't like he carried the thing about with him all the time, just that I have a more vivid recollection of those visits when he had his violin with him.

Parlabane looked to Mairi, who was reading over his shoulder, her eyes almost on stalks.

'MHTB,' she said in a stunned whisper. 'Monica Halcrow's Tour Blog.'

Redacted Details

There were times when, despite your best efforts and your most cherished principles, you still ended up having to act as much of a sleazy prick as any Dacre disciple or Murdoch minion. There was no sugar-coating it. Sure, he had been pushed in front of a train and chased all across Berlin; the stakes were undoubtedly high, with a bright young woman still inexplicably missing. But what he was perusing right now was not the hacked laptop of some spoiled Tory or the incriminating data files of a thuggish sex trafficker. He was reading the candid and intimate private journal of a vulnerable girl half his age.

They sat in Parlabane's hotel room like two wretched reviewers speed-reading a Harry Potter novel so that they could fire out a pointless five hundred words in the next day's paper. *Monica Halcrow and the Fiddle of Sappho* was light on spells and boarding schools, heavy on jealousy and sexual tension.

Parlabane was scrolling through it on his Ultrabook, Mairi on her iPad. Every so often one of them would look up and tantalisingly ask 'Have you got to the bit where . . .?' but ultimately it offered precious little insight. The blog just seemed to flesh out details of what they already knew, with the only revelation to carry genuine shock value being that an innocent abroad on her first tour had taken a remarkably short time to plumb the true depths of rock depravity in shagging a drummer.

Both reviewers also felt compelled to conclude that the ending was a bummer.

'It looks like Heike was in a very bad way, psychologically,' Mairi observed, concern bordering on dread creeping into her tone.

'No shit,' Parlabane agreed. 'She's talking about disappearing and letting a myth grow up around her.'

'I can't help thinking this can't be the whole story, though. Or am I looking for something that isn't there because I don't want to accept what is?'

'It's not the whole story,' Parlabane stated. 'For one thing, it ends in Rostock, with several dates still to play. And look at *how* it ends: with Monica beating herself up that she didn't do enough to intervene in Heike's downward spiral, like she's writing this after the fact.'

'You're right. I mean, I've not spoken to her in a while, but as far as I know, Monica isn't even aware that Heike's missing. And yet the final thoughts on her blog imply she's guilt-ridden, saying if she'd done things differently, Heike would still be here today.'

Parlabane pointed to the last paragraph on Mairi's iPad.

'Specifically it says: "Maybe she'd still today be here". And that wee bit of Yoda-speak follows on from "I didn't feel such a thing was any more my right". These last few paragraphs Monica's writing are not.'

'It's been edited,' Mairi said, shaking her head in mild irritation at how obvious this should have been. 'Of course it's been edited. But why would you censor someone's private journal?'

Parlabane knew a reason, and it wasn't reassuring.

'I think Monica Halcrow is in a lot of trouble. Bodo leaks this blog and the whole world has a poignant and compelling portrait of Heike Gunn's potentially suicidal state of mind, including her stated intention to pull a vanishing act and never be seen again. It would be the perfect cover for them having killed her and disappeared the body.'

'But as soon as it appeared on the web,' Mairi reasoned, 'Monica would be able to tell everyone the whole story.'

'That's why she's in a lot of trouble.'

Mairi stared at Parlabane with an expression he had seen too often down the years: that look of distress at having discovered precisely how deep the rabbit-hole goes, and what darkness lay at its end. It hadn't been him who had brought her to this place, although he had been her guide on the descent. He felt guilty, but knew that wasn't right. Responsible, then. Responsible for what she was going through now, and responsible for getting her through whatever happened thereafter.

By her own admission, Mairi had come out to Berlin expecting a peaceful and satisfactory resolution: they would track down her missing singer, clear up whatever mess had been left and move on towards the album launch and the US tour. Instead it now looked like one of Mairi's young charges was dead and the other in imminent danger of following her.

At this point her response was still in the denial phase.

'Damien said Monica was always tapping away on her laptop, on the bus and in the dressing room. Everyone must have been aware of that. So this document must have been copied by Jan or another of Bodo's Bad Candy crew while she was on stage, presumably post-Rostock. But if these people suddenly made Monica disappear, surely the police or her family would check her computer and find the original? Then the discrepancies between the full account and the edited one would only draw attention to Bodo.'

'I don't think they copied it from her laptop,' Parlabane replied. 'She calls it a blog. That implies web-based.'

'That could just be a modern term. She mentions how "diary" sounds too old-fashioned.'

'This wasn't written on Word. There's weird line-breaks all over the place. It was copy-pasted from another source, like WordPress or Movable Type. I think somebody – on the bus or in the dressing room – surreptitiously watched her log in and clocked her password.'

'What difference does that make?'

'It means it's stored online and they can access it at any time, from anywhere. Bodo can erase the original from his office desk in Berlin, replacing it with this version as the definitive. Then suddenly you don't only have an explanation for Heike vanishing, you've got a guilt-racked suicide note from Monica as well.'

Mairi closed the document on her iPad and opened up her browser.

'I'm booking us on the first flight home. We need to reach

289

Monica and find out what's missing from that blog. I doubt she'll spill anything over the phone because she did a very good butter-wouldn't-melt act the last time I spoke to her, but we can prove that it's in her best interests to tell the truth.'

'Plus we can threaten to leak scuddy photos of her if she doesn't play ball,' Parlabane suggested. 'Just saying.'

Mairi glared at him in momentary incredulity, then laughed with exasperated relief. It had taken her a while to decide he was joking, but to be fair, Parlabane couldn't have said for certain that he was.

'Oh, Jack.'

She rested her head on his shoulder as the tension of the last few minutes gave way to a moment of welcome levity. This in turn precipitated a few gentle tears, but she was more determined than upset.

She selected flights for the next morning, leaving Tegel early and changing at Heathrow for Glasgow. He watched her book them on her iPad, saying nothing to remind her that there was a good chance he'd be arrested once he was back in the UK. He'd known there was no avoiding that: it wasn't like he was planning to flee to a non-extradition country. If it was going to happen, it was going to happen. He just hoped it didn't happen before they found Monica, and saw no need to further worry Mairi.

'Bit of a red-eye,' Parlabane noted. 'We'd better get some sleep. It's been a long day, and tomorrow could be longer.'

'Yeah,' Mairi agreed, standing up and stretching with a yawn.

She lifted her iPad and Parlabane stepped to one side to allow her to pass on her way to the door. He got it wrong, both of them stepping the same way in the narrow channel between the bed and the dressing table.

Mairi stopped and looked into his eyes, their faces only inches apart once again.

'Maybe . . . I don't need to go to *my* room to sleep,' she said quietly.

There was nothing coy or playful in her voice; her tone sincere, vulnerable.

'And maybe we could just . . . sleep,' she added. 'Together.'

Parlabane closed his eyes, hating this, hating himself.

She read it in his face before he had to say anything.

'I'm sorry,' he told her. 'And I have absolutely no doubt that "just sleeping" would feel good. I'm just not sure it feels *right*.'

'Is it because I'm employing you?'

'No, it's not that. It's a lot of things. I feel responsible for you.'

'I'm big enough to look after myself. I've survived in this business long enough.'

'I know. But we aren't in your business any more. We're somewhere more dangerous, and I can't shake the image of you as Donald's wee sister back in your parents' house. I can't let anything happen to you.'

'Because you couldn't save him?'

'Partly, maybe. But mainly, dating back to those teenage years, there was a barrier erected in my mind to put you off limits: my pal's wee sister. It was to stop me doing anything I'd regret. And to stop me torturing myself with possibilities.'

'You *fancied* me back then?' she asked, with genuine surprise.

'Jesus, are you kidding? Was I that good at hiding it?'

'Maybe you didn't have to be that good because I assumed you'd only see me as Donald's daft wee sister. Back when I was torturing *my*self that you might notice me.'

Christ. Half a decade suddenly revised itself in his head: things he'd missed, things that could have happened differently.

Nah. He'd still have fucked it up.

'Maybe that's still the problem. Even now you see me as trivial and immature.'

'That's absolutely not—'

'I've seen the look on your face when I pitch up with a Starbucks, or when I was picking out clothes for you yesterday. It doesn't mean I'm shallow. I'm not engaged in politics and causes, but I'm no stranger to fighting battles. And, unlike you, I'm mature enough to know I can't fight everyone else's.'

'Mairi, honestly, I . . .'

'Good night, Jack.'

As soon as the door closed he felt an urge to go after her: catch her in the corridor, make the grand gesture. He'd never know whether he'd have acted upon it, because his mobile rang at that moment.

As he read the name on the screen he felt everything pause for a microsecond – his breath, his heart, even time.

It was Sarah.

An image flashed through his mind: he could have been kissing Mairi as this call came through, breaking away to see who was trying to get in touch in case it was urgent. Christ, how would that have felt? He didn't believe in fate, but he couldn't help interpret this as an indication that he'd made the right choice. He'd turned Mairi down and finally Sarah was getting in touch.

He hit answer.

'Sarah,' he said, trying to sound pleased but not overexcited. He just couldn't wait to hear her voice.

There was a long pause. Long enough for him to worry. Then eventually she spoke.

'Jack.'

Her voice was flat and emotionless, hollow and distant.

'The police were here,' she said. 'They just left.'

She sounded wrung-out: nerve-frayed and simmeringly angry.

'They were asking where you were. Asking when I last saw you. They were from London.'

'It's the Westercruik Inquiry,' he said, his tone low and apologetic.

'I know who they were, Jack. They came *here*, to the hospital.'

'Oh, God, Sarah, I'm—'

'They weren't discreet. Bustled in flashing badges and making a big show of demanding to see me. They did it in front of everybody. They were here for ages. Question after question regarding stuff I knew nothing about. I think they were asking things just for the sake of asking things.'

'Did they put you under caution?'

'No, but what difference does that make? My colleagues saw me being escorted to a private room by detectives, then I spent the next hour being treated like a criminal.'

'I'm sorry,' he said, but there was no apologising for this.

She wasn't calling to warn him or to ask for help. She was calling to let him know what he'd brought to her door.

He felt completely empty inside. He'd been trying to protect a guttering flame for months, and this was the moment he had to accept it was dowsed.

'So, apart from the police harassment, how are you?' he asked, some last ember inside wondering if the gallows humour could still spark a moment of connection.

'I'm tired, Jack. Tired of treading through your wreckage. And tired of you pretending that this isn't over.'

Intervention

Heike poured herself another worryingly big measure of malt and swigged back about a third of it in one go. It must have burned, but there were harder things to swallow.

'We're already booked to play Letterman, did you know that?'

I didn't. And now that she'd told me, I couldn't wait. America had been on the horizon as another big block of tour dates: more buses, more hotels, more soundchecks, more hangovers. Suddenly I saw it for what it really was: a unique and privileged opportunity. I'd never even been there, and on my first trip I'd get to play on national TV. This was huge, scary in a good way. And Heike had lost sight of that because she felt the burden was all on her.

More than ever, she needed a friend. More than ever, she needed someone who would cut through her bullshit and take her just a bit less seriously.

'I'm on the verge of this massive exposure, this major breakthrough, and I just feel adrift. I'm not sure I can face what's in front of me, but I do know that once I've had it, losing it again would be unbearable.'

I knew what I ought to say, which would be kill or cure for our relationship. I was scared to say it because I wasn't sure I had the right, after all that had happened since Zurich. I was afraid she'd kick off or even storm out. But I knew I had to risk her anger because I cared enough to do so.

'Catch on to yourself, Heike,' I said.

Her eyes bulged a bit, a look of disbelief forming. For just a split-second it was identical to the surprise it provoked that night in Berlin, except that then it had turned into laughter. This time it turned into growing outrage.

But I stayed the course. I had no other option.

'You're living the dream,' I added, repeating my words from Frauen Frei. 'And if the dream falls apart again, then you'll want to be able to tell yourself you rode the hell out of it while you could. You don't need to hold anything together. This band would run through walls for you.'

She stared at me almost helplessly, having gone from defensiveness to drinking in my words.

'We're not just your musicians, Heike, we're your friends.'

She continued to look at me in silence, her lower lip quivering. Then she managed a hint of a smile and a gentle nod.

'I know that,' she eventually said. 'It's just . . . Everybody assumes I'm thick-skinned and have this haughty conceit of myself, but I'm really a shambles. I'm so afraid that people only like me for who I'm pretending to be or for what I can give them, and you can multiply that insecurity ten times over when it comes to the band. I think, They're only putting up with my bullshit because they want to be rock stars and I'm their best bet.'

'That's not true, Heike. Nobody would put up with your bullshit just to be in a band.'

She gave a small, grateful laugh.

'I become this nightmare control freak because you guys are all I have. I get obsessed with anticipating anything that could damage us, individually or collectively. I never had any brothers or sisters, I never had a mum, and now my dad's gone. This band is as close as I've got to a family.'

The tears came now, from both of us. We fell into a tight hug, clinging on to something we valued.

'I'm sorry about the photos,' she said, sniffing. 'But I swear, I had nothing to do with it.'

'I know. I'm so sorry I accused you. I wasn't equipped to deal with that kind of thing, I was totally reeling and I got confused because you were so short with me that day.'

'I was reeling too, and I felt terrible for you because you were new to it all. But to get you through it I had to be your band leader rather than your BFF. Plus, I felt so awkward in front of the guys, like they were a microcosm of the whole world that was suddenly staring at us.'

'Why didn't you tell me all this?' I asked. 'Why did you let me go on thinking you'd done what I accused you of?'

She gave me a regretful look.

'The worst part about the whole debacle was that it made me realise we could never be, for so many reasons. That hurt. It was easier to let you think I had screwed you over, because then you would keep your distance and I wouldn't be left feeling tantalised by what I couldn't have.'

I gave her a sad smile, understanding.

'I missed you, though,' I told her.

'I missed you too.'

Wherever the moment was going, it was disrupted by a girl in a white denim jacket similar to Heike's coming to our table. She wasn't sporting the cream-blonde crop but she did have the fangirl look about her, even if she was maybe on the old side for that. I'd have put her mid-to-late twenties.

'Heike, I need to speak with you,' she said. Her English was strongly accented, her tone somewhere between desperate and insistent.

Heike turned around to face her, with a polite but regretful smile.

'I'm sorry,' she said. 'But my friend and I are in the middle of something quite important and we really need some time to ourselves.'

I spotted the bouncer who was manning the chill-out area casting a glance. He was under orders from the management to make sure we were left alone, but was looking for a nod from Heike instead of acting automatically.

I normally felt extremely awkward whenever I was being in some way 'protected' from the public, but this time the intervention would be welcome. Heike and I were actually putting our difficulties behind us, so the girl's timing was really bad.

Then she said the three words that changed everything.

'It's about Hannah.'

Lost in Translation

The brightness of the morning sun through the towering wall of glass was making Terminal 5 seem less gruesomely purgatorial than usual, in almost wilfully drawn contrast to the prevailing mood. Parlabane sat next to Mairi in one of the common waiting areas, opposite a departure monitor, waiting for a gate to be assigned to their flight to Glasgow.

Mairi hadn't said anything since they sat down. She had been quiet all morning, but not silent like this. Things had felt slightly awkward between them, but they had made small talk on the way to Tegel and on the flight to Heathrow. Something was different now, though. She had been sitting with her magazine open at the same page for at least twenty minutes. She wasn't reading, just staring, unfocused.

Parlabane turned to look at her face, and saw that tears were starting to form in eyes already red and puffy from fitful sleep and an early rise. She became conscious of his scrutiny and turned her head away so that he wouldn't see her.

He wondered what it looked like to the people in the nearby seats, what stories they might imagine for the weeping woman and the torn-faced prick sitting beside her.

'Back in a minute,' he said, getting up and walking away.

He wanted to give her privacy. It might seem futile in a place as public as this, but he knew the strangers didn't matter. It wasn't them she wanted to hide her upset from.

It felt like it was all he could do, and yet it felt worse than doing nothing. He wanted to give her more than privacy, he wanted to give her comfort. He wandered through the departure area, weaving through the streams of passengers and suddenly hit upon the way he could best demonstrate his solicitude right then.

He bought her a Starbucks.

Mairi acknowledged it with a sad and knowing little laugh.

'Thanks, Jack,' she said warmly, with a sniff.

'I willingly sacrifice my principles on the altar of your comfort.'

'I know you didn't do it lightly.'

She took a sip and gave his knee a pat as he sat down.

'You okay?' he asked.

'Been better. It was looking at the departure board that brought it home: I saw the flight to LA that we're all booked to be on in a couple of weeks. I'm due to go out for the first part of the tour, and to have some meetings with the US label. Heike and I had fun talking about it, how that was proof that we'd all truly made it: we'd be sitting in business class, heading for Hollywood.'

Mairi glanced at the board again. Parlabane could see the LA flight listed, three below theirs. She turned to look at him.

'She's dead, isn't she, Jack?'

Parlabane held her gaze, took a breath. He didn't want to answer and he didn't want to lie.

His phone began to ring.

When he saw who it was from he knew he had no option but to respond.

'I'm sorry,' he said, standing up. 'I have to take this.'

Mairi nodded, hugging the coffee cup to her like it was a comfort blanket.

Parlabane touched the little green handset icon as he walked to a comparatively quiet spot, out of anyone else's earshot, particularly Mairi's.

'Hey, Scoop, how's it going?' asked Jenny cheerfully.

'Well, I'm still alive and I haven't been arrested, so by those measures fortune has been smiling upon me. Are you calling to tell me that's about to change?'

'Not that I've heard. Word is there's been a delay in getting that warrant and there's some very frustrated Metbots as a result.'

'A delay?'

'Yes. The kind of thing that mysteriously happens when very connected people have an interest in the polis not talking to somebody.'

So that was why they'd been hassling Sarah: trying to turn up the heat on him in other ways. A delay was finite, though. They would clear the obstacles soon enough; he just wondered who specifically had thrown them in the police's path.

'Where are you?' she asked.

'Heathrow. On my way back from Berlin.'

'Any luck finding your pop star?'

'Not so far.'

'Well, fortunately your Auntie Jenny's got some information you might be interested in. It's a bit of a quid pro quo deal, though, so I'm expecting you to sing for your supper.'

'As long as it's not about Sir Anthony Mead's laptop, you can order off the menu. What have you got?'

'It's about Ms Gunn. I've managed to get hold of her credit card transactions. Her other financial details are on request, but I got these first because I've a contact. This stuff is inadmissible until it comes through legit channels, but you know the score.'

'Sure: an unofficial wee heads-up to point you in the right direction. You did this for me? How big a favour am I going to owe you?'

'Don't flatter yourself, Scoop, this isn't about you. My Borders Agency query got flagged when her name popped up in another investigation. But on the day you say she disappeared, there was major activity on her card. The final use was at Berlin Haupt . . . Haub . . .'

'Hauptbahnhof.'

'Aye. She made a payment to ICE – that's Intercity Express. I chased the transaction and it turns out she bought a one-way ticket to Copenhagen. Absolutely nothing since then.'

'Denmark. Interesting.'

'Does that track with you?'

'A wee bit. Anything else? You said major activity.'

'Yes. Earlier the same day she spent seventy grand on two designer watches. You know what that's about?'

'Not a clue. But thanks.'

'Oh, don't thank me. In a second I'm going to put you through to a nice lady called Detective Superintendent Catherine McLeod, and you're going to give her absolutely anything she asks for. And when I say nice, what I mean is a black-belt ball-crusher Glesca Polis high heid-yin who, unlike me, will not be so indulgent of your more, shall we say, colourful traits, so step lightly.'

Before he could say anything else the line clicked and the tone changed as he was transferred. He heard a woman's voice a few moments later. She didn't sound as scary as Jenny was making out, but to be fair they were only at the sniffing-butt stage, and fore-warned was fore-armed.

'Hello, is this Jack Parlabane?'

'That's right.'

'I understand you've been looking for Heike Gunn, who I believe has gone missing.'

'She hasn't been seen or heard from since failing to turn up for the last night of her band's European tour in Berlin,' he clarified, in full best-behaviour mode, as though Jenny might be listening in. 'What do you want to know?'

'We've found a body,' McLeod said, her tone firm and even.

Shit.

He glanced across to where Mairi was sitting. She seemed to sense his attention and looked up, restless anxiety in her eyes. He turned his head away. He couldn't let her see his face right then.

'You've found Heike?' he asked.

'No. That's why I need to speak to you. We found someone dressed to *look* like Heike, right down to the creamy-blonde hair. She was discovered in a shipping container in Rutherglen. She had been stabbed.'

'A shipping container? Shipped from where?'

'The goods were despatched in Kiev, but its sea port of origin was Hamburg.'

Germany.

When the call was over Parlabane hurried over to Mairi.

'Have you still got a copy of that leaflet? The one from the Brauereihallen?'

'I think so,' she replied, beginning to sift through her Mulberry shoulder bag. 'What do you need it for?'

Parlabane glanced up at the departure board and scanned it for a German-bound flight. There was one going to Frankfurt in half an hour, preparing to board.

'Come with me.'

They hastened towards gate A10, looking like they were running to catch their connection. When they got there the Frankfurt flight was at pre-boarding, dozens of passengers grasping their passports and looking up expectantly towards the departure desks.

Parlabane approached a grey-haired lady who was conversing with her travelling companion in perfect but discernibly accented English.

'Excuse me,' he asked. 'We don't speak German and we need to know what this says. Would you mind telling us?'

'Not at all,' she answered, glancing at the leaflet in Parlabane's hands, the word VERMISST leaping out in its block capitals.

'Missing,' she said.

'And the lines beneath the picture?'

She took it from him and looked more closely this time.

'It says they are searching for a girl who looks like the one in the photograph.'

'*Looks like?*'

'Yes. They are worried about her. "When she was last seen she was dressed like Heike Gunn, from the band Savage Earth Heart. Her name is Anezka, but she is also known as Hannah or Anna." It asks if you have seen a girl who looks like this to please call the number on the leaflet.'

'Thank you,' Parlabane said. 'Thank you very much indeed.'

'You're welcome,' she replied, wandering off to join the queue as her flight was called.

He turned to Mairi.

'Bodo said on the phone that I ought to learn some German. He knew I'd misunderstood the flyer. I asked him why he was looking for Heike, and he said he wasn't. He was telling the truth.'

'So what does this mean?' Mairi asked.

'It means you don't need to start organising the memorial tribute concert just yet.'

New Life

The girl sat down at the end of our table, perched on a low pouffe. She kept glancing towards the exit as though concerned who might be about to walk in.

She introduced herself as Kabka. She was attractive, if skinny, and had the most impossibly black hair, swept back behind a headband and reaching down between her shoulder blades. The phrase "bride of Dracula" popped uncharitably into my mind, maybe because I was resentful of the interruption and partly because she had an Eastern European look to her.

'Hannah is in Berlin,' she told us.

'We're going there in two days,' Heike replied, her tone asking the question why Kabka had come to Rostock instead. I supposed the answer would be complicated, but could never have anticipated the extent.

'Yes. She hopes to see you. She did not get the chance to explain when you were in Madrid.'

Kabka looked anxious and apologetic, like she was keen to please but didn't fancy her chances of getting a result.

'Explain what?' I asked. 'Who those men were that took her away?'

'That is not why I am here. This is for Heike,' she added. 'I do not know if I am allowed to say to another.'

'It's okay,' Heike assured her, resting her hand on my thigh out of sight and giving it a squeeze. 'We're all friends here.'

Kabka nodded uncertainly.

'Okay. Hannah said she ran away when you . . . you try . . .'

She looked really uncomfortable, like she was intruding upon something.

'To kiss her,' Heike said firmly.

Kabka nodded again.

'Yes. To kiss her. I am just . . . the messenger, yes?'

I wondered why a messenger was needed, given Hannah had Heike's mobile number.

Kabka sent another glance towards the door, then reached inside her jacket. She produced three photographs and placed them down on the table, sliding them towards Heike with an expression of the utmost gravity.

The light was dim in the low-ceilinged room, but Heike saw enough in that first second to make her cover her mouth and shudder with shock. She glared at Kabka, so many questions in her eyes. Kabka guessed the most important, though.

'These are Hannah's pictures of her mother. Please be very careful touching them. They are all she has left of her.'

Heike reached out to lift one of them, her hand shaking like she was cold. Her breathing became smothered, choked in a sob as her eyes filled.

I had only seen Heike's treasured Polaroid briefly via her phone, but even I recognised that it was the same face staring back at us from these dog-eared prints. She looked a little older, more soberly dressed. In one she wore a winter coat, her face peeking out from a hood. In another she wore a pale dress, looking skinny; underfed, I thought. The clothing was so cheap and careworn, though maybe it was just the age of the photos.

In the shot Heike had picked up, gripped delicately in trembling fingers, she was holding a baby.

'That is Hannah,' Kabka said. 'When she was about three months of age, in Bratislava.'

Heike was struggling to speak. I wanted to put an arm around her but it didn't feel right: it would have been like I was trying to make myself part of this.

'These are pictures of . . . This is . . .'

'Your mother,' said Kabka. 'Sieghilde. This is why Hannah ran away from you. She had not been able yet to tell you the truth: she is your half-sister.'

Heike put the photograph back down, as though it was too heavy a burden to hold up for long. Her eyes went back and forth from the three pictures on the table, trying to make sense of what they were telling her.

'How is this possible?' she asked. 'My mother died when I was a baby.'

Kabka shook her head. Her voice was low, as though afraid of being overheard, but also like she was aware of the impact her words would have, and the need to lay them down gently.

'Sieghilde let your father take you away because she was too weak to resist. Heroin was killing her, and your father gave up trying to get her off it. She had tried, when you were born. She got a tattoo. Do you know of this?'

Heike took a mouthful of whisky then wiped her eyes with her sleeve.

'Yes. She got the letter H tattooed on her forearm, where she liked to shoot up. It was a declaration that I was the only H she cared about now.'

Heike rolled up her sleeve and revealed a similar mark. I had seen it plenty of times but never guessed it had a deeper meaning. It wasn't something she had chosen to share with me, far less mentioned in any interviews.

'I had this done as a kind of, I don't know . . . remembrance, tribute. It didn't work for her, though. She was back on the stuff within weeks, I was told.'

'Yes. But losing you was . . . *die Wende*, the, what do you say, the turn-around point. She got clean. And then the Wall came down. She had a friend in Bratislava, so she moved there looking for a new life.'

Heike placed a finger softly upon the shot of her mother in the winter coat, and whispered the single word: 'Bratislava.'

I imagined her thinking about where she was when that photo was taken, what age she'd have been.

'Once the Iron Curtain came down there was soon a heroin scene in Bratislava. Her old life found her once more. She got pregnant, but Hannah does not even know his name. Sieghilde called her Hannah because she wanted a name that started with H. She was trying again to stop.'

304

'With the same success,' Heike suggested, sounding numb.

'Yes. And when Hannah got taken by the authorities, this time she did not escape the spiral.'

'Hannah told me she was raised in care homes,' Heike said.

'That's right. Before she died, her mother wrote her a letter. It told her she had a half-sister whose father was an artist. She never expected she would find this half-sister, but years later she discovered your music. She found out your father had lived in Berlin, and the dates matched up. She feared it was just a coincidence, until she saw a photograph of you playing your guitar. You were wearing a T-shirt, so she saw your arm.'

Heike stared at her tattoo, like it had just appeared, or she was only seeing it for the first time.

'Hannah has this tattoo also,' Kabka went on. 'She had it done when she was thirteen.'

'I didn't see it,' Heike replied. 'Although I recall she kept tugging her sleeve down like she was self-conscious about something. It was warm in Bilbao that night too: short-sleeve weather.'

I knew it wasn't my place, but there was a very big question that still needed an answer, and Heike seemed too emotional to raise it.

'Why isn't Hannah the one here telling us this?' I asked.

From the way she kept glancing at the door, I strongly suspected the answer would have something to do with the two men who had taken her away so easily in Madrid.

I wasn't wrong.

'Hannah . . . the reason I know her, we were in the same situation. She is from Slovakia, I am from Bulgaria. I was offered a job by an agency in Sofia. They said they recruited for waitress work in Berlin. They said they could fix the legal things, the documents, but only if I paid five thousand euros. I did not have this money, but they say it's okay, I pay five hundred euros as a deposit, then pay the rest once I am in work.'

She looked down at the table, her face flushing. I wanted to look away too. I knew what was coming, and I felt dreadful for her.

'When I get to Germany there is no job. They take my passport, they take me to this house, and they . . .'

She sighed, steadying herself. Her voice wavered but she carried on.

'They raped me. Three men. Several times. After that, they make me work as a prostitute. Until I pay back the debt, they say, which keeps going up. I lived like this a long time. Almost four years.'

She sounded hollow, suddenly very old, but from what she was saying I knew she was probably not much older than me.

'How did you get out?' Heike asked.

'They like the girls young: healthy and attractive. They are not streetwalkers, they operate at the top end.'

I thought of the Eastern European-looking girls in Madrid, and realised Jan wasn't lying when he said they were going to the Fiera in Milan.

'Once you start to look too old they are finally ready to let you pay off the debt. They like the girls to know they *can* buy their way out, so that they will work hard and be obedient. In the end, all the money still comes back to the bosses. But if they decide you are too old and you cannot pay the debt they ship you off to work in brothels, where there will be twenty, thirty, forty men in a day. This is also how they keep the girls in line: the threat of something worse.'

'You paid off your debt?' I asked.

She nodded solemnly.

'I worked very hard,' she said, looking me in the eye. I felt about one inch tall.

'This is why I am here, and why Hannah is back in Berlin. She made them angry because she went missing while she was supposed to be working in Spain. And she spent a lot of the money she had saved on travelling to follow you around, working up the courage to speak to you. Now her debt is very high, and she is not so young.'

Heike was still trembling, but from anger. I thought of the men we had seen at the museum in Madrid, and for the first

306

time in my life I wished real, brutal violence upon another human being.

'How much does she need?' Heike asked.

Kabka paused, readying herself to break it to us.

Preparing to Fly

They picked up a hire car at Glasgow Airport, Mairi having booked it online the night before along with the flights. She'd neglected to mention this to Parlabane, who was on his way out towards the taxi rank when she hauled him back to the rental desks. It just wouldn't have occurred to him to hire a vehicle when he was flying into Glasgow or Edinburgh, cities he thought of as home, so he was grateful that it was standard practice for Mairi as a London-dweller.

The rental firm gave them a Volkswagen Scirocco. When the woman on the desk told them this, it felt like Europcar had done their research and calculated specifically which vehicle would psychologically goad him the most by forcing him to recall happier times. He had owned a Scirocco when he first lived with Sarah, a late-eighties model purchased second-hand from a guy in Lochgelly. He'd loved that thing, hadn't he?

No. It wasn't the car that he'd loved, nor the flat they'd lived in or the work he'd been doing.

They took the Clyde Tunnel exit off the M8 and headed for Partick, Mairi barely restrained by the speed cameras in her conspic-uous urgency to reach Monica's flat.

'One thing I don't get,' she said, turning on to the Clydeside Expressway. 'If it was Bodo who put out those flyers, why did he print Heike's picture rather than the girl he was actually looking for? Surely he'd have a photo of her; she was probably in his database.'

'He was playing the percentages. You see a picture of a complete stranger you've never seen before, you won't remember the face even if you walk past her the very next day. But if you see that flyer and then you see a girl who looks like Heike Gunn ...'

Parlabane could hear strings playing from an open window above as they walked from the car to the door of the red-stone tenement.

'Sounds like she's home, anyway,' he observed.

Mairi looked at him like he was a puddle.

'That's a cello, cloth ears.'

They climbed the stairs to the second floor and rang the bell, Mairi giving it a long, firm press to make sure it was heard over the music.

The cello ceased, and a few moments later the door was opened by a young woman in deck shorts and a No More Page Three T-shirt, clutching a bow. She had long, flowing but unkempt red hair, indicative of someone either not long out of bed or not expecting to be dealing with visitors.

'Hello. We're looking for Monica?' Mairi said brightly, as though trying to jog the girl's memory regarding who she lived with.

'Oh. She's not here. You're . . . Mairi, is that right?'

'Well remembered. We met at the party after the show at Barrowlands. I'm the band's manager. This is Jack. Isobel, isn't it?'

'Yeah. Why don't you come in? I'm just putting the kettle on.'

She opened the door and led them into the living room. It was bright and warm, sun streaming through the bay window where Isobel's cello was resting on its stand.

'You and Monica were both in the RSNO, weren't you?'

'Aye. Found this place together when she first moved down from Shetland and I came through from Edinburgh. Have a seat. Let me move some of this crap.'

Isobel reached down to the settee and picked up a basket of ironing, tossing a couple of magazines into it as well to clear space.

'Did Monica just nip out?' Mairi asked optimistically. 'Will she be back soon?'

Isobel bit her lip apologetically.

'I don't think so. She left about half an hour, forty minutes ago. I don't know where she's gone, but it wasn't round the corner for a pint of milk.'

'But she's okay?' Mairi said. 'I mean, she *has* been here. It's just that she's been ignoring my messages.'

'She's been here, yes. Okay's another matter. She's been very weird since yesterday but she wouldn't tell me what was wrong.'

'Weird how?' Mairi asked.

Isobel shrugged.

'Everything was fairly normal: we were having a bowl of pasta and watching the tennis, then she got this phone call and it was like she'd seen a ghost. She went off to her room to take it. I went to see if she was okay a bit later and I found her packing a bag. She said she was going to Shetland, but she's just back from there two days ago.'

'A family emergency?' Parlabane suggested.

'If it was family she wouldn't have reacted like she did, going off so I couldn't hear her. Monica's mum is on the phone all the time, and she sits and jaws to her in front of me, you know? But the other reason I know she hasn't gone to Shetland is that when I was in her room I saw what was on her laptop; it looked like she was hiring a car. She was out this morning: she didn't say where, but she could have been picking it up.'

'Has she been secretive like this in the past?' Mairi asked. 'I mean, has she been behaving any differently since she returned from the tour?'

'Well, obviously things were a bit touchy when she first came back, given the fallout from what was in the papers and her breaking up with Keith. She was very withdrawn. I'd been looking forward to hearing all the tour stories but she didn't want to talk about it. Of course, it didn't help her frame of mind that Keith kept calling and sometimes showing up.'

'He came here?'

'Aye. She let him in one time because he'd come all the way from Aberdeen, but it ended in a row and her threatening to get the polis if he didn't leave. It was borderline stalking after that. Lots of phone calls and him turning up at the front door. I think I was more upset about it on her behalf than Monica was herself: she's a tougher cookie than folk assume. But the call last night: whatever this was, it really spooked her. I've never seen her being evasive like that. We're normally quite open with each other.'

Mairi looked towards the window. From her expression, Parlabane deduced she wanted to lean out of it and scream.

Mairi tried calling Monica's mobile but predictably reported that she was getting shunted to voicemail.

'If it wasn't Shetland,' Mairi asked, 'have you any notion of where she might have gone? It's really important.'

Isobel looked pained. Parlabane had no suspicion that she was holding something back.

'I'll have to have a think. Let me get you both that cup of tea.'

'That's very kind,' Mairi replied, 'but there's no need. We're imposing enough.'

'Not at all. Besides, ever since moving here I've been on a mission to debunk the Edinburgh stereotype, you know? *You'll have had your tea, then,*' she mimicked.

She went off to the kitchen, leaving the two of them in the sudden silence of the living room, where they had to contemplate the fact that the one person they could have finally leaned upon to tell them the whole story had just driven off, and they had no idea where.

It was Mairi who spoke first.

'We're screwed, aren't we?'

Human Worth

'Twelve thousand euros,' Heike said. 'I don't know which is the more sickening insult: that her life can be for sale so cheap, or that it's a figure way beyond her means.'

It was the first time she'd spoken since last night. The bus had been on the road more than an hour, during which Heike had stared out of the window or at her phone. We were on our way to Hamburg, but her thoughts were already in Berlin. She looked like she'd barely slept; how could she? I asked myself. I couldn't imagine the emotional torment she had gone through: to learn her mother had been alive when she was little, years when she could have been with her; but more happily now to find out she had a sister.

('I won't tolerate the word "half",' she had said. 'We have the same mother: we're not half anything.')

She had begged Kabka for one of the photos, just until we met up again in Berlin. But Kabka wouldn't. She looked torn, saying, 'A promise is a promise – trust is everything to Hannah. You must understand what these pictures mean to her.'

Heike had settled for taking a photo of one using her iPhone, but in the dim light of the bar, the flash had produced only a bleached-out ghost of the original. Heike had spent much of the journey looking at it.

Twelve thousand euros. It sounded like a lot of money to me, but it was nothing to Heike. She had let slip once that her credit card limit was in six figures. She was more worried over how soon a wire transfer could be arranged.

Kabka promised that Hannah would pay it back. Heike told her that wouldn't be necessary, but Kabka had insisted that it was important to Hannah that she did so.

'It's a matter of pride. Hannah is smart. She knows she could earn money if she was out there in the world and free to prove herself. She's just never had that chance.'

I hadn't slept brilliantly either, and I sensed it was going to feel like a long day. I knew that in Heike's mind the Hamburg show was now simply an unnecessary inconvenience, a diversion to be got through on the way to her true destination.

So far on the European tour Heike had been the consummate pro, putting her game face on and delivering a performance whatever was going on behind the scenes and beneath the surface. But everyone has their limit, and in Hamburg I saw hers.

Her mind was elsewhere all day. We were both late for the soundcheck because we went to a Western Union office to organise the money transfer, and it was agonisingly slow, thanks to a computer problem with Heike's bank back in the UK. She became almost irrationally agitated when they said it would take twenty-four hours, then I reminded her she could pick up the money in Berlin. To my mind this was a better arrangement, as travelling with that much in cash seemed too precarious to somebody who never took out more than fifty quid at a time from an ATM.

The show was fraught, the atmosphere tense and awkward long before we hit the stage, with Heike and me being AWOL. Jan had been getting grief from the venue management, and there was an A&R guy from the German support band's record label kicking up aggro because their own soundcheck was getting shorter by every minute Heike was late. Angus lost his opening slot as well, so he didn't exactly add a note of harmony either.

The show felt flat from the off, Heike barely talking to the audience between songs. Then she had a minor breakdown during 'Dark Station': arpeggios she could pluck in her sleep suddenly misplayed or missed out as her fingers turned to jelly; her voice wavering as she fought tears.

We didn't play an encore. The audience didn't exactly clamour for one, but they did wait around expectantly after we left the stage, only to shuffle off when the house lights went up. The band knew something was wrong, but Heike wasn't saying what. I told them she was just a bit burned out – she'd perk up in Berlin, as that was the end of the line.

The taxi dropped us off at Alexanderplatz, which I found difficult to picture as a centrepiece for the civic pride of the old East. It was vast, bustling, bright, loud and a bit vulgar, reminding me of Piccadilly Circus. There was trashy pop music coming from storefronts, smells of fast food on the breeze: the kind of place my mum would find nightmarish, but which would have been irresistible to me around the age of fourteen.

The Wall fell before I was born, and it seemed impossible as I looked at my surroundings, to imagine half a city cordoned off.

Needlessly separated.

I had been warned that Berlin was a place you could feel stalked by history. Given all we had been through together, I felt like I was being stalked by Heike's personal history.

As we passed the World Clock I looked for the café where Heike had agreed to meet Kabka. I saw it further along the tramlines on Rathausstrasse, close to where the television tower poked up at the sky like some gigantic cake decoration.

We stepped inside and scanned the tables for Kabka. She wasn't here yet, but we were a few minutes early. We grabbed an empty booth and took a seat, Heike bagging the side with a view of the door.

The waiter took our order and quickly returned with two coffees. I heard the door open behind me as he put them down, and when he cleared Heike's line of vision she looked on in obvious alarm. Before I could turn to look there was someone sliding into the booth beside me, a burly and shaven-headed figure I recognised as one of the men who had taken Hannah in Madrid.

He sat with his back straight and stared directly across at Heike, like I wasn't even there.

'Where is Kabka?' Heike asked.

Her voice caught a little. She was trying to hide fear and anger, and not succeeding.

'She is not coming,' he replied. 'You have the money?'

314

Heike opened her jacket and let him see the plastic wallet stuffed with hundred-euro notes.

He gave a patronising nod, like he was surprised or impressed or something. Like he was amused. I didn't take it to be a good sign, and nor was the fact that he was on his own.

'That's as close to it as you're going to get until I see Hannah,' Heike told him. 'If you don't produce her, and her passport, then there's no deal.'

He seemed to ponder this, then nodded.

'You are right,' he said. 'There is no deal. Not for that price.'

'This is twelve thousand euros,' she stated. 'That's how much Kabka said Hannah owes. You can have it in your hand *today*.'

He looked like he was mulling it over, or actually he was making a show of mulling it over, which meant he wasn't. The fact that Heike had turned up here so smartly with twelve thousand in cash must have told him she could get more.

'Things change,' he said.

'Hannah's debt just went up?' Heike asked acidly.

'No. It is not about Hannah's debt. It is about Hannah's worth.'

'She's getting *older*,' Heike replied, dripping venom. 'She's a declining asset in your evil little business.'

'Like I say, things change. Not many men want to fuck a girl like Hannah when there are younger, prettier girls on the menu. But maybe they want to fuck a girl who looks like a famous rock star, yes?'

In that moment it all changed quite terribly for the worse. I wouldn't have taken him for a Savage fan, but Heike's face had been on a lot of magazines and TV screens. Still, it could have been much worse: if he had known the truth about why Heike was here, he really could have named his price.

'She looks a lot like you,' he went on. 'Even naked.'

I saw rage burn in Heike's eyes, and I was a second or so behind in working out why. He was letting us know he had seen the photos from our bathroom in Nice; maybe he was the one who had them taken.

'A girl like that could earn me a lot of money. Many men will want to fuck her after they see you on television. So you want to rescue her, be her saving angel, you must pay what she is worth. How do you say in England? Give until it hurts, yes?'

He chuckled, a weird gurgle like blood down a drain.

'How much?' Heike asked.

'Seventy thousand euros. Tomorrow. You give me your number, I call you later with the where and when.'

'How do I know you won't turn up tomorrow and say now it's a hundred thousand?'

'I don't have time to play games. Two days from now, I have business in Sofia. Two days from now, Hannah goes back to Madrid. Is tomorrow, or no deal.'

'I can't get that kind of money in cash so soon,' she said.

'I do not want cash,' he replied. 'Too complicated.'

'So what the hell *do* you want?'

Smuggler's Soul

'We've wasted our time here,' Mairi said with a sigh, keeping her voice low so that Isobel didn't hear from through in the kitchen.

Parlabane didn't answer. A thought was nagging him, a connection just beyond his grasp, all the more tantalising because something in here had sparked it and he wasn't sure what.

He looked around the room, at the framed prints and posters on the wall, then towards the window, where his eyes lit upon Isobel's cello. He glanced immediately at the basket full of unironed dresses, T-shirts and trousers. They had passed a laundry airing stand in the hall, hung with towels, bras and knickers. Women's clothes. Young women's clothes.

Parlabane stood up as Isobel returned with two mugs of tea.

'I know where she's gone,' he suddenly realised.

'What, did you just channel it?' Mairi asked, though he could tell the sarcasm was to repress the fervency of her hope.

'A cup of tea,' he said, the connection coming into focus. 'She never offered me one.'

'Who didn't?'

'Flora Blacklock. I went to her place on Islay.'

'So?'

'So she was nice as could be: completely open and helpful. And yet I'd come all the way to the arse end of nowhere and she didn't offer me a cup of tea. She said she was on her way to Port Charlotte to prepare her boat for the next day. We talked on the boat instead, but she sat fixing ropes: nothing urgent.'

Mairi got it, her features suddenly animated.

'She didn't want you inside the house.'

'She would have had very little notice, maybe just spotted my car approaching. No time to hide all the evidence, like maybe T-shirts and underwear belonging to a younger woman.'

'Heike.'

Parlabane nodded.

'That's where Monica's going,' he said. 'Heike's been hiding on Islay this whole bloody time.'

'But the Border Agency told your cop friend she never came back to the UK. How did she get there?'

'Fiona Blacklock is the closest person Heike has to a mother in this world. She also just happens to be a highly accomplished sailor, from an island with a long, rich history of maritime smuggling.'

Normality

We got through the penultimate gig on fumes and the promise of what tomorrow might hold. Heike sounded pretty phoned-in to my ears, but it was better than Hamburg, and the audience didn't seem to notice how disengaged she was. Some nights you can tell they're only there for a good time and are happy enough to see the band in the flesh. They're often belting out the songs so loudly they barely notice how well we're doing them.

It could have been a lot worse. We were fifteen minutes late going on because Heike had a serious wobble. I found her vomiting in the ladies and had to talk her down from abandoning the show.

'I can't think about anything else,' she said. 'I don't *care* about anything else.'

'You need to see it as a dress rehearsal for tomorrow night,' was my winning gambit. 'That's when you'll give the performance of your life because Hannah will be standing right there, watching from the wings.'

When it was over I just wanted to get to my bed. I wanted the next day to come around without delay. I wanted Hannah to be safe for Heike's sake, and I wanted this tour to be over. So as I entered the hotel through its revolving doors I was totally unready for the sight that was waiting for me in the lobby.

It was Keith. He was sitting on a couch to the right of the reception desk, scrolling through his phone as he passed the time while waiting for me to show.

It felt jarring to see him, and took me a moment to accept its reality. He belonged in another time-line of my life, and seemed as out of place here as had he been a character from some old TV show I used to watch suddenly made flesh and blood.

I stopped in my tracks, then went forward hesitantly as he got up and strode towards me.

He tilted his head and gave me a bashful smile.

'I did say I'd fly out and surprise you,' he offered by way of explanation.

I couldn't think of anything to say. 'It's good to see you' popped into my head, but under the circumstances it really wasn't. I felt ambushed.

'I'd booked the flights before . . . you know. Never got around to cancelling them because in my head, I think, that would have been symbolic of . . . I don't know. Anyway, instead of moping around and feeling pissed-off about what happened, I thought, if this is worth saving, I need to prove it.'

'Let's get a seat,' I said, urging him back towards the couch. I felt uncomfortably visible standing in the middle of the lobby, and all the more on the spot for it.

I plonked myself down on the edge of a couch, my head spinning. I chose my spot so that Keith would sit on the couch opposite, but he came around the low table and sat beside me.

'Look, things were said, in haste and in anger,' he told me, friendly but firm, like we both knew this was difficult. 'It was all such a shock. I'd never had to deal with the press before, and I was dropped into all of that because of what you'd done. But now I've had time to reflect, and that's why I'm here to forgive you.'

To be honest, it took me a moment to remember why I was supposed to be in the wrong. So many other things had been to blame that my own guilt got lost in the fog.

'See, being exposed to the media like that was actually what made me understand what a mental world you've been caught up in, so I realised it was no wonder you had your head turned. But it's time to get real now, Monica. You can fly home with me tomorrow, and once you're back in normality we can put all this behind us.'

I wondered if he'd got his dates wrong, but another part of me suspected that in Keith's mind this wasn't an issue.

'I still have a show tomorrow,' I told him.

He shook his head.

'I think they've had quite enough out of you already. Dragged you from pillar to post for a month and made a fool of you in front of the whole world.'

He still didn't understand. I wasn't on a fucking hen weekend here.

'That comes with the territory,' I replied. 'But it *is* my territory. This is my job, Keith.'

'It's *a* job, yes, but it's not where you belong, Mon. This is what I mean by having your head turned. And I know who bloody turned it: that lassie Heike. She's had her claws in you, seduced you into joining this band and seduced you into God knows what else. She's used you and humiliated you.'

'Nobody has used me, Keith. I'm a grown adult. I'm capable of making my own decisions and taking the consequences. I'm happy to talk things through when the tour is over, but that isn't until tomorrow night. You know we've the US tour coming up in a few weeks as well, don't you?'

'Christ, Monica. You should hear yourself. You're losing sight of who you are, and you're giving up a great life that we could have together. This is why you have to come home now. We can put all of this behind us, and I won't hold any of it against you, I promise. Trust me, everything will look different once you're back in the real world and *she's* out of the picture. Everything will make sense once she's no longer part of your life.'

The more he talked, the more I realised this was so over. He wasn't offering a chance at making up: he was laying down the terms of my surrender. And boy had he ever picked the wrong day.

I felt bad about him having come all the way over here, but only until I realised what was going on in his head. He kept talking about me having been made a fool of, but this was because he was the one who felt humiliated, and now he needed to put that right by proving to the world that I was back in my place. He still didn't understand what this band meant to me, or who I really was. I saw an ugly side to him, one I realised I had always been aware of but had either been in denial about or maybe thought I could

321

control. I wondered how often I had modified my behaviour to prevent that part of him from revealing itself, how much of the real me I had subconsciously sacrificed.

'Where are you staying?' I asked him, derailing his rant.

'At the Radisson. I splashed out on a junior suite for us back when . . .'

'Nice,' I said, standing up. 'Stay there. It's late, Keith, and I've a busy day making a fool of myself tomorrow. Good night.'

Catch of the Day

Mairi maintained a heavy right foot where the open road invited it, but she didn't take any risks. Monica had a head start of anything up to an hour, but as long as they made it to Kennacraig for the same sailing, they knew they would catch up to her on the boat.

Mairi stayed in the car at the ferry port, keeping her head down while Parlabane, whom Monica wouldn't recognise, bought the tickets. Until she was on board and thus had nowhere to run to, they couldn't afford to let her spot the manager she'd so studiously been blanking.

They cornered her in the observation lounge, having watched her return from the bar with a coffee and pick a table on the port side. Her attention was focused on ripping open a sachet of sugar and pouring it into her drink when they made their move, Mairi slipping into the seat alongside and Parlabane taking his place opposite.

'Monica,' Mairi said neutrally. 'Fancy meeting you here.'

She looked trapped and panicky, genuinely horrified. This wasn't merely a surprise: clearly it was a disaster.

'I've been trying to get in touch for days,' Mairi went on. 'I left messages.'

Monica stared down at the table, cheeks burning.

'I'm sorry,' she said. 'I should have replied, I know. But it's complicated, and it's personal, and it's private, okay?'

Mairi shrugged.

'Okay,' she conceded, looking to Parlabane. They'd agreed on how they'd play it, and he was up.

'It's funny how these things come around, though, isn't it?' he suggested. 'I was on this same ferry less than a week ago, and I took this photograph.'

He placed his phone on the table and turned it around so that Bodo's picture was the right way up, facing Monica.

'Do you recognise this guy?'

Parlabane saw the impact on her face like a boulder dropped into a millpond. She wasn't anywhere near as good at hiding it as the guys at the Brauereihallen.

Monica shook her head.

'His name is Bodo Hoefner. Funny thing is, after seeing him on this boat we ran into him again in Berlin, where it would be fair to say wackiness ensued, some of it the homicidal variety. You definitely sure his face doesn't ring any bells?'

'I've never seen him before. I swear.'

She looked around pleadingly at Mairi, like she could call Parlabane off.

Mairi sighed.

'You know, Monica, you're a quite brilliant violinist, but a rank amateur at lying.'

'I'm not lying,' she insisted, tears beginning to form. 'I don't know who this guy is'

'I think you do,' said Mairi softly. 'And I think you're very scared of him. That's okay. We can help you, but only if you talk to us.'

'About what? I don't know anything about what happened to you in Berlin.'

'Then let's talk about something else,' said Parlabane. 'Such as what you know about this guy being in possession of naked photos of you and of Heike coming out of the shower in a hotel bathroom.'

She shook her head, wiping away the tears that all three of them knew were betraying her. Parlabane knew the retreat into silence was still an option, so it was time to close that one too.

'Or we could talk about a dead girl dressed to look like Heike, stabbed to death and left to rot in a shipping container in Germany.'

Underworld

Heike received the message by text as we stood on Kurfürstendamm. The tree-lined avenue had the most exclusive retail outlets in the city, and I'm sure if you scanned CCTV images going back years, you wouldn't find photographs of two women looking less pleased about having just spent a fortune on designer gear.

In the café yesterday, the thick-necked creep had produced a card bearing the name of an upscale jewellery business. There were some details scribbled on the reverse.

'You go here. You buy these: precisely these. Thirty-five thousand euro each. You text me when you have them, then I give you the rendezvous.'

He was demanding two Cartier watches. It was only when Heike referred to them as a ransom that it really sunk in how out of our depth we both were. I was surprised that he wanted something so apparently frivolous, and wondered if he was doing it to make a point, trading Hannah for trinkets he didn't even need.

Heike explained otherwise. High-end designer watches were a common and valuable commodity in the world of organised crime. They held their value (sometimes even gained more), they were easily transported and they came with receipts and paperwork, meaning that the money was laundered whenever they traded them in for cash. These days jewellers were supposed to tell police who they had sold them to if they had suspicions. This was why Heike being a rock star was the perfect cover.

As instructed, she sent a photograph of the goods to the number she'd been given. A few minutes later her phone chimed with the response.

'We meet him in ninety minutes,' she said.

I glanced at my watch, which looked pitiful after what we'd been browsing.

'Exactly noon,' I said. 'Where?'

There was an unnerving inevitability about her answer:

'Zoo Station.'

His choice was insulting, by implication: Heike was literally buying Hannah at a place synonymous with prostitution. I just hoped this was all I was supposed to read into it. If he somehow knew about Heike's mother, then those two watches were never going to be enough, even after his talk of having to do the deal today.

The location wasn't all bad, as far as I was concerned. It was public – bustlingly so – meaning lots of witnesses. It was also the ideal place for a getaway: as soon as we had Hannah and her passport we could jump on the first train out of there.

Heike started walking back towards Adenauerplatz station.

'Is it far to the Zoo?' I asked.

'It's a ten-minute walk that way,' she replied, pointing in the opposite direction. 'But it's a long time to wait. I want to ride the U-Bahn for a while. It helps me think.'

Heike didn't say much after that, other than to tell me when we were changing trains. I had never done this before: travel with no destination, drifting like litter. Having grown up on Shetland, the first time I had ever travelled on an underground train I found it shockingly noisy, and that was just Glasgow. My first time on the London Tube was overwhelming: buffeted about by crowds, in danger of being swept away from my dad by all the bodies.

Heike seemed calmed by it. She watched the passengers, stared at the walls and billboards as they zipped past. She was miles away. Did she have a memory of this, sitting on a U-Bahn train with her mother? It seemed impossible, but I didn't know how old she had been when her father took her away. My earliest memory – merely shapes and impressions – was of my parents putting lights on our Christmas tree, when I was coming up for two.

Maybe it was simply that on a day like this, it was better to travel hopefully than to arrive.

As the clock ticked towards noon we finally headed out towards Zoo Station, changing for the S7 line at Brandenburger Tor. Heike told me it used to be called Unter den Linden, before the Wall went up, after which it had become a ghost station. I had read that when people first re-entered these places late in 1989, they found all the ads and signs had stayed unchanged since 1961. The thought gave me a sense of what Heike must be feeling, having this preserved but hidden past suddenly revealed to her.

The train stopped between stations for a while due to a signalling issue, so that it was a couple of minutes after twelve when we got there. Heike strode urgently down the stairs, gripping the straps of her shoulder bag. Somewhere inside it were the two watches. We entered a big concourse, and saw the large white clock hanging over the middle. I could see benches beneath it, in a circle.

I scanned the figures seated there, looking for cream-blonde hair or a gorilla in a suit. Instead, I spotted Kabka waiting for us, leaning against an advertising billboard. She hadn't seen us, and there was an anxious look on her face as she searched through the flow of passengers, looking for Heike.

Neither Hannah nor the gorilla were anywhere to be seen.

Kabka hurried forward as soon as she spotted us.

'Where's Hannah?' Heike asked.

'I am to take you. The exchange is not to be here.'

Heike and I traded looks. Neither of us liked this, but what choice did we have?

'Where, then?'

'It is not far.'

She led us out through the wide swing doors and on to a busy pavement.

'I am so sorry,' she said. 'When Hannah told him she had the money so soon he knew someone else was giving it. He remembered seeing you with her in Madrid.'

Heike grabbed Kabka by the arm.

'Does he know Hannah is my sister?'

'*No*,' she replied forcefully, like it was an accusation from Heike.

'Hannah said he thinks you two were maybe lovers. That's all. I would not tell him. I fucking *hate* him.'

'What's his name?'

'I only know him as Boris. It is not his real name, I think. Everyone calls him it, though. The other men, I mean. It is because he looks like KGB.'

We followed Kabka across a dual carriageway and around what looked like an old department store ready for demolition. Behind its wooden fence, on boarded-up frames that were once display windows, were signs showing digital impressions of the new development. Plastic tubes fed through holes in the walls like the building was a patient in intensive care.

Kabka turned right on to a narrow back alley, stopping at a plain doorway in the rear of the building opposite. She gave it a nudge and it swung open, unlocked. On the inside of the door, there was a green panel showing a white stick figure in a running pose, the word 'NOTAUSGANG' printed above it in large letters. I could see stairs beyond it going down into gloom. This was an emergency exit, but from where?

'What is this place?' I asked.

'It was a nightclub. Closed down now. Sold. This whole block is going to be rebuilt.'

Heike stepped inside, but stopped at the top of the stairs. The passage was dimly lit by three fluorescent tubes. Several others remained dark or smashed, the darkness deepening the further the stairs went down from the open door.

'I don't like this,' I said, the words coming out before I could stop myself.

'It will be okay,' Kabka told us.

'I'm not so sure,' replied Heike.

'It will be *okay*,' she said again, this time holding open her jacket. Kabka had a handgun tucked into her waistband.

If it was intended to stop me worrying, it worked. I was no longer worried: I was terrified.

The stairway smelled of urine and damp. It felt cold as we descended, in contrast to the mugginess outside. I wondered how long the place had been closed. The electricity was still working, though, and I could see light coming from double doors at the bottom, one side of which was ajar.

Kabka pulled the door all the way open to reveal a low-ceilinged interior, a place both cavern-like and claustrophobic. Many of the bulbs had died, meaning the lighting was random: some areas in dark shadow alongside pools of harsh brightness that showed up the peeling walls and dog-eared carpet tiles.

The place had split levels, ramps leading to concrete platforms with aluminium barriers. I had heard many a club described as a cattle market: this was the first time I'd seen a place actually modelled on one.

I heard a door open somewhere and looked for the source of the sound. It came from next to the bar, a roller-shuttered gantry alongside which Boris had emerged. He strode to the crush barrier and stood with his arms folded, looking down at the three of us. He was alone, but he had left the door open. I couldn't see where it led.

'You have the watches?' he asked. His voice barely carried, swallowed up by the soundproofing effects of the low ceiling and the carpeted floor. It was almost like a studio or a rehearsal room. The worrying implication of this was that if something bad happened down here, nobody was going to hear a cry for help. Nobody was going to hear a scream.

Heike removed the leatherbound boxes from her bag, flipping one open to show the goods.

'Now where's Hannah?' she replied.

Boris called out a word I didn't quite catch; could have been a German name, could have simply been a command. A moment later, Heike and I gasped as one.

Hannah appeared from the doorway, gripped from behind by a tall and muscular man in a light grey suit and white shirt. It was the other guy from Madrid, the one who had blocked our path as Boris dragged Hannah away.

He had his left hand over Hannah's mouth, and with his right he held a huge knife across her throat. While Boris was squat but powerful, this guy looked like he could pick him up and throw him. I gazed at the blade and the creature holding it, and I knew he could decapitate Hannah with a flick of the wrist.

But there was something even more frightening about him. He looked totally psychotic, like he was on coke or steroids or both. He was giving off so much aggression his whole body was shaking, his eyes bulging, knuckles white.

'You bring the watches here now,' Boris said. 'Or Gerd may get angry.'

Heike stood there for a second longer than Gerd was happy with.

'DO IT NOW!' Gerd boomed, his voice an explosion even inside this dampened vault.

Hannah shook in his grip, her head tilted away from the blade.

Heike obeyed like a robot, helpless even though she was giving up her only leverage. We had walked into this with our eyes half shut, and now I'd have been happy just to get out of there with both of us still alive.

At his gesture she walked to the barrier and placed the boxes on the floor at his feet, eighteen inches up from where she stood. Boris lifted them and placed each in a separate pocket.

'Documents,' he ordered.

Heike handed over the receipts and certificates, the last things she could have withheld. She wasn't for calling anybody's bluff.

As soon as Boris had the paperwork in his hand he turned and made for the exit next to the bar, where he had come in.

'Now you give me Hannah's passport,' Heike shouted at him.

He didn't even glance over his shoulder. I watched the door close behind him, leaving us alone with his snarling, drug-wired partner.

Gerd began to back Hannah away slowly.

'You leave now,' he commanded. 'You do not fuck with me, understand?'

There was a moment of total silence in which all I could hear was Hannah's unsteady breathing.

Then Kabka spoke.

330

'Fuck you,' she said in a furious whisper.

She drew the gun and pointed it.

'No,' Heike protested, turning around to face her, holding up both hands.

Gerd's already wild eyes burned in response.

'You going to shoot me, little girl? Huh? You going to fucking shoot me?'

Hannah whimpered as his grip tightened over her mouth.

'Let her go,' Kabka commanded, still holding the gun in both hands. 'Give us her passport. The debt is paid. Let her go.'

'You think you can tell me what to do? You think a whore tells me what to do?'

'LET HER GO!' Kabka screamed.

'FUCK YOU!' roared Gerd.

For a fraction of a second I thought her goading had worked, or that his bluff had been called. He took the knife away from Hannah's throat and held it down by his side. At the same time he removed his hand from her mouth and put it on her shoulder.

I thought he was about to push her away. I can still see that moment so clearly: the last time I believed everything was going to be okay.

His grip tightened around her upper arm and he spun Hannah around to face him, thrusting upwards with the blade. Her feet were lifted from the ground by the force of it.

He withdrew his right arm and let go with his left. Hannah fell to her knees, holding her stomach. She was side-on to me, but I could see the blood coming through her fingers. Then I saw it seep from her mouth, a trickle at first, then a choking surge before she fell forwards.

Kabka screamed and dropped to her knees. I heard a clatter of metal as the gun fell from her hands. Gerd was a clear target now, but she was useless with shock.

'That's what I do to whores,' he spat, pointing with the blade to the body at his feet.

He had killed her right in front of us.

And we were witnesses.

Kabka must have realised the same thing. She fumbled for the gun, but could barely hold it.

'I am sorry. I cannot do this,' she said, dropping it on the floor a few feet from Heike.

Heike picked it up, backing away from the barrier. Behind it Gerd was moving, striding towards the ramp.

She raised the gun, her arms shaking.

'Stay back,' Heike said. Her voice was a whisper.

'Or *what*? You think I'm afraid of another fucking whore?'

Still he came forward, the knife in his hand.

His eyes were wide, his pupils huge. His mouth was an angry, twisted sneer.

'Put down the gun,' he commanded. 'And maybe I won't fuck you before I kill you.'

That was when she shot him.

It was shockingly loud, and yet the room was quiet again instantly. Deathly quiet.

It seemed incredible that this little object in Heike's trembling hands could put such a big man down, but down he went. He was thrown back by the impact and crashed to the floor, the knife sent clattering behind him.

I watched him roll himself painfully from his front on to his back, blood staining his chest, more coming from his mouth. He was reaching into his jacket, climbing to his knees.

'I think he has a gun,' I yelled out.

Heike shot him again. He fell backwards, spinning as he tumbled, sprawling face down on the carpet tiles. The hand that had gone into his jacket was now stretched out at his side, holding something small and black. It didn't look like a weapon.

Kabka sprinted up the ramp to where the two bodies lay.

Heike remained frozen, paralysed by fear and disbelief.

'Stay back!' Kabka urged, though there was little chance of either of us moving.

She knelt over Hannah, putting a hand to her neck to feel for a pulse.

Kabka remained still for a few moments before I watched her

eyes close in grief. She looked up disconsolately at both of us. Hannah was dead.

Then Kabka's expression changed to concerned curiosity about whatever was in Gerd's outstretched hand. She scrambled across to where he lay and pulled a little black wallet from his grip, folding it open.

She said something in a language I didn't understand. It could have been German, it could have been Bulgarian, but it didn't matter. The emotion was obvious enough: impossible as it seemed, the situation had just got worse.

'What is it?' Heike asked.

Kabka's voice was flat and hollow.

'This guy was a cop.'

Zoo Station Departures

Kabka dropped the black wallet like it was toxic, then looked suddenly alert, like a deer that had just sniffed a lion.

'I think I hear someone. We have to go.'

Heike remained rooted to the spot. The gun was no longer raised but she was still focused on the two bodies on the platform. Her face was a portrait of anguish and disbelief, a mirror of my own.

Kabka all but rugby-tackled her to get her moving again, taking the gun from Heike's grip against no resistance.

'We need to get rid of this,' she said. 'I'll drop it in the river.'

Instinct overcame Heike's paralysis as she hit the stairwell. She lunged up the steps three at a time, as though she had been submerged since we entered and needed to come up for air.

I half expected to find we were surrounded when we rushed out through the door, but the lane was deserted, the city obliviously getting on with itself in the background.

Heike looked totally blank, as though overwhelmed by what she had been asked to process. I didn't feel like I was doing much better, as I had to go lean against a wall and throw up.

'You have to act normal,' Kabka urged, leading us out towards the main thoroughfare where we could melt into the crowd. 'Like nothing happened.'

'Normal?' Heike said. 'That guy Boris knows who was here. He's in with corrupt cops.'

'This is a mess for them too,' Kabka reasoned. 'He'll want to cover it up and deal with it himself. That's why I have to get out of the city: Boris will come after me. He'll think *I* shot Gerd.'

'Why?'

'Where were *you* going to get a gun? He'll know I brought it.'

Kabka swallowed, wiping at her eyes with her sleeves.

'Plus he knows how close I was to Hannah.'

The last time I saw Heike was when she disappeared through the doors into Zoo Station.

Kabka was no longer with us. I hadn't noticed her leave. The three of us had been walking along the crowded pavement: one second she was alongside us, the next she was gone, like we'd only imagined her being there. I just hoped she was as good at making the gun vanish too.

'Take a taxi back to the hotel,' Heike said.

'Why, where are you going?'

'I'm going to protect you. You don't deserve any of this, Monica. I've never known anyone like you, anyone who would do so much for me, and this is what you got.'

'Whatever's going to happen, we can get through it together,' I reasoned. 'It was self-defence. He killed Hannah.'

'It doesn't work like that: he was a cop. I did this, and I have to deal with it.'

'I want to help you.'

'Good, because I need you to do something: I need you to say you weren't with me in that nightclub. I need you to lie for me once, and then whatever you say after that will be the truth. When they ask, you'll say you came with me to Zoo Station because you wanted to see the shops on Ku'damm. You'll tell them I wanted to come here because I'm interested in *Christiane F.* When we got here, we split up, and the last thing I said to you was I'll see you at the soundcheck.'

'But Heike, I want—'

'Promise me, Monica.'

She held me with both hands, squeezing my upper arms as she stared into my eyes, tearful and begging.

'I promise.'

She hugged me then, pressing her body into mine and her cheek against my neck.

It was the way she held me and the way she looked at me afterwards – the sorrow and regret – that told me she wasn't coming back.

'I'll see you at the soundcheck,' she said, then walked away.

Run to Ground

Monica's coffee had sat untouched since she took her initial sip. Once she started talking, everything that she'd been carrying gushed forth in a torrent, words spilling on top of one another with such haste that it was as though she couldn't speak fast enough to cope with the pressure that was forcing them out.

Parlabane truly felt for her. Everything that she had told them was gut-wrenching. It must have been eating her from the inside to keep it secret while having no clue as to Heike's fate. But whatever Monica had been through, it had to have been far worse for Heike.

'Heike must have assumed she had limited time before the German cops came for her,' Parlabane suggested. 'She probably guessed they would put a stop on her passport, and she'd be arrested if she tried to board a flight. So she headed for Denmark and made an SOS to Flora: speed bonnie boat indeed.'

'She needed somewhere to retreat to,' Mairi said. 'Where she could lie low and consider her options. Maybe one of them was the rock 'n' roll mystery disappearance. Quietly liquidise her assets and fade away into mythology, like she was contemplating in Rostock.'

Monica's eyes flashed in accusation.

'How do you know what we discussed in Rostock?'

'We'll tell you later,' Parlabane replied, not wishing to frighten her with the implications. 'Short version is Bodo hacked your blog, then I hacked Bodo.'

'She's definitely planning *something*,' Monica said. 'I hadn't heard from her since Zoo Station: that wasn't a lie. Then, last night, out of the blue my phone rang and it was her, though not from her usual number. A landline, I think.'

'There's no mobile reception at Sanaigmore,' Parlabane said.

'That's the place, yes. She gave me the address and told me she needed me to come to Islay. She said she had found a way out of this.'

The sun was still high and bright as their two cars rounded the headland and trundled steadily along the narrow track towards Flora Blacklock's house. It was after six, but from the light and warmth in the blue sky above it could have been any hour since the sun burned off the coolness of the midsummer morning. It was only a few days since Parlabane had last been here, but the weather was about ten degrees warmer.

They parked nose to tail a few yards shy of the property's walled borders, the closing of their car doors muted by the light breeze coming off the sea, but doubtless loud enough to carry inside and herald their arrival. Parlabane looked towards the bay beyond the rear of the L-shaped cottage.

The boat he'd boarded in Port Charlotte was tied up at the little wooden jetty, dwarfing the careworn yacht alongside it. He guessed it was the *Hecate* that had recently served the rescue mission across the North Sea. He wondered why it was moored here now.

Flora emerged as they walked down the path, intercepting them before they could get close enough to peer inside the building. Her arms were folded, ready to bar their way, but there was conflict in her face. Parlabane could tell she knew Monica was expected, but she wasn't supposed to be accompanied.

'We know she's here,' Parlabane stated, making it sound like a polite but unassailable assertion of fact rather than a challenge or demand.

'She phoned me last night,' Monica added, almost pleading. 'She asked me to come.'

'I asked you to come *alone*,' said a voice, hurt and vulnerable.

Heike appeared from the side of the house, dressed in a most atypical – and even less rock 'n' roll – ensemble of navy linen trousers and a white cotton blouse. She was taller than Parlabane had imagined, and yet she still looked slight and fragile. Her body language was meek and defensive, a husk of the strident figure who stalked the stage, thrashing her guitar as she howled into the mic.

She took in her other two visitors briefly before focusing her gaze upon Monica, her expression searching and confused. It might have been one of betrayal, but Parlabane wasn't sure she still trusted anyone enough to even feel that.

Mairi read it too.

'Monica didn't bring us here,' she said. 'We met her on the ferry. We had already worked out where you were.'

Heike looked suspiciously at Mairi, distrusting of her motives.

'You went missing, Heike,' she said softly. 'That's why I hired Jack to search for you. I was worried. With very good reason, it turns out.'

Heike looked to Monica again.

'You told them,' she stated, crushed and disbelieving, her voice breaking up from the dryness in her mouth.

'We didn't give her much choice,' Parlabane explained. 'We had most of the picture already: Monica only filled in a few blanks.'

Heike's left hand slowly rose to cradle her face. She was a pale flower wilting in the sun.

'Oh my God,' she whispered, grasping how much they knew. 'Oh my God.'

'You only have friends here, Heike,' Mairi assured her.

'He's a journalist,' warned Flora, in tones firm enough to reveal what a consummate performance she had given the last time in order to allay his suspicions. 'He's nobody's *friend*.'

'Actually, my trade has largely decreed that I'm an ex-journalist, but that's beside the point. Do you see anybody here running to tell the polis?'

'We're all on your side, Heike,' Mairi told her. 'We're here to help, however we can. We heard you might have a way out of this. Care to tell us about it?'

Heike weighed things up for a moment, then let out a resigned sigh.

'You'd better have a seat,' she said.

Flora gestured towards a weatherbeaten wooden table, pulling out a bench for Parlabane and Mairi to sit on.

Heike began making her way towards the table. Her route took her close to Monica, who remained rooted to the spot, trembling slightly. Heike stopped a couple of feet away and they gazed uncertainly at each other, a fleeting moment to the observer but doubtless a lot longer to the pair of them. Then they all but flew into an embrace, holding each other tight for what seemed bloody ages to the observer but doubtless a fleeting moment to the pair of them.

When they finally broke apart Monica took a seat next to Flora, but Heike remained standing at the end of the table, arms folded. Parlabane recognised it: she would feel vulnerable sitting down, subconsciously more comfortable upright with an eye on the horizon and no obstacles, should she need to start running.

'I wasn't sure what I was going to do once I got here,' she said. 'I wasn't really thinking that far ahead. I just needed somewhere I'd be safe for a while. Part of me thought that maybe the cops would be clueless as to what had happened in that basement, while another part of me was expecting a knock at the door any moment. It turned out to be the latter.'

'I saw them coming,' said Flora. 'There were two of them, two men saying they were looking for Heike. I said I thought she was away to America, same as I told you, but they said they knew she was here. They were police, from Berlin. Well, one of them was.'

'SEK,' said Heike darkly. '*Spezialeinsatzkommando.*'

'He told me he was investigating the murder of a fellow officer and needed to speak to Heike. He said it would be better for everyone if she cooperated. I admitted she was here and I let them in. I think we both knew it would come to this.'

'So I walk in, thinking I'll be led away in handcuffs, and who's standing there but that jowly bastard: Boris.'

'Bodo,' said Parlabane. 'His name is Bodo Hoefner.'

'We heard his nickname was Boris because he looks like KGB.'

'He's actually an ex-cop.'

'That would explain a lot,' Heike said, nodding to herself. 'Anyway, soon as I saw him it struck me: why aren't there Scottish polis here too? That's when the SEK guy told me they could make it go away.'

'How much?' asked Parlabane.

Heike swallowed, clearing her throat.

'Two million euros.'

'Fuck me,' said Mairi.

'Have you got that much?' Parlabane asked.

Heike nodded.

'It's cleaned me out, but I do have it. It's been a profitable couple of years, and I guess they knew that. They said if I paid them the two mill, they'd make the whole thing disappear.'

'The cover-up would have been under way already,' Parlabane suggested. 'The last thing these guys would want is the Berlin police following the threads from a mess like that: a drug-crazed corrupt cop with links to a Europe-wide sex-trafficking operation.'

'I suggested as much,' said Heike. 'Told them they had as much to lose as I did from the deaths coming to light, and I had witnesses that it was self-defence. They just laughed. The SEK cop told me they could frame the investigation any way they wanted. They had found Kabka and she would say anything they commanded to stay out of jail. However it went down, nothing was going to touch them, but if I wanted to avoid a murder rap I had to pay up.'

'I saw Bodo on the ferry from Kennacraig the day I came here,' Parlabane told her.

'He'd been tipped off that you were looking for me: that's why he was following you. He came here again after you'd gone, to make sure I hadn't been seen and to remind me that the deal was off if I did anything stupid, like pre-empting an investigation by going public with my version of events. He knew it was going to take me a while to get the cash together, and he insisted I stay incommunicado in the meantime.'

'But it's here now?' Mairi asked. 'Two million in cash?'

Heike nodded slowly, her expression grim.

'Where do I come in?' asked Monica.

'When I called to tell him I had the money, Bodo insisted that you be there also for the handover. He wants to talk to you face to face.'

'Why?'

341

'Because you were a witness. I was adamant there was no way you'd have told anybody, but he said the stakes were too high to rely on second-hand assurances. He claimed he was very good at spotting a liar. He said there's no deal until you look him in the eye and tell him you haven't spoken to anyone about this.'

'Guess that's going to be tricky now,' Monica said apologetically.

'Bollocks,' said Parlabane. 'That's not why he wants her there. He's asked for this exchange to take place at sea, hasn't he?'

'How do you know that?' asked Flora anxiously, giving away that she would be the skipper.

'I saw Bodo's emails. He's chartering a vessel from Esbjerg, on the west coast of Denmark, and your boat is sitting out there ready to set sail. How soon?'

'Tomorrow morning, first thing.'

'Why by sea?' asked Monica, who didn't look keen to get on board.

'Two reasons that I can think of,' Parlabane replied. 'One is that you can't just take a suitcase filled with two million euros through customs at the airport. And the other is that neither can you take firearms. Trust me on this: if you sail out to meet this guy, he's going to take the money then kill all three of you, weight your bodies and drop them into the sea.'

'He's already laid the groundwork,' added Mairi. 'He hacked your tour blog. He got hold of your password and he's been working on an alternative version ready to upload, edited to suit his narrative. There will be no mention of him or of the sex trafficking or the killings in Berlin. Instead it will read like an account of Heike descending into a despair deep enough to be contemplating suicide, and you blaming yourself for not preventing it.'

'If you get on that boat, you'll be gone for ever,' Parlabane stated flatly.

'And if I don't get on that boat, I'll be gone for about two decades. It was a *cop* I killed. They're not bluffing: if there's nothing in this for them I'll be spending the best years of my life as a prisoner.'

Heike ran two hands over her head in exasperation.

'That's unless anybody's got a Plan C,' she added.

342

Plan C

The good weather had broken overnight. Flora's boat struck steadily north beneath grey skies, Scottish smir occasionally spraying the windows of the bridge. At least there wasn't much chop.

Flora stood impassive at the helm, Heike out on the foredeck despite the drizzle, looking ahead from near the prow like an imperious figurehead. Her face was solemn, her thoughts unshared.

Parlabane mostly kept his eye to the horizon, but every so often he took a glance below decks, checking on their undeclared and very precious cargo.

Bodo had hailed them over the radio, later than the appointed time, to give them the precise coordinates. Flora plotted them on the navigational computer and gave her passengers an ETA.

'You know it?' Parlabane had asked as she pored over the chart table to the left of the console.

Flora nodded.

'It's a rocky bay on Colonsay. He's recce'd it, the bastard: that's why he was late calling us. No houses, no jetties, no landing points.'

No witnesses, Parlabane thought.

The coastline was just a vague shape, a denser band of grey in the distance as viewed from the starboard bow.

Nobody spoke. From the moment Flora had pushed the throttle forward and the engine growled in response they all knew the countdown had begun.

Parlabane wondered if it was worse for Mairi: not being here; not knowing. He was glad she was safe on dry land, though. There was no reason for her to risk herself, and she'd made her contribution.

It had been Mairi who had initially come up with an idea to give Parlabane some negotiating leverage and stay Bodo's trigger finger. Unfortunately, there was always the possibility that Bodo would decide that having one million euros and leaving no living witnesses was an acceptable result, so the obvious weakness in Plan C was that it essentially relied upon his avarice to prevent this thing ending in a bloodbath. Parlabane had little doubt that Bodo was as greedy as he was ruthless; he just didn't want to bet all their lives on it.

Flora eased back on the engine as they neared the south-western tip of Colonsay, a treacherous-looking miniature archipelago of thrusting rocks jutting from the waters like they had crumbled from the headland. She wasn't simply slowing to navigate around this hazard, however. Their destination was close.

A few minutes later the vessel tacked starboard around a towering outcrop and their rendezvous was in sight: a powerful cruiser bobbing in the bay. Figures were visible on the foredeck and open bridge. Even at this distance he took one of them for Bodo: that broad body, thick neck and a domed head you could smack with a fence post for hours before you got bored.

Glances were shared, mutual checks and assurances. Parlabane felt a tightening in his gut and read the anxiety in Heike's expression as the moment drew near. It was a cue to get in character, hiding his own nervousness behind a mischievous grin that had fooled so many before her into believing he knew what he was doing.

Flora glided them into the bay slowly, a growl of reverse thrust rising from below as she brought the *Hecate* alongside Bodo's hired vessel.

He witnessed the moment Bodo scanned who was on deck and recognised the unexpected member of the crew. All things considered, the guy did well to conceal his pleasure. Given what he was planning for everyone on board the *Hecate*, he must have thought it was his birthday to have the pain in the arse he'd been chasing all over Berlin suddenly show up here, where there was nowhere to run, climb or abseil.

Flora killed the engine.

There were two others with him: Gove-Troll and Spike, standing at the prow and stern respectively. Ropes were thrown across to the *Hecate*. Flora reciprocated, tossing a coil across to the other boat before crouching to tie a line to a port-side cleat. Parlabane scanned the waters around Bodo's vessel. It didn't look like it was anchored.

'What are you doing here?' Bodo asked, as Gove-Troll wrestled with a gangplank. His tone was suspicious, the initial delight giving way to more cautious instincts.

'I came along to make sure everybody gets what they want from this exchange.'

'I don't see the other girl, Monica,' Bodo stated.

'She's down below,' Heike replied, coming to stand next to Parlabane on the waist in front of the bridge. 'She'll be up in a minute. She was feeling seasick.'

Gove-Troll secured the gangplank on a detachable hinge at his end, then tipped it towards the *Hecate*. It came down with a clatter, its edges scraping gently back and forth along the gunwale as the two boats bobbed just out of synch.

'Where is the money?'

Bodo's voice carried crisp and clear upon the air. The only other sound was the lap and splash of the waves in the little channel between the two boats.

Parlabane looked to Heike then back at Bodo.

'Shit, I knew we'd forgotten something.'

Bodo glared and pointed a stubby finger like it was a blade.

'Don't try to fuck with me, *Kotzenkopf.* I ran out of patience with you a long time back.'

'Yeah, I get that a lot,' Parlabane replied, holding up his hands. 'Don't worry, we do have the money. But here's the thing: there's a slight change of plan.'

He saw the consternation in Bodo's face and stole a glimpse down at the cargo. Bodo's patience might be wearing thin, but he wasn't going to do anything rash until he was sure they'd brought the money.

'See, no offence, and we're not in any way trying to imply that you're an evil cunt who exploits young women and murders anyone who gets in his way, but we had this frivolous notion that you might just kill us all once we'd handed over the cash. Call us paranoid, but we thought it might be safer if we came up with a kind of staggered payment scheme. So the new deal is one million today, then, if you deliver on your end and the cop-killing gets covered up, another million in six months. And, obviously, we all have to still be alive for that to happen.'

Bodo's eyes narrowed.

'I'm starting to think that killing you would be worth the other million euros. Where is the fucking money?'

Parlabane folded his arms.

'First, do we have a deal?'

'Yes,' he grunted impatiently. 'One million euros now.'

'In return for what?'

'The dead cop never comes to light. The girl stays out of jail.'

Parlabane gestured to the gangplank.

'You said the magic words. Come and get it. And remember to lift with your knees. A million euros is heavier than you'd think.'

Gove-Troll and Spike began to move, but Bodo halted them with a gesture.

'No,' he ordered, staring first at Parlabane and then at Heike.

'You bring it to *us*. You and her. If you managed to carry it on to your boat, then you can carry it off.'

Bodo then issued something in German, causing Spike to join Gove-Troll at the bow, where the latter was hauling open a canvas bag.

It was full of plastic sheeting.

They began rolling it out, covering the foredeck.

Fucking bastards.

Bodo was opting to stick instead of twist. He had either decided one mill was a good enough return on this venture, or reckoned Heike hadn't been able to raise as much as she'd claimed and was stalling over the rest. Either way, he was going for the 'bird in the hand and no living witnesses' option.

It was incongruously calm, unnervingly quiet. Parlabane felt profoundly aware of how isolated they were. Bodo had picked his spot well.

Bodo pulled out a handgun from his jacket. He didn't point it, just held it close to his chest by way of warning.

'What are you waiting for?' he asked. 'Go and get my money.'

'You know, you're in Scottish waters,' Parlabane advised him. 'Possession of that handgun is a strict liability offence. Could be looking at five years if the police see you. I'd stick it away if I were you.'

'I'll take my chances.'

'No, seriously, I'd put the gun down. Spoilers: the cops are a lot closer than you think. Closer than you would believe.'

Bodo looked confused, lots of calculations going on busily behind his eyes.

'Yeah, sure they are,' he decided. 'It's a little late for bluffing, *Kotzenkopf*, especially when we've seen each other's hands. If you went to the cops then she would go to jail. It's . . . what do you call it? Mutually assured destruction.'

'Yeah,' Parlabane said, putting on an exaggeratedly torn expression and pulling at his chin. '*About* that . . .'

A Square of Captured Light

'I'll be spending the best years of my life as a prisoner,' Heike had said. 'That's unless anybody's got a Plan C.'

Mairi was the first to break the silence, offering her idea that they hold back half the money. Parlabane heard her initial suggestion but was barely able to parse anything she said after that, nor any of the brief discussion that followed. It was just white noise, as though all sensory input was being deliberately scrambled by his brain in order to prevent any cognitive resources being diverted.

Everything he had learned in the past few days was being broken down and rapidly reassembled in his mind, a single word from Heike suggesting a possibility so shocking that he had to test it to destruction before he could consider presenting it to anyone else.

He became aware of someone saying his name, a hand being waved impatiently in front of his zoned-out face.

'Hello?' said Mairi in irritation. 'Jack? Looking for some feedback here. Care to tell us what you think?'

Parlabane took in the expectant faces around the table. It was time to file.

'Aye. I think rather than one million, we give Bodo fuck-all.'

He looked straight at Heike.

'You're not going to end up in a German prison,' he told her, 'because the prisoner in this scenario isn't German. She's Spanish.'

Several faces stared at him in confusion.

'Heike, you'd better sit down.'

'I'm good here.'

'Seriously. You had really better take a seat.'

Heike stood her ground, giving him a look that had no doubt delivered the same message to producers, musicians, photographers and roadies down the years: leave it.

Parlabane shrugged. This was going to be rough on her, but she'd been through worse of late.

'Jack, what's going on?' demanded Mairi. '*Who* is Spanish?'

'Tell you in a minute. Meantime, think about this: any time we saw Bodo he had the same amped-up wankers with him, right?'

'Not all of them every time,' she replied, 'but always two or three from the same pool.'

'Except there was one guy we saw once and then never again.'

'Sure. In Alexanderplatz, before it all kicked off.'

'Somebody tried to push me under a train minutes later, then after that Bodo was desperately trying to get hold of my phone. But I've just realised that it wasn't because I took *his* picture; it was because I had photographed the guy he was with.'

'What's so special about him?' Mairi asked.

Parlabane produced his phone and scrolled to one of the photographs in question, holding it out towards Heike.

'Ask Ms Gunn.'

Heike took the phone and came very close to dropping it when she saw what was on the screen. A shudder shook her from head to toe, though this wasn't why he'd suggested she have a seat. That was still to come.

'This is the cop I shot. He's still alive.'

Monica grabbed Heike's arm so that she could see it too.

'Oh my God. He must have survived it.'

Parlabane took back the phone.

'He didn't *survive* anything. He was never shot. Heike, I can absolutely guarantee that you haven't killed anybody. I can also guarantee that you're really going to want to in about two minutes.'

Parlabane took a breath, all eyes on him.

'It's known as the Spanish Prisoner. It's a long con that dates back nearly five hundred years, but somebody's always got a new way of working it. The principle has never changed, however: get a wealthy mark to part with money in the belief that it will secure the freedom of a wrongly imprisoned nobleman or a damsel in distress.'

'Or a victim of sex-trafficking,' suggested Mairi, working it out.

'With most marks, the incentive is the promise of a big reward once the prisoner is restored to his or her rightful riches and power. But with others, they have to dream up a prisoner for whom the mark would be prepared to pay a ransom purely for emotional reasons. Such as a half-sister you never knew you had.'

Heike's eyes looked hollow, her legs suddenly weak beneath her. She took a short step forward, putting a hand on the table for support, then succumbed and took a seat on the bench alongside Monica.

'No,' she said. 'It can't be. Her face was familiar from the first time I saw her. I felt a connection, something instinctive, fundamental.'

'She was familiar because she was probably somewhere around the fringes on your last European tour, one of Bodo's girls. And, sad to say, she'd have spent a long time learning how to make people feel instantly comfortable and at ease around her.'

Heike looked exasperated. She wasn't fighting it now: she just needed to know how it was possible.

'She had photographs of my mother, photographs I'd never seen, from her time in Bratislava.'

'You only saw them briefly, in a club, in the dark. Kabka didn't let you take any away. They'll have been Photoshopped.'

'From what source? I've got the only surviving picture of her.'

'They hacked Monica's blog: how hard would it have been to copy that photo from your phone?'

Heike's eyes were dead, her expression numb.

'Fucking bastards,' said Mairi.

'Historically, the con men would fake some kind of tragedy at the ransom handover, leaving the mark implicated in a killing so that he wouldn't tell the authorities. One of them would pretend to be stabbed; they used to burst a bag of blood in their mouths to sell the illusion. The blood-bag even had a name: it was known as a cackbladder. But in this case the ransom itself – the high-end watches – was only the set-up, and the fake killing was the basis for the real sting.'

'So if nobody got shot or stabbed in that basement,' asked Monica, 'what about the dead girl in the shipping container, dressed to look like Heike?'

'What?' Heike demanded.

Monica briefly filled her in, Mairi producing the flyer from her bag.

'Sadly, I think that *was* your Hannah,' said Parlabane. 'I think we can assume she's the girl Bodo was looking for when he circulated these. For whatever reason, she must have run. Maybe she realised she was a potential risk to the success of the scam if she was seen alive. Maybe she was playing her own angle, threatening to blow it open unless she got a bigger cut.'

'Or maybe she felt guilty about what she'd done and was trying to reach Heike,' Mairi suggested. 'She was found in a crate bound for Scotland, after all. That can't be a coincidence.'

'So what do we do now?' asked Monica.

'Simple,' said Heike, the tremble in her quiet tones betraying the rage beneath. 'We do the one thing that ugly fucker was relying on me *not* doing.'

Lifted

'What about it?' asked Bodo, the first hint beginning to show on his face to indicate that he suspected all might not be well.

'Never mind,' Parlabane told him. 'I think we've got what we needed. So we'll just go and get you what you've been asking for.'

Parlabane followed Heike as she stepped carefully down the stairs, silently venting a sigh through pursed lips before they both stepped to the side to leave the passageway clear.

Upon a signal from Detective Superintendent McLeod, armed police erupted from below decks at both ends of the boat, pointing their Heckler & Koch fully automatics at the three astonished figures on the other vessel.

Commands were barked out, loud and frantic.

'Get down. Get down on the ground. Faces to the deck, *faces to the deck.*'

Parlabane heard the clang of boots on metal as they rushed across the gangplank. He looked through a porthole and saw one of the officers standing with his weapon pointed at Bodo as he lay flat-out on the deck. Another cop had a boot on his neck as he restrained him, grinding his face roughly against the polished wood.

Could have been a lot worse for the bastard. The armed cops had had a bead on him through the portholes the whole time. If Bodo had actually pointed the gun, rather than merely brandishing it, they'd have taken no chances. His brains would be lobster food by now.

Such had been their assurances anyway. Last night Heike had understandably been all for letting the cops swoop in as soon as Bodo gave them the rendezvous coordinates, but McLeod warned her that they didn't have anything concrete on him at this stage.

If a police launch intercepted him, he and his men could make up any story about why they were there, after quietly dropping any weapons they were carrying into the sea.

McLeod explained in depth about the evidence they required, and went to great lengths in describing how the police marksmen would act instantly if they believed there was danger to those on board the *Hecate*. She added that she would entirely understand if Heike didn't want to put herself at any risk, or found it too difficult to consider confronting Bodo again.

Having heard all of this, Heike was thoroughly emboldened, and according to Mairi looking a lot more like her old self.

'You had me at "that prick might get away with it",' she told McLeod.

They climbed back up on deck as two police launches buzzed into the bay, ready to pick up their wretched cargo. The prisoners were on their knees, hands cuffed behind their backs. Gove-Troll and Spike looked shell-shocked. This was supposed to be an easy gig, but after years of growing used to getting away with it, the crash had come out of nowhere.

Their boss, by contrast, looked satisfyingly furious: his face ruddy and his eyes boiling.

Heike made her way to the gunwales of the *Hecate*, as close to the gangplank as the cops would allow her. She stared across at him, a quiet satisfaction on her face.

Home from War

The sun was starting to break through as Flora guided her boat smoothly back to Islay. Heike sat on a bench on the foredeck, looking towards the horizon, saying nothing.

Detective Superintendent McLeod had opted to come back with them, deputising her assistant, DI Thompson, to accompany the prisoners on one of the police launches. She took the opportunity to remain above decks on the return journey, having been confined below on the way out.

She stayed on her own much of the time, fielding lots of messages. She had a standard-issue combined radio and mobile, but with no network coverage out here it was all old-school comms protocol. It was also largely incoming info: Parlabane heard lots of 'received' and 'acknowledged' and 'understood'; very little else.

She did wander over to speak to him at one point, though.

'I want to say thanks,' she told him. 'You did well back there. Got Herr Hoefner to say what we needed him to.'

'Eliciting just the right quote is a trick of the trade.'

'I gather you know more tricks than most in your trade. Jenny Dalziel has been filling me in on your rather chequered history.'

'And I thought she was a friend.'

'Relax. It wasn't all bad. For one thing, you appear to have provoked the displeasure of our esteemed colleagues in the Met, so props for that. It surprises me, though.'

'Why?'

'Well, for one thing, you're not black. What's the problem: did you forget to bribe them like all the other journalists?'

'Miaow,' he replied. 'Actually, I'm not being persecuted. I really did do what they think I did, and it's not really me they're after.'

'So why not do a deal, cooperate?'

He thought about it, measuring what he could tell her.

'Two reasons, I suppose. One is that I'm protecting a source, and that's sacrosanct.'

'What's the other?'

'It's just so much fun *not* to give them what they want.'

Mairi and Monica were waiting on the jetty as the *Hecate* rounded the headland and Flora slowed the engine. There had been a cop with them the whole time, keeping them up to date, so Parlabane guessed they weren't standing out there like fishermen's wives after a storm, waiting for the sight of their loved ones' boats to confirm they were still alive.

Parlabane and Heike threw out the lines as Flora expertly manoeuvred her vessel into parallel with the pier, old tyres flanking the wooden beams as buffers. DI Geddes, the cop who had stayed with them, tied the rope to a cleat at the stern end, Monica jumping to it at the bow with surprising speed.

Shetland girl, Parlabane remembered.

Heike didn't wait for the gangway. She hopped down almost directly into Monica's arms. He didn't stare, wanting to afford them their privacy, but they didn't seem very concerned about who may or may not be watching. They both had their eyes closed, tears on their cheeks. It was all pouring out now. They knew the danger was past and they could start looking forward again.

Mairi looked relieved to see him, but there were no tears or hugs. She was keeping her distance, and not because of who might be watching. There was something self-conscious about how she stood her ground, as though conspicuously aware of the contrast between them and the other reunited couple on the jetty.

Whatever had been sparking between them was over. Perhaps it had derived from the other tensions they'd been feeling, meaning now that the fear was gone, so was the thing they were confusing it for. Or maybe he had simply succeeded in blowing her off. He didn't know. He just knew that she wasn't looking at him the way she had done in Berlin.

He knew it was better this way. It just didn't *feel* better.

'You okay?' she asked him as they all began wandering back up the path towards Flora's house. Heike and Monica walked in front, Flora and the two cops at the rear.

'Well, I didn't get shot. That's always a plus.'

'You don't sound exalted,' Mairi observed, picking up on the ambivalence in his tone.

'No, I'm happy it's worked out for everybody. But I just realised this means I'm out of work.'

Heike's ears pricked up.

'Hardly,' she said acidly, turning around. 'I'm sure you've got a drippingly juicy story to flog all over the media. Give them an excuse to run those fucking pictures of us again.'

Jeez, she was just hoaching with gratitude, wasn't she?

He maintained a sincere expression but he was smiling inside. He'd have cut her some slack anyway, given all she'd been through, but Mairi had already warned him that Heike seldom went out of her way to ingratiate herself with people, especially journalists. He couldn't help but admire her for it.

'Actually, I've got nothing,' he told her. 'Biggest story of the year: rock stars, sex trafficking, drugs, murder, blackmail, and I won't be telling anybody a bloody thing.'

'Jack signed an NDA when I hired him,' Mairi explained. 'This story will not be reported.'

'Yeah, but it'll all come out when it goes to court,' Heike reasoned.

'No, it won't,' McLeod weighed in. 'Assuming you seek an injunction, your identity will most likely be subject to reporting restrictions. In cases involving blackmail the judge will usually grant an anonymity order. You and Monica are both victims here, so it would defeat the ends of justice if your details were dragged through the court and the media.'

'Like I said,' Parlabane told her, 'I've got nothing.'

Heike looked relieved, then, for a moment, as close to sheepish as she probably ever got.

'One day,' she said, 'when it comes time to do the official book on Savage Earth Heart . . . you'll definitely be on the shortlist.'

Parlabane smiled at that.

'Of how many?'

'Five or six. Definitely not more than ten.'

He really did like her style.

McLeod's mobile-cum-radio buzzed to hail her as they approached the back door of Flora's house. She stepped to one side and held it to her ear: more 'received,' 'acknowledged', a 'good work' and a 'keep me informed'.

'That was DI Thompson,' she reported. 'Just to let you all know: the suspects were transferred into separate police cars at Kennacraig and are currently en route to Glasgow for processing.'

'Good,' said Heike. 'So does that mean you're all clear to go after the sleekit bastard who put them up to this?'

It was the last piece of the puzzle. The previous night, once Parlabane had outlined the nature of the con, it hadn't taken long for Heike to deduce that the whole thing must have been predicated upon personal knowledge that Bodo and his cohorts could not have garnered for themselves. Nor could it have been cooked up at short notice: this had been long in the planning and painstaking in its execution.

There were only a handful of people who even knew that the photograph of Heike's mother existed, and they had been shown it in the strictest confidence. This entire charade had been built on details that were nowhere near the public domain, such as the real meaning behind her tattoo.

Calling it a betrayal of trust didn't come anywhere close to describing what had happened here. This was something far more bitter, vengeful and cold, and Heike could only think of one bastard who fitted the description.

Last night Heike had been about ready to put out a contract on the guy, never mind have him lifted by the polis, but McLeod told her the cops would have to hang fire. They couldn't make a move until Bodo and his men were in custody, for fear that any pre-emptive action might cause word to filter back up the chain.

'You can't afford to scare off the big game by shooting at a snake,' was how McLeod explained it, and Heike had accepted this.

The big game had been bagged now, however. Snake season was officially open.

'I already made the call from the *Hecate* on our way back from the bust,' McLeod informed her. 'Alistair Maxwell was apprehended at his home in Glasgow ten minutes ago.'

The Guilty Ones

We got out of taxis at roughly the same time in front of Govan police station, the first time we'd seen each other since getting back from Islay a couple of days ago. Neither of us said much. There were a lot of charged and confusing emotions going on after all that had happened, and now that we'd both had some time and space I really didn't know where we stood.

Heike was looking surprisingly prim and sober in her appearance, like it was a dress rehearsal for the court appearances that would come later. That's not to say she didn't totally *sell* it; you wouldn't think a grey wool top and a waterfall cardy was a look that could drip style and attitude until you'd seen Heike rocking it.

She seemed restless and anxious as we waited in the reception area. I was nervous too, and not only on her behalf. I found McLeod quite scary. She wasn't brusque or unpleasant, but nor was she going to be mistaken for anybody's favourite auntie.

We were escorted up to McLeod's office by the male cop who'd been with her on Islay, DI Thompson. He was good-looking in a boyish and easy-going way, not striking me as somebody who took himself at all seriously. I could see myself going for him under other circumstances, but that aspect of my life was too much of a mess right then to think about complicating it.

Once McLeod started talking I felt much more at ease than I had thought I would, and I could tell Heike was less on edge too. I had been expecting McLeod to be all business and very direct, like she had been a few days ago, but she was calm and compassionate. I noticed a photograph of two young boys on her desk, and guessed she must be their mother. She understood fear and vulnerability, but it wasn't just about what she already understood: it was what she was *wanting* to understand.

She talked to Heike for a long time about what it had done to her to have believed she had killed somebody.

'I knew I didn't have a choice,' Heike told her. 'And I knew what he'd just done. But that didn't make it any better. I barely slept in days, and when I did I kept having dreams about it. Even in daytime I kept imagining there was blood on my hands. I felt like Lady Macbeth.'

'You need to forgive yourself,' McLeod told her. 'Not merely tell yourself it doesn't matter because it was all fake: you need to forgive yourself for what you *believed* you'd done. There have been times in all our lives when we wish we could turn back the clock and find that something awful was no longer true. You've been given that chance, but it doesn't work unless you can wipe away what it did to you.'

It sounded so much more convincing coming from her than if I or anyone else had said it. She had gravitas or authority or something. It didn't just come across as well-intentioned advice: it was like she'd lived it.

So we were both in a much more relaxed and thoughtful frame of mind by the time she started filling us in on the investigation. I guessed this was intentional, as nothing she told us was easy to hear.

'Our colleagues in Germany have been moving on this with great speed and . . . well, I'd love to avoid using the word "efficiency", but it is what it is. They believe they've identified the suspect photographed by Jack Parlabane in Alexanderplatz. Can you confirm that this is the man you saw in Madrid and later believed you had shot in Berlin?'

McLeod spun her laptop around to face us. She must have seen it in our expressions, though she still needed us to say it. There was no question but that we were looking at the coked-up psycho we'd seen stab Hannah in that basement.

'I can reassure you that not only is he not dead, he's not a cop either. His name is Gerd Augenthaler. He's officially a Bad Candy employee and unofficially one of Bodo's gangmasters, managing groups of girls on tour at expos and conventions. He was last known to be in Cologne, where he is now believed to be lying low since word got back that his boss's trip to Scotland was a bit of a disappointment.'

McLeod turned the laptop again and worked the keyboard.

'If you don't mind, Heike, I'd like you to look at some more pictures they've sent us and tell me if you see the man who accompanied Bodo Hoefner to Islay.'

McLeod went through several mugshots, getting no response until the fourth one, at which point Heike said: 'That's him. The oily prick.'

'Jackpot,' McLeod confirmed. 'The other shots were control pictures, so the Germans will be pleased you picked him out so unequivocally. This man actually *is* a cop. He isn't from the unit he claimed, but he is a serving officer in Berlin. They have long believed that the reason they've struggled with monitoring Bodo's activities is because he had a man on the inside, feeding back information. They just didn't know who or from where.'

'Well, they do now,' Heike said, bitterness mixing with some satisfaction.

'The UK Border Agency can confirm that he entered and left Glasgow on the appropriate dates, plus Caledonian MacBrayne are supplying CCTV footage that should, we hope, put him on the ferry to Islay, but the German police may require you to give evidence in Berlin.'

'If it's to bring down this sex-trafficking operation, they can name the day and I'm there. I don't care where I have to fly from.'

McLeod shifted a little in her chair and cleared her throat. It wasn't like some obvious calling-to-order moment, the conductor rapping his baton on the stand, but it definitely sounded like an overture to something.

'At the German end it's looking like a very complex case, but the web is starting to unravel. With a sudden collapse at the top of the management structure the police in Berlin are getting the sense that some of the girls may be feeling emboldened to give evidence. One in particular has already come forward.'

'If it's that bitch Kabka, you can't trust her,' said Heike. 'She'll lie to save her own skin. She was in on the con. She brought the gun along and all but put it in my hands.'

'Heike's right,' I added. 'She's a liar, and a convincing one too. Back in Rostock she was the one who spun Heike the whole story. I guess they played it that way because it's harder to press someone for details when it's second hand.'

'It isn't Kabka,' McLeod told us. 'She's in the wind, and she's left fewer traces than your man Gerd. From what we've learned about her, that's not surprising. She's a survivor. She wasn't lying about most of her own story. She was a prostitute, but what she neglected to tell you was that she has moved up to management, shall we say. She's manipulative and resourceful, but to be honest I'm finding it difficult to judge her too harshly, given what she's been through.'

Heike gave a small nod, her rage partly derailed by this thought. I didn't have a lot of charitable feelings in my heart for Kabka either, but I felt the gas get turned down a notch on my anger too.

'The girl who's been speaking to the police is called Lenka. She was close to Hannah, or Anezka as she knew her. They were both Slovakian, and they shared digs. Anezka had confided in Lenka about what she was involved with. She had been offered a deal for the return of her passport and the cancelling of her debt if she carried off this deception. However, according to Lenka, she became very conflicted.'

McLeod gave Heike a sympathetic look, but somehow I could tell not all of it was for her.

'She had to listen to all of your music and learn everything she could about you, and according to Lenka she became genuinely fixated.'

'A method performance,' Heike suggested, her voice sad and quiet.

'To say the least. Anezka began to feel that there truly was a connection between you as a result of the time you'd spent together, so she felt awful about what she was involved in. Then, perhaps unsurprisingly, once the charade was over Bodo reneged on his end of the deal. According to Lenka, he genuinely did mean to make more money from Anezka by trading off her resemblance to you. Bodo confiscated her phone, in case she tried to double cross him by calling you to prove she was alive. That was when she decided to run away and find you. Ironically, she thought you could save her for real. If she tracked you down and told you the truth, blowing the lid off the scam, you would help her escape her life in Berlin.'

'Jesus,' said Heike, no trace of anger now, all passion spent.

'We know she travelled to Hamburg. She was hoping to stow away, get across to the UK; get to Scotland, then find you somehow. That was as far as she got. Police in Hamburg have been interviewing freight terminal staff ever since this body showed up at our end and we discovered the container's port of origin. They traced the guy who was handling the bookings for that particular shipping, and he admitted he had caught her sneaking into the terminal. Initially he said he had been moved by her story and therefore turned a blind eye, but under pressure he admitted she had sex with him in order to secure her passage.'

'Fucking bastard,' said a voice that I was surprised to discover was my own.

'But having allowed her to sneak into a shipping container bound for Glasgow the next morning, he spotted one of those flyers Mairi showed us. They'd been distributed at ports, railway stations and bus terminals. He figured there might be a reward, so he phoned the number and told them where she could be found. Someone arrived within the hour, which shows the reach this operation has. He admitted he took a pay-off to say which container she was in, but swears that's all he saw. He said a man showed up claiming to be a worried relative, and he assumed he would just be taking her away.'

'How did they know she was a threat?' Heike asked.

McLeod looked regretful, almost apologetic. None of this was easy. None of this was good.

'Lenka told them. When Anezka went missing, they threatened her, knowing the two of them were close.'

'That's how they work,' muttered Heike.

'She's crushed,' McLeod said. 'That's why she came forward. She blames herself for what happened to Anezka.'

Heike gave a sharp sigh.

'The wrong people always feel the guilt,' she said. 'Let's talk about the *right* people. Tell me about Maxi.'

McLeod made a face, wincing. It made me tense instantly. This wasn't going to be good news.

'You'd best prepare yourself,' she told Heike. 'You're likely to find what I'm about to tell you upsetting.'

Heike sat up a little straighter in her chair, her expression suddenly stony.

'We've released him without charge.'

Heike's mouth fell open.

'Jesus Christ, *why?*' I asked for her.

'For one thing, we had no evidence against him. Maxwell did admit that he was the one who tipped off the photographer in Berlin, but as collaborating with the *Daily Mail* is unfortunately not against the law, we had no reason to hold him.'

I was more reeling with outrage on Heike's behalf than she was herself. But she had been paying closer attention than me. She was calm, bracing herself for what was still to come.

'That wasn't the part that's going to upset me, was it?' she asked, her voice flat. 'What else has come to light?'

McLeod looked her in the eye.

'Someone else has confessed.'

McLeod said nothing more. I wondered why she was drawing it out, then I realised she was giving Heike time to get there by herself.

Heike responded with a slow, solemn nod, then spoke a single word.

'Angus.'

'Our mutual friend Mr Parlabane has an associate with whom I believe you might be familiar: a Mr Cameron Scott.'

'Spammy,' Heike said quietly.

'Mr Scott informed Parlabane a couple of days ago that he had heard a rumour Angus had been caught dealing on the side while on tour with Shadowhawk a few months ago. We suspected this might have put him in a vulnerable position with certain of his Bad Candy colleagues, so we leaned on him. We didn't have to lean very hard. He was weeping out a torrent.'

Heike looked away, like she needed a moment's respite from facing anyone. When she turned back again, she seemed more sad than angry; disappointed rather than surprised.

I recalled that night in Valencia, when Heike had gone off to bed early: Angus drunk and railing with bitter envy about Heike's good fortune.

'He was jealous and resentful,' McLeod said. 'He hid it well, but he told us he found it very hard having a close-up view of your success given that you had started off together.'

I expected Heike to explain how her work ethic had a lot more to do with their different paths than luck, but she said nothing. She knew she didn't need to justify herself to anyone over this.

'He thought this up a long time ago as a kind of revenge fantasy, but he never really envisaged carrying it out. That was until he got greedy with his side-action on tour and suddenly Bodo Hoefner was threatening some truly savage stuff *pour encourager les autres*. Angus panicked and told them he could help them scam you on the forthcoming tour. He was painfully aware of how much you had been making, so he knew it would be well worth their while.'

'I did everything I could to help Angus,' Heike said, tears in the corners of her eyes. 'I brought him on board as guitar roadie. I was the one who got him the opening slot as well.'

'He said in his statement that he thought you were only doing all that in order to underline how far you had come compared to him.'

'That's bullshit,' she protested.

'He knows. As soon as you went missing, the scales fell and he saw how things really were. Up until then he'd told himself it was just about money, and that you'd be making plenty more. But after Berlin he was terrified that something awful would happen and he'd always know it was his fault. That's why he tipped off Parlabane that you might be with Flora. He was trying to derail it, hoping the whole scam would fall apart without the sabotage being traced back to him.'

We sat quietly for a while, McLeod giving Heike time to take it all in.

'What about Jan's role in this?' she eventually asked. 'Have you interviewed him?'

'According to Angus, Jan had nothing to do with it. He does what he's told by Bodo, but he wasn't in on the plan. He didn't need to be, and the first rule of any conspiracy is that you don't involve anyone unnecessarily.'

'It was all Angus,' Heike said with hollow resignation. 'He had access to all our stuff every night.'

McLeod confirmed this with a nod.

'He copied the picture of your mother from your phone and gave it to Bodo to have Photoshopped. He also said that he only hacked Monica's blog so that he and Bodo could monitor how the charade with Hannah was playing out. He says he didn't know what else Bodo planned to do with it, and to be honest I believe him. He's wretched with remorse, which is not a sight you see that often in Govan nick.'

'Rooting through our stuff while we were on stage was the least of his sins,' said Heike. 'He ransacked my memories. He knew all those things about me because I'd shared them when we were growing up. He got himself in trouble and did something desperate to save his skin: I can forgive him for that. But what I don't think I can ever forgive is that he knew how much I would want Hannah's story to be true.'

The air felt thick and muggy as we stepped back outside the police station, denying us the sensation of release you sometimes get when you escape from a place that's made you feel claustrophobic. Heike looked wrung-out, like somebody had taken her and squeezed until all the colour and joy were drained from her whole person.

'You look like you could use some serious coffee,' I said, hoping she would agree rather than pour herself into a taxi and retreat into solitude.

366

'How about a drink?' she replied.

I looked at my watch. It was only five to eleven.

'Is it not a bit early?' I suggested.

'We're in a fucking rock band, Monica. There's no such thing as early.'

Damage

'Can I offer you a dram?' Mairi asked, getting up from the table.

They had finished the wine about ten minutes ago, and though he could see another bottle on the worktop he had been glad that she had thus far made no moves towards opening it. It was getting late and he had a big day tomorrow. Plus there were, of course, other reasons.

Mairi was opening a cupboard, ducking so that the door didn't hit her head because she had so little room to manoeuvre inside the tiny kitchen. Parlabane reckoned that with a stretch she could have reached it without getting up from the table.

Fucking London. Maybe at some point it would send a hint to the government that people living in half-million-pound broom cupboards was a sign that they were concentrating too many resources in one place, but successive administrations had proven impervious to such signals.

He had recently heard some chinless Tory fuckpuddle say that London was a world-class city being held back by the rest of the UK. Parlabane had reckoned that if he poured all his money and efforts into fitting out his toilet he could almost certainly have himself a truly world class shite-house. Obviously there would be little in the way of cash or other physical resources for the development and upkeep of the living room and the kitchen, etc . . . but if anybody asked, he could tell them he had a world-class bog and it was just a shame the rest of the house was holding it back.

She held up a bottle of Bowmore.

'I think I've had enough of Islay,' he said. 'Plus you've an early start.'

'That's true,' she decided, putting the bottle back. 'Might be wisest if we both called it a night.'

Mairi had said she would cook him dinner to say thanks for everything, but she had ended up running late and still had to pack for her flight, so she'd phoned out for pizza instead. He wasn't complaining: it was good pizza, and she was doing him a favour anyway by having him here tonight when she was off on tour in the morning.

He was crashing with her in Hoxton as he had to be in central London the next day. It was not so much a meeting as a secret rendezvous, necessitated by him fast and unavoidably approaching the jaggy end of the Westercruik Inquiry.

His contact had called two days ago.

'You know who this is?'

His phone hadn't registered the number and she didn't identify herself, but he recognised the voice instantly.

'Yes.'

'I need to see you. Same time, same place. Same day as our first meeting.'

She knew someone might be listening, which was why she gave away nothing. They could follow him, and they very well might, but for all they knew they'd need to follow him for days. Was it worth those kinds of resources? He knew *he* wasn't.

Mairi stuck their plates in the dishwasher and led him into the shoebox of a living room, piled everywhere with CDs and band T-shirts. There was a two-seater couch, its edge so close to the telly on the wall opposite that the 'remote' control was a misnomer.

'It's snug, but I'm told it's comfy,' she said. 'I'll just get you some sheets.'

She went off towards her bedroom, leaving him standing next to the turntable on which she was playing *Damage* by Jimmy Eat World. He picked up the album sleeve, not having had such an object in his hand for years, and glanced at the once-familiar sight of a twelve-inch vinyl disc spinning beneath the stylus arm. It took him back to his teenage bedroom, to Donald's teenage bedroom: listening to songs, talking about gigs, and all the time distractingly aware of the trendy wee sister who was through the wall festooned on her side with Depeche Mode and Tears for Fears posters.

He wondered if Mairi had looked out this record specifically or whether it was just what she'd felt like playing. Either way, it definitely wasn't an overture towards romantic intentions. It was an entire album about the break-up of a relationship, one that had given him a sometimes melancholy and sometimes defiant solace throughout the final days with Sarah.

It was on side two right then, probably the most poignant number: a song about a late-night drunk phone call suggesting they could still make it work, when deep down the caller knew they couldn't. It was called 'Please Say No'.

Mairi returned with a set of cotton sheets pressed between her hands.

'I didn't think you'd be needing a duvet,' she said, in reference to the fact that it was about eighty degrees in there, even with all the windows open.

Their hands touched as she passed him the bundle. She looked up from the sheets and into his eyes.

'Mairi,' Parlabane began, but she put a finger to his lips before he could go on.

'I just need to ask: does it change anything that I'm no longer employing you, and you no longer have to feel responsible for me?'

'It's not that. It's not about you at all. It never has been.'

'I know. It's about Sarah,' Mairi stated, nodding in a way that suggested she had always known this and was pleased to see he was catching up. 'If you kiss me now, if you admit you want somebody else, then you can't keep telling yourself it's not really over with her.'

He gave a sad smile by way of confirmation that she was right.

'You don't want her back, Jack. Part of you thinks you do, but you don't. Part of you believes that if you get her back it means you're still the man you used to be before it all went wrong. It means *you're* back. But the problem was that she never wanted that guy. I liked who you were when I was fifteen and I like who you are now.'

She squeezed his hand and he felt himself melt.

'Trust me on this,' she whispered. 'Parlabane's back.'

They were moments from a kiss, but some emergency reserve of willpower allowed him to seize control before he was dragged under.

'Mairi, this is not the time to start something. You're off to America with the band tomorrow, and you'll be gone for, what? A month? More? A lot can change in that time.'

She sighed, conceding the point.

'It was going to be less, but after everything that's happened I thought I should keep a close eye.'

'Tell you what. When you come back from the States, if you still feel the same way, then we'll talk.'

'Sounds annoyingly sensible. But I'll settle for that over nothing. It's a deal.'

'Of course,' he added, 'this is assuming I'm not in jail . . .'

Gods and Mortals

We were sat on a low and comfy couch in a basement bar Heike liked, a place that was already serving at this hour because it also did coffee and food. So I could tell myself this was an early lunch, although I'd have to order something more solid than another bottle of Dead Pony Club.

Heike had gone quiet, looking blankly past the table towards some unknown point: possibly ten feet in front, just as possibly ten days behind.

'I can't get her out of my mind,' she said eventually. 'Hannah, I mean, or Anezka rather: both versions are equally tragic. I relived Hannah's death over and over for days, and what I've learned doesn't change how I feel. She wasn't who she pretended to be, but I liked her. Whoever she really was, it burns to know how she was chewed up and spat out by those people.'

'Her and how many others?' I said.

'That's why I don't want her to be forgotten. I'm going to ask McLeod for her full name. She was the inspiration for "Gods and Mortals", though I'm going to rework the lyrics. When we record it, I'd like to include a sleeve note dedicating the song to her memory. We can't tell anybody why, other than that she was a victim of sex-trafficking, but if it's on the next album then her name will be written somewhere it will be seen around the world. Better than some anonymous headstone – if she even gets one. I mean, if that's okay with you,' she added.

'Of course,' I replied. 'But why are you asking me?'

'Because it's your song too. My lyrics, but the music was a collaborative process. You ought to be credited.'

She was looking intently at me, slightly worried. It was almost like she was afraid I'd refuse.

I thought carefully about what to say. Thanks seemed obvious, but maybe wrong, as the point wasn't that she was giving me this, was it?

'It's very much appreciated,' I said.

'It's only fair. Especially as I've decided to credit Maxi too. Not fifty-fifty like his lawyer is demanding, but he never expected to get that.'

'You're giving him a share, even after . . . well, I know that turned out not to be him, but he was the one who tipped off . . .'

'I spent a lot of time thinking about things while I was hiding out at Flora's place. When I was forced to contemplate losing everything, it gave me a different perspective upon what I had and what really mattered. Maxi did play a big part in the songs he claims, even "Dark Station". Partly for reasons of self-defence, I had kind of blinded myself to how things were between us in the past. I missed him while I was hiding up there: not the wanker he turned into, but the guy he was, and the guy he was deserves his cut.'

She took a sip of beer and giggled, the first happy sound I'd heard from her since I couldn't remember.

'I missed everybody. Mostly I missed you, though,' she said, giving an apologetic little smile: no angle, no agenda, no assumptions.

'I missed you too,' I replied. 'It was horrible not knowing where you were. But it was more than that: I missed the person *I* am around you.'

'I'm sorry about everything I put you through.'

'Don't be crazy,' I protested. 'What *I* went through?'

But Heike put a hand on my arm and dropped her voice, stressing that she needed to be heard.

'Yes, what you went through. I never meant to let myself get close to you, because right from the off I wanted it too much and you weren't available. But we got forced together like we were driven by the swell. Christ, I don't even know what I'm trying to say, apart from that I didn't want you to get hurt. I want to explain, but this is so hard for me. Part of me hoped you would work it all out with Keith while I was gone. Then I could tell myself I'd done the right thing by pushing you away, but here you are and I still don't know how you feel about me. About . . . us.'

I was reeling, grateful I was sitting down on this big soft couch. Emotion and instinct were already at odds, my desires muted by a fear of flying too close to the sun.

All I could do was try to be honest.

'I know what you mean about us being driven by the swell,' I told her. 'But my worry is that it was only circumstances that drove you towards me, and I'm wary of where that leaves me now that things are less crazy.'

'Oh, it will always be crazy, one way or another. But no matter what happened between us, I wouldn't kick you off the tour, if that's what you're worried about. I'd let you stay on the bus, at least until the next town.'

'Joking apart, that's it precisely. We're about to start a two-month tour of the USA, with all the stress and pressure that goes with it. I don't think, under those circumstances, that a relationship between us would be a good idea.'

Heike took a long drink of her beer then let out a sigh, sounding resigned.

'Probably not a good idea, no,' she admitted, slumping back on the couch.

I slumped back too.

A couple of moments later, our feet touched under the table. I couldn't say whether Heike reached to mine or I to hers; maybe they just kind of brushed halfway.

Futures

He kept his head down as he entered the gardens between Temple Place and Victoria Embankment, ever mindful of drawing attention to himself and in particular to who he was meeting. This was where she'd first told him about Anthony Mead, and where they had hatched their conspiracy to expose him.

It wasn't long past nine but it was already shaping up to be very hot. There were about a dozen under-fives running about the place, shrieking joyfully as they evaded the clutches of the nursery teachers who were trying to slap some suncream on them. None of them looked like they worked for the Met or the MoD.

He glanced towards the spot where they had always sat. She was there, but she was not alone. Trying not to overreact, he reminded himself that it could be a perfect stranger sharing her bench, but all of his instincts told him otherwise, and when his contact spotted him, her worried expression confirmed it.

She was sitting next to another woman: ten or fifteen years older, soberly dressed and exuding authority. A quick scan of the gardens revealed two men in close proximity: two men he hadn't even seen until they wanted him to.

There was no point in turning back. They already had his source, and it wasn't like he would be able to give these people the slip. He maintained his direction and his pace, slaloming some of the nursery kids before arriving at the bench.

'I didn't give you up,' he stated. It wasn't going to make any difference to the outcome, but it felt important to tell her this.

'She knows you didn't,' replied the older woman. 'Kendra, you're free to leave now,' she added.

The woman he had only known as Kay got to her feet, giving

him a helpless but apologetic look. She didn't say anything, just walked away with a hesitant gait in the direction of the river.

'What's going to happen to her?' he asked.

The woman eyed him with a penetrating but inscrutable gaze. This was no cop, he guessed, but an altogether more exotic and dangerous species.

'A less noble individual might have enquired as to what *she* gave up about *you*.'

He shrugged. He genuinely didn't care. Not about that.

'You're not with Westercruik,' he ventured.

She responded with a thin smile and patted the bench, inviting him to sit. He got the impression there wasn't really an option to refuse.

'You didn't answer my question. What happens to her?'

'If she was going to be thrown to the lions it would have happened before now. I've known she was your source for some time. It's you I'm interested in at the moment.'

'Well, you'd better hurry up. They're dangling the electrodes pretty close to my bollocks.'

'Relax. You won't go to jail. That's not the game here, believe me. Not now, anyway. They'll be ordered to leave it. They won't be given a reason and they won't be happy about it, but they'll do as they're told.'

He was about to ask how she could possibly know this when the answer hit him like a sledgehammer.

'You're the one who set the whole thing in motion.'

She said nothing by way of response, simply held him in that unnerving stare.

'You played me,' he went on. 'When the intel on that laptop turned out to be bollocks I knew I'd been used, but I assumed it was about finding leaks. You've found them all now. What else could I give you?'

'It *was* about finding leaks,' she replied. 'But it was about exposing them too: making sure there was no option for an internal cover-up. I used you to take it public.'

'So I was your useful idiot. Why are you showing me your hand now?'

'Because there was more than one game being played. Your involvement with Kendra brought you to my attention. It's true I set you a trap, but it wasn't to see whether you'd take the bait: that part was a given. I was more interested in finding out how you'd respond *after* the jaws snapped shut. So now I know I can trust you,' she added pointedly.

'Why would you care about that?'

She watched the children for a moment, making him wait.

'I was hoping you might help us out.'

Parlabane almost choked.

'Me, help you? Did you actually *read* my file? That would be like the Catholic Church reaching out to Richard Dawkins.'

'No, it really wouldn't. You're a man of principle, Mr Parlabane, you've just proved that. You think we're on opposite sides, but you're drawing the line in the wrong place.'

She looked out towards the river, and Parlabane felt relieved at the reprieve from her regard but no less anxious about where this was going.

'There's a new game kicking off,' she said, 'and it's going to be between those of us who believe in common responsibility – in nations, in government, in democracy and accountability – and those who believe they are above all of those things. The bad news is that we're the underdogs. *They've* got all the money and all the influence: that's why we need all the help we can get.'

'You'd have to be pretty desperate if you're asking me.'

'Hear me out,' she insisted. 'I've not told you what it would involve. You would be lied to, double-crossed, misinformed, manipulated and, if necessary, disavowed. Plus the money's shit too.'

'You're really selling it.'

'I don't have to sell it, Mr Parlabane. You made up your mind thirty seconds ago.'